SHADOWS FOR A PRINCESS

DOMINIQUE KRISTINE

This novel is a work of fiction.

Names, characters, places, and incidents are the product of the authors' imaginations or are used in a fictitious manner. Any resemblance to real persons, events, and locations are coincidental or used in a form of parody.

ISBN-10: 0-9903817-8-1
ISBN-13: 978-0-9903817-8-5

www.dominiquekristine.com

TERRAINA

NARKANTH

Fort Stonewall

Ashdale

Shadeglen

Lakeshire

Weathermore

Eastmark

Stormwatch

FAS PERRA

Nirmashire

HINDERA

Riverdale

Kirkwood

Lorwick

FELLWOOD
FOREST

Ackleton

Easton

Brychas

VASTHAS
DESERT

CRESTOLI

THE MAGISTERIUM

• TOWNS
● CITIES
● CAPITALS
◆ POINTS OF INTEREST

250 MI

THE RUNAWAY GIRL

A bitter wind cut through Ysolde's traveling cloak, the fur-lined garment as useless as silk. She shivered and warmed her chilled fingers against Tikiina's neck to no avail—her three-year-old filly was also frigid.

With the feeling lost in her hands and fingers, she would soon be forced to stop. Take shelter. Rest for the night and hope the men pursuing her had also become hopelessly lost in the storm. By now, they had to be making camp in one of the many towers littered across the heartlands.

Above her, the sky remained a perpetual state of gray. The wind howled, shrieking around her and whistling through sparse trees jutting like naked toothpicks from the rocky soil. With the exception of the river dividing the country, hard terrain stretched between the coastline and eastern mountain range, separating the kingdom from its neighboring, enemy nation.

Ysolde pursed her lips. She turned her face against the lining of her hood, felt the black bear fur against her cheeks and nose, and closed her eyes. For all her suffering, it would be worth it to see her mother again.

Ten months ago, Tegau had left to rejoin the Marcogh tribes, leaving behind strict instructions: her child was not to accompany her. Ysolde, barely turned eighteen, had been left behind in the castle with her adopted father, stepsiblings, and vindictive stepmother.

By now, he would have realized his daughter was gone, and there were no doubt hundreds of royal guards combing through the countryside for her. They'd ride over the hills and fan out toward the south, north, and west, hoping to find her.

With each hour of travel, her arguments became more convincing, a self-deprecating determination that the man who raised her had done so out of obligation alone.

It was the right thing to do. Her father's legitimate queen had never wanted Tegau or Ysolde in the castle, although they had been there first for many years as consort and adopted child. As far as Ysolde was concerned, Queen Rhonwen was the usurper who swept into their happy lives and unbalanced their world.

Why had the nobles forced the king's hand and made him marry such an awful woman?

Although the weathermages had forecasted clear skies, the threat of a storm loomed above them on the horizon. She cringed, wishing she'd donned more than riding leathers and a cloak.

The wind howled, seeming to scream, "Turn back! Turn back, child!"

And she wanted to heed the wind's warning. After all, didn't her people worship the winds and the sky? Surely the wind knew more and had seen more than her in all of its many millennia of existence, but more than she desired safety, she wanted to see her mother's smile and feel Tegau's warm, inviting embrace.

It was the right thing to do. Without Tegau there, the king would sleep beside his wife, rather than his consort. Without Ysolde in the home, Aldemar would no longer divide his love among three children, rather than the two born from his seed.

Had he even loved her?

No, it was obligation, responsibility to keep her mother happy, and with Tegau gone, Ysolde would force him no longer, even if he'd been the only father she'd ever known.

And she missed him. She missed him so much that burning tears obscured her vision and great sobs made her choke unsteadily atop her mount.

Sensing her rider's distress, Tikiina veered off the trail to the remnants of an old travelers' encampment. She'd been bred by the wilder tribes, a mere foal when she'd been gifted to Ysolde by a Marcogh chieftain when they'd crossed paths while vacationing in a southern province years ago. One of their children should ride one of their horses, the man had said before he and his people continued on their trail.

"Thank you, friend," she whispered.

She dismounted and kissed Tikiina's velvety nose then made use of the camp. It was an eyesore, but it would do, and by the time she'd collected enough wood, her fingers felt waxy, uncooperative, and stiff. They hurt but were required for magic.

Reaching deep, she summoned a spark of mana from the renewable fount of energy within her soul. Magic bloomed at the tips of her fingers and spiraled in a blaze of red. This she directed to the twigs until they caught and became a magnificent glow.

Ysolde added kindling to the fire and waved her hands, weaving together spells and mystical power until the flames roared. She spread blankets over the cold ground and invited Tikiina to lie with her.

"Come, come," she urged the filly. "It's safe. I'll keep you safe."

With promises and gentle coaxes, the copper-furred creature lay beside her. Ysolde snuggled against her side and tossed a blanket over them.

Could she keep them safe?

She thought so. Why else had she endured years of tutoring at the behest of her adopted father to hone her magical talents?

Although her belly protested its empty state, beast and human companion slept.

Hours later, she roused and packed her belongings. She rolled the blankets, kicked earth over the campfire's embers, and walked beside Tikiina until they found a pasture with a pitiful covering of grass. While the horse pulled up mouthfuls of clover, Ysolde nibbled berries she'd packed from the castle pantry.

Was her father worrying by now? Guilt flooded her. He'd have never allowed her to undertake the journey with permission, and traveling with a retinue of soldiers would have slowed her down.

Their second day went the same as the first, and this time as she made camp, she began to doubt herself. She had no idea where to find the Marcogh, memories of the nomadic tribe hazy at best, and their only city was a distant dream at the end of two or three weeks traveling by horseback. Would they even accept a girl among them who couldn't recall the simplest words in their language?

Ysolde guided them toward a pair of large rocks jutting up from the ground at diagonal angles. Loose shale crunched beneath Tikiina's hooves. Cold and numb, she slid down from the mare's back and began the laborious process of clearing out a spot for them both to lie down. With Tikiina settled, Ysolde collected twigs and sticks for a fire. She managed a few feeble sparks then gave up and tried to keep her meager campfire alive.

"We'll be closer to the forests tomorrow," she told her horse, teeth clattering together. "I think. We'll cross the river and find warm pastures."

She dozed off and on, curled into a tight ball against Tikiina's side.

Awakening to the sound of men in her camp, Ysolde's drowsy eyes opened and took in a blurry sight. Men moved freely in her camp and spoke in low tones. Among them, a familiar voice whispered, "By Ashta's breath…she'd have died of cold. Kinsley, fetch wood for the fire. Trevor, see to Tikiina."

It couldn't be.

King Aldemar himself had come to retrieve his child, and Ysolde had never been happier to see him.

"Father?" She pushed up, blankets falling.

"Ysolde, sweetheart, bless Ashta you're all right."

Worry creased his brow, and shadows stood out beneath his gray eyes. He was dressed for a prolonged hunt, in rich furs and thick leathers. After taking a seat on the cold, hard-packed ground, he put his arm around her to lend his additional warmth. A soldier from his retinue covered Tikiina's back with another blanket and tended to the chilly mare.

"I'm sorry. I'm sorry, Father. I was such a f-fool. I thought…"

"No need to apologize," he said in a quiet voice, more concerned with draping his cloak around her shoulders. "Please never do this again, Ysolde. I beg you."

She could only shiver at first, huddling within the enchanted garment. Her teeth chattered. "How did you find me?"

"I saw your campfire from the hilltop. At least, I thought it was yours I saw, but this couldn't have made so much light." Aldemar rubbed his bearded chin, laced with more silver than brown in recent years. They were stark opposites, she and her fair-skinned father.

"Are you taking me back to the castle? Even af-after I ran away?" Another wave of sadness clenched her throat, ushering in a fresh series of sobs. "I didn't think you'd want me anymore without Mother. I th-thought you'd be glad to be rid of me."

"No, my dear. No," Aldemar said firmly. "I'm bringing you back home. I'm sorry you felt unwelcomed. I *never* meant for that to happen."

Ysolde had no survival skills, but in minutes, the guardsmen had erected tents, fanned out to collect wood, and set a kettle to boil above the fire. Without the wind cutting through, she warmed more quickly.

Safe and warm, the exhaustion of the day took its toll, weighing down her eyelids. She fought against it and turned her face into her father's shoulder.

"Are we going back now?"

"No, my child, you sleep. We'll head back in the morning."

"But what about Mother? I didn't find her."

Aldemar paused. At first, he said nothing then, in a quieter voice, said, "She'll return one day. When she left the castle, your mother promised she'd come back to us. We must trust in her."

As he gazed into the fire, Ysolde saw more than the monarch of Wysteria's wealthiest kingdom. She saw a lonely man, a man who missed his beloved as much as she missed her mother.

She'd been such a fool.

"I love you, Father."

"I feared the worst when we discovered you missing, Ysolde. Please never do this again. If you have grievances with Rhonwen, bring them to me, and I shall deal with her."

"I promise."

He pillowed her head in his lap and stroked her dark hair, humming the song her mother used to sing to the best of his ability. His familiar, off-key rumble reassured her. As she drifted toward sleep, she overheard low murmurs among the men guarding the camp and feeding her fire.

"It truly did appear larger," one knight mused.

"Like a summer bonfire," another agreed.

"Then let us take it as a sign from the goddess that our princess is to return home."

"Princess?" Ysolde questioned, her voice a sleepy slur. She'd never had a title, only called Lady Ysolde by respectful members of her father's court and servants who tended the castle.

"From this day forward, you will always be equal to my and Rhonwen's children in title. You have always been my little princess, and now the rest of the kingdom shall know it too."

ROYAL BURDENS

1

For Princess Ysolde Westbrook, freedom came at the cost of embarrassing a handful of her personal bodyguards. And for all of her privilege, she wanted nothing more than to walk in a normal woman's shoes for only five minutes.

She longed to shop without an armored guard lurking over her shoulder. She wanted to wander the docks and breathe the salty mist without bored defenders palming their sword hilts each time a dockworker strayed too near to the invisible perimeter the guardsmen visualized in their minds' eyes.

It didn't make much sense to Ysolde that she should be treated like a known criminal perusing the fine silversmith's wares, always followed, always scrutinized and under watch. So she had developed a reputation for occasionally throwing her guard from the trail when she no longer had the patience to be their hapless princess in distress. Sometimes she used magic, and other times she devised a plan with her chambermaid, who crept into Ashdale in advance and paid a handsome reward to a citydweller, who eagerly made a diversion. Such planning wasn't necessary this time.

During the height of the harvest season, their abundant yields always brought eager merchants from distant lands. Traders and buyers haggled over exotic silks, while the fishmongers called to the hungry with their smoked delights.

Foreign spices perfumed the air, wafting to Ysolde on an early autumn breeze. She inhaled the rich aroma and paused to purchase a jar filled with her favorite dried herbs. She loved them and had long ago adopted her mother's habit of placing a sachet of thyme and lavender inside her pillow each night.

"You bumbling imbecile," one of the guards roared to his comrade. "How did you lose her?" The voice, sharp and panicked, came from the tightly packed throng of people behind her.

"She was here only a moment ago," the second guard replied defensively. "Then I had a look around again, was sure I saw her. Turned out to be some elderly bint with the same pattern over her hair."

"Check the back alleys. She can't have gone far," a third voice said.

Ysolde slipped into pockets in the crowd, grateful for the anonymity of traveling without the usual guards assigned to shadow her. The new men, chosen by her steward, were too inexperienced to keep speed with her and ignorant of her usual tricks. With a hand-painted, silk scarf covering her sable braids, she blended in with any other woman on the city streets as long as she didn't make eye contact. In a crowd of native Hinderans, she stood out as unique, her darker complexion and ethereal eyes singling her out from the fair-skinned citizens of Ashdale. Her eyes marked her as different, their ever-shifting color the same shade as the skies above.

For a while, she traveled alone through the market district. One of Ysolde's favorite pastimes was to spend and filter her money into the city's economy.

Half of the fun of visiting without her usual escorts was to watch them scurry about harried and upset that they were unable to find her again. For the first month of her rule as Princess Ysolde, Duchess of Ashdale, she had also put her knight protector through the very same ringer. Unlike most, Geoffrey Ashcroft had never failed to find her in the four years since her appointment. He paid attention to the subtle things, like the way she moved and which scarf she wore, a lesson her current guards would do well to learn if they expected to stay in their commander's good graces.

For a man who'd built his career around bashing people with a shield and a lance, Geoffrey matched her intelligence with charm and wit. They'd even become friends, once she ceased the effort to elude him at every turn. In fact, he was the only man among the guard able to keep up with her on horseback.

He was due to return by nightfall, exhausted and starving after a long journey on the road, and he wouldn't be pleased to discover she'd shaken off her guard retinue. Hoping to greet him with a peace offering, she stopped at a favored vendor for her usual order.

"Two cherrydrop chocolate pastries please," Ysolde requested politely. "One wrapped as usual." She passed a single silver coin to the clerk behind the table and accepted a fluffy, chocolate-iced tart in exchange. The clerk wrapped the second in a piece of wax parchment.

"I didn't mean to steal it, honest, sir. I was just hungry. Haven't eaten a thing in days. Please, I'm sorry!" A cry went up behind her at another market stall.

Alarmed by the sudden clamor, Ysolde hurried to the side of the street.

"Listen, you little gutter rat, I couldn't give a damn if your belly is empty. If it's not filling my pockets, I'm not filling your stomach," the owner rumbled dispassionately.

"I'll take this little waif to the gallows. He won't bother you anymore." A bored city guardsman stood beside a table with his hand on a child in threadbare clothes. He gripped the little one by the shoulder in an unforgiving hold.

A child to the gallows? With no greater reason to break disguise, Ysolde stepped forward and cast the veil back from her hair.

"I demand you release that boy." Authority infused her voice and carried the instantaneous effect of pulling all eyes toward her.

The guard's mouth dropped. He bowed his head but kept his grip on the dirty child. "Your Grace."

"Since when do we punish children as we would their elders?" Ysolde asked.

"This little urchin is a thief, and he'll grow up to be a bigger thief if we ignore him. We nip them in the bud now before they're a blight on society."

Ysolde set her lips in a firm line and straightened her shoulders. "You may have handled things that way with your previous duke, but so long as I oversee Ashdale, you obey my

13

rules. Report to your watch captain and relay that he is to meet me at my audience chamber within the hour."

"Yes, Your Grace. As you wish. I'll just take this—"

"You will leave him here."

"Aye, of course."

As the watchman hurried away, she turned to the youngster left in her care. She bent her knees and smiled at him. "Hungry?"

"Yes, madam," the child mumbled, too shy to meet her eyes.

She offered her pastry to the boy. "Slowly," she cautioned when his ravishing hunger nearly caused him to choke. "Do you have a name?"

"Crispin, madam." He'd at least swallowed before answering her.

"Crispin is a fine name. Do you live nearby?"

The boy shook his head and shied back. Dust and ash smudged his nut-brown skin, and tangles matted his curly hair. Ysolde wasn't quite sure of the color, it was so dirtied. It could have been anything from ash blond to chestnut brown.

"Parents?"

"No, madam," he whispered. "Just me."

Poor soul. "Well then, I suppose you will have to come home with me. It will mean some small work. Do you think you can do that?"

Crispin nodded his little head, cheeks stuffed with food. She chuckled at the sight of him and wiped his face with her sleeve.

A masculine voice spoke up behind her. "Your maids will foam and froth at the mouth when they see what you've done to that dress."

Ysolde sighed. She would recognize Geoffrey's placid baritone anywhere, but she simply hadn't expected to hear it so soon. She turned to face him, head tilted up to make eye contact with the enormous Hinderan man.

"Perhaps I'm mistaken, but I was under the impression that wardens were assigned to escort you for your safety." A fan of the theatrical, Geoffrey exaggerated a look in either direction down the market street. "I see no guards, but I do see a lone princess standing where she ought not be."

"Look, Crispin, my shadow has finally caught up to me."

"Indeed he has," Geoffrey replied. A grin made his rugged, road-weary features all the more handsome and softened the edge from his next words. "Are you in the business of adopting stray urchins now?"

"When they are in need, yes." She smoothed a hand over the boy's head.

Apparently, Geoffrey had expected another response. His brawny arms folded against his chest, and he frowned. "All right. You've saved the young one. Now send him away before he infests you with lice."

She placed her hands over Crispin's ears and shot a displeased look at Geoffrey. "If lice are your concern, perhaps you should follow your own advice and remain clear of the brothels."

"You wound me," he muttered in a dry tone. He shook his head and trailed at her side. Road dust clung to his dark blue traveler's cloak, and a day-old golden shadow colored his strong chin and the cheeks of a square jaw.

"How did you find me so swiftly? Have you traveled home yet?" she asked.

The knight shook his head. "As I reached the estate, two frantic wardens intercepted me. Imagine my surprise when the pair of them informed me that our princess had gone missing in the markets." Speculative, he raised his brows. "Or my lack of surprise. Must you?"

"I must. I am quite capable of protecting myself, or have you forgotten?"

Geoffrey became her silent companion for a few paces. He gazed thoughtfully into the distance instead and chose not to speak until they nearly reached their destination. "During my travels, I crossed paths with a messenger from Eastmark. Baron Paddleton has been assassinated."

She slanted her gaze down at the boy traveling beside them then back up to Geoffrey. "Troubling news. We can speak of it further when you're rested from your trip and after I see Crispin settled with the chamberlain."

"There is a city orphanage, you…" The words died on his tongue. He sighed, shook his head, and continued alongside her. "As you wish, Your Grace," he agreed with grudging reluctance.

To soften her knight's defeat on the matter, Ysolde removed the wrapped pastry from her bag.

"Oh, before I forget." She held out her peace offering and smiled at him. "Welcome home, Geoffrey."

He accepted it without delay. "Ah, bribery. Reminds me of my days on the city watch."

***

A cool breeze snaked beneath Ysolde's silk scarf. She traveled a winding pathway within the rear garden, its stone path bordered by trumpet-shaped pink lilies and plum-colored roses. Their fragrance surrounded the princess and reinvigorated her mood, restoring the pleasure she'd initially felt upon leaving the estate.

Ever since her betrothed's abrupt departure from the land, she'd taken up the hobby of tending his old garden. At first, she'd wanted to set fire to it, but too many memories dwelled there of their long nights talking beneath the stars for her to let it die; likewise, she couldn't bear to assign its care to one of the servants.

The path provided the most direct route between the northern and southern wing of her estate. After seeing Crispin settled with the housekeeper and shooing Geoffrey off to his personal quarters, she wanted a moment to herself before she returned to her duties.

"There you are."

The disapproving voice, all too familiar, pulled her from her quiet contemplations.

"Hello, Fingall," she called in greeting to the dour elf.

"Greetings, Princess. New missives have arrived with need of your attention."

"Thank you."

Fingall held a prestigious duty as Ysolde's seneschal and had served the duke before her. And the duke before him and many more, though she had never been so bold as to ask the elf his age. However old he was, his features remained deceptively youthful, his indigo eyes clear, and his golden hair full. He wore it in elaborate braids gathered at the nape of his neck above the stiff collar of robes woven from azure shadesilks, a fiber spun from the giant moths of Fellwood's murky forest.

"The taxes have been collected in full, Princess, and all records are present for your perusal."

"Any trouble?"

"Only the usual sort."

She had yet to see the elf crack a smile or show any emotion for that matter. He was perpetually calm, always unruffled, and impossible to read, yet he was such a fixture of the estate that she didn't dare relieve him of his duty.

"And the usual sort is…?"

"The nobles are displeased. You bleed them for your charity work to benefit the city's derelicts," he said.

Ysolde arched a brow. "And yet the markets swell with trade. Crime has dropped because the people have wages to feed themselves. Why tax the poor heavily when they cannot afford it? Hungry men and women are peasants who cannot labor to provide for the city or themselves."

"I have served as advisor to many before you, Ysolde." Fingall only ever used her Ashtarian name when matters became dire. The rest of the time, she was *Princess this*, or *Your Grace that*. "No one else has ever enacted such stringent taxation against the nobility. You risk alienating them all if you continue. I beg you to reconsider your course of action."

"I will not allow them to pay a pittance, Fingall. They complain, but look out at the city and tell me things are not better."

The old elf sighed. "I can see your mind has been made. Tread with caution, child. I care for you dearly, but times are dangerous."

"You spoke with Geoffrey."

"I have," Fingall confirmed.

"Has the watch captain arrived?" She cut him off, quick to avoid another lecture following Geoffrey's doom-and-gloom warning. She tired of tax talk, bickering nobles, and assassination conspiracies.

"In your audience chamber, as requested," Fingall replied.

"Good."

"Shall I summon Ser Ashcroft? I am told they are acquaintances."

Wispy tendrils of dark hair drifted into her face as she shook her head. "No. Geoffrey is due for some rest, and I am quite capable of handling this on my own."

Ysolde delayed the meeting for as long as it took to set her flowers in a water vase. Afterward, she moved into the audience chamber and settled into her throne. Two men awaited her, one the nervous fellow from the city, the other a broad-shouldered, familiar man clad in the black armor of the city watch. The one with whom she took offense wrung his leather-gloved hands and snapped to attention in her presence.

"Gregor Lansford," the captain introduced himself, as he bowed deep. "It's a pleasure to have your company. How may I serve?"

"You can begin by carrying forth word to your watchmen regarding the barbaric practice of brutalizing children."

"Your Grace, I assure you, while my men do have autonomy to handle incidents as necessary, it is not and has never been the policy of the guard to execute little ones. He ought to have taken the little sprog to the orphanage." Gregor clapped a hand upon his underling's shoulder. The man flinched. "Isn't that right?"

"Aye, Captain. Very correct. I behaved beyond my boundaries, and I apologize to Her Grace."

"And those who are older?" Ysolde asked.

"Adults?" Gregor's brows rose. "Begging your pardon, Your Grace, but we execute thieves on the morrow following their arrest. What else are we to do with them?"

"They will be brought before me." A forward lean followed her decisive words. "No more deaths unless *I* decree it.

"These are criminals. They would say anything to walk away with their lives." He didn't appear convinced. A heavy furrow wrinkled his brow.

"And I have a knight captain capable of telling truth from lies," she countered. "I wish to know why a thief resorts to the trade so I can fix it."

"Aye, he does. Geoffrey had my job before he came into the old duke's service," Gregor replied. His brows furrowed. "Your Grace, there are quite a few thieves in Ashdale. You'll have your hands full quickly."

"Then I will be sure my schedule allows for them," she replied, unruffled. "You have my orders, Captain Lansford. Let this be a step toward a safer city."

"As you wish." The dumbfounded watch captain and guard bowed deeply then exited the audience chamber.

All that was left was to inform Geoffrey of his expanded duties, which he would no doubt despise but accept without argument. His days were filled with enough work, and now she had inadvertently added more.

***

From the doorway, Ysolde watched the weary knight settle into his armchair. Geoffrey was a large man, a giant among the many soldiers in her employ, and she'd once thought his armor composed his bulk. She was wrong. He remained broad in the torso without the metal chestplate.

After pouring a generous helping of white-honey into his steaming tea, Geoffrey leaned his head back and shut his eyes, as if the weight of the world balanced precariously upon his muscled shoulders. His cherry tart rested on a white linen beside his over-sweetened tea, and its untouched state told her all she needed to know about his trip.

"Would you like some tea with your honey, Geoffrey?" she asked playfully as she entered the room. "Maribeth told me you were in the sitting room. I thought I'd join you and catch up."

"Of course. You need not ask me permission to occupy your own sitting room, Your Grace." Ever the gentleman, he rose from his chair until Ysolde took a seat opposite him.

"Is it not polite to ask before invading someone's private time?"

Geoffrey returned her warm smile. "If I sought private time, I would retire early to my room. Your presence is always welcome."

"How was it?" Ysolde stirred a spoonful of red sugar crystals into her tea. Geoffrey frowned as if she'd ruined it. He didn't appreciate the spicy bite of the sugar extracted from Crestolian red peppers, but to her, it was the perfect complement to the smoky flavor.

"Your lead took me to a dead end," he reluctantly admitted. "For all of your witchcraft and sorcery, it's done little to guide me to Ashlynne."

"I'm sorry. Scrying has never been my strength, I admit." She'd tried though, using every trick she'd picked up during her years at the palace.

"Not that it's your fault," he quickly said, waving a hand. "You've done all you can for me and even spent money from your own coffers to aid my futile search. I could ask no more of you."

"Even so, I wish there was more I could do."

Geoffrey chuckled quietly, a bitter sound that squeezed cold fingers around her heart. For months, Ysolde had borne silent witness to his pain and felt helpless when no amount of money or spell found his lady love. Ashlynne was a ghost.

"I miss her deeply, but I've always known finding her would be a fool's errand."

"Has your mother said nothing? Offered amends?"

Ysolde's knight commander came from a distinguished family of nobles who lived in the valley where the finest steeds in the country were bred and raised. She had enjoyed many lively debates with him on the quality of Hinderan's horses compared to those from her homeland.

"Admit to any wrongdoing? Of course not."

Her quiet sigh accompanied a droop in her shoulders. "I'm sorry. Truly."

Geoffrey waved off her concern. "You have nothing to apologize for, Princess. My mother's cruelty chased Ashlynne from the estate despite your attempts to dissuade her."

Experience gave Ysolde an acute understanding of his pain. Three long years had passed since the day Rhun had packed his belongings and taken the road leading back to their people. He had hated living in the city, too uncomfortable with the massive estate and servants underfoot. After a year of enduring for her sake, he had kissed her brow, apologized, and never returned.

Like her mother.

"How is your urchin?" Geoffrey asked abruptly, changing the sore subject.

"Crispin is doing well," she replied, emphasizing the boy's name. "Not a flea on him." Anymore. Her chamberlain's complaints had no end, however, and had endured through much of the afternoon. "We also discovered something."

"What's that?"

"He is one of the fey folk. His horns are mere nubbins, hidden in his hair."

"Great," he said without humor. "A fairy child. Let's hope that come morning, you'll not find the boy gone and most of the silverware missing." He raised his tea to take a sip.

Ysolde discreetly flicked her fingers toward him, using magic to send a small wave of his cup's sweet contents lapping over the edge and onto his thighs.

It didn't escape his notice. Sighing afterward, he touched a napkin to the wet spot on his trousers. "And now one brat plans to play at mothering *another* brat."

A playful smile touched his lips. No one but Geoffrey dared to adopt such a relaxed manner of speaking with her. He'd earned it, and Ysolde wouldn't have it any other way.

"He is without a home, Geoffrey. You know as well as I that sometimes all a person needs is a chance at a better life."

"Did you not have a pleasant life before our impetuous king whisked you away from your people? You speak very little of home."

"Do I?" She reflected on their past conversations and realized she had spoken very little of her life before court, beyond her knowledge of horses.

"It was only a curiosity."

"No, it's fine. My people don't live in cities like yours, but I wouldn't call it unpleasant. Not really, anyway. Our towns are actually temporary settlements since we follow the wild herds. Our only city, Brychas, is to the deep south on the border of Fas Perra and Crestoli, where we dwell for a portion of the year during the cold months."

In her fondest memories, Brychas shone like a beacon. It was an oasis of beautiful green, isolated from the rest of the desert, and while many knew of its presence, few could penetrate the powerful veil of illusion to enter.

"Brychas is certainly different," he agreed. "My father took me once as a boy. We bought our stallion there, and he has sired many fine foals since."

Ysolde leaned forward, expression full of mirth. "So you admit Marcogh stallions are the finest."

"I admit that they breed quick-footed stock," he corrected her. "But their endurance pales in comparison to a well-bred Hinderan coldblood."

"A sentiment the Hinderan nobility seem to share." She smiled faintly. "Even after these past few years, they still complain that I, a foreigner, hold a seat of such esteem and rank."

"My lady, the people love you. You're a virtuous champion of the just. King Aldemar would be a fool to remove you from rule to satisfy the cries of a few spiteful noblemen."

"Father wouldn't do that, but he has devised another option." Ysolde waved the parchment in her hand. She hadn't let it go since its arrival. "Our king has decided to take it upon himself to send marriage prospects for a visit."

Geoffrey laughed. "Sounds both interesting and absurd. Who has he named?"

"The usual bevy of lords, old and young. I begged his indulgence and requested that he withhold Crowley from the list. It would be too much like marrying family." The queen's brother gave her the chills whenever they met at court. He was also a consummate brat.

"I am not yet convinced he is not a pig transmorphed into the guise of a man and placed in royal clothing. Of course, I've paid a terrible insult to all pigs, haven't I? They can at least be lovable creatures to their caretakers."

Her laughter felt like a release, chasing away her immediate worries. Geoffrey never failed to lighten the mood and often adjusted from the role of stalwart protector to humorous best friend.

"And with that said, I should retire to my bedchamber. It's been a long day, and I set out early to return at an appropriate hour.

"Of course. I've kept you up long enough," she replied.

Ysolde watched him leave for his bedchamber with guilt gnawing her insides. Tomorrow would be a new day and a better one to let her knight know she'd added more work to his already heavy burden.

Unsuitable Suitors

2

When Shyla shook the princess awake, Ysolde's sleeping mind was on the cusp of a satisfying dream. Warm arms had surrounded her and held her close, strong arms that made her feel secure. She clung to it initially until Shyla's voice broke through the dreaming fog.

"Ysolde! Ysolde, wake up, please! The duke is here!"

Then Ysolde roused, and the morning dissolved into panic as they rushed through bathing, dressing, and scurrying down the steps to greet the man.

As far as the nobles went, Gared Bowman, Duke of Lorwick, was among the youngest of his peers and hadn't yet reached his middle years. He had a strong jaw, thick and full dark hair, and gorgeous, baby blue eyes like the summer sky. If Ysolde were to judge her male peers purely on the merit of their good looks, she would have chosen him at once.

Unfortunately for the duke, it wasn't a pageant, and pretty eyes weren't enough to win her affection. She'd met goblins with better manners.

"What a pleasant little estate. Some time has passed since I last paid visit to Ashdale, and it does my heart good to see it grown and powerful. I assumed King Aldemar had placed you within a quiet backwater, perhaps a quaint hovel with a platoon of two dozen city watchmen," the man joked. "But the city thrives against all odds."

"On the contrary, Ashdale has a thriving trade route and lively community." Ysolde's pleasant smile wavered as the duke stretched the limits of her patience. Her mouth felt strange, her uncooperative lips resistant, until at last, she quit the attempt to put on a friendly countenance.

Was it too early to open a bottle of wine? She'd need it if she intended to bear a day of entertaining the duke and ignoring thinly veiled insults.

"Rather amazing when the city's duchess remains in bed long past the start of the day. I'm impressed." Duke Lorwick glanced over the dining room, his nose in the air.

Despite his words, Ysolde had the distinct impression he meant the opposite. His clear disdain left her wondering at his true reason for coming to Ashdale.

"Does your knight protector not find it necessary to perform his duties?"

"Pardon me?"

"Your knight. We have sat here for a time while you remain undefended by your guard. Perhaps I misjudged Ashdale after all, if your primary knight's manners are so lacking."

Ysolde pushed her seat back from the table with an abrupt shove, rose from the chair, and tossed her napkin to the table. "Perhaps he has overslept this day, but my knight's manners are impeccable. And he certainly does not arrive unannounced before the breakfast chime has even rung." She stepped away from the table. "I trust you will see yourself out as promptly as you barged in."

"How dare you leave without permission—"

"Permission?" Ysolde whirled to face him. Fury churned in her gut and spiked her pulse to a feverish tempo. "This is *my* home. My city. My province."

"And it's no wonder your father seeks a man worth his salt to take possession. You have run this place into the gr—"

"Piss off," Ysolde said hotly, opting for the coarsest word in her vocabulary. Manners, refinement, and hours of training in courtesy and eloquence flittered away in the figurative breeze.

One of Geoffrey's new recruits stepped in, wearing a dubious yet wary expression. Were the guest anyone but a duke, the young man would have shown him the door. Lorwick didn't move, and so he and the young guard stood in a bitter stalemate, each one eyeing the other.

"No, Oswald. Return to your post," Ysolde said. "As Duke Lorwick feels disinclined to honorably leave, *I* will show him the door."

"I am a guest, sent by the king himself. You cannot kick me out."

She didn't bother with a verbal reply. A graceful wrist flick stoked the flames in the low-burning hearth. Red-hot cinders swirled into the air and rushed toward the table in a spiraling cone.

Duke Lorwick stumbled from his seat, escaping the attack. Her stride brought her closer to the man, and with the next casual gesture, a gust of wind blew the ember cloud toward him again. The unprotected nobleman evaded it by hurrying to the door, as a sheep would when herded by a shepherd's hound.

"I will report this to King Aldemar!" he cried.

"Good. Tell him everything. Tell him of your ugly spirit and piss poor behavior. Tell him all of it."

"It's no bloody surprise a Marcogh would behave this way. One of your kind could never become a true lady. You don't need lessons in eloquent behavior—you need an animal trainer!"

"Get out!"

The next plume of fire came dangerously close to setting Lorwick's face aflame. Frantic, he patted his beard with both hands and slapped his cheeks until the embers died out. He rushed from the dining room without another word.

"What's wrong? What's happening?" Geoffrey's alarmed voice called from the hallway. He charged into the dining room with his sword in hand seconds after Lorwick had hightailed it from the chamber.

"Good morning, Geoffrey," Ysolde greeted him. Her enthusiastic tone made him double take and lower his sword arm to one side.

"I seem to be at a disadvantage. I heard the shouting and came at once. Was that Duke Lorwick? Why did he rush from the dining room as if Nox herself chased at his heels? Why was there fire?"

"Nox would have been kinder, I think," Oswald offered reluctantly. "Duke Lorwick has had the privilege of discovering our lady's temper, Ser."

Geoffrey turned to Ysolde and raised a brow. "Was that necessary? Truly?"

"He insulted you," she defended herself.

"Ah." Geoffrey blinked. "Excellent job then." The knight sheathed his sword, no longer concerned with the events.

Ysolde beamed at him. "I thought so too, but it's good you arrived when you did. I have a matter to discuss with you, so we may as well speak now."

"Oh no. I don't know whether to ask what I've done or," he hesitated before adding in a jovial voice, "what else you've done in my absence."

He had a knack for predicting such things, and sometimes she wondered if precognition was another of his odd gifts.

"It's nothing terrible," she voiced with caution. "Have a seat and join me for breakfast."

Geoffrey expressed his skepticism with a raised brow before his gaze lingered on the door. "All joking aside, you have my apologies for oversleeping. I should have been awake when the lout arrived to stall him with a tour of the premises until a decent bloody hour."

"But you weren't, and you have a valid excuse for your tardiness. Please, join me now, and we'll put it behind us."

As they settled in their designated dining chairs, a servant hurried away with Lorwick's picked-over meal. Apparently, he hadn't appreciated the customary breakfast of poached eggs, delicate crepes filled with fruit-studded cream, and thinly sliced ham. One returned moments later with Geoffrey's usual preferences, a plate piled with fluffy skillet cakes and thick chunks of glazed ham to accompany his hardboiled eggs.

"So, tell me what I've missed while I was away." The knight tapped an egg against the edge of the table and peeled it, all the while never taking his green eyes from her face.

Sometimes, Ysolde was positive Geoffrey, Fingall, and her direct relatives were the only men capable of remembering she had eyes. She chuckled at the thought and raised her tea for a sip, letting it warm her insides.

"Tell me, how well do you know Gregor Lansford?"

"Gregor?" His confusion grew. "We're as close as brothers without the blood tie, I suppose. I think highly of him, my lady." He didn't take a bite of his food, favoring the chance to study her closely instead. "Has he done something to offend you?"

"No, no, nothing of the sort," she blurted out quickly, waving a hand.

He sighed his relief.

"What were you going to do if he had?"

"Beat him," he answered without pause, wearing a too-serious expression. "But why are we discussing my friend Gregor?"

"Yesterday as you were unwinding after your travel, I spoke with him and another member of the watch in my audience chamber. I told him I find the current regulations unsatisfactory and would like to hold court for the thieves—myself."

"We have a magistrate for that."

"One who sends everyone to the gallows, young or old, innocent or guilty."

And it wouldn't do anymore. Although Ysolde had yet to determine if her plans to assume the man's role were realistic, she knew without a doubt she couldn't allow him to hold the life of every supposed criminal in his hands.

Everyone couldn't be guilty. They all didn't deserve to swing.

"Ysolde," Geoffrey said in a gentle voice. He turned to reach for the coffee, only for a standing servant to dart in, seize the pot, and fill the mug for him. He flashed a charming smile at the young woman who nearly overflowed the cup.

Ysolde rolled her eyes. Four years and the servants still swooned in his presence. "Yes?"

"Magistrate Wicksham is a good man. A fair man. I have always trusted his judgment and felt absolute confidence in the old duke's decision to appoint him to the chair. I began as his bailiff, after all."

She bit her lower lip. If he thought the magistrate was a good man, then the magistrate was a good man. He'd never lie to her.

Geoffrey had a natural gift, and it had been honed during his time in the monastery as one of Ashta's Chosen. His ability to know the truth from lies made him invaluable wherever he worked in the kingdom.

"And you're one hundred percent confident only the rightfully accused died while you were bailiff."

"And while I was watch captain."

"And now?"

He sipped coffee, silent. When he didn't answer, Ysolde leaned forward and pressed again.

"Tell me, Geoffrey, do you honestly believe no innocents have died? Do you truly approve of the changes since my father stole you away from the watch?"

"He didn't steal me, my lady. I humbly accepted the king's request to guard his most valued treasure—you. I have no regrets. If I'd told him no, he would have understood." He paused, a thoughtful expression coming to his features. "And chosen someone lesser, of course."

"Of course," she agreed with a laugh. "But answer my question."

"I agree with you, all right? But without any other way of judging the accused, the guards do what they must in my absence." He shrugged and raised a cup of coffee. "It's unfortunate."

"Which is why I'd like you to stand with me during court each day."

"Each day," he repeated.

"Yes."

"I am to stand beside you as you hold court *daily?*"

"No, not daily. Perhaps three or four days a week. Is that too much to ask?" Her confidence dwindled in the face of his overwhelmed expression.

The knight shook his head. "No, my lady. Of course not. At what hour should I make myself available to you?"

"Before afternoon tea." Ysolde pressed her lips firmly together and watched him. "For no longer than an hour. With your talent, things should proceed smoothly."

She didn't bother to ask if the time was acceptable—Geoffrey would have told her anything she wanted to hear. Instead, she would simply watch the knight and make adjustments accordingly if it appeared to cut into his schedule.

"One can only hope, my lady."

***

To Ysolde's great relief, Lorwick set the bar low, and the rest of the suitors who trickled in over the course of the next month displayed cool heads and civil tongues.

Or maybe the word of her incendiary response to disrespect warned them to behave.

They were all unsuitable for one reason or another, and after they would leave, she would have the honor of listening to Geoffrey's comical observations. They were all uptight, too old, military-minded, or some other unacceptable combination of traits.

"Count Saddlesworth has plans of making Ashdale into a proper military garrison. I thought you should know."

Ysolde scoffed and stabbed at a piece of roast quail on her plate. "Except we are not meant to be a military outpost. It would stifle all the trade we've finally drawn in."

Geoffrey barked out a laugh. "He plans to squash this trade nonsense and direct it all to Fishwell."

"Over my dead body."

"Ysolde, while I do feel sympathy for you, I hope your father sends a never-ending stream of these buffoons. They're hilarious." He grinned and finished his wine, completely unapologetic.

His views changed a few nights later. In lieu of high noblemen, her father sent the best knights and land-holding lords in the land.

"I think highly of Ser Cadby." Geoffrey approached her after supper in the sitting room one evening.

A small fire flickered in the hearth, and the lamps burned low, providing a cozy atmosphere to Ysolde's favorite room. For once, he sat beside her on the settee instead of occupying his oversized armchair. He relaxed against the cream cushions and appeared well-at-ease.

"The man stinks like a horse's arse." She passed him a teacup and saucer.

"But he's unrivaled with a sword, a great military leader. You could use someone like him around here. He wouldn't be the sort of duke to sit idly when the people need him, and he has no interest in changing Ashdale. We talked at length."

"He doesn't need the sword to strike fear into the heart of our enemies. Only a strong wind."

Geoffrey choked on his drink.

Ysolde reached over and thumped his back. When he was done coughing, she offered a napkin and a smile.

"Besides, if I have need of a sword, then I can think of no one better than you. Perhaps you should be the new duke."

Startled by the compliment, he stared while wordlessly opening and closing his mouth.

"Thank you," he said after recovering his wits. "Not that you need my sword so much these days. When am I going to get you outside onto the training ground with the rest of us?"

"I hardly think it would be appropriate to slaughter me in front of the men."

"It'll be fun," he insisted. "Maybe you can teach them a thing about archery."

Her light laughter and smiles faded away. "No, I don't think that would be a good idea."

"My apologies, Ysolde. I didn't mean…" He sighed. "At any rate, I should meet with Gregor to discuss your most recent edict. Andras shall remain in the estate and will be here in my stead until I return."

"Is it really so terrible, what I ask?" She latched onto the topic change, eager to leave talk of training and archery behind.

"Ashdale's dungeon lacks the proper quarters to secure the abundance of criminals serving their time, Your Grace, and it's been this way since you abolished our—*his* standard execution policy." Geoffrey cleared his throat and glanced away.

She knew her knight well, and more than anything, he hated to challenge her authority or to give unsolicited advice.

"What would you suggest I do?" If he wouldn't offer alternatives on his own initiative, then she would ask outright.

"With all due respect, Princess, there are some criminals beyond the scope of your new rehabilitation ideals. Gregor is under the impression that you desire no executions at all."

Ysolde sighed. "No, I said that I wish to be informed before an execution takes place."

His apologetic smile didn't alleviate her concerns. "They're accustomed to exercising complete autonomy over their duties. The old duke was not one for holding court."

"No one should die in obscurity, not even a thief. How many people have been killed in my name, I wonder." Her pensive gaze focused on the mountains beyond the window. "Expand the dungeons."

"Pardon me?"

"You heard me. We can expand the dungeons or build a jailhouse. Those who are sentenced will work off their debts. They can help repair the roads, fortify the walls, and sow the fields."

"And where will— Yes, of course, Princess. As you say. I'll relay your directives at once." He stood, ready to make good on his word.

"You dislike the idea."

Geoffrey lacked talent for concealing his thoughts, and during the years of their partnership, she'd come to learn his body language and mannerisms. She was "Ysolde" when her knight was at ease, which quickly became "Princess" again when he felt he'd overstepped his bounds.

"I said nothing of the sort, my lady." He fidgeted like a little boy, shifting his weight from one foot to the other before he resumed his tall stance.

"You didn't support it, either."

He opened and shut his mouth, a silent testament to his disapproval. "Please, my lady. If you desire advice, you should seek Fingall."

"Fingall will say I'm behaving foolishly. I'm not asking the old elf; I'm asking you."

Geoffrey ran his fingers through his blond hair and frowned. A flash of guilt twisted her gut for putting him on the spot. "It is a very noble plan. We will make it work. It's our job after all."

It was the most she could ask for, and at the very least, she knew in her heart she could count on him for anything.

THE PRIMROSE

3

Years ago, long before Ysolde's time, the city's founding nobleman chose to erect a majestic tower to overlook the city. The duke built it at the heart of Ashdale, accessible to the old, the poor, and the wealthy, so that one and all could spectate the morning hangings. It was as much for public enjoyment as it was a tool to deter the city's criminal element.

In the time since then, the watchtower had been affectionately named the Spire of Suffering for its grisly reputation. Each duke before Ysolde upheld the city's unforgiving practices by executing accused thieves and murderers by the morning.

And for nearly five years prior to Ysolde's appointment, Geoffrey had served as captain of the watch. The tower was a second home to him, and its watchmen were as much family as the siblings conceived by his parents.

He slammed his fist into the top of Gregor's desk. The man behind it, slumped in his seat with his head tilted back and eyes shut, jerked forward and went for his sword. His startled blue eyes flew to Geoffrey and filled with recognition before it cleared the sheath.

"You arsehole. Haven't you got anything better to do than ruin my good rest?"

"You're sleeping on the job, mate."

"I've got to sneak it in at some point. Your bloody duchess has us all pulling extra work."

Geoffrey grimaced. "You'll be pulling a little more. She plans to build a prison of some sort and to extend the dungeons."

Gregor swore out loud. "Does she believe us to be golems?"

"I don't know," Geoffrey admitted. "She's wide-eyed and optimistic about turning the city around. I don't have the heart to tell her it's beyond saving the way she wants."

"Why don't you tell her the godsdamned things you hear when people lie to you? For the love of Ashta, you're a former paladin. You can see what lies in men's hearts, and you know the evil that's out there."

"And she doesn't. It's my job to guarantee she never does."

Gregor spat to the side. "She's your princess, not your wife. Shielding her from the truth seems rather foolhardy."

"She'll learn it on her own in time. Eventually. But that's neither here nor there. I can loan you some additional men from the estate, some of our guardsmen perhaps. We'll appoint them to this new prison."

"And who will train them to maintain a prison?" Gregor demanded. "It isn't the same as holding a watch post in the markets or at Her Grace's estate."

"Must you nitpick everything?"

With the city map spread over the table, the two men sketched out ideas and began the initial planning stages of how to spend Ysolde's money. They divided the tasks between them of who would contact the laborers, inform the magistrates, and spread word to the authors of the *Ashdale Chronicle*, alerting them that change was coming.

"I appreciate your help in all of this."

"I hope your princess certainly appreciates it. Now, if you don't mind, I've got a wife to get home to."

"She's your princess too. Now come on. We've worked hard. Let's have a drink or...seven first."

"Fine, but you're buying."

Noise drifted from the windows of the Goose and Tap and only intensified once they stepped inside the familiar establishment. Fiddlers played from the low stage in the corner while a raucous game of cards carried on near the room's rear. Someone would be thrown out before the night ended.

"Bar?"

"Not if I can help it. Harol's been a bit on the chatty side lately," Gregor explained.

They veered to the rear, closer to the card game and away from the music. Once they settled into chairs, Geoffrey whistled for the first skirt-wearing bar wench to pass by. His favorite serving girl jerked toward the sound and nearly spilled ale over her current customer's lap.

"Geoffrey?" Ignoring the rest of the thirsty men waving their empty mugs, Anatha rushed over to greet him instead. She scooted onto Geoffrey's lap and slung one arm around his shoulders before flashing a red-painted smile up at the knight. "What's kept you away from us for so long?"

"Business out of town."

"For the duchess?" she asked.

"Personal matters, lovely. All personal."

"Aren't you going to serve us our drinks first?" Gregor demanded.

"Man's got a point." Geoffrey chuckled and shook his head. Anatha planted her bottom a little more firmly in Geoffrey's lap until he spanked his palm against her thigh. "Drinks first, then you can settle as long as you want."

Sulking, the bar wench abandoned her seat. "Same as usual for you blokes?"

"Aye," Gregor said. "And a fish stew."

"Make that two," Geoffrey said.

Moments later, she returned to set heavy ale mugs on the table. She placed a smaller glass of whiskey beside each. "S'on the house tonight, gents. Harol decided to serve all members of the watch for free on Solinday."

"He's not even a member of the watch anymore," Gregor muttered.

"Ser Ashcroft was our captain for years before you came to this bloody town, Gregor, and he's still captain in the eyes of many. I say he gets his drinks for free." Anatha flipped her blond hair over her shoulder.

Geoffrey fixed his friend with a smug look then raised the drink to his lips.

They were on the fourth round before Gregor squinted across the table and stared his friend down. "All right then. Out with it. You're slamming back the drinks as if liquor is a brand new concept to you. What happened when you went home? Did you find her?"

"Would I be here drinking this cheap ale with you if I did?"

"Blast."

"I'm going to take your advice and move on. It's done and behind me. Ashlynne's gone, and no amount of searching will ever find her if she wants to remain hidden." All because his mother had gotten ahold of her and shown the girl the worst side of the haughty nobility.

He tried to tell himself that if Ashlynne had truly loved him, his mother's words would never have driven her off. In the end, he blamed himself for not seeing that truth.

Gregor nodded, but his eyes remained unconvinced. "Glad to hear it then."

"You don't believe me."

"I'll believe it when you're no longer sulking over your ale. Drink like a man."

They drank until alcohol sloshed in their bellies with only steaming bowls of fish stew and hard bread to dull its edge. Afterward, the two friends spilled a generous amount of coin onto the table, waved to Anatha, and traveled a tedious path to the door.

"How do you walk such a straight path after outdrinking me?" Gregor demanded.

"You don't feel the effect of alcohol when you're disciplined."

Gregor grunted at him. "You barely finished the bloody training at the temple, and you're waving that in my face now?"

"But the point is that I *did* finish it. Besides, I haven't done too poorly for myself."

Geoffrey's chuckle and smug grin earned him a punch to his unarmored shoulder. They laughed on their way to the intersecting street corner further down the road where a single red lantern glowed brightly beneath the starlit sky.

"You could be a paladin of Ashta. Instead, you're bowing and scraping to a spoiled girl on a throne—"

Geoffrey adjusted his stride to bump into the watch captain, sending the man off course. Gregor toppled into the lantern post and clung to it for balance.

"The rules were too stiff for me, mate," Geoffrey replied. And their superiors too disingenuous. His memories of the final days in the Order sobered him.

"Like what? Be a good man? Abolish evil with impunity? Sing the praises of our goddess Ashta? Things you already do."

"Vows of celibacy," Geoffrey lied through his teeth, plucking the first excuse for his abrupt departure from the warrior priesthood.

"Only until you're married."

"Who wants to get married for the privilege to have sex?" Geoffrey demanded.

Years ago when the temple of Ashta had accepted him into her holy order, he'd wanted nothing more than to serve on the side of justice and good. Now he looked at the warrior priesthood with bitterness.

Gregor shook his head. "So you're planning a visit to the Moonlit Primrose instead, are you? You poor bastard. Get it wet for me then, will you? My missus is probably fast asleep by now."

"Wake her."

"Aye, I can do that and pay a visit to Madame Maybell's Dispensary for a poultice to soothe the knot she beats into my skull."

Chuckling, the two friends parted ways, one to his home and wife, the other to visit another old friend. From the exterior, the Moonlit Primrose resembled any other well-to-do estate. Its high, wrought-iron fence sported a sturdy gate. Beyond it, two brawny hired hands flanked the manor's door. Employed muscle kept the customers in line but was often an unnecessary feature for intimidation only.

Rose protected her employees more fiercely than any guard. Geoffrey witnessed it once when a drunk slapped around one of the girls for failing to please him just right. By the time the city guard arrived, they'd had to toss him into a wheelbarrow and literally cart him off.

"Evenin', Ser Geoffrey," one of them greeted him kindly. Mert and Joffren, if Geoffrey's memory served him correctly.

"Evening. Quiet night?"

"Bloody boring as usual. Business is slow, what with the princess raising taxes and all," Mert said.

"What's that got to do with business here?" Geoffrey asked.

"Rose had to raise rates. Some of the clients ain't liked that much, and now they're off gettin' their pickles dillied elsewhere," Joffren explained. "They ought be real glad to be seein' you."

They stepped aside and let him into the brothel. Through no small amount of willpower and focus, Geoffrey made a straight line to the front desk, where a buxom half-elf filed her nails.

"Pansy, that's your name, right?"

"Actually, it's Lily, and—"

"I want to see Rose," he interrupted her.

Lily undressed him with her lilac eyes, roaming her gaze up his body from booted feet to his face. "She's not taking customers. Might I recommend Magnolia?"

"Bullshit." A surge of sobriety struck Geoffrey with the effective force of ice water to the face. He glowered at the petite woman behind the desk. "I don't do business with anyone but Rose. Tell her that I'm here."

"All right then. As you wish, Ser Geoffrey."

Lily abandoned her seat at the desk and traipsed away. The seductive sway of her hips entranced him until she disappeared around the corner. Then he snapped out of it and bided his time. She returned moments later and shook her head.

"Rose won't be able to take you this evening, Ser. Might I—"

"Is she busy with a client?"

"No, but—"

"Tell her that I've come as a customer. Only a customer."

Lily's pink lips bowed into a pout. "I'll try again."

When the girl returned a few minutes later and beckoned Geoffrey to follow her into the back, his eager steps overtook her down the familiar hallway. He knew the way without her help.

Once inside, he stripped off his shirt and dropped onto the edge of the bed to wait. Long days of riding by horseback, training the men in the yard, and the overall stress associated with his duties had tightened Geoffrey's back muscles until they were as rigid as bowstrings.

The flowers of the Moonlit Primrose were more than highly paid prostitutes. They supplied any earthly pleasure a man, or woman in some cases, dared to ask for. From visual entertainment that didn't involve physical contact to their luxurious massages, their ideal goal was to create a satisfied customer.

Geoffrey drowsed for a second, but he awakened to light pressure unsettling the bed. He opened his eyes to the sight of Rose peering down at him.

"I almost didn't have the heart to awaken you. You seem to be in need of the rest." Her cherubic smile put him at ease.

"I seem to be in need of quite a few things," he replied. "Hence my presence in a brothel."

The brothel mistress giggled. "And so you are."

Rose was blessed with the kind of timeless beauty that made her true age indiscernible—late twenties, mid-thirties at the very most, but her eyes held wisdom beyond those years.

The casual visitor to the Moonlit Primrose didn't know that the brothel's proprietor was the sixth Rose to operate the establishment. Her bright blue eyes and wild mane of red hair alluded to foreign origins of the kingdom Crestoli to the east.

"So…" Her fingers walked down his chest. "It's been quite a while since you've come to my door as a client. What'll it be tonight, love?"

"Whatever you've got for what ails me."

As she leaned over him, her sleek strands of vibrant red hair skimmed his chest. She inhaled the lingering scent from his ale. "I'd offer you a drink, but you're ahead of me."

"I am," he agreed. Her topaz eyes held his gaze, and all of his guilt welled to the surface. "I'm sorry for how I treated you. I know it's not your fault."

Rose nodded, never losing her sympathetic smile. "I was never upset with you, Geoffrey."

Her deft touch made quick work of the ties to his breeches, and then she made him forget his troubles.

Unexpected Guests

4

Ysolde hadn't held such an ostentatious, exorbitant dinner since her arrival to the estate as its duchess. It was absolutely outrageous, a waste of money needlessly spent to awe a man she had no desire to impress, despite Fingall and her father's best hopes.

The sweet blend of honey and herbs wafted toward her from the steaming seafood platter where a yard-long ocean bass lay upon a crisp bed of tart greens, its orange flesh laid open and stuffed with seared yellow peppers. The castle's chef, Madame Quirre, embellished the expensive catch with red sea cucumber. It was a decadent meal accompanied by a basket of honey-glazed rolls.

Warm colors favored by south Hindera had been the theme of the night, celebrating the attendance of their esteemed guest, Baron Easton. The man came from lands bordering the harsh desert, where winter didn't exist and the flowers always blossomed.

She detested his exaggerated battle stories and the idea of organized wyvern hunts for pleasure. The miniature dragons weren't good for eating, and their tough hides, while durable, made ugly armor that was outperformed by other materials.

Geoffrey's forced smile reached its limit. Her knight, ever devoted to his duties, remained in his seat despite the boisterous company shadowing their dining table. He had finished his meal nearly a half hour ago, and she'd lost count of the number of times he'd glanced at the door with longing to leave.

"What manner of creature inhabits this region compared to our wyverns, Ser Ashcroft? Any good for sport?"

"I wouldn't know," the knight answered honestly.

"How could you not know of the beasts in your own backyard?"

"I don't hunt for sport." Geoffrey bit into his fourth roll, concealing his apparent disdain of the conversation by eating.

"We do not conduct pleasure hunts in Ashdale," Ysolde informed the baron, plastering a smile on her face. "Geoffrey has led a few in the rare event of a dangerous beast or when food and fur become scarce, but otherwise I see no need to decorate my halls with the heads of deceased animals."

"Ashdale is home to several talented local artisans," Fingall chimed in. "You will see many examples of their work gracing our halls. Our snow festival is one of the most beautiful times of the year, when the streets fill with ice sculptures."

"A northern Hinderan winter brings no less than a meter of snow. In a day. They're quite unforgiving, and the livestock are few," Geoffrey cut in. "The mountain goats aren't so plentiful by then, so once the lakes freeze, the city fishermen conduct their work on the ice."

"Ice fishing?" the baron asked uncertainly.

"Naturally. Did you not realize Ashdale's seafood is our finest commodity?" Andras, Geoffrey's second-in-command, replied. "We stockpile it in the fall and salt it, of course."

"A peasant's dish." Easton waved a dismissive hand.

Ysolde nudged her wine glass in a subtle queue. Shyla moved over to refill it and offered a brief sympathetic glance.

"Oh no. Kippered fish is our chef's finest meal," Geoffrey said, putting on a brighter smile. "At least thrice a week come the winter months. Our princess doesn't believe in wasteful, extravagant meals. This is quite the rarity."

Andras chuckled and joined in. "She certainly doesn't. The old duke ordered meals befitting King Aldemar himself. Not our princess. We often eat like the commonfolk."

Their sudden, inexplicable praise over fish brought a smile to her lips, which she hid by sipping from her glass. Geoffrey tended to complain about their lack of variety during the winter months. Whatever their reason for making mischief, she had no drive to discourage them.

From the corner of her vision, a rounded, pale face peered back at her from the doorway. She twisted to see

Crispin holding one of her favorite cups between his small hands.

"Crispin, come in. Don't be shy." Her fond expression came naturally, easing the tightness in her cheeks and the ache in her jaw. The boy's appearance served as a welcome distraction.

"I brought you a pot of tea from the kitchens, ma'am. I brewed it all myself," Crispin told her gleefully. He offered one of Ysolde's hand-painted, porcelain teacups imported from Sarangi. It rested upon a matching saucer traced with intricate patterns of flower petals and branches.

"And who's this?" Easton asked.

"A page in my household," Ysolde replied. "Crispin, this is Baron Easton. He's come to visit us all the way from Ackleton."

"Ysolde has become popular among the little ones of our city. Some of the staff have speculated about her desire to adopt a half dozen more like Crispin into our service."

Ysolde's head whipped around to face Geoffrey. She had made no such claims on the subject of orphans. Where had Geoffrey gathered the preposterous notion?

"A half dozen?" Easton echoed.

"He jests," Fingall hurriedly replied. "We have a fine orphanage in the city, but the princess took a shine to this one."

Geoffrey didn't provide another witty retort or lie. He stared quietly at Crispin instead. In the time since the young child had come into her service, his opinion had wavered from disapproving to indifferent.

Crispin offered the mug again. "Your tea, ma'am. It'll get cold soon—"

Geoffrey, who sat beside her on the left, lunged forward from his seat. Before Ysolde could protest, he backhanded the mug of steaming tea from Crispin's grasp, drew his sword with the other hand, and shoved the blade through the young boy's chest.

"Crispin!" As Ysolde cried out her ward's name, Shyla shrieked.

"Geoffrey! What in Ashta's name are you doing?!" Andras lurched from his seat as if to stop his commanding knight from taking further action.

Baron Easton almost toppled from his seat in his attempt to distance himself from the scene. His fancy sword remained sheathed at his side.

Ysolde's chair clattered against the floor. Her horrified gaze moved from the slain child to Geoffrey. Seconds later, she collided against him, a steam locomotive wrapped in an elegantly dressed package. For such a slim woman, she struck as hard as any man, enraged and beating against his chest like a mother bear defending her cub.

"How could you? He was just a boy! Only a little boy!" she yelled.

Her strikes didn't budge Geoffrey, who proved to be as solid as a brick-and-mortar wall despite her blows.

"Princess, look."

"You killed him!" She struck out at him again. If she'd been rational and of a thinking mind, her knight might have had to fend off against fire and lightning. Magic was the furthest thing from her mind. Flashes of pain danced across her knuckles, minor compared to the still, little body on her dining room floor.

"Look!" Geoffrey caught her wrist and spun her around. He trapped her against him with one arm and forcefully directed her face toward the corpse.

Whatever it was that Geoffrey had slain, it wasn't Crispin. Black blood seeped from the wound and spread into the rich carpet. The eyes, wide open and staring, promptly clouded gray as the color leached from the child's skin. His flesh wrinkled, his hair silvered, and eventually the scrawny remnants didn't resemble Crispin at all.

"It's a doppleganger! Look at it!"

She went limp in his arms and leaned back against him, the fight drained from her. Geoffrey smoothed his hand up and down her arm.

"You just skewered him," she whispered.

"I'm sorry I terrified you, but I would never harm Crispin," Geoffrey assured her.

45

"If that isn't the young boy, then where is he?" Andras crouched beside the mess made by the supposed tea. Foul-smelling vapors arose from the liquid, which had eaten straight through the carpet to the wood beneath.

"Good question," Geoffrey muttered. "He could be anywhere. Search the stables, check his quarters, and look in the kitchens."

Mention of the boy's uncertain fate roused Ysolde. She tensed up and turned in Geoffrey's hold. "By the goddess, we have to find Crispin. They might have hurt him."

He nudged her toward a seat. "My lady, please sit. We'll find him. Fingall, I want you to remain here with the princess. If an assassin can get through the elven wards on the castle, then there's no stopping them."

"Please, he's just a boy. I won't sit here when he could be hurt somewhere."

"All right," Geoffrey agreed. "Wherever he is, he's alive. Of that, I have no doubt."

"He is correct, Princess. A doppleganger cannot maintain an illusion once the source has died," Fingall confirmed.

Geoffrey nodded. "Baron Easton, would you escort the princess while Andras and I give our commands to the guard?"

"Of course." The baron appeared uncertain or in doubt of his own ability to protect.

"I'll search the kitchens and east wing," Geoffrey stated. "Notifying men as I go."

"I shall search the grounds and spread the word," Andras volunteered.

"We'll head to his quarters and then to the stables," Ysolde said next. "Fingall, you're to remain here to relay any news if we return or to meet him if he should come through."

"Of course." Fingall nodded and returned to his seat. His body angled toward the only two entrances to the great dining hall. Power emanated from him, a contained hurricane awaiting freedom.

As they all divided to conduct their searches of the grounds, Ysolde scurried down the corridor toward the servants' wing. Its close proximity to the stables allowed her to rush into his room first.

"Crispin? Crispin, are you here? Now's not the time to play, love," Ysolde called out.

Three tidy beds in a neat row bordered the wall, one belonging to her stablemaster, another to her lead groundskeeper, and the last to Crispin. All were empty.

Baron Easton shot her an uncertain look. "He isn't here, my lady. Perhaps this is a job best left to your—"

"I will find him," she interrupted him.

Without waiting for him to object again, she hurried into the corridor and down the hall to the wing's exit. A small door let out onto a narrow path tucked to the rear of the majestic estate.

The fine hairs at the nape of her neck rose. A pins-and-needles sensation spread over her limbs and raced down her spine, a chill she couldn't shake no matter how she tried. The stench of evil permeated the air, its foul odor invading her nostrils.

Something was here.

As Easton shrieked behind her, providing the warning she needed, Ysolde lunged to the left as a whistling noise cut past her. Quickly, she spun back to the right, pivoting the final time to face the incoming arm hurtling toward her face.

The creature attacked in repetition with its hooked appendages, stabbing downward with insectile limbs like sawblades. She ducked around behind it.

Almost invisible to the eye, splashes of color in a circular pattern on the pavement indicated a perfect demon-binding rune. Her steps had released it and triggered the trap.

"Princess!" Easton cried from behind her. Rather than rush to her aid, he trembled beside the door.

Ysolde remained between him and their attacker with a brilliant dome of magic bubbled around her. The creature skittered left and right, striking with mantid claws but always meeting the shimmering protection barrier.

A ring of fire blazed around her feet, only to spiral higher with each pulse of her heart. With her increasing fury, the column of fire rose until it completely surrounded her.

"Easton, take cover!" Against her better judgment, Ysolde spared a glance over her shoulder to see the door hung open. Easton was nowhere in sight.

The coward. The bloody coward. She seethed inside.

As she released the spell, it blazed outward in a controlled explosion, washing over everything in its wake. Magic incinerated the grass at her feet, scorched the stepping stones, and seared into the foul creature standing in front of her.

It went up like tinder. Shrieking in pain, the beast streaked across the grounds as a white-hot blur with flames trailing behind it. Cinders and specks of black ash drifted in the wind, and seconds later, there was little more than a pile of smoldering ruin left behind.

More mindful of her steps but giving the slain demon no further thought, Ysolde raced across the grass toward the stables. With the stableman missing from his post, she found the doors wide open, revealing anxious horses in their stalls. One nickered nervously and stamped the ground.

She stumbled over a body half buried in the hay strewn across the floor. Catching herself on her hands, she looked down to see the barn filth mixed with a dark puddle of red. Her stableman's throat had been cut, and his unseeing eyes stared up at the wooden ceiling.

"I'm so sorry, Huxley," she whispered. Tears wouldn't serve her or the dead, so she pushed herself up and hurried forward. "Crispin? Are you here? It's only me."

No answer.

"Please come out if you're hiding, love."

Blackjack, Geoffrey's enormous stallion, whinnied loudly from the rear of the stables. He was a unique mix of Hinderan coldblood and Marcogh swifthoof. The result added a layer of muscle to the latter's svelte physiques and two hands of height.

As she searched for Crispin, the horse put up a racket and kicked the reinforced stall door. He and his son, Zephyr, were the only animals that required one after countless breakout attempts…and successes. Once she'd walked over to soothe Blackjack, she saw what had stirred him. A small body lay crumpled on the floor in the storage nook across from the riled horse.

"Crispin!"

Ysolde rushed over to the boy's limp form, oblivious to the equine tack and old tools in her path. She dropped to her knees beside the child and pressed her ear to his chest.

A weak and thready rhythm assured her the boy lived, prompting her to weep in relief. "Still alive. Thank the gods, still alive. Crispin, love, wake up, darling."

He didn't stir. He lacked color in his cheeks, and his skin felt cool and clammy.

"Ysolde?!" Geoffrey shouted from the pathway beyond the stable door. He barged inside with his sword drawn and gleaming red. Black ichor ran down the pristine steel but failed to dull the magical luster it exuded. His fine tunic clung against the contours of his muscled chest, heavily soaked with sweat. Even his fair curls slicked against his brow and temples.

"I'm fine, but Crispin isn't. Please, do something!"

"I haven't healed anyone in years."

"You have to try," she pleaded. Tears streaked her sooty cheeks. She wiped them with the back of her hand and left a black smear on her wrist.

"I don't…" He tossed his sword aside and scooped the boy into his arms. "I need sunlight."

In the time it took her to move to her feet, he was already crossing the barn and stepping outside into the afternoon light. Consternation etched his grave features as he stretched Crispin across the grass and knelt beside him.

All of Ashdale knew Geoffrey to be a former paladin of Ashta, but Ysolde had never received the honor of watching him put his training to use. She'd listened to cheerful jests about his talent on a horse and his skill with a sword—even overhearing boisterous talk among the men about their expertise in the bedroom—but Geoffrey was uncharacteristically humble when it came to the temple.

"Please, Geoffrey." From the corner of her eye, she saw Andras galloping across the grounds, Zephyr's black mane flying in the wind. A small squad of guards rode in his wake. He dismounted upon arrival as understanding of the scene dawned on him.

"Shall I fetch a healer?"

Geoffrey shook his head. "They'll never arrive in time. The boy's almost gone." He opened the leather pouch attached to his belt and removed a string of pale green and white pearls. They glistened in the sunlight, throwing off dancing beams of light across the grass.

The appearance of the prayer beads took her by surprise, but she'd never been more thankful to see a token of faith to Ashta. Whatever the prayer was he uttered, Geoffrey kept the words to himself. His lips moved in silence, and with his head bowed, he placed both palms over Crispin's fragile chest.

At first, nothing happened, but then a glow spread around his hands. It intensified and grew, creeping from beneath Geoffrey's hands until the boy was alight with color and the two of them were engulfed in golden fire.

Crispin drew in a gasped breath, his tiny body curling in on itself as he coughed up whatever foul concoction had been given to him. Ysolde dropped beside him, frantic hands smoothing up and down the child's back. When his breathing came easier she pulled him into her lap and cradled him close.

"Thank you," she whispered.

"That was miraculous, Geoffrey," Andras said, awestruck. The other observers nodded, murmuring agreement.

"It was nothing," Geoffrey said modestly. "I'm surprised it worked."

Andras offered him a hand up from the grass. "Perhaps the Lady still watches out for you after all."

Geoffrey gave his cousin a weak smile. "Perhaps. Allow me a moment to fetch Blackjack. I doubt it'll be any use, but we should secure the perimeter. I want three of you to remain with Her Grace in the event that our assassin hasn't yet left the grounds. You three come with us."

***

Geoffrey's heavy footfalls announced his arrival hours after the assassination attempt. Ysolde glanced up to find him framed in Crispin's doorway, his tired features appearing more worn than usual and lined with exhaustion.

"We found nothing. The doppelganger may have been alone, which isn't unheard of. They work best that way and don't draw attention to themselves."

"Any sign of Easton?" She stepped away from the bed where Crispin lay in a deep sleep.

He chuckled. "When I last saw him, he was hiding at the garrison. Claimed he only wanted to find one of us to report you were under attack. That's how I knew where to find you. Now the old sod won't leave, claims the attack on you could have been meant for him. He fears an ambush."

"I understand demons are frightening, as is magic in general, but the man should be ashamed of himself."

"A point on which we can both agree."

Ysolde sighed but said nothing more on the baron or his cowardice. "Demons were the last thing I expected. At least what I faced was low level."

"Andras and I dispatched the remaining traps, so there should be no fear of them coming in the night. The castle is secure again. Come. You look exhausted, my lady." He offered his arm and another weary smile.

"No more than you," she protested but took his offered arm.

"Magic has a way of doing that, as you well know."

Their walk to the upper level was brief, Geoffrey her silent escort to the third floor. They stopped in front of her bedchamber door, where the man stood still as a statue, hand resting over the pommel of his blade. After a tense moment, his hand lowered.

"Ysolde," he began gently. "Someone tried to assassinate you, and we'll do everything within our power to maintain security of the estate, but until further notice, you're not to leave this castle without me in your company. Under any circumstance."

She stiffened. The rational part of her mind understood his caution, but she had always hated being told what she could and could not do.

"If I am unavailable, Andras is allowed to join you in my stead, but that should be rare."

"Are you dictating to me?"

He lacked humor in his voice as he said, "I am."

"I will not be held a prisoner in my home, Geoffrey. What sort of message does that send to my attackers?"

"If you are a prisoner, then consider me your warden. It sends the message to your attackers that if they want you, they'll have to come through us to have you. There's no need to stand alone when our duty is to be by your side."

Her lips twisted downward in a frown. "It makes me look afraid."

"When I first swore my oath to your father to protect you, he told me you were a fan of melodrama. Nothing holds you to the castle, Ysolde."

Geoffrey sighed and took both of her hands in a rare display of affection. Or reassurance. She couldn't determine which, only that his ungloved hands were strangely comforting against her skin, rough and calloused fingertips hardened from training.

"Does it truly trouble you that much to travel with your guard?"

She sighed and shook her head. He wouldn't understand her reasons, she was sure. Sneaking out would only create unnecessary friction

"Have I asked too much?" he asked, breaking the silence again.

"No."

"I will always make time for you, or have I not made that apparent by enduring court each day?" A fragile smile broke through his stoic mask. Geoffrey couldn't pass up any opportunity to tease.

Impossible man, she thought with exasperation. "Because you see that as a duty. My wanting to wander the market or to attend a play is an…indulgence. One, as you may recall, you were once quite keen on curbing when I first arrived."

The corner of his mouth twitched. Then both dropped back into a frown. "I was accustomed to dealing with criminals and had no experience escorting a young girl."

Young girl. She'd been twenty-four when her father bestowed the duchy to her, hardly a child. Old enough to have been engaged. "And now?"

"While you may be my princess, Ysolde, I also consider you a friend. I would give my sword arm before I saw you harmed. Please. Allow us to do our duty. Let me protect you."

His unexpected words caught her off guard. "Of course. I'm sorry for— Geoffrey?"

His eyes glazed over, appearing to look through and past her. Then his tall frame swayed. As Ysolde reached out to steady him, he toppled to the floor with a thunderous crash. The silken runner meant to muffle footsteps provided no cushioning, and his head cracked off the hardwood floor beside it.

"Geoffrey!" With her heart jumping inside of her chest, Ysolde dropped to her knees beside him. "Shyla, I need you!"

A pale face peeked out from a doorway further down the hall. Her maid kept a room attached to her own. "Ysolde? What's happened?"

"Send someone for the healer and find Andras. Hurry!"

Shyla rushed off while Ysolde checked Geoffrey over. Her heart wouldn't stop slamming against her ribs until she found his pulse. Thankfully, he hadn't donned full armor while storming around the estate grounds, and the lack of it let her place an ear directly to his chest to hear the strong heartbeat beneath. Its rhythm soothed her. Unlike Crispin, he didn't appear to be at death's door.

"Foolish man," she mumbled as she maneuvered his head into her lap.

A few minutes later, three of the guards burst to the top of the stairs, Andras in the lead.

"Is he alive?" he asked, clearly winded. "We've sent a rider to the temple district for a healer. Shouldn't be long."

"We were talking, and then he collapsed without warning," she explained.

The knight's brow wrinkled with consternation before he crouched beside Ysolde to study his commander.

"He must have overtaxed himself reviving the young boy, Your Grace," Andras said in a quiet voice. "Magic isn't without its costs, even when it comes from a goddess."

"Do you think it safe to move him?"

Uncertainty crossed over his face. "I'm not a healer, but I am not inclined to leave him in the hall."

Ysolde glanced over her shoulder to a door a few feet up the hall. "We'll put him in the chamber adjoining mine until the healer deems it safe to move him further. If it is mere exhaustion, he will benefit most certainly from a soft bed."

"I'll turn down the blankets and ready the fire." Shyla had hovered on the fringes of their small gathering, ready to offer aid at a moment's notice. She moved ahead of them to prepare the room.

With the combined help of three men, they were able to get Geoffrey into the adjoining master suite. The room had once been one immense bedchamber until a former duchess, exhausted with her husband's snoring, had stonemasons divide the bedroom in half in the custom of southern Hindera. There, it was uncommon for any members of the nobility to sleep alongside their spouses at all.

And all the easier for philandering noble husbands to receive visits from their mistresses.

The room remained furnished to the preferences of Ysolde's predecessor, displaying a fondness for dark colors, blue wool, and heavy drapery. A fire drake's head decorated the mantle above the fireplace. According to the plate beneath it, the great grandfather of her predecessor had slain the young dragon with a single arrow while on a hunt in southern Fas Perra.

Ysolde thought it was despicable and felt ever more thankful sport hunting had never caught on in Hindera. Her father preferred to study animals that lived, and his educational pursuits had led him to seek and befriend the Marcogh years ago.

"Heavy bloke, isn't he?" one of the guards muttered. "Will you need us for anything further, Your Grace?"

"No, that will be all."

As the two guardsmen left, Andras offered a soft spoken, "I'll stay. Go to take your rest, Your Grace."

She shook her head. "I'd like to stay and hear what needs to be done for him."

"Then we'll both watch until the healer arrives," he said, never raising his voice.

The knight captain, much like his commander, had a gentle personality until riled. He offered her the chair from the desk, and together, they waited.

An Act of Defiance

5

Andras had nothing but the utmost respect for Geoffrey, and that respect kept him glued to a seat at the bedside, Ysolde occupying a chair opposite him. Once the last healer was gone, assuring them nothing could be done for the knight with their magic or talents, he remained under the pretenses of keeping her company.

"Overtaxed," he muttered after a headshake. "It could have been worse, I suppose, with patronizing comments about him being in the gods' hands now."

"They had better not. They only tell us that rubbish when they've no idea what's wrong or how to fix it."

He chuckled. "Well, in this case, it seems they knew for certain. I had no idea Geoffrey was capable of such an amazing feat of magic."

"Nor did I," Ysolde said. "But it is an admirable gift, and the Order is poorer to have lost him as one of their number."

The princess leaned across and swept Geoffrey's tousled hair from his brow. The touch was tender, rife with undisguised affection.

If Andras hadn't known with absolute certainty his cousin was still devastated by his lover's disappearance, he would have assumed the two were engaged in a secret, illicit affair. They were close, closer than what was both accepted and permitted in Hinderan society, but their friendship had become so commonplace among members of castle staff that no one questioned it any longer.

As the hours dwindled, Ysolde's darkening eyes shut for increasingly long intervals. She napped on occasion, unaware of her own dozing, only to snap awake and touch Geoffrey's brow.

Occasionally, Andras drifted to the hall and lower level to pass instructions along the chain of command, but for the most part, he remained a guardian fixture to Geoffrey's room.

If another threat remained on the grounds, it would have to swath through a few hundred guardsmen and cut him down as well to reach the indisposed commander.

By dawn, Ysolde had begun to fret. She paced the room, eventually calling Shyla for tea, and the young woman returned with trays bearing breakfast. Andras shot her a grateful look, thankful she knew his preferences.

"Watching over Geoffrey is a duty requiring only one of us," Ysolde said after Shyla took away their trays. "I know that you love your cousin dearly, Andras, but your time would be better served elsewhere."

"What would you have me do, Princess?"

"Command the guard in his stead," she decided after a hesitation. "It's what he'd want. If anything should happen, Shyla will fetch you with haste. I promise."

He rose and bowed. "Of course, Your Grace."

"I'll accompany you and bring warm drinks for the men," Shyla offered.

He caught her gaze and smiled. "Thank you."

Andras and Shyla slipped into the hall and shut the door behind them.

After a quick glance down either length of the corridor, Andras crushed Shyla against him and kissed her neck. "See to it the princess has a rest soon. Even if it's only a few hours."

"I will," she whispered. "I expect you to do the same. Don't run yourself ragged."

"I'll rest once I'm certain the castle is secure. It's what Geoffrey would do if he could." Certain of their privacy, he leaned in and stole another quick kiss. "I have to go."

"Be safe."

They split ways once they reached the ground level, Shyla to fetch drinks and Andras to muster their guards. Morning orders went out, and within the hour following breakfast, the guardsman present on the castle grounds lined the courtyard in neat rows numbering over five hundred. Even more patrolled the countryside, occupying the watchtowers of the north, east, and southern folds.

"We need to understand why a doppelganger was able to penetrate the castle defenses. How did he enter, and better yet, was he alone?" Andras announced to the platoon of guards.

Three men stood before him, Knight Lieutenants Nedic, Harrigan, and Torrance. While they were all upstanding, proud men, the former had little more than contempt for Andras. Nedic would never accept Geoffrey had chosen Andras for his work ethic and not their blood connection.

"The little rascals are masters of illusion. I want you to ride the castle perimeter and inspect every inch of the curtain wall."

"Ser Andras, we inspected the wall yesterday," Nedic said.

"And you'll do it again, each of you with hounds and a dozen men. Take a bit of cloth from the creature's corpse, and investigate thoroughly. If they've chiseled and concealed holes in the wall, it won't fool a hound. I want to know how it happened."

A deep furrow lined Harrigan's brow. "What good is it to search now when we searched yesterday? Did we not deactivate each of the demonic sigils left behind?"

"Illusions are crafted in many ways, and what's hidden in the evening may be revealed by daylight," Andras replied. "Besides, doppelgangers aren't demons. You, most of all, should know that."

The half-elven lieutenant grumbled under his breath. "My elven blood hardly makes me all-knowing in these arts. It's unnatural."

"The little arsehole somehow got past the lot of us and into the castle. You want we should check the entrances to the residence again?" Piers asked.

"Concentrate your search on the stables. It was there that Huxley was slain and Crispin poisoned."

"As you command. Will Ser Ashcroft be leading the search?" Nedic asked.

"No. Ser Ashcroft overtaxed himself when he brought Crispin back from the brink of death. Until further notice, I am in charge."

Nedic's jaw clenched.

"Is there a problem?"

The grizzled war veteran stared at Andras head on. "No, sir."

"Excellent."

The morning passed without incident, and by afternoon, Ysolde appeared in new clothing, her hair freshly braided—signs of Shyla convincing the woman to part from dispensing Geoffrey's care.

Andras rose from his chair and bowed. "Taking a break from your bedside vigil?"

"Maribeth chased me away." She gave him a strained smile. "Then Crispin and Shyla took her side. They're all sitting with him now."

A guard rapped on the door frame and leaned in. "Ser Everly, there's a messenger at the gate."

"Send him in," Andras said. "We'll meet him in the yard."

Ysolde at his side, they crossed the courtyard to meet the courier halfway. The young man, short of breath, delivered a quick bow.

"Post from Weathermore, Your Grace, for Ser Geoffrey."

"Ser Everly will take it, thank you." She gave the messenger a coin and sent him on his way while Andras broke the seal. His hands shook as he read the contents.

"Andras?" she whispered. "What is it? You've gone all pale."

The knight cleared his throat and swallowed the lump of sickness rising in his throat. He tasted bile. "There's been another slaying, Princess."

"Who?"

"Count Weathermore."

Ysolde's face blanched. "He was my strongest supporter. I… We dined with him mere days ago. Dead?"

"I'm afraid so."

"What happened?"

"A gentleman could not repeat the atrocity done to Count Weathermore," Andras told her.

"May Nirmad take his soul to a better place," she whispered.

"I'll see to the investigation until Geoffrey is awake and able," he assured her, aware of her troubled expression and the dark circles beneath her eyes. "Please don't let me keep you."

"Thank you. I should rest for a moment, after all."

"Then allow me to escort you."

After Andras saw her back to her room, he cut a quick path from the castle residence and into the barracks. If he was to assume Geoffrey's mantle, the duty wouldn't be complete until he took action for Weathermore's murder.

It couldn't wait. He called in the three lieutenants and relayed the gruesome news.

"If Geoffrey were awake, he'd send a hundred of you to investigate what's happened on Weathermore Island. So it's what I'll do. Harrigan, prepare a ship and set sail. You're to accompany them and lead the charge."

"And what do you believe we'll find? The man's dead now and his murderer long gone."

"No." If only it were so easy. Andras read the summary of events again then he crossed to Geoffrey's workstation. "We must take action. Whoever murdered him, they didn't merely despise him, Harrigan. Weathermore's death was an act of absolute defiance."

Harrigan snorted. "How do you know that?"

Andras lowered to the oversized chair behind Geoffrey's desk. It felt alien, strange to claim his cousin's seat. "Because, my friend, when someone takes the effort to stuff a man's balls in his mouth and leave his decapitated head in a chamberpot, there can be no doubt about it. It wasn't a mere execution. It was a murder of the most profound contempt."

***

Geoffrey awakened to a splitting headache, the sort that made it easy to sympathize with melons on a chopping block.

His eyes opened to an unfamiliar, blurry sight, a ceiling he didn't know and a bed he'd never slept in.

He squeezed his eyes shut against the light pouring through the window and tossed the covers back. Cool air touched bare skin. Someone had undressed him from the waist up only but removed his boots and woolen socks.

"You should be resting." The soft, concerned voice came from his right, a whisper in the still room.

Bright, morning sunlight lit the feminine figure seated by the bed, brilliant rays pouring through cracks in the curtain behind her and casting fiery, golden highlights in her hair. He squinted against the glare from the window, and his heart lurched in his chest.

Ashlynne had returned. Or so he thought.

The illusion of his lost lover was shattered when the woman leaned forward, bringing her face into view.

Ysolde. Her eyes shone bright as a cloudless dawn, their colors mirroring the sky beyond the window, hints of gold within a blue and pink canvas.

He'd never seen her more breathtaking. More beautiful.

He felt a fool for even thinking of Ashlynne, for even allowing her to surface in his thoughts. And he would have laughed at himself for mistaking his dusky-skinned princess for the porcelain beauty of his past.

"How do you feel?"

Geoffrey countered her question with his own inquiry. "What happened?"

"You, my reckless knight, worked yourself to the breaking point and collapsed at my feet. Gave us all quite the scare."

"I didn't mean to frighten you," he said in a genuine apology.

The prayer must have taken more out of him than he thought. A seasoned paladin with years of practice could have healed the boy without blinking. But he hadn't worked holy magic in close to a decade.

"For a little while there, I was afraid you'd hit your head too hard," she admitted with a faint smile. "You've been asleep for over a day. Nearly two now."

"What?" The knowledge was enough to jolt him into an upright position, a move he regretted in an instant. The room spun. Ysolde's hands guided him back down to the soft mattress and down-filled pillow.

"A full day has passed since you collapsed, and the healer expects you to remain in bed for another day at the very least."

"And who will take my responsibilities?"

"Andras took charge, and everyone performed their duties as if the words came from your lips to their ears. You have no fear of the guard falling to pieces during your sickbed absence."

"You expect me to remain in this bed while there's—What bed is this, by the way?"

"The late Duke Ashdale's bed," she replied. Her predecessor and adopted uncle was the king's younger brother by two years. Of all the extended family connected to her through the king, Benedict Westbrook had loved Ysolde the most.

Whenever she'd visited him at court as a girl, activities in the city came to a screeching halt. On top of Ysolde's usual retinue, the duke had requisitioned several of Geoffrey's men to accompany her. Even Geoffrey at times. At first, he'd resented being pulled from his duties as Watch Captain to babysit the strange girl who was neither Hinderan nor Marcogh but a strange mix of both worlds in mannerism.

When Benedict Westbrook passed from an abrupt wasting sickness, few members of the royal family had been shocked to discover his favorite niece had inherited every mile, all with the king's blessing.

It hadn't surprised Geoffrey much at all when the king approached him at the watchtower and asked if he would accept the position of his daughter's personal knight guardian. He hadn't ordered him but asked, with all of the love of a doting father. It was Aldemar's concern, the open honesty, that had led Geoffrey to accept the role without question.

"No wonder everything smells of tobacco," he grumbled. "Has no one washed these linens or opened a window since the man died?"

"Of course things were washed, but I suppose the scent has infused everything."

At least Ashdale hadn't died in the room. In the final days of his illness, he hadn't been able to ascend the stairs to the upper level and had received his nursing care from a healer on the ground floor.

But the smell of the man's disgusting habit had permeated the walls and stained them an awful shade of dark cream.

"Geoffrey, when I asked you to save Crispin, I didn't know it would take such a toll on you."

Sighing, he repositioned his head against the pillow. Smell or no smell, it was undeniably soft, better than where he slept at present. "One day. Promise you'll stay indoors or leave only with Andras. Please. Someone attempted to assassinate you, Ysolde, and we can't take this lightly until we've gotten to the bottom of it."

"You have my word, so long as you promise to not put up a fuss and recover your strength." She paused, and he could see the gears turning in her head before she added, "In bed, as the healer directed. Trust that the tables have turned and until you've recovered, you shall be the one watched like a criminal."

He scowled. "What of your father? Has the royal guard been notified?"

"I penned a letter and sent it by eagle. His response should arrive shortly."

Geoffrey sighed. Writing the king was necessary but a duty he ought to have performed once the imminent threat was over. Instead, he'd been on his back.

"Do you suppose he'll sack me? I did, after all, allow an assassin onto the grounds."

"Geoffrey," Ysolde said sharply, taking his hand and squeezing it. "You killed the assassin before it could do me any harm. You saved a little boy's life. If my father arrives with any intention of sacking you, he'll have to remove me as well. I won't allow it."

"Your father rarely listens to you. Spoiled princess you may be, but we both know once Aldemar's made up his mind, there's no dissuading him from his goals."

"For you, I would give him no alternative but to allow you to remain. After all, this is *my* duchy." She squeezed his hand again and leaned forward to brush a rampant wave of blond hair from his brow. "And you are my friend."

WEB OF TREASON

6

G ared Bowman, Duke of Lorwick, stared at the disgusting creature in front of him. It was short and squat with curved legs and sooty skin. Resembling a hideous cross between a turkey and naked mole, its wrinkled jowls shook with each spoken word, and its beady eyes never made contact.

"You promised results." Lorwick folded his arms against his chest. Two of his personal guard—the best the city of Lorwick had to offer—flanked him on each side. They were hulking brutes, chosen for their brawn as well as their talent, outfitted in shining mail and dark red cloaks bearing his crest.

All parties involved had agreed to meet in the northern section of the city sewer under the cover of dark, the echo of dripping water in the distance.

"We did; we did. But the princess has a strong protector. Quite a strong one. He saw through the guise and killed my friend. I had no choice but to flee, else he would have seen me too." The creature cowered in the face of Lorwick's silent rage.

Kelren, the knight to his left, chuckled while circling his thumb over the hilt of his sword. The fond gesture had polished a smooth indentation. "The failed paladin?"

"Failed he may be but skilled enough to see through our magic."

"Clearly I underestimated him, a mistake I won't make a second time," Lorwick said. "If he sees through doppelganger illusions, he isn't to be trifled with."

"It's true; it's true," the creature agreed. "Your payment has been refunded, Your Grace. We have failed; we cannot keep it."

Lorwick shook his head.

"It would hardly be appropriate to send you away without proper payment, my friend. See to it that he receives all he's owed, Lester," Lorwick said to the wall of muscle standing to his right. The knight nodded and followed the doppelganger from the chamber.

"Of course, Your Grace." Lester led the pathetic creature away.

"And what of you? What news do you bring to me?" Lorwick asked the other visitor.

Lord Shadeglen straightened his spine. The noble bore the rigid posture of an aristocrat and scrawny physique of a scholar—too young to have seen battle in the last wars with Fas Perra, of course, and too cowardly to have engaged in any violence outside of a fencing session.

He looked out of place, uncomfortable with their chosen surroundings, and his eyes darted toward every moving shadow. A rat scurrying along the wall made him leap out of his skin.

Lorwick would have loved to see what would happen if one of the filthy vermin actually touched the baron.

"The nobility tire of her childish games. She brings increased taxation to fund her social experiments. Prisons," he said with undisguised disgust. "As if thieves deserve to be given a second chance."

Another visitor cleared his throat.

"We don't mean you," Lorwick said with a sneer. He glanced at the mercenary leader standing near the entrance, a late arrival to their conference. The man was a mobile mountain in black leather, his stoic features carved from stone, skin the color of obsidian—a half-orc from a nation across the ocean. "You're a reputable businessman as far as we're concerned, Tuwaktu."

"Excellent. I would hate to assume services from the Iron Fist are no longer needed or wanted." Tuwaktu chuckled in a deep, rumbling baritone.

Lester returned to Lorwick's side, wiping black blood from his blade with a cloth. He sheathed the sword and retook his stance.

"How many are behind us?" Lorwick asked Shadeglen.

"I will give no names, but you have the support of many. If you should move against her and Aldemar, I give my word others will follow. A rolling tide of dissent will sweep across Hindera from the greatest houses to the small."

"If I may, Lorwick," Tuwaktu interrupted. "There is no need for either you or the other nobles to trouble yourselves over this matter just yet. Allow my brother to continue the plan we discussed and to make contact with my associates across the border. We need only force this king's hand. If she is not dead by the Festival of Giving, she shall certainly be wed to you."

"And this is guaranteed?"

"My men will create trouble for you to help abolish, of course. King Aldemar will have no choice but to defer to your superiority, and once the two of you are wed, we may renegotiate the terms of our financial arrangement."

"I like this plan." Duke Lorwick stroked his chin. His eyes darted to Shadeglen. "Will I face opposition if I pursue the princess again?"

The lord chuckled. "None from the rest of us, though I might suggest you take on a sweeter manner for the time being until you have what you want from the girl. Good luck with taming her."

Once the meeting adjourned, Gared emerged from the sewer and returned to his residence by carriage. The estate grounds spanned several miles throughout the countryside, situated on a hillside in the outskirts of the city. It was a duchy known for its grape industry, the fertile valleys producing the finest wines in Hindera.

But Lorwick's province lacked the wealth of Ashdale. Gared coveted their rich fur trade and healthy alliance with the elven isles of Iluminarel. He hungered for their trade agreements with the snow elves of the mountain peaks, who supplied Ashdale's healers with a bounty in medicinal herbs. If the kingdom's capital, Stormwatch, was Hindera's soul, then Ashdale had certainly become its heart.

All in the hands of a brown-skinned savage who could never appreciate the city's worth. His blood boiled at the thought of Ysolde controlling the province's wealth, displacing a worthwhile duke. Aldemar's progressive steps had gone too far.

He'd marry the wench and mold her into an obedient wife, and he'd have her father's blessing every step of the way.

With a grin on his face, Gared poured a glass of port and settled behind the walnut desk to read the fresh post, only to discover his writing station in the same state as the prior day. It was woefully lacking in mail.

"Fiona!" he roared.

His maid scuttled in from the adjacent room, her head bowed and hands folded primly before her. "Your Grace, how may I serve you?"

"Where is the post?"

"I hadn't the chance to fetch it yet, Y-your Grace."

"Haven't the chance to fetch it," he repeated, voice low and malicious. Rising from his chair, he stepped over and backhanded her across the cheek.

Fiona made no sound. She'd been taught well.

"You'd be wise to remember who rescued you and your horse-faced mother from the brothel before I have a change of heart. If not for me, you'd be sucking every knob in this city and hoping for two silvers to scrape together once done."

The magenta of a developing bruise arose on her cheek, spreading like watercolor across an ivory canvas. Her large eyes shimmered with unshed tears. "I'm sorry, Your Grace." She gasped. "Please. I'm sorry. Don't put my mother on the streets. Please!"

Lorwick caressed her injured cheek, drifting his knuckles over her skin. "I won't, love. After all, what kind of son would I be to shove my father's favorite whore and her spawn onto the cruel streets? Now fetch the post."

"Right away, Your Grace."

"Good girl," he crooned while delivering a soothing stroke through her curtain of ink black curls. Hair as dark as his own. "Bring it to my chambers and make yourself ready in the bed. It's been a good day for House Bowman, and I would like to celebrate."

POOR WEATHER

7

 Despite all forecasts of pleasant weather, it rained on the day of Count Weathermore's funeral, as if the gods themselves wept for his loss. Ysolde certainly cried during the eulogy.

In life, Charles Homerton, Count of Weathermore had been an exceptional man, beloved by commoners and nobles alike, for he gave freely of himself *and* his money. If a fellow member of the gentry required a loan, he gave it—with no villainous intentions of usury or sly plans to benefit from their misfortune. If times fell hard and food became scarce, he imported it, too soft-hearted to allow his citizens to go hungry.

Geoffrey wouldn't tell her how he'd died, and looking at his body now, seeing the state of it in the preserved stasis wrought by the temple sisters of Nirmad, one would think he was simply resting.

It had taken days for Geoffrey to return to his former vitality. Enough time passed for the temple to send the proper notifications, prepare the corpse, and for Weathermore's next of kin to occupy Fair Weather Park.

The new Count Weathermore's stoic countenance bore no resemblance to the man on the funeral pyre. His hair was glossy, chestnut brown rather than salt-and-pepper black. He had his father's thin, severe mouth, but it wasn't prone into spontaneous outbreaks of smile—and why should it be when his father had been brutally murdered?

Fresh tears seeped, leaving wet tracks on Ysolde's cheeks. Geoffrey nudged her and offered a handkerchief she graciously accepted.

They all said words, as was customary, while standing beside the deceased and leaving a gift for him to take to the beyond.

All of Ysolde's father figures were leaving her. First Benedict Westwood, now Charles, who had been a gentle, flawless human being and philanthropist. The hysterical part of her craved humor to deaden her pain and wondered if she should mandate round-the-clock protection for Fingall. If she lost him too, she'd be devastated.

The remainder of the crematorial ceremony passed without incident. The air was humid and damp, and fresh logs had been brought for the pyre. Each had been treated with an alchemical substance to expedite the burning.

Afterward, the ashes of his remains and their gifts—hers had been a tome on Sarangese herbs she'd once promised to give him when she finished with it—were gathered into a bronzed urn and presented to his heir.

"Will you remain as my guest, Princess?" Count Weathermore asked. His features were pinched and tired, his face crinkled with the exhaustive weight of assuming too much responsibility too soon.

"No," she murmured in a gentle voice, "but thank you." She moistened her lips and gazed up at the taller man. "We will find who did it."

"Please find them before I do, or nothing shall remain of the monster to stand trial. My father was a kind man. He did not deserve this. He should have died surrounded by his grandchildren, in his bed, loved and adored."

The impassive facade became a fragile thing, threatening to splinter before her, like so many pieces of shattered glass.

"We will find them," she assured again. A tight hug accompanied her words. Then she kissed each of Richard's cheeks.

They sailed for home that night, and during their voyage to Ashdale from the island, Ysolde sobbed herself to sleep in her cabin. While boarding the boat, she'd overheard two barons gossiping, their voices hushed but too loud for keen Marcogh hearing. If Geoffrey and Andras had thought her too sensitive to know the manner of his death, they'd been right.

The late Weathermore's fate tortured Ysolde, and in her dreams, she saw him risen from the grave and pointing a white, skeletal finger at the source of all Hinderan's problems in the north: her.

***

Two men made their way down the dusty road, riding side by side on two slender destriers. Fas Perra was known for its slim warmbloods, the fleet horses bred for speed with nimble legs designed for distance running. They rode at a sedate pace, protected from occasional gusts of biting wind by their woolen traveler's cloaks and eager to reach their destination to take shelter from the cold.

"Why must these people pre-fix everything with 'Ash?' From their names to their cities, it's all I hear," one complained.

"Aren't you cheerful company?" the shorter of the two men said to the other. He rode with the reins looped around the saddle horn, freeing both hands to cup an arcane sphere in his palms, its ember glow emitting a personal globe of warmth to cut through the unnaturally frigid day.

"I can't believe this is harvest month," the second man muttered. He grimaced as the mountain air breached his layers of protective clothing.

The man holding the sphere glanced at him, chuckled, and offered a sympathetic smile. "I swear to you, brother, this will be the easiest job you've ever worked. You will earn more coin beside me than you've ever attained at the Magisterium as a slave. It'll be worth it."

"Technically, earning two coppers to rub together would be more coin than I've ever earned at the Magisterium, Etienne."

"Smart arse."

The younger brother chuckled and steered his chestnut stallion within reach, nudging his sibling with an elbow. "Share some of your warmth with me. I'll be an icicle long before we reach Ashdale to deal with the princess and her mess."

"I'll pass it to you in a moment. Be a man, Laurent, and show some patience while I charge the bloody thing."

After all, he'd only removed it from his pack after watching his warm-blooded, half-elf brother shiver for the thousandth time since they ascended the mountain trail. Desert elves were known for their intolerance to the cold, preferring the scorching climates of the Vastitas Desert to the south.

While he loathed his brother's suffering, Etienne found his hands were tied. Hindera was the safest place for Laurent, and the only place where he could protect him from the Magisterium.

"How well do you speak Hinderan?" Laurent asked suddenly.

"*Na thydd na voy asha to bochyn*," Etienne replied in the tongue. As well as I live and breathe. "And you?"

"Decent enough to hold a conversation with a commoner. The Magisterium made Hinderan an elective, and I wasn't privileged to sit the class while on the island."

"So how did you learn it?" Etienne glanced at his brother and saw the man staring down at something concealed in his gloved palm—a secret something he'd gone to great efforts to hide.

"A good friend taught it to me. A voluntary student who joined under contract to save her family from going into debt."

"Ah. Have no worries. Stand beside me, look important, and pretend to understand everything we say. You're my brother, you work for me, and I couldn't function without your unique set of skills."

"You'd function quite well without me, and you know it."

"Hardly, and I'll be happy when the day arrives that you come to understood we need one another. I promised four years ago to guard you with my own life and..." Etienne trailed off, staring at his brother's shoulder-length waves of black hair. He fit every stereotypical description of a bard to ever circulate through the kingdoms. "For someone wanting to avoid possible recognition, you certainly haven't changed your appearance. If you'd let me cut your hair—"

"It was short when I fled the Magisterium. You know that."

"Shorter than you're accustomed to wearing, no one would recognize you," Etienne finished. "Laurent, it's only hair. It'll grow back again someday."

"I like the way I look now. No one will recognize me," he insisted.

"If you say so, little brother." Etienne stole another look at his younger sibling, letting his brows furrow in consternation. Maybe Laurent was right; maybe he had changed dramatically since his miraculous escape from the Magisterium. "You're certainly much taller than you were the day you left them."

"Taller than you now," Laurent said with a chuckle.

"By three inches. Big damned deal," he muttered under his breath. "Isn't my fault your bloody desert elf ancestors are tall as hill giants."

"We're not so tall. It's only that you Fas Perrans are obnoxious imps."

Etienne shot him a dirty look. "You're half Fas Perran."

"Only half," Laurent retorted. "Anyway. I hope this is the prosperous opportunity you claim it will be."

"She's a child on a throne playing at a game she doesn't understand," Etienne said.

"And her knight? He's a former paladin. The moment he has a look at us, we'll be fucked sideways and tossed out the door," he muttered.

"I have a way of foiling his magic. Trust me."

"The last time you told me to trust you, we spent an hour fleeing across the plains of Crestoli from two dozen angry gladiators on horseback."

"This time is different. Besides, my wit got you out of the Magisterium, didn't it?"

Laurent quieted. "You did," he agreed following a long pause. "At great personal peril and risk to your own safety, you did. I can never understand why you'd do such a thing for me, a mere stranger with whom you share a few drops of blood."

Etienne didn't answer him. Instead, he passed the warming globe to his brother and pointed to the smoke rising in the distance. "Look up ahead. We're nearly there, and we'll be in warm beds by nightfall. Warm beds, brother. I'm told the

Moonlit Primrose has the sweetest wenches in the northern half of the continent."

Laurent made a face at him. "I don't need to pay for sex, you git. Maybe you do, but I'll get by on my own."

"What they see in you, I'll never understand."

"It's the hair." To illustrate his point, Laurent tossed back his dark locks and flashed his brother a grin. "And my charming wit."

True to Etienne's prediction, they reached their destination as twilight arrived to spread a blanket of lavender across the darkening sky. Tiny stars winked into view and shimmered above them, worsening the extreme chill of the mountainous landscape.

At first sight, the city lived up to her intimidating reputation. Ashdale's city gates loomed over them, an impressive construction of stone and mortar that connected both sides of the mountain pass. Etienne eyed the thick doors as they passed through, both surprised and impressed at their quality.

"Gnomish? I didn't think those brainy gits came this far west," Laurent muttered to him.

"No, they're dwarven," Etienne corrected. "They must be centuries old and still look brand new."

His brother loosed a long, low whistle.

They followed the hard-packed earthen road through the lower town into the central markets. Despite his mention of the brothel, they both checked into a shared room for the night, and Etienne devoted his evening to penning a professional letter to the duchess and her steward.

Dear Princess Ysolde Westbrook, Duchess of Ashdale,

I contact you with only the most generous and heartfelt intentions. Upon learning of the recent setbacks to your security and safety, my brother and I have traveled from our native land of Fas Perra to offer our unique services. We have both studied extensively in the fields of supernatural creatures and subterfuge, thus believe we may be of assistance to your recent plight.

We request your audience to discuss the matter in person.

Your humble neighbor, Scion Etienne Dufresne, Shade Knight of Fresna

"I don't know about that. Should you reveal your title and that you're the son of a regent? She may distrust you, genuine or not," Laurent muttered as he read over it.

"She'll distrust me more if I'm anything but transparent. I'm told she's Marcogh. They have a knack for reading dishonorable intentions in others. Between her and the paladin, it's best we're absolutely upfront regarding everything we plan to do for her and the duchy. You see, I plan to reveal so much of myself they have little interest in delving into your history. It's a trick I've learned."

"*Excessimo,* brother."

Etienne bent at the waist in a mock bow then folded the letter. He sealed it with a drop of wax garnished with gold dust, the mark of wealth, and strode to the door. "I'll find a messenger for this. You keep your bloody hands to yourself and try to resist the urge to nick everything that isn't nailed down."

"Damn. You wound me."

Etienne chuckled as he shut the door behind him. The two of them stuck out like a bent nail among the common folk of Ashdale in their wool tunics, leathers, and clothing designed to break the cold. The wind cut right through his trousers and the extravagant brocaded waistcoat he'd worn. Fas Perra's best winter dress wasn't enough for Hindera.

He made his way into the unforgiving night with his cloak drawn tight. If their plan was to work, their arrival to Hindera had to remain low key.

Laurent's safety depended on it. The Magisterium couldn't discover one of their servants had escaped with his life.

A BENEFICIAL PARTNERSHIP

8

"Are you certain of this, Princess?" Fingall asked for the dozenth time. "Are you up for meeting with an audience so soon after Count Weathermore's funeral? You've only just returned as of this morning. You must be exhausted."

"Whether it's one day or fifty, there's work to be done, and I aim to see it completed. If we have Fas Perrans here, then we must discover why. I will hear them out because words on paper cannot show me a person's true intent."

"Neither can conversation," Fingall pointed out. "As we have recently learned."

"Of course not. That is what Geoffrey's for."

Geoffrey sighed. "There *is* a limit to my gift, Princess. I can only tell you so much about a person, after all. I've learned evil to be quite subjective. But as you wish. Send them in, Fingall."

The elf stepped from the room momentarily. When he returned, he strode down the aisle of the throne room, his spine straight and eyes unimpressed by the pair moving behind him. There was a particular tension to his frame that set Ysolde on edge.

"I present to you, Etienne and Laurent Dufresne of Fas Perra," Fingall announced in a dry, disagreeable tone.

Although the brothers differed in some ways, they were like mirrored images in a carnival glass—one long-haired and tall, the other shorter and neatly groomed. Of course, short was a relative term, as they both would have towered over her if she were standing. They had the same eyes, bright as turquoise jewels within their tanned, impossibly handsome faces. The taller brother wore his facial hair closely trimmed, but the other was clean shaven.

Both bowed deeply, but only one spoke.

"It is a pleasure to stand before you on this day, Princess Ysolde. Thank you for accepting our request," the shorter brother said, whom she assumed to be Etienne on account of the other man's pointed ears.

"And it is a pleasure to have you in my court...Scion Dufresne?" she guessed.

He smiled. "You would be correct. This one is my brother, Laurent, and his knowledge of your language is clumsy at best, so you must excuse him if he—"

"Hello," Laurent said, looking abashed.

"Says nothing more than that."

"You've met my steward, Fingall. Beside me is Ser Ashcroft, my Knight Commander.

"A pleasure," Geoffrey muttered.

"Charmed," Etienne said, his tone a cheerful contrast. He looked too friendly to be Fas Perran. Her father had always told her they were a nation of cutthroats and demon worshippers, praying to their seven false gods.

"Please, tell me what brings the son of a regent to our kingdom."

"Straight to the heart of the matter." The man smiled pleasantly at her and nodded in respect. "I will be honest with you, madam. I believe we may form a beneficial partnership."

"I have little interest in aligning myself with Fas Perra. That would be an offer to take to my father, the king."

"No, you and I. I have no interest in serving my country at this moment. Nothing matters to me more than my own brother's safety, and as you can see, he is clearly not a legitimate heir to House Dufresne."

Ysolde studied Laurent, who merely smiled at her in a disarming way that sent heat curling into her lower belly. He had an attractive smile, reminding her of Rhun with his healthy, golden glow and mane of jet hair. But the resemblance between her former betrothed and Laurent ended there, particularly due to the pointed tips of his ears. He was half-elven. "Yes, I can see."

"This places him in a very dangerous position. His existence to our social world remains my dearest secret, and I have entrusted it to you."

She turned her glance toward Geoffrey first. Since her recent decree, she'd come to learn his body language. A hand on his hilt meant he was tense. Meant there were dangerous intentions and dubious thoughts on his mind regarding whoever stood trial.

So far he had been silent, an impassive guardian standing beside her with his hand nowhere near the hilt of his sword. With the brothers, he appeared to be completely at ease.

"Do you mean to imply your father would slay his own son rather than claim him as a bastard?"

Laurent's eyes widened. Etienne touched him on the arm and spoke for him. "I do not think my *father* would kill him, but it is always a possibility, and thus a risk. He has remarried in recent years, and I believe my stepmother once moved against me to secure the inheritance for her own spawn. She would have no qualms about removing Laurent from the equation too."

"I see." She frowned as she considered his words. There was more in what he didn't say, and the knowledge unsettled her. "Why then have you sought me out?"

"In exchange for asylum in Ashdale, we offer you protection of our own. I am an accomplished sorcerer and have dabbled in many studies you may find useful. My brother, though he speaks your language very poorly, is skilled in the arts that best belong in the shadows."

"A thief, you mean?" Geoffrey spoke up.

Etienne and Laurent exchanged looks. Ysolde could almost hear the gears turning in the older brother's head. His eyes darted to Geoffrey, lingered, and then settled on Ysolde. "An assassin of the best caliber. And it will take one assassin to outwit another. If someone has summoned the *devae* against you, one failure will not discourage them. They'll only try again."

Geoffrey didn't flinch. Again, the sorcerer had told them only the truth.

"And your House? Will your father come seeking his heir?"

Etienne shook his head. "I renounced my claim to the inheritance, and while he is not obligated to accept my decision, by our law he cannot force me to return. I suspect he will attempt to sway me with flowery letters and enticing promises."

"How do we know this isn't some elaborate plot from Fas Perra to gain access to the royal family?" Geoffrey asked.

"With all due respect, Ser Ashcroft, if we wanted to harm her, no one would know of our presence. This I say, not with arrogance, but with complete confidence in my brother."

Geoffrey stiffened, hand hovering over his blade hilt. "Your honesty is refreshing and alarming," he said drily. "Certainly you are both aware of the skirmishes between Fas Perra and Hindera recently in the Riverdale province?"

"We were long clear of the area when it happened, but the news did reach us," Etienne said.

"Can you grant us any insight into these attacks?" Ysolde leaned forward. "Such as which of your seven Houses authorized them?"

"That is not information I am willing to grant without a compromise between us guaranteeing asylum, Princess. I have nothing but love for my country, but I despise what we have become in the past decades. As you know, war began between our kingdoms under the rule of Regent Sabatois, and her insanity seems to have carried to the rest of the council. With my father next in line, I would prefer to see peace between us again."

"A wish I'm certain my father would reciprocate, were his borders not under constant attack."

"Then perhaps as their children we should take matters into our own hands."

Ysolde darted her eyes to Geoffrey, searching for cues, but looking at him gave her nothing but the stoic profile of his face.

She'd have to make the choice on her own.

"A final question. How did you hear about the attempt on my life?"

Etienne's eyes drifted to his brother. He opened his mouth to speak then paused, and when he did, Geoffrey's expression transitioned from indifference to skepticism.

Immediately, the two had a heated exchange in their language. Of course, everything spoken in Fas Perran sounded passionate and filled with tension. As if men were either one breath from ripping off their clothes to seduce their audience or challenging one another to a fight.

"I will explain," Laurent said in heavily accented Hinderan. He turned to Ysolde and bowed again, his poise bringing further attention to the attractive qualities of his face. "In my work, such information is worth of many gold, Princess Ysolde. It is… ah, how do I say this? Difficult job, it is thing common to reach ears of best assassins."

"You're saying you heard about the price for my life?" she asked sharply.

"A man approached me a moon cycle past."

"He declined," Etienne offered up quickly. "When I told you I have nothing but complete confidence in my brother, I meant the words. You will find no better assassin in all of the western continent. More than that, I cannot reveal."

"And you sent no warning?" Geoffrey demanded.

"Would you have believed word of an attempt on the princess's life from a stranger? A Fas Perran stranger at that? Beyond the obvious, one does not earn prestige in this business by unveiling plots on a whim. Reputation is everything. He would have made enemies and, of course, would never work again."

Geoffrey said nothing. Ysolde took it as a good sign. While she sensed the anger simmering off of him, she also knew him to be a rational man. The brothers were right, and it would be foolish to expect them to behave in any other way. Their lives were worth as much as hers.

"I am not certain I have need for a mage."

"I am aware of your ability with magic, madam, but you will find no one more willing and accomplished in the art of summoning the *devae* than me. I am told your father, the king, has a royal spymaster. Together, Laurent and I will fulfill the same role for you from within the safety of your own domain."

What a cocky bastard. She eyed him warily then glanced at Geoffrey to find him staring at the two brothers. His thoughts remained a mystery.

"I will have my answer for you tomorrow."

"Thank you. Your valuable time has been most appreciated. Good day to you, Princess and Ser."

Both men bowed deeply and strode from the room.

"You can't be serious," Geoffrey started once they were alone. "A bloody demon summoner and a murderer? Why didn't you send them on their way?"

"At least they're not from Narkanth. We're at least civil with Fas Perra. Besides, you had ample opportunity to order them out."

Geoffrey blinked. "That isn't my responsibility. How would it look if I were to presume and act for you in the presence of foreigners?"

She lifted a brow and stared up at him. "Your responsibility is to protect me. If they were threats such as their countrymen who were slain near Riverdale, then you would have every right to toss them out or clap them in irons."

"Don't remind me of that," Geoffrey groaned. "Leave it to Lorwick to be at the right place at the right time to aid Crowley when the whining brat needs him."

Ysolde wrinkled her nose. "I dislike it as much as you. A letter from Father arrived yesterday with nothing but praise for the rude cretin. He said my treatment of the man was harsh." She sighed and dismissed the topic with a wave of her hand. "Tell me what troubles you about the two brothers—excluding their nationality. At least Hindera is on civil terms with Fas Perra. It could be worse; they could have been from Narkanth."

The monotheistic, mountainous nation on their northern border despised magic in any form. Each of their attempts to overthrow the southern kingdoms had been thwarted, a century of failure and animosity resulting in the previous King of Hindera severing all trade agreements.

As the seconds passed in silence, Ysolde knew she had him. A thick wrinkle creased his brow before he finally mumbled, "They're hiding something. They may not have outright lied to us, but they're concealing something."

"So I wasn't the only one to sense something is amiss?"

He shook his head.

"Your honest answer, Geoffrey: can we trust them to keep their deal, secret or no?"

He hesitated to answer, reluctance on his face. "We can. They don't intend to harm you or Hindera, but I'd like to know what they're keeping from us."

"Then if they mean me, my people, and our country no harm, let them have their secret." She smiled up at him and placed a hand on his arm. "The gods know we each have our own."

THE TROUBLE WITH WOMEN

9

G eoffrey folded his arms against his chest and scrutinized the assortment of men standing on the castle's training yard. The Ashguard were considered one step above Ashdale's city watch, each member an extension of Ysolde's will, the personification of her rule.

As a part of the hiring process, each season Geoffrey and Andras hosted an open call where they allowed men from all walks of life to present themselves to numerous challenges. They sparred, ran, and performed feats on horseback. He tested them to the limits of their endurance in a variety of ways, but most of all, he kept his eyes open for *potential*.

In the two weeks that had passed since his time abed, the dangers had only grown in the heartlands beyond Ashdale. They were no closer to discovering the killers of Baron Paddleton and Count Weathermore than they were to finding Ysolde's own assassin. When Ysolde wrote her father, requesting permission to enlist more troops, he'd surprised them by, not only granting his blessing, but encouraging her to abandon all limits previously imposed.

Geoffrey had his work cut out for him.

"Varied lot we have this time, despite the gloomy weather." Andras peered up at the gray sky and frowned. The threat of rain was a constant in northern Hindera, but on training days, it was a cruel misfortune to men performing feats of endurance in the muddy sand. "Lots of new faces, both out here and within."

"You mean our new Fas Perran guests."

Andras grunted. "Why didn't you convince her to send them back to where they belong?"

"I didn't believe it would be necessary this time," Geoffrey admitted.

83

"And now they've been here a week but act as if they've always been, sauntering about, free as you please."

A silver-blue cat leapt onto the wrought-iron rail beside them and sat grooming herself. She had a tiny stub of a tail and two lynx point ears with tiny tufts of black hair at their tips. By all rights, she was adorable, and Geoffrey had found himself petting her on occasion since her first appearance in the halls of the estate.

"Go on, shoo." Andras scowled down at the feline. She gave him a lazy blink and yawn but remained on her precarious perch. "Blasted thing belongs to them. I've seen it with the mage. I tell you now—the man gives me the creeps."

"So long as he isn't summoning *devae* in the streets."

"Demons, you mean. Don't start using their fancy words."

Geoffrey chuckled and gave Andras a clap on the shoulder. "If I didn't know better, I'd think you were jealous. I've seen Shyla and some of the other maids eyeballing the taller one since his arrival. And no shortage of them tiptoeing out of his bedchamber at night."

He crossed his arms and shot a sidelong glance at Andras, studying him.

The other knight grumbled. "As if I'd be intimidated by a man with a woman's hairstyle. It's unnatural, hair that long on a man."

"Sounds like jealousy, mate. Don't fear. Shyla only has eyes for you."

Andras jerked his head toward Geoffrey, blue eyes narrow. Intense. "What makes you think I care who Shyla gives her attention to?"

"No reason."

"The one over there is worthless," Andras said in a sudden change of topic. "He balks around the horses, has dropped his sword at least three times, and is generally uncoordinated."

"Send him home then. You know I trust your judgment as well as my own. Who do you have your eye on otherwise?"

"That little one over there has some fire in him," Andras nodded to a slim warrior in shiny, low quality mail. "Must have spent his family's monthly earnings to impress us today. The mail is new. Cheap but new. I expect it to split like tinder beneath an axe's blade."

Geoffrey snorted. "A bit on the small side, but he fights better than you while wearing trash. Think I should take him, then?"

"Arsehole," Andras muttered and shot him a dirty look. "But yes, I believe you should accept him and his opponent, though he's equally small. They both handle a sword well enough."

"Agreed." Geoffrey struck his sword pommel against a nearby bell, signaling an end to the trials. "You, you, and you over there. You're dismissed to the infantry. See Knight Lieutenant Nedic." He sent another four home.

A few glum-looking men, exhausted and sweaty after the day's ordeal, made their way from the sparring ground.

"You've broken that one's heart," Andras uttered in a low voice. A man trudged from the field, letting the practice blade slip from his listless fingers. "He's here every call. Why haven't you given him a chance?"

"Look at the way his fingers shake."

"Think he's on the glow?"

"I know he is," Geoffrey whispered. The fungi, named for its telltale glow, only grew in the depths of the dwarven caves. "I won't have an addict in our ranks."

"Maybe some discipline is what he needs." Andras shrugged. "He fights well, and he shows perseverance the others lack. This marks the seventh time I've seen him over the past two years. Usually they give up after the second refusal, but what do I know?"

Geoffrey glowered at him. "Go catch him at the gate then. I'll give him one chance."

While Andras set off to retrieve their final candidate, Geoffrey turned to appraise the remaining individuals. Eleven stoic faces met his watchful gaze, perspiration dotting their brows and redness splotching their faces. All but one man, at least. One of them had yet to remove his metal helm for air—in fact, he'd wore it since the day's exercises began.

"The last of you are the ones who interest me as members of the princess's personal castle guard, for reasons which I may share with you during the interview process," he announced. "You know who I am, and you know of my training, so it would behoove you to speak with absolute honesty. I will not abide liars, but I am willing to overlook past indiscretions—criminal and otherwise."

He walked down the line of them, feeling the apprehension in the air, mingled with currents of pride and confidence. At the end, he paused in front of the boy in full platemail.

"Take off your helm, lad, and let me see you."

The swordsman hesitated but only for a brief moment, and it didn't take long to understand why. Auburn hair tumbled free around a pretty, oval face. A palpable hush fell over the guardsman spectating the event.

"I thought so," he murmured in a gentle voice. "What's your name?"

"Raennia, Ser. Raennia Cassii," she answered, chin lifted.

Geoffrey had to admire her spirit. Already there were whispers among the guard and the other recruits.

"Why do you want to be part of the Ashguard?" he asked her.

She eyed him with wary caution. "My father served in the king's army, a long time ago. Since his death, it's been on me to help out my mother and siblings."

"How many?"

"Two sisters and a brother."

"And your father? What happened to him?"

"He was killed during a bandit raid this past summer. They tried to steal our goats."

It wasn't an unusual story or rare occurrence. As the city grew and fewer of the guards patrolled the lowlands, they received increased complaints about bandits roving the highways. "I suppose he's the one who taught you to swing a sword?"

"He did, Ser, yes."

"Who will protect your mother if I give you this job?"

Her expression faltered. "My family had to move to the city, Ser."

Geoffrey didn't ask her to elaborate. With her father gone, he could make the proper assumptions.

Andras returned with their misfit and gestured for the man to join the line. The second-in-command stared at him. "Surely you don't plan to give this any serious consideration. She's a *woman*."

Geoffrey grunted. "You've never had the honor of watching the female gladiators of Crestoli fight in the arena. They're bloody vicious, mate. You couldn't get me to take one on for a thousand gold solans. Besides…" He dropped his voice. "When she's on the rag, we'll know the princess couldn't be safer."

"And where will we house her? With the men?"

"Why not?"

"A beautiful, young woman housed with several hundred men in the barracks?"

"If we can't trust them to respect their fellow guardsman, we can't trust them to protect our princess," Geoffrey said with a shrug. He turned back to the young woman who watched their deliberation. Despite her straight spine and the stoic set to her jaw, he saw anxiety in her pale eyes. "You're hired."

He watched her closely, all the while aware of the changing mood in the squadron of guards. Surprise and indignation roiled together, charging the air with turbulent emotion.

"Thank you, Ser. I won't let you down."

"You're a guardsman now, Raennia. I won't dishonor your accomplishment by coddling you, but I expect to be told if any of your peers behave in a way unbecoming their rank and station. Better yet, I trust you to put them to shame."

"Yes, I can do that."

Geoffrey turned to address the men. "You know my policies and the rules I've set. There will be no leniency. We are all brothers here. If I hear a single whisper of indiscretion or unbecoming behavior toward our female recruit, I will hang the guilty party by his balls on the city gates. Am I understood?"

"Yes, Ser!" voices chorused.

"As for you." Geoffrey crossed his thick arms in front of his chest while he approached the lanky man brought back from the gate. He'd ridden a horse between the obstacles like he was born in the saddle. "You have Ser Everly to thank for this *single* opportunity. What's your name?"

"Marik."

"Why are you here?"

"Because I have nothing else to fight for, Ser Ashcroft."

"No family, no wife? Parents?"

"All gone."

Geoffrey circled around the man, assessing him with the critical eye of a swordsman as much as a former guard. He had the particular straightness of the spine associated with a soldier. "Have you been a guardsman before? City watch? A town militia?"

"I was a soldier in the king's army, Ser Ashcroft. I served for eleven years. Left my wife, children, and mother on our farm. Bandits raided our home while I fought in the skirmishes with Fas Perra." Marik swallowed, the action bobbing his Adam's apple and creating tension in his face. Emotion broiled to the surface, bringing with it pain that couldn't be numbed without a healthy dose of glow in his system. "There was nothing left when I returned."

Geoffrey grunted. He couldn't feel disgust for the man after receiving such open honesty, but he didn't want to deliver a strike to his pride by pitying him either. "Kick the habit. You'll have one chance to get clean, or you're out on your arse."

It didn't take long to narrow down the rest.

"I will now leave you in the hands of my second-in-command. Training begins at the top of the sixth hour each morning. You have what remains of this evening to say goodbye to your loved ones, for you will not see them until you have failed or we've made a proper warrior of you."

Ysolde stood above them on the balcony overlooking the field, waist length hair free and loose around her shoulders. She never wore it completely down, usually maintaining braids in some form as homage to her Marcogh ancestry.

He caught her gaze for a brief moment until an approaching courier drew her attention away. He studied her face from below, watching as her pleased smile faded into a frown and then an incredulous stare.

"Andras," Geoffrey spoke up for his friend's attention. "Can you handle the rest of this?"

"Of course. Is there something the matter?"

"Possibly," he answered.

The younger knight nodded and turned back to the group. "Go on. I know what to do."

After a quick washdown and a change of clothes, Geoffrey tracked the princess down to her study and rapped his knuckles against the closed door. "Ysolde?"

"It's open," she called out.

He pushed open the door and stepped into the expansive space. It was any scholar's dream, more similar to a library than an actual gentleman's study. With an upper level accessible by a narrow staircase, it led to several shelves of ancient books, old lore collected by the former duke.

With a roomy desk and alchemical lab at one side and a massive hearth at the other, Ysolde trusted him to share in its comfort from time to time, allowing Geoffrey to lounge in the massive armchair while a fire crackled in the hearth. Behind him, she'd toil over scrolls or magical experiments.

Sometimes they talked, and sometimes she worked in silence while her ever-present protector warmed by the fire.

He hesitated to speak at first and only watched her. She paced back and forth in front of the cold fireplace, a letter crumpled in her clenched right hand.

"More bad news?"

"He's horrible," she spat.

"Who's horrible?"

Ysolde offered the paper, letting it roll from her shaking fingers into his palm.

Geoffrey smoothed out the parchment. His eyes dropped to the official script of a royal missive from King Aldemar himself, written with all of the familiarity and love of a father with the rigid, no-arguments wording of a monarch.

My daughter,

I have graciously allowed you plentiful time to select a worthy husband of your own choosing. Instead of decisions, I receive news of childish tantrums, assault, and deceitful behavior unbecoming of you and my reputation. You have left me with no alternative but to make the decision for you. We will announce the banns in a month shortly after my arrival. Expect Duke Lorwick to be in my company if he does not reach Ashdale ahead of the royal ships.

With love and warm regards,
Father

"When have I ever showed deceitful behavior? And my treatment of Duke Lorwick was well deserved, as the man refused to leave when asked politely."

Geoffrey frowned. "Never, my lady. Perhaps your disappointed suitors have returned to the king with falsehoods."

"They were unsuitable, and they should accept that. *You* would never go spewing lies for being spurned."

"No, I wouldn't," the knight agreed quietly. Because I'm not a spineless arsehole, he thought. "He loves you, Ysolde. He won't force you to marry."

"He'll do whatever he wants. We're not even blood, a fact the nobles bring up at every chance."

"He may not be your father by blood, but the man loves you. I've seen it in his eyes when he looks at you. He placed you here on this throne to rule when there were a half dozen other qualified nobles eager to assume the role. Surely you can understand what that means."

Her pacing never paused. She wrapped her arms around herself and shook her head. "Obviously nothing. I cannot even be given proper time to find a husband of *my* choosing. And why should I even need one?"

"Here. Sit down." He stepped in to halt her stressed walk and guided her to a chair. "I'll be back in a moment, and I hope to find you here."

Geoffrey left her in the chair and returned to his room. The door was half ajar, as if someone had been inside. He frowned at that, as well as the leather dress shoes beside the door.

"That isn't where I left them."

He shook it off, deciding one of the maids must have tidied his room and taken the time to shine his shoes as well. He'd never seen them glow with such luster in the past. Once he fetched a large bottle of plum brandy from his stash, he returned to the study with two glasses.

Ysolde looked up at him with red-rimmed eyes. She'd obviously cried in the time he was gone. "What is that for?"

"To have you deep in your cups by this night's end," Geoffrey replied bluntly before offering the bottle. "I find this is most enjoyable when ice cold. Would you do the honors?"

While she did give him an uncertain look regarding getting drunk, she also leaned forward and touched her fingers against the glass bottle. Her brow furrowed with concentration until delicate traces of frost bloomed from her point of contact.

Geoffrey admired the chilled exterior, though it had only come with effort. "Your skill with ice magic has improved."

"I suppose so," she agreed in a quiet voice. "Why are you doing this?"

He poured generous glassfuls of liquor and pressed one into her hand. "Because I have the rather enjoyable task of being more than your loyal knight, my lady. I am also your friend. Andras can handle the new recruits—I am needed here."

She took a small, dainty sip from her glass.

"No, no, no," Geoffrey said. "Drink like a woman, not a girl. This isn't wine."

His heckle worked. Ysolde glared at him before she tipped the contents of her small glass down her throat in a single shot.

Geoffrey matched her, tossing back his glass with a grin. As far as he was concerned, nothing cleared the mind like a good, stiff drink.

"I saw your newest batch," she said after their glasses were refilled. "I was surprised, and pleased, to see you accept a woman into your training."

"I always endeavor to accept only the best men into our ranks." He gulped down another swallow. "One simply happened to be a woman this time. Hindera is behind in the times, my lady. I traveled to many places with my father over the years before I became a squire. Did you know the women of Valekesh run the household? They make all decisions down to the children and who their sons will pursue for marriage."

"I've heard as much, but I haven't had the good fortune to travel there."

"Civilized Valekesh is a beautiful place, my lady. In Crestoli, there are women gladiators. My father took me to a tournament once. They're beautiful *and* deadly.

Interest lit up her blue eyes. "Truly?"

Her second glass disappeared, and she held out her cup for more. He topped it off with a grin on his face.

"Yes. Absolutely lethal. It's a sight you'll have to see one day with your own eyes. I saw a woman take on two men much larger than her and outmaneuver them with a blade."

"Father would think that quite unsuitable." She hiccupped.

"Perhaps I should teach you. Have you ever handled a sword?"

"Not well. Who needs a sword when I can…" She gestured and produced flame at her fingertips.

"Let's do it for fun," he insisted. "Just you and me outside in the training yard one day. Only us."

Her quiet, amused giggle brought a grin to his face. "I'm not sure I've had enough brandy to agree to such a thing."

"Have some more."

Ysolde had even more, and soon the hours had passed in conversation and babble about the country and places he'd visited, surprising him that a woman of her refined culture had traveled so little. When he reached the bottom of the bottle, he tilted it toward a light and frowned.

"We're out, and it's for the best, I suppose. Come on, Princess. Let's get you to your room."

"Are we done so soon?"

"Soon? The clock is well past the eleventh evening chime."

The moment she stood, she swayed on her feet, plopping right back down into her chair. She giggled, a sound he'd never had the pleasure of hearing before.

"You're a bloody lightweight. Up you go, lass. Come on." Geoffrey hefted the princess to her feet and guided her to the study door.

Within seconds of reaching the hallway, she stumbled over her slippers and tumbled against him. Fortunately, he was prepared to catch her. He wrapped both arms around her slender figure. Like the rest of her Marcogh brethren, she was athletic and lithe, but she fit against his body as if she belonged, soft in all the right places.

"The house is spinning. I demand you make it stop."

"Geoffrey?" Andras called from the end of the hall.

He glanced behind him to see the other knight approaching them, his brows raised.

Ysolde attempted to draw herself up in a more dignified pose, but she ended up leaning against him with a smile on her face. "Oh lovely, there are two of you to fix it all now."

"Er…" Andras froze, his gaze moving between their drunken princess and Geoffrey. The corners of his lips twitched, but he kept his amusement at the situation off his face. "Fix what, Your Grace?"

"My floors and walls keep moving," she answered. "Quite unacceptable of them, don't you think?"

"We had a few drinks," Geoffrey admitted, finding himself under the heavy weight of his cousin's stare. Andras eyed him with unconcealed suspicion.

"Am I to assume I have your duties for the morning?"

"No, no. I'll be there, mate. Were you looking for me?"

"As a matter of fact, I was, but you appear to have your hands full." Andras smirked. "We'll speak later then. No worries. Good eve to you both."

He bowed and stepped away, whistling.

Geoffrey sighed.

"Come on, lass. This way," he murmured, coaxing her to continue.

When he tired of Ysolde's uncoordinated steps, he plucked her up in his arms and held her. Progress moved along quicker then, and he took the stairs two at a time, praying to Ashta no one else encountered them and asked questions. Most of the help had their evening duties to perform prior to bed or were already tucked in.

Except for Shyla, he thought. He kicked the chambermaid's room door in passing on his way to Ysolde's bedchamber. The door creaked open.

"It's about time that you arri— Oh, Ysolde!" She hurried over, concern written across her face.

"You may want to get her tucked into bed," he said. "Because I doubt she'll manage on her own. She's your responsibility now. Goodnight, the both of you."

Before the girl could protest, he transferred Ysolde to her possession and strode away.

He may have been down a bottle of his favorite brandy, but at least Ysolde would have more urgent matters on her mind than her marriage troubles—like an unrelenting hangover.

If only another stiff drink could wash away the feelings Ysolde had invoked in him when he'd held her in his arms.

HERS UNTIL DEATH

10

B linding light pierced her lids and throbbed with a merciless pulse that ebbed across her skull. With a groan, Ysolde rolled to her side and pressed her face against the pillow, and when that failed to help, she flipped it to the cooler side.

"Good morn, Ysolde. Would you enjoy breakfast in bed today?" Shyla asked, her voice a whisper beyond the heavy curtain.

"Is the room sitting still?"

Amusement and sympathy both reflected in Shyla's gentle voice. "Quite still, I promise. I've also brought some water for you."

Refreshing sips of water alleviated her parched throat, but it did little to curb the pounding behind her eyelids. She should have known better than to rise up to Geoffrey's challenge, but she'd done it anyway, too headstrong to humbly decline.

Sourly, she thought Geoffrey was probably outside pretending to wage war while she suffered in bed and wished for death.

"A bite to eat will help with it," Shyla promised as she parted the curtains and placed the lap tray. Removing the silver dome revealed Ysolde's usual preferences. She nibbled on some toast with jam and ignored the rest of the plate. The idea of eggs turned her stomach.

"Where's Geoffrey?"

"Training the new recruits. They've been outside for a few hours now," Shyla said. "Perhaps you'd like to watch for a time? I can run a hot bath and prepare your dress for the day."

Ysolde grumbled a few uncomplimentary names for Geoffrey beneath her breath.

"Yes to the bath, please. I am less certain about watching the training." The thought of clashing swords and ringing steel held less appeal.

In the room adjacent to Ysolde's bedchamber, there was a spacious tub of pristine, white porcelain with gleaming, silver handles and gold embellishments. It was deep and wide enough to seat three or even four. And unlike Stormwatch Castle, it sported brand new gnomish plumbing. Hot and cold running water came through a device that may as well have been magical in nature, as she understood none of its workings.

There were racks of fluffy towels featuring the Westbrook crest—a stately dragon and a gryphon on opposite sides of a beveled shield—and a few yards from the basin, a plush chaise waited beside the window where Ysolde often settled to brush out her hair. From there, she could watch the horses prance and play in the fields below whenever the stableman allowed them from the barn to graze.

It turned out her predecessor had squandered a gross amount of the city's taxes on remodeling his home, adding features her father deemed unnecessary. The bathroom was merely one among many.

Still, Ysolde didn't miss waiting for servants to pour buckets of boiling water into a clawfoot tub. At the turn of a polished knob, a low hum came from beneath her feet and in the surrounding walls. Then steaming hot water poured from the spigot into the deep basin. She could have done it herself, but Shyla always insisted on setting the towels and pouring fragrant oil blends into the water.

"Thank you, Shyla. That will be all."

"But, Ysolde—"

"I won't slip and drown. I promise."

"If you do slip and injure something dear, Geoffrey won't forgive me if he's the one to heal your broken bits," Shyla reminded before she dipped into a playful curtsy and left the room.

Ysolde waited until the door was shut before stripping off her shift. Stepping down into the hot water brought an immediate sense of relief.

Her thoughts turned to the prior evening. To endless pacing as she raged in silence against her father's decree.

She wouldn't be the first Hinderan woman to suffer the indignity of an arranged marriage, but she'd never imagined the man she'd loved as her father since childhood would force one on her. If Geoffrey hadn't distracted her from her dark thoughts, she probably would have paced through the night.

She only wished he hadn't seen her at her worst, but what was done was done. With a sigh, Ysolde sunk up to her chin in the fragrant water.

A flash of memory slipped through her mind of his strong arms cradling her against his chest. Her fingers were no longer a stranger to the hard muscles of his broad shoulders. She recalled the herbaceous scent of soap clinging to his skin, a pleasant counterbalance to his natural musk.

It was such an inappropriate thought to have about her knight that she flustered and felt a hot rush of shame.

"I will never drink brandy again."

She lingered in the tub until her skin pruned, but she couldn't remain forever. Cool air kissed across her damp body as she stepped from her bath. She never called Shyla in to help with drying her hair, preferring the time alone and the absolute privacy. A small touch of magic warmed her towel. Then the princess applied a few drops of scented oil before buffing herself dry.

Ysolde ran her fingers over the shiny map of tight skin stretching from the under curve of her left breast to her navel. She closed her eyes and sighed. Sometime soon, Lorwick would be discovering the disgusting sight too, the realization bringing a shiver to her body.

She was lucky to be alive. The people able to claim surviving a dragon attack were few, but the number able to boast standing up against a dracolich were even fewer.

Sometimes at night, she still felt the heat searing into her skin, and her memory came alive with the phantom sensation of clothing fibers roasting into her flesh.

Ysolde chastised herself for dwelling in the past, pushed the black memories away, and donned a clean shift. Shyla waited in her room with all of the fastenings, ribbons, and laces for her wardrobe.

"Has the morning training routine ended?" she asked once she squeezed into her fitted dress bodice. The rich plum and green looked good against her warm ochre skin, and the boned bodice accentuated her slender curves.

She'd never have a voluptuous body for other women to envy, but she admired her shape with confidence. She felt powerful, her legs strong from daily riding, her poise flawless. Ysolde pushed her shoulders back and raised her chin, shaking off the dredges of the hangover with determination.

"No, I believe they have taken a moment to allow the new recruits to catch their breath," Shyla told her.

"Excellent. I'd like to see my future guard, after all."

In lieu of spectating from her usual balcony overlook, she headed downstairs, coming across Etienne on her way. His furry friend darted out from behind the sorcerer's feet and twined around her ankles.

"Oh, hello there."

"Adrienne, please love, don't trip the princess."

"No, no, she's fine. It's been a long time since I've had a cat around is all. I forgot how quick they are." Ysolde crouched to give the purring furball a scratch beneath her chin. "Are you and your brother finding everything to your liking?"

"You have been more than generous with your acceptance and welcome, madam."

"And your duties?" With proper affections offered to the friendly cat, she rose to her feet.

"I've come from the training outside. You and Ser Geoffrey may rest assured that none of your newest recruits bear any taint of the *devae*."

"You think whoever wants me dead will try again."

"Oh, most assuredly," Etienne said with a calm, chilling smile.

While the man was handsome, she remained on guard whenever in his company. The stories she'd heard of Fas Perrans conflicted with his casual and friendly nature. Was it a ruse so she'd lower her defenses?

"Considering the vast sum of money offered for your death, I plan to leave nothing up to chance. My brother believes they'll take any opportunity they receive for further infiltration, which includes the call for knights in your security detail."

"You say none of them are touched by demons, but is there anything else of interest?"

"On the contrary, madam, there is much of interest but nothing to concern you. Have no fear. Laurent may not speak your tongue as well as I do, but his powers of observation and concealment are unrivaled. There are times when even I forget he is present in the room, and if anyone plans to move against you, he will know." He smiled again. "Then we will handle the issue as desired."

Ysolde shivered, imagining the handsome younger brother could be hiding in every corner. Usually, she found Laurent to be earnest but enjoyable company over breakfast, and his poor knowledge of Hinderan led to humorous miscommunications.

In fact, she'd taken the responsibility of teaching him the language. Following the morning meal, they met for an hour in her study where she instructed him as her governess, Shyla's mother, had once instructed her in Hinderan.

"But do not let us keep you, Princess Ysolde. Please." He stepped aside with a flourish of one robe-clad arm.

"Good day to you then."

Sunshine warmed her face the moment she stepped outside. The bright sky gave her a momentary pause while her sensitive eyes adjusted, a sharp reminder that too much brandy, no matter how sweet, carried a bitter price.

"You're no good to me if you've collapsed on the ground," Geoffrey's voice resonated across the training yard. "The safety of the princess is your primary duty at all times when she is in your company, and no exhaustion, however dire, should lower your sword."

Some were bent with their gauntleted hands on their knees while a servant passed out heavy, wooden cups of water. No matter how he worked them, Geoffrey always saw to their needs.

"When you don the armor of the Ashguard, you are more than a weapon—you are the embodiment of her will. You are the fist of righteousness, and what you do in uniform reflects upon Princess Ysolde's reputation."

The hypocrite. On deeper consideration, she realized Geoffrey never made his visits to the brothel while wearing the cloak bearing her crest. Still, the city knew the handsome knight's face regardless of the attire he donned.

He turned around, as if sensing her, and she wouldn't be surprised if he'd realized she was present all along.

"Greetings, Your Grace. Have you come to meet with your new guardsmen?" he asked. "One or two even appear to be knight quality, upstanding individuals with experience in battle."

Those who were able to stand straightened quickly then dipped into courteous bows. The others managed clumsily, still winded from whatever rigors Geoffrey had put them through prior to her arrival.

Of the lot, only the lone female guardsman seemed to have her breath. She stood proudly after a deep, respectful bow, her features stoic, despite the sweat beading from her brow and dripping into her eyes.

"I did," Ysolde confirmed with a pleasant smile. It came naturally when she watched the young woman standing among strong men. She felt a kinship with her, a sort of secret camaraderie, as one woman clawing her way into the world of men facing another.

"I am certain you have heard it all from Ser Ashcroft, but I wished to bid you my personal welcome. It took courage and skill to make it this far, admirable qualities both, but there are others you will need to display to keep your place here— honesty, trust, and loyalty."

She walked down the line and met the gaze of each trainee in turn. At first glance, at least two of them didn't bear the image she expected for knights. Then again, Geoffrey created a proud example few men could emulate, and she trusted his judgment.

"Listen well to Ser Ashcroft," she continued. "For you could have no better commander. I look forward to watching your progress, all of you. In the meantime, I hope you find Ashdale Castle to be a home filled with family and friends."

Afterward, once the men were dismissed, she took Geoffrey's arm and beamed up at him. "Walk me from the courtyard to the garden, would you?"

"Of course, Your Grace."

Once they left the training ground, Ysolde felt the weight of his silence crushing her prior excitement with the strength of a magistrate's hammer. At first, she said nothing, longing for the companionable mood of the previous evening. "I feel as if I owe you an apology. Was I a terrible bother last night?"

"Hmm?" Geoffrey blinked at her, and she realized he'd been lost in his own thoughts. Not silent, not morose, but merely thinking. She sighed in relief.

"Was I much of a bother last night?" she repeated.

"No, far from it. In fact, I no longer need to waste my coin at the Goose and Tap for my debauchery now that I have you for a noble drinking partner," he teased.

"You probably have more fun there not having to play nanny." She tucked a stray wisp of hair behind her ear. "Still, I wanted to thank you."

"Wrong, Your Grace. I find any conversation with you enlightening and enjoyable. No appreciation needed."

"Which is why you're back to my title." She gave his arm a light pat.

He grinned at her, eyes twinkling with merriment. "I've returned to using your title to lead by example, Ysolde. Think nothing of it. With so many new faces on the premises, it's best for them to learn now, rather than later, to always maintain proper decorum and respect for you. It'll save me the efforts of thrashing them later."

"Speaking of new faces, with my father's imminent arrival, things will be busy around here. I know you will want to oversee everything yourself, but I'd like you to focus on your new recruits. Andras can handle the guard arrangements."

"That was already my intention. Ever since my hiatus, I've filtered more responsibility to him and freed my time to attend duties as your escort. Which brings me to another matter. Would you like to attend a show at the theater?"

"What?"

"The theatre," he repeated with slow emphasis. "I know you've felt restricted, and you and Shyla are always chattering on about this play. I saw the flyer you tried to hide beneath your book, so I thought you might like to attend."

"I'd love to," she blurted, filled with a rush of giddiness and delight. "But I thought, with everything that has happened, it would be a poor idea."

"With everything going on, you should take a few happy moments when you can," he countered. His atypical behavior caught her off guard.

"Thank you, Geoffrey. I'd like that."

"Good. Is there anything else?"

"Yes." She moistened her lips with the tip of her tongue and drew in a deep breath. "I wanted to let you know that, should you wish to leave my service after the wedding, I will grant you the freedom to do so with my full blessings."

Stunned, Geoffrey stood beside her without uttering a word, stricken mute by the sincerity of her words. By the words themselves. By all of it.

She regretted the offer when he finally inhaled and spoke in a too-quiet voice, "You are firing me."

"I know your thoughts regarding my husband-to-be, and I wouldn't wish you that hardship day after day."

"I swore my service to *you.*"

"I know, and you've become a dear friend to me. Too dear to see unhappy."

"I swore until death. Where else am I to go, Ysolde? Should I return to my father's lands, perhaps?" His voice began in his usual peaceful and reserved tones, only to rise in volume with an abrupt flash of irritation.

"You're his heir, Geoffrey. You'll be Baron Lakeshire one day."

"So you'll send me back to a spiteful mother who chased away my bride-to-be? I certainly can't return to my post as watch captain. Who will have me?"

"Geoffrey…" She hadn't expected anger when she had concocted her idea.

"What hardship shall I be avoiding by leaving the only home ever to welcome me as I am?"

The tirade came to an abrupt end, the indignation replaced by silent reticence and color on his cheeks. Ysolde listened to the wild drum of her heartbeat while Geoffrey visibly struggled to find words. "Forgive me, Your Grace. I've spoken out of turn."

"No, I am the one who is sorry. Geoffrey, your place here is secure and always will be. I only thought, if you *wished* to go, to serve someone you didn't loathe on principle, then I would not stop you."

"Nox herself could not dislodge me from this post, Your Grace, and if Lorwick wishes to remove me, he will find formidable opposition." He bowed stiffly. "I will leave you to your time in the garden. Do you require anything else?"

"No," she said with a heavy heart. She'd upset him enough. "Nothing right now."

"My apologies again, Your Grace." He bowed deeply and returned to the trail, taking swift strides on his long legs.

Everything had gone wrong. She went back over her words and wondered if she could have phrased them better but could only sigh. In her efforts to bring peace, she had only caused more strife. Worse, she had hurt Geoffrey, and that pain squeezed at her heart.

THE VOIDWALKER

11

Ashdale was home to a large, indoor theatre, a rising edifice of marble and stained glass sponsored by the princess. The local nobles enjoyed taking turns, each one eager for the prestige of being the theater's patron for a season. Winter was her turn.

Geoffrey had attended many shows and concerts over the years thanks to Ysolde's love for the arts. She kept a private balcony with comfortable chairs, but he preferred to stand watch from the rear of the viewing box. From there, he maintained constant vigilance and never enjoyed the production below.

According to Andras, the play was worth their time, and Geoffrey had originally set out to sweep his princess away for a private night on the town. Now, he could scarcely enjoy it.

How could Ysolde believe for a moment he'd happily enter the service of another noble? His thoughts proved to be an unwelcome distraction from his duties as her guardsman.

He had to focus, had to place one hundred percent of his attention on their surroundings. The theater made for the ideal place for the next assassination attempt, if the brothers were correct, which also made it an unnecessary risk to her safety.

But they couldn't stuff the woman into a dwarven lockbox and toss away the key until all threats of murder were behind them. He wanted her to live, needed her to enjoy life and all it could offer.

"Geoffrey?"

The whisper lanced through his thoughts, disrupting them. He snapped his attention back to Ysolde, saw her twisted in the seat, worried eyes studying his face.

He stepped forward, leaning down closer to her. "Yes, Your Grace?"

"We can go. I don't need to see the play."

Her lie was a poor one. Her buoyant smile was gone, replaced by worry lines etched on her brow.

"With all due respect, Your Grace, I've heard better lies from tots."

Since his irrational explosion at her in the garden, he'd walked a line of absolute obedience. There was no excuse for his behavior, and she'd had every right to remove him from her employment.

Geoffrey didn't want to leave Ashdale Castle. It was home. Worst of all, he couldn't imagine entering the service of another duke or even a lesser noble. Ysolde had ruined him for all others, her too-bright smiles, her generosity, and even the niggling personality traits he'd once loathed, all culminated to the only woman he ever cared to protect.

He'd be lost wearing another duke's crest or commanding some other noble's army.

"Please. Enjoy the show. It begins on the hour," he said amicably.

"Only if you do as well." She patted the bench.

At her invitation, he eyed the seat with resignation.

"For the love of Ashta, Geoffrey. It won't bite you. It's only a chair."

"Perhaps it isn't the chair I fear, but Your Grace's appetite once dinner hour arrives."

Her expression fell, filling him at an instant with regret.

"I was teasing," he said, voice barely audible. "I know you wouldn't bite me."

"You're still angry with me. You never refer to me as 'Your Grace' unless you're troubled."

He removed his shield then sighed in relief as he lowered into the seat. It creaked beneath his additional weight but held firm, unaccustomed to bearing armor-clad knights.

"No. I'm far from upset at you, Ysolde. *You* didn't anger me. The situation angers me, that your father could even require you to marry that arse—" He bit the word back with a growl.

"It is what it is, and there is nothing we can do to change it. He's been lenient with me all these years. He married Jocelyn off when she turned eighteen."

"I know," he replied grudgingly. "But I don't care about Jocelyn."

Would it bother him at all if Ysolde were some other woman, the daughter of another nobleman? Doubtful. Arranged marriages were a natural part of life, something members of their high society expected since birth.

Then why did it trouble him?

Was it the man chosen by the king, or was it the looming promise to cast Ysolde into a loveless marriage for the sake of creating more noble progeny? He shivered, pained by the fleeting glimpses of the future—Ysolde unhappily sitting court beside Lorwick as he imperiously ruined all she'd built with tenderness and love.

"I think I'd like to return home now," she said in a soft voice.

"Ysolde, no, please." He took her hand, cradling it between both of his heavily gauntleted palms. "Don't let my foul temper ruin your evening. I'm sorry."

"One day I'll get you to come for enjoyment without resembling a man in the middle of a battlefield."

"How could I appear any other way when Hindera's most troublesome noblewoman is in my care? Danger is attracted to you as iron to a magnet." He said the words playfully before releasing her hand, realizing the gesture between them was too familiar. Too personal. He counted himself lucky when she didn't take offense.

It shouldn't have surprised him that the play was a comedic romance, as Ysolde had a fondness for them. She was a dreamer, filled with naivety he'd once held in disdain in the days of their initial acquaintance and later appreciated as their friendship blossomed. He wouldn't have her any other way or change her for all of the gold in King Aldemar's royal coffers.

It was a shame her father didn't agree. A shame he'd rather change her with marriage, tying her to a man who would consider the task of breaking her spirit a hobby no more difficult than hunting geese.

"Ser Geoffrey." The voice was a whisper, an audible breeze across his senses. "Do not panic. There is no need to fear me."

He didn't panic. Oddly, he didn't sense a lie in the disembodied voice's words.

"Who are you?" he whispered.

Ysolde gave him an incredulous look, raising her brows. "You know who I am."

"Not you. The little voice in my ear."

She squinted at him. "Are you feeling well?"

"Say nothing," the voice continued, quiet and disarming. Something tickled Geoffrey's ear, an invisible presence he couldn't see. It reminded him of kitten whiskers. "She'll only worry. Assassins have come for the princess, and you must not allow them to know you are aware."

Geoffrey stilled. His eyes darted to Ysolde's concerned face to find her twilight-hued eyes focused but oblivious to the creature on his shoulder, a being he felt but couldn't see.

"Remain where you are; know you may trust us to handle the assassins. If they become aware of your discovery, their plans will change, and innocents will be harmed. Act naturally, Ser Geoffrey."

"I'm fine," he lied before attempting to steer her attention back to the play. "This is a fantastic show. Absolutely amazing effects." He turned to Ysolde and retook her hand in his, stroking the leather side of his heavy gauntlets over her knuckles. "I'm glad we came tonight."

A hint of her smile returned, and she turned her hand over, her smaller fingers slipping between his as far as his gauntlets would allow. "Thank you for bringing me. I know you'd prefer I stay within the castle after what happened."

"I overreacted, so think nothing more about it."

Ysolde didn't respond well to threats and orders, as he'd learned from their tumultuous first year together.

"What shall we do once the curtain falls?" He hoped the voice understood it was a question for it, and not Ysolde.

It did. "Your only duty is to deliver her to the coach awaiting you outside. Exit through the theater staff entrance."

His senses told him to trust the voice, and although its identity was concealed, he planned to do exactly as it bid him to do. His second sense had never steered him wrong in the past.

"I'd say we could share a drink, but you saw how well that went the last time," Ysolde answered with a nervous chuckle. She ducked her head, and a stray curl drifted into her face, resting against her cheek.

"I'm amenable to another try. Maybe the night will end without you becoming completely soused."

To Geoffrey's great fortune, it was a short play and part of an ongoing serial currently driving the city mad with anticipation. With actors performing each new script as quickly as the playwright could pen them, it meant eager fans waited no more than a month before receiving new material.

"That wasn't what I expected," Geoffrey said once the curtain fell. He rose from the seat, restored his shield to his back, and offered Ysolde an arm to lead the princess from her private box. "I regret missing the first part while away from town."

"I can tell you about it if you like."

"I'd like that."

"Perhaps over our drink."

"Drinks, love. One drink is only a tease." Despite his lighthearted tone, his heart pounded.

The forewarning had him jumping at shadows, and Geoffrey came close to drawing his sword on an innocent cast member who crossed their path.

"Why are we leaving this way? We told Elric we would meet him at the front of the theater where he left us."

"Less crowded this way."

"But Elric won't know where to find us."

"He will," he insisted.

At least he hoped so. Relying on the dubious words of an invisible stranger was among one of his foolhardier decisions. He opened the door, and rather than allow her to step through before him, he clutched the princess close—to hell with propriety—and shuffled them both through the door at once into the narrow alley.

The air in their surroundings hummed with malevolence, a foreboding presence that lanced spikes of dread into his subconscious.

Had the voice led them into danger instead?

"They are here," it whispered, as if reading his thoughts. "Two of them. In the shadows to your left."

"Ysolde," Geoffrey spoke quietly.

"I feel it," she whispered.

The coachman awaited them in Ysolde's handsome, two-horse carriage. He faced forward, sweating profusely despite the cool weather of the evening, and upon their arrival, he jerked around and leapt down from his seat.

"Ser Ashcroft, what's happening?" Elric asked while pulling open the door. "Why were those oddball Fas Perrans adamant that I come here?"

A dark shape lunged from the darkness, robbing Geoffrey of his chance to answer the man. Instincts guided him, and with one step, he maneuvered his body between Ysolde and her would-be attacker.

A weapon clashed against his shield, and then he skewered the masked swordwielder.

Another assassin came from the other side, but Ysolde was there, a formidable opponent in her own right. Before he could spin, she released a wave of flames.

She was powerful, but magical spells were risky in close quarters. The backdraft of the heat tightened Geoffrey's skin. He patted out his cape before it became ablaze with fire.

In the distance, someone shrieked, and voices called out in alarm.

Then the sky roared and ripped open, the tear revealing a glowing gateway into a world of nightmarish creatures. One squeezed through, more teeth and fangs than body, easily as large as a horse. Its slavering mouth opened wide, and two clawed arms extended toward them.

Fire welled up from Ysolde's palm and swirled in an upward funnel. It crashed with a roar into the descending beast, igniting it in brilliant, white flames.

"Take cover within the carriage!" Geoffrey yelled, thrusting Ysolde behind him with his shield out as fiery debris rained toward them from above.

"But Geoffrey—"

Another man leapt out, only to be felled by an invisible force, an unseen protector. Geoffrey heard a choked gurgle, saw a splash of blood, and watched the futile clawing at the dagger hilt protruding from their assailant's throat.

"Go! I'm behind you, love."

Ysolde was nimble, even in the full dress of a proper lady. She leapt into the coach without an assistive step, and Geoffrey boarded behind her.

The carriage lurched forward at speed and jostled them in their seats. Geoffrey reached out an arm to steady her as it raced down the cobblestone streets.

"Don't stop until we've reached the castle, Elric!"

A loud thud followed by a scream echoed into the carriage. The vehicle veered sharply, threatening to topple off balance. Then an unearthly howl sent cold shivers racing down his spine.

"Geoffrey, look out!"

The creature leaning through the window was all gaping jaws and jagged teeth. Black talons clutched at the frame, splintering the wood as the demon snapped at Geoffrey's shoulder. His pauldrons crunched beneath its fangs.

The pain was indescribable, fire in his veins coursing through every fiber, every inch of flesh. With a shout, Geoffrey dropped his sword and thrust his gauntleted hand into the beast's throat, his fist surrounded by holy flames. An agonized scream preceded the monster tumbling loose from the carriage door and striking the street.

Black flames burned behind them, and lightning split the sky. Their carriage continued on for its destination, and despite the occasional thump or shadow gliding past the window, they saw no further harassment.

"Open gate, we have princess!"

Through his pained haze Geoffrey recognized Laurent's accented voice, though he had no recollection of the man being on the carriage when they departed the theater.

The castle landscape raced past the windows when the coach sped inside its perimeter. Startled shouts and cries of surprise came from all around them, guardsmen rushing forward from all sides as Geoffrey shoved open the door and staggered down.

"Nox have mercy!" Andras exclaimed from the path leading to the courtyard. He rushed up to them on foot. "What's happened?"

"Call the healer for Geoffrey," Ysolde instructed.

Geoffrey spun to face her.

"Forget me. Are you hurt? Are you injured?" He asked the questions while touching her, thoroughly checking the woman for injuries without waiting for a response, running his hands everywhere and down the circumference of her arms.

"Geoffrey!"

To the void with propriety and rules, he thought. Her gown, formerly a lovely emerald, was a casualty of the night's events, stained dark with blood soaking through the crushed velvet.

He spun her, searching where the demon claws had rent the dress.

"Where are you hurt?" he demanded again.

"Nowhere. They barely touched me, thanks to you. This is *your* blood."

Indescribable relief swept over Geoffrey, leading him to do something he'd never done, in all of their years of friendship, in all of the time he'd served as Ysolde's faithful guard—he hugged her. Tightly. Crushing. He enfolded her in his arms and pulled her against him, unconcerned with the onlookers at the gate or the watchmen hurrying toward them from the gate.

"You may want to save the celebration for later, mate. Look behind you," Andras said, spoiling the moment.

Ysolde gasped. A quick glance over the shoulder revealed Laurent stepping down from the driver's seat, his leathers glistening and wet. Elric was dead, eviscerated during the escape.

"The *devae* kill your driver. I took over for him."

111

"Appreciated, Laurent. Thank you." With the excitement dwindling, Geoffrey felt the pain in his shoulder again, an acidic burn radiating down his arm, reaching his fingertips. "Where's your brother, by chance?"

"Etienne deals with more problem at theater. There is much work to do. Take safety indoors."

Before anyone had the chance to commend him for his efforts, Laurent stepped backward and vanished, becoming an insubstantial, dark shadow and disappearing completely from sight.

Perhaps the sight would have shocked Geoffrey more if the blood loss hadn't left him unsteady. When he staggered and went down to a knee, hands caught him from every direction.

"I've got him from this side," Andras said. "Do you suppose the two of us can get him inside, Raennia?"

"I have him." She pulled Geoffrey's uninjured arm around her shoulders. "Come on, Commander, lean on us."

With their guidance, Geoffrey reached the receiving room beyond the oaken doors. Ysolde rushed ahead and readied the couch, and by the time they reached it, its plush, velvet-encased cushions resembled the best seat in the house. His legs had a mind of their own, and the world spun, making him wander off course despite the two guards flanking him.

"Ysolde, I'll bleed over your nice things."

"Cushions can be replaced. You cannot, Geoffrey. So sit down and let me call in the healer for you."

He gave a dry chuckle, amused but hurting, his shoulder ablaze with agony he concealed beneath a strained smile for Ysolde. He settled heavily, clumsily into place, and then Andras helped remove the layers of shredded metal.

"Jory went to ride for a healer. One should be here soon," Raennia said.

"Head to the barracks and tell everyone currently off duty to assemble and form a perimeter around the castle. No one comes in or leaves without my authority," Andras said to her.

"Aye, Ser."

Andras and Raennia went their own ways, one to alert the other guardsmen, the other to fetch a stiff drink for the suffering commander. While his cousin was gone, Geoffrey leaned his head against the cushions and inhaled measured breaths to control the pain.

"You saved my life."

"Your skill with magic remains admirable," Geoffrey raised his head slightly, letting a weak smile accompany the compliment. "It's fair to say we saved one another."

His father, a respected baron himself, had once shared a secret with his only son, and Geoffrey had discovered the truth in it. Most members of the high nobility were no different from Lord Easton—frauds unable to lift a sword in battle. The Ashcroft family took great pride in proving the opposite true.

As the only solution to their dilemma became clear, the knight made his decision. Ysolde needed more than a husband and more than a defender. She required respect, and as the knight charged with her protection, the responsibility fell to him to find that man.

Even if Geoffrey had to become him. No one could ever love her more than a man who had sworn his own life to protect her.

***

While he wasn't the worst patient the healers had ever treated, Geoffrey also wasn't the best. He'd insisted on waiting up for their new friends, so after the priestess did her work, Ysolde had Andras assist him to her solar where they waited together for the two Fas Perrans to return.

Larger than her private sitting room, the solar had large windows overlooking the garden on one wall and the training yard on the other. There were books, a harp, and a collection of embroidery supplies all kept in neat array—distractions for Ysolde's varying moods or the entertainment of her guests.

Crispin sneaked in not long after, with pockets full of Geoffrey's favorite sweets. The three of them shared miniature tarts bursting with berries and then settled in to wait.

Etienne and his brother appeared two hours after the failed assassination. While his proud posture never drooped, Etienne's tanned skin had gone ashen, his eyes bearing dark circles as if he'd been awake for days. Ysolde knew the appearance of an overtaxed mage well, having worn it herself many times over the years during her period of study.

"Quick, Shyla. Fetch a sweet drink for Lord Dufresne."

"That won't be necessary," Etienne quickly said, waving the girl off. "There are far more important matters at hand than my exhaustion at the moment."

"Tell us everything." Geoffrey sat forward, eager, only to grimace in pain. Ysolde touched her fingers to his uninjured shoulder and urged him back again.

"We believe this was more than an attempt on her life. In fact, I believe only you and your guards were marked for death, Ser Ashcroft. As for you, Princess, abduction seems to have been their goal."

"Abduction?"

Laurent unfolded two matching handkerchiefs. "Infused with dust from the night-blooming shaderose. It is native to Fellwood."

"I've heard of it." Ysolde frowned. "A mage in my father's court tried to cultivate it once, but it never took."

"They only bloom in the presence of wood elves and fey." Crispin surprised them by speaking up.

As if noticing the boy for the first time, both Etienne and Laurent looked down at Crispin, where he sat at Geoffrey's feet.

"While he is correct, this is perhaps not a topic to discuss in front of the boy," Etienne offered in a polite voice.

"You're right," Ysolde agreed. "Crispin, why don't you head to bed? I promise Geoffrey is fine."

"No, no," Geoffrey said. "Let the lad stay."

He ruffled Crispin's curly hair, making more of a mess of it. At some point, he'd gone from being "her urchin" to a member of the household, seemingly overnight. He made no trouble and cleaned after himself. Geoffrey had surmised the boy to be the one behind the sudden rash of shoe shinings and mendings.

"As you wish." Etienne nodded.

Ysolde steered the conversation back on track. "Do we know who these attackers were?"

"Yes and no." Etienne set two blades on the table. They were slender weapons with basketweave guards protecting the hilts, and their enchanted blades gleamed in the lantern light of the solarium.

"Fas Perran steel," Geoffrey said. "Duelist blades, if I'm correct."

"That it is," Etienne agreed. "And they are. But what an outsider would not notice is that these are more than mere enchantments."

He ran his thumb over the flat of the weapon, imparting enough magic to make the sigils blaze with power. "These are runes favored by agents of Regent Mystere."

At first, she didn't want to believe him, until she realized Etienne had shown them nothing but honesty, earnest to the point of courting treason with his own people. Fury built within Ysolde as she realized the implications. Years of peace between their countries would come undone, their fragile truce shattered.

"That's an act of war!"

Her father would have to be notified at once, requiring her to send a second letter.

"Regent Mystere is a humanist. He would have nothing to gain from such an endeavor to harm you. None whatsoever. When we went to war with your country, the most outspoken voices against invading Hindera came from him and my own father. They were outvoted."

"Then how do you explain the evidence?"

"I can't. Not yet, at least." The man paused, thoughtful eyes gazing at something unseen on the floor. "Something about this entire situation troubles me."

Stress always led her to pacing. Her steps carried her back and forth across the room while she considered not only her options but her obligations.

"I know you must bring this news to your father's attention, but I ask you to grant me time to speak with Regent Mystere."

"That will take days. Weeks even," she countered. "He'll be furious if I put it off so long."

"Days at the most. We have a saying in Fas Perra that the fastest letter arrives by twilight. Adrienne, would you please?"

"Your cat?"

Adrienne had become a familiar face among the castle residents. The cute, long-furred kitten had crept out of hiding when they arrived, sticking by them during Geoffrey's healing and trailing in Ysolde's footsteps when they relocated to the solar.

"More than a cat, I assure you. And while I apologize for the deception, I trust you will honor our secrecy."

The kitten curled by the fire raised and stretched, arching her back. Her form elongated, enlarged, and bled from subdued grays to deep violet streaks in pitch dark fur. She became a murky shadow shaped into an enormous feline, her amber eyes bright as two burning coals. Her head came level with his waist, which she bumped against his side while purring.

Geoffrey didn't move, and neither did Ysolde, the two of them stunned into speechlessness.

"Adrienne is a talented voidwalker. She'll have the letter to Regent Mystere by dawn."

"Pah. I will have it there within hours."

The spell was broken when the void creature spoke, and the fear that had held Ysolde paralyzed sent her stumbling back a step. Its voice was youthful, high-pitched like a child. And it spoke their language.

"She's a demon," she breathed. "You've had a demon in the castle all along."

Etienne appeared unrepentant. "For our protection as well as yours. Adrienne has been my lifelong companion, and I trust her with my very life."

"And you?" Ysolde turned toward Laurent. "Do you keep another?"

"Ah, no. I have not same calling."

"A demon," Geoffrey said. "This is the creature who spoke to me in the theater, isn't it?"

"Yes," Etienne said, unmoving and unflinching. Despite the visible fatigue in his frame, he stood on guard and held a white-knuckled grip of his staff. "She warned you when I could not."

"And you saw no reason to share this with us?" Geoffrey continued, his voice low, with barely restrained menace.

"No, I did not."

The silence returned and held. As the inky, catlike outline slid her body against Etienne's shins, Ysolde watched from a distance, her back stiff and shoulders tense.

At any moment, Geoffrey was bound to explode into a frothing rage. During his years as a paladin, he'd sworn an oath to abolish anything unnatural from the void. Fine hairs raised on the back of Ysolde's neck, and her legs tensed, prepared to leap between the men.

"Etienne," Geoffrey began, dropping the title between them. "I find myself without the words to convey my gratitude for all you have done. I owe you and Adrienne both our thanks."

The palpable tension in the air popped, dismissed in an instant with Geoffrey's words. Ysolde's shoulders relaxed as she released her pent breath, and from the corner of her eye, she noticed Laurent mirrored her.

She wasn't the only one who'd expected a fight.

"Had we been alone—"

"Had you been alone, you would have no doubt prevailed in some other way, Geoffrey," the sorcerer said gently. "You have a great power of your own, and the princess is not without her own abilities. We merely made your job easier."

"Perhaps."

"Exactly so." Etienne winked then turned the subject. "Now, with Adrienne as my eyes, I only ask you give me time to discover the truth."

The decision belonged to her, yet Ysolde looked to Geoffrey. Not for guidance but for reassurance. His steady gaze lent her strength.

"Very well, do what you can, Etienne. It's the least I can do after what you both did, and I would rather present my father with facts, not guesses."

"Those were my thoughts precisely, Ysolde… May I call you Ysolde?" Etienne asked, in a pleasant voice, featured serene despite the weariness lining his features.

"Yes, of course. You've earned the privilege to my Ashtarian name," she said.

Laurent nudged his brother.

"Also, I thought you should like to know Duke Lorwick is in the city vowing to uncover the parties responsible for the attack," Etienne said. "As we left the theater, Laurent overheard him mentioning he would be on his way shortly to speak with you regarding what's happened."

Geoffrey swore under his breath.

"Thank you, Etienne. Now please, take your rest, both of you."

"I'll send Adrienne by nightfall. For now, I have a letter to pen. Good eve to both of you, may it fare better than this afternoon."

The two Fas Perrans bowed to them and filed from the room, their cat following behind them.

With the adrenaline and excitement over, Geoffrey's wounds no longer placing him in danger, and the worst behind them, Ysolde excused herself from her knight's company under the pretense of tidying her appearance and wanting the healer to attend him again.

In the privacy of her bedroom, she wept and wished for the second time in all of her years that the king had never taken her from the Marcogh tribe.

**

"Once again, you arrive without announcement or warning," Ysolde said, voice tight with unconcealed disapproval. She joined Lorwick in the receiving room where the footmen had directed him.

She'd exchanged her bloodstained evening dress for a masterpiece of rich, cocoa velvet. A hint of cream, lace underskirt peeked around the hem, barely concealing her forest green slippers.

If she'd had any choice in the matter she wouldn't have donned anything new at all, but Shyla had insisted they follow the rules of proper decorum, and that she greet her "guest" in clean attire.

What would she ever do without Shyla? Her faithful friend had seen her through every up and down in her life, ever since she was a five-year-old girl. Twenty-three years of loyalty, fidelity, and mirrored respect.

"I was concerned for your safety and welfare, Princess. With your father's arrival imminent, it is my responsibility to see you well taken care of."

Did he know Aldemar had sold her off to him like a piece of chattel? Whatever the truth, she decided not to speak of it or draw his attention in any manner to the idea.

"As you can see, I am fine."

"I am told you have entertained two visitors on the premises since we last met. I should like to meet these men. It isn't proper for an unmarried woman to entertain male guests."

Ysolde's lips pressed into a thin line. It didn't surprise her to learn gossip had reached the city about the two Fas Perrans in her home, but she wondered if Lorwick had also discovered their identity. "Are you not a male guest?"

Lorwick's charming smile never faded. "I am, but I ask these questions for your safety, my princess. Only for your safety. There's been an attempt on your life, and I must know who dwells within these walls.

"I entertain no guests," she countered. "I have employed two men into my service among a few hundred others who fight beneath the Ashguard's banner. Anything more you have no need to know."

"For now, perhaps." His phony but pleasant smile set her on edge. "I find any potential threat to you to be my business now after what has occurred this evening in the city, Princess. Where is your knight?"

"The healer tends to him. Ser Ashcroft sustained a wound in my defense."

"His injury provides further truth to my words. Please. I should like to meet these two men."

"Would you also like to meet every new guard my knight has hired into our service?" she countered. "If it is my state you worry about, then do take notice that I've suffered no harm due to *his* valor. I will not have you dismiss his efforts."

Lorwick tensed. The jovial, albeit well-practiced smile faded from his face, and tension clenched his jaw. "I see."

Meow.

Ysolde's eyes darted to the open door. Adrienne trotted into the room on light and tiny feet, and without invitation, helped herself into the woman's lap.

"I don't recall you keeping a pet."

"I do now," Ysolde said defensively. Without hesitation she stroked her fingers down the kitten's gray-furred back. "There are over a dozen watchdogs on the property and nearly as many horses. Why shouldn't I have a cat as well?"

"Hrm. Well. It looks common is all." Lorwick leaned forward, and in those seconds Adrienne was under his quiet scrutiny, Ysolde's heart pounded. Could he see through her illusion to the beast residing beneath her magical disguise? "Rather homely, isn't it? Had I known you were fond of such animals, I would have brought you a finer creature, one of impeccable lineage. A Narkanthi Mountain cat, perhaps."

Adrienne hissed at the man, causing him to lean back before he had the gall to touch her. The move endeared the creature to Ysolde in an instant.

"How would you attain such a creature when our kingdoms no longer engage in trade." Although decades had passed since the awful war between Hindera and their northern neighbors, enmity remained between them."

"For you, I would brave the frigid borders to capture one with my own two hands."

"I like this one." She smiled brightly. "And I think she's lovely. Almost blue. I've never seen a cat so fair a color."

She and Adrienne would have to visit the larder before Etienne sent the cat on her journey into the void. She deserved at least half a rack of lamb.

"Well," Lorwick grumbled. He sat still, his back rigid in the seat. "I'm pleased to see you without injury following your ordeal."

"My thanks for your concern. However, if there is nothing else of importance, I hope you will excuse me. I have many matters to attend to."

With Adrienne in her arms and lacking further inclination to remain cordial with Lorwick, she strode from the room before he could respond. She didn't look back, but in her mind's eye, she visualized the scandalized expression on the duke's face. It brought a smile to her lips.

The insufferable ass.

One day, she'd be forced to entertain him, but that day hadn't yet come. For now, Ashdale Castle remained her home and hers alone.

She fed Adrienne well and watched the cat, in her larger form, savagely rip into a portion of cured pork. It brought Ysolde pleasure to imagine her future husband had changed places with the ham shank.

A Good Heart

12

They had played their card game for at least an hour, or perhaps closer to two. Raennia had lost track after a fourth mug had been foisted on her by the other guards, the wooden stein overflowing with dark ale.

After dark, the barracks became a den of activity, so the group of them had requisitioned the wine cellar and estate pantry for their nefarious card-playing needs.

Rae had been disappointed to find Geoffrey absent from the table when she'd arrived. He'd joined them a time or two, looking cheerful and playing the part of the good sport whenever he lost his coin to them.

While he was honorable and undeniably attractive, Rae couldn't see beyond the way he treated her. When Geoffrey was near, she was a comrade in arms, another soldier-in-training, more than what the other members of the Ashguard perceived when she removed her mail.

He treated her like an equal. And Rae loved every second of it.

When her turn came around, she rolled the dice and laid her cards across the table. Four Stars and a lonely Crescent faced upward. "This round is mine."

The half-elf sitting to her right made a grumpy noise in his throat. She stole a glance at him, admiring chiseled features and a strong jaw adorned by a neatly trimmed goatee. It hadn't taken long for Rae to determine his eyes were his best asset.

Every maid in the household whispered about Laurent, and each one of them tried to catch his eye in some manner. Since his arrival with his brother, Rae had noticed the staff tending better to their dresses and hair.

A quiet sigh escaped her. She didn't have time for such trivialities as flirting, not when her days were full of sparring and marching in full armor. They'd had her fitted for a proper set, and she'd never been prouder than the day she showed her mother the fruit of her hard work.

Nothing could have improved the moment more than having her father present too, but her little brother was a close second. His eyes had widened, and he'd worshipped the very ground beneath her booted feet.

Rae smiled and pushed away her thoughts of him.

"Lucky hand is all you have this time," Laurent said to her with a good-natured grin. "Why do we play for coppers? Real money will give excitement to game."

"We're not all as rich as you, pretty boy," Jory said with a sharp laugh. "Why do you think I'm playing here rather than visiting the Primrose with Caven and Lieutenant Torrance?"

"Because you wouldn't know what to do with a whore, lad!" Everyone laughed at Piers's teasing, Even Raennia. The bearded guard slapped the blushing Jory on the back. "Don't you worry, son. We'll get you sorted. I bet even our Raennia here will have a useful bit of advice."

"Sure, I do. Don't listen to these louts, for a start." Rae winked and scooped up her winnings, adding them to her measly pile. "Anyway, Laurent, unless you have a suggestion for a different type of wager, shut up and drink. All of you take your shots."

Small glasses filled to the brim with amber liquor waited for them on the losers' tray. The taste of the Nymphalian fire brandy was still on her lips from the last round, an expensive purchase Laurent had donated to the games.

The generous move had earned him the favor of all men in attendance, but she was happy to sit out on the next required drink of the spicy stuff.

"Gods, it burns," Jory complained. "I think I rescind my gratitude to you, Laurent. It's like someone poured a volcano into a shot glass."

"No shame in dropping out, little girl," Nedic said with false sympathy.

"Watch it there," Rae reminded him. "Girls are plenty tough."

"You're not a girl, Raennia. You're a woman," the old lieutenant said with a wink.

"She certainly is, so perhaps we should give little girls more credit," a voice spoke from the entrance. "If they develop into fine women willing to join us in battle."

In the flickering light from an enchanted lantern, she made out the silhouette of the slimmer brother. Whispers around the castle called Lord Dufresne a necromancer, a mage who dealt with demons and worse. The ominous skull atop his staff and his habit of keeping to the shadows did little to improve perceptions of him. He'd never said a cross or impolite word to her, but there was something about him, an impression of power that was vastly different from what she sensed around Geoffrey.

Laurent twisted to look behind him. "Come to join us?"

"Is there room for another player?" Etienne countered.

The laughter in the room quieted, wary glances exchanged between the players. The tension rolled through the room, a cloud of discomfort settling on Rae's shoulders that had nothing to do with the sorcerer's polite inquiry.

Nedic spat into a nearby pot as he rose to his feet.

"Late for me," he said in a gruff tone.

He brushed past Etienne without a word. Piers followed in his wake, giving the taller mage a scathing look.

"Looks like there's room now." Jory studied Etienne with unabashed, open curiosity, exhibiting the fearlessness of youth. He was the youngest of them, a tender nineteen years, with strawberry blond hair and freckles.

Rae nudged a chair out from the table with her foot and set the dice on the table.

"Appreciated." Etienne bent into a courteous dip before he dropped into the seat. He leaned the staff with the misshapen skull against the wall nearby, staring vacantly at them with its empty sockets.

"You come to win all the money, yes?" Laurent teased lightly.

Etienne dropped his eyes to Laurent's pile of coins. "I came to let the air out of your overinflated ego, but from what I witnessed a moment ago, someone has beaten me to it."

"It's about time someone beat him," young Jory chimed in.

The fifth game player grunted. Marik spoke little, leading Rae to wonder if the man remained silent to avoid trouble. He kept to himself, and it surprised her as much to see him at the game as it did to see Lord Dufresne.

While Rae dealt the next hand, Jory fetched refills and included Etienne on the drinks. Dark brown ale with creamy foam sloshed within the clay tankard as the young man set it in front of their newest player.

After a few hands, they learned the game played faster without Nedic and Piers. They also learned Lord Dufresne had a good head for cards and luck comparable to his brother.

"Ha! Looks like your luck is up for the night," Jory crowed after Rae made her worst roll of the night.

Raennia glowered at the double daggers she had rolled and eyed Etienne to her left. He offered a pleasant smile while he filled her waiting shot glass with two measures of sweet-smelling liquor from his flask.

She studied the green-tinged liquid. What new and evil delight had the mage concocted for them? To her surprise, it went down smoothly, leaving a cool, tingling feeling in her mouth and throat.

Within moments of Raennia setting down the empty glass, Laurent suffered an abrupt outburst of laughter.

"What's so funny?" she asked.

Etienne raised one shoulder in a shrug. "My brother is an obnoxious child. Nothing unusual."

She shot a glance between the two brothers. "What is this stuff anyway?"

"Nothing that would hurt you, of course. It's fermented from the juice of a mint plant found in southern Fas Perra. I once read that the natives of Fellwood prefer to smoke it."

Marik chuckled, and Jory's face took on a greenish tinge.

Etienne steepled his fingers. "You are in for an interesting evening."

The bastard.

Poor Jory fell victim to the same fate when he rolled a skull and a star. Etienne grinned and poured the kid a single measure of his strange drink.

"If I might ask, what magical service do you provide, Lord Dufresne? I fear my experience with true sorcery is limited to the occasional healer and hedge witch," Raennia said.

"Surely you've met a magic user of some variety in the past, excluding our dear duchess." He didn't answer her question, cloaking himself in a veil of mystery.

"No, none, I think. Though, there was this one time I'm certain I saw magic. It was after my father…" Her voice cracked, and she paused, drawing in a quiet breath before continuing. "It was after my father offered shelter to a passing traveler, some three years ago. She was a mercenary, I think, or at least armed like one. Anyway, I saw her out at midnight in our fields with her sword, a blue glow around her and wind in her blond hair. The next morning when she bid us farewell, rain began to fall."

"The ability to create rain is a rare gift," Etienne commented. "I would be inclined to believe it an act of coincidence."

"Maybe. Still, I know what I saw."

The round circled the group, and Rae tossed in her second bet before rolling the dice. A sun and a crescent, both of which she had in her current deck. Despite having a strong hand, she slanted her gaze toward Jory and then set her cards face down.

"I fold," she said with false disappointment.

When she glanced up again, she found Laurent's eyes upon her, watching her closely with unconcealed interest.

He knew. She didn't know how, but there was no mistaking the understanding in his eyes.

Laurent also set down his cards. "I fold. Bah."

"Are you going to answer my question?" Raennia inquired again, irritated Etienne had brushed her off.

"You truly wish to know?" Etienne's brows raised. "In Fas Perra, I am the firstborn of Regent Fresna, which granted me a vast number of responsibilities related to my father's office. Here, I serve as the magical advisor for the duchess," he replied. "Although she is quite accomplished as a sorceress herself, my talents cover a wide range of practices often neglected in Hindera. There should be no more demons while I am in her employment at least. As for your mystery mercenary, you may have crossed paths with an agent of the Magisterium. I'm told they're quite formidable, but I haven't had the good fortune to meet one. Have you, Laurent?"

A change came over Laurent's face, but she had no idea what caused his handsome features to twist into a frown.

He must have had a sour hand after all, and it was about time, since he'd played throughout the night with the luck of a fey and exhibited the drinking constitution of a giant.

She'd felt compelled to keep up with the men in drinking, aware of the eyes on her. She was a woman in a man's world. Laurent looked as if he had been drinking spring water the entire time, despite having at least two mugs more than she.

"Well, whoever she was, she claimed no credit for it and saved our crop, so for that I'm eternally grateful. I can't say I know much about the Magisterium though, beyond rumors. They say only the best sorcerers come from there but that they have ice in their veins and no compassion."

"I myself was tutored privately at home, so I couldn't tell you truth from rumor regarding them. It would seem they're not as heartless as the stories say."

Etienne glanced down at his cards and casually laid them on the table after Jory and Marik lowered their hands. He smiled despite his losing hand.

"I take it you have no love for the Magisterium," she wagered a guess, looking to Laurent.

Of the two, he was the more approachable for sure, though Etienne's smile was more handsome. Maybe, she thought, because Laurent reminded her so much of a courtier. Or a bard—all smiles and silken talk.

"Magisterium is not nice people," he explained, appearing uncomfortable. "I am finished for night. I bid you all good evening."

"Done so soon?"

"Soon?" Laurent looked down at her and managed a quick smile. "It is well past the midnight chime, no?"

"He's right." Marik stood and stretched, limbs popping. "Even with a full day off tomorrow, I imagine we should all get some sleep."

"I can see you safe back to your room, Laurent. It's awfully dark." Whether appreciated or not, Jory scrambled after the man, reminding Rae of a faithful puppy chasing a big dog.

Marik gave them all a nod and headed out into the night, leaving Rae alone with the rumored demon summoner. As she counted her winnings on the table, the weight of his staff bore into her, oppressive and dark. Unlike the men who fled when Etienne entered, she refused to shift or squirm like a frightened child.

Rae ducked her head instead, sweeping her humble pile of coppers into a coin purse as an excuse to avoid eye contact. Like some of the other men, she had plans for her coins, none of which would benefit her on a personal level. She wanted to provide a good, full meal on the table for her mother and siblings. And a warm blanket for the baby, with winter approaching.

"That was a good game. Is there a name for the drink you shared with us?"

"It's called a Fellweed Cordial," he replied.

"It was pleas—" She'd raised her head to see an empty room. Etienne had retreated soundlessly from the cellar without even a footstep, gone so swiftly the shadows themselves may have carried him away.

"Well goodnight to you too," she muttered.

On her way upstairs, a whiff of baked bread turned her from her path to the barracks, bringing her to the kitchens instead. Her stomach grumbled. A peek around the corner revealed a quiet, dim-lit room, but her gaze fixated on the trays set to cool on the wide prep table.

Their breakfast. From what she'd learned since becoming an inhabitant of Ashdale Castle, the cook staff awakened early to bake the day's first bread.

In the meantime, she needed sustenance for her own growling belly. Once Rae determined there were no witnesses to her crime, she plucked a gooey sweet from the tray.

Chopped nuts and a liberal dusting of scarlet sugar covered the thick icing.

Food had never tasted so good. So rich, the sugary-spiced topping more decadent than the finest treat purchased in the market square. She stuffed the remainder of the first in her mouth and snatched a second. Her unbearable hunger made short work of it.

"You too?" Jory called from the doorway.

She froze, wide eyes turning to the young man standing to her right. The panicked quivering in her chest settled when she saw him alone, Laurent gone to bed or off to chase pretty maidservants.

"Hungry?" she asked, offering Jory a roll.

"Bloody starved is what I am. What do the elves put in their alcohol? It's evil."

"Elves and fey. Who knows which of them made that stuff?"

"Blessed Ashta, have you had any of the milk?" Jory had the jug from the cooler tipped to his mouth.

"Well don't drink all of it. Save me a taste—"

"Isn't it late for the two of you to be out of bed?" Geoffrey's voice boomed through the kitchen.

To her credit, Rae didn't leap out of her skin again. She stood tall, despite the icing on her fingers or the smear of cinnamon and candied peppers on her lips. The chef used it liberally on most products Ysolde favored.

"We were hungry, Ser Ashcroft," Jory said.

"So I see."

Crap. They'd been caught. Ever since the events of the previous evening, none of the guard had expected to see Geoffrey out of his bed. For once, he'd taken the healers seriously.

Bites from demons were dangerous, easily infected and often lethal if left untreated. Several of the guardsmen, Raennia included, had visited their commander in his sickbed to bring him reading material and play games of chess throughout the day. He hadn't made his trip to the kitchen without difficulty. Dots of perspiration lined his brow.

"You're eating us out of house and home, so I assume Dufresne must have shared his booze with you." Geoffrey smiled. "I sympathize. Andras and I made the mistake of gaming Doubles with him two nights ago."

Both culprits shared a nervous laugh.

"This is all my fault," Rae confessed with a nod toward the half eaten tray. "I started in on them first."

"Oh, don't be mistaken. I wouldn't be bothered if you eat this pantry to the last crumb. The gods know I've had my share of food. You'd just be wise to avoid allowing Madam Quirre to see you doing it. You've got roughly thirty minutes before she makes rounds."

The man claimed a sweetroll of his own and paused in the kitchen doorway. "I know tomorrow is your day of peace, but I'd like to see you in private once you're well, Raennia. I should be on my feet again." He groaned and held his side. "I hope."

When he was gone, Jory collapsed against a table and leaned on the marble slab. "That was a close call."

"Then let's heed his warning. We won't be so fortunate next time," Rae said.

They found a shank of lamb and a hard cheese wedge, which they took back to the barracks. Fearful of awakening their fellow guardsmen, they ate by a single candlelight, huddled on the floor by their beds. Jory kept the milk jug tucked beneath his arm.

"Can't remember the last time I've ever had a meal so grand. I don't think I ever have," Jory admitted.

"You come from a family of farmers, right? Like me?"

"Shepherds," he corrected. "We sold off the best of the flock and only kept the old, gamey ones for ourselves. Not the best meat, but you get used to it when the alternative is tuber soup."

Rae smiled. "Things will be different for your family now. And mine too."

There would be no more humble days and hungry nights for the Cassii family. And she'd do anything for their luck to remain unchanged.

***

Sobriety gave way to worry, and anticipation made a jumble of Rae's insides, twisting her stomach into knots.

Raennia couldn't fathom what Geoffrey wanted her for, as he rarely took any of them aside in private conversation. Did he mean to chastise her for imbibing on Lord Dufresne's strange alcohol, or was there some other infraction against her flawless record?

She crawled from the bed shortly after the tenth hour, feeling like she'd been worked over by Andras again in the ring. The second-in-command and Geoffrey had similar views, and he took no pity, treating her like a man.

Groaning, she lowered to the edge of the mattress again and returned to her sprawl. On top of a hangover, a sensation of turbulence rolled through her stomach.

"That won't help," Jory said from the adjacent cot. He lay curled on his side, miserable features pinched, eyes shut tight. "Ate too much. I feel like a tick beneath a heel."

"You overdid it with all of that milk," Rae mumbled.

"Yeah, probably so. Aren't you supposed to be meeting with the commander today?"

"He said when I was up and about. I'm not sure I'm in a rush to go if I'm going to get yelled at."

"Can't be because we raided the kitchen. He'd be calling me in too," Jory pointed out.

"You're right." Rae crawled off the sheets and pulled a tunic from the chest at the foot of her bunk. While she had declined preferential treatment on account of her gender, she'd accepted the offer of allowing her to share the facilities in the servants' quarter where the maids changed and bathed. "I'd better see what he wants before he hunts me down instead."

"I'll be here." Jory burrowed beneath his covers, and seconds later, he was snoring. Noisily.

Raennia chuckled at her friend and then headed out with clean clothes bundled beneath her arm. A quick, hot bath helped wash away the final vestiges of sleepiness and eased the remainder of her headache.

An hour somehow passed between her awakening and finally entering the main floor of the castle. Nameless, faceless maids scurried about in the usual hectic and busy midday rush. The staff was too many, and Rae had no head for recalling all of their names. Save one.

"Shyla, have you seen Ser Ashcroft about?" she called to the woman in passing.

Shyla paused. "Oh, yes. He's in the solar with the princess."

"Oh." Raennia hesitated.

Anyone with half of their wits could tell Geoffrey and Ysolde were madly, deeply in love. Or so she'd assumed despite the rest of the men in the barracks waving off her theories with laughter. According to them, Geoffrey lived only for some artist who had escaped the city and flown off to parts unknown, and with every telling of the story, the breakup became more outlandish.

At one point, Piers had told Rae the girl had taken Geoffrey for every coin, down to his last copper, and fled to Crestoli where she began a business in their lucrative slave trade.

Nedic claimed the woman's disappearance was due to foul play. Geoffrey's mother had the woman slain, and now her parts were moldering beneath the castle.

Whatever the truth, Raennia stood by her own observations, even if no one else noticed the stolen glances between the two. The way Geoffrey admired Ysolde behind her back reminded Rae of the way her father had always looked at her mother.

Not that any of it mattered now that Duke Lorwick was to become the woman's husband and assume control of Ashdale. She'd felt pity for Ysolde then and wondered how any free woman could envy Hindera's gentry when they were confined by the laws of their noble ranks.

"What's wrong? Don't know the way?" Shyla asked.

"I wouldn't want to interrupt."

"You won't be. I took them tea a moment ago. You'll be welcomed, I think," the lady's maid urged.

"Thank you."

Going by memory, she made her way upstairs. Part of guardsmen training required them to know every square inch of the castle down to its most disused stairwell, and with a destination in mind, her confident stride took her down the corridor.

Geoffrey's strong voice drifted into the hallway before she reached the door. "The boy would make a good stableman or kennel master one day. Gods know we've got enough bloody dogs now after that last litter to need the helping hand there. Would it be too much pressure to ask him to train with Birch and learn to handle the guard hounds?"

"Crispin loves animals of all types, so I don't imagine he'll feel put out at all."

Rae announced her presence with a knock at the open door, rapping her knuckles against the wooden frame.

Geoffrey stood, the way she'd expect him to rise and welcome a refined lady instead of a farm girl from the hills. "Ah, please come in. Ysolde, you remember Raennia, don't you?"

"How could I forget the first woman in Hindera to ever receive a guard post? She has my deepest respect. Good day to you, Raennia."

That's it. She'd fallen last night. Tumbled and hit her head along the way to the barracks. Her eyes fell upon Ysolde, taking in her fine state of dress, the rich, plum velvet and satin trim shirring her shoulders and the polished stones shimmering around her neck. The woman made elegance appear as simple as breathing.

"Good morning, Your Grace. Ser Ashcroft." Delivering a stiff bow borne from nerves, she wondered if her attire was suitable. Her tunic, corseted vest, and pants paled in comparison to the attire of the other two.

She hadn't donned a dress since her father's funeral, and even more years had passed before.

Much to her surprise, Ser Ashcroft wore something more than his usual armor or plain tunics. The man looked like a noble, clothed in a handsome, bronze doublet over a cream shirt. Even his hair was groomed and neat, tamed from its usual unruly mess of dark blond curls.

"You arrived much earlier than I expected. The princess and I actually had a wager that you wouldn't emerge from the barracks for at least another two hours." Geoffrey's welcoming smile alleviated her fears. "You lost me five silver."

"Sleeping all day would be a waste, Ser."

Sleeping in as late as she had was a rarity, but she had no chance to fret about the hour of her arrival since Ysolde patted the seat beside her.

"Come join me, please. Tea?" A convenient service for four occupied the rectangular table between Geoffrey's oversized armchair and Ysolde's lounger.

"Oh, um, I would be honored, Your Grace."

The moment struck Rae as surreal, royalty playing hostess to her, pouring her tea and serving it to her on a tiny, exquisitely crafted porcelain saucer with a probable worth greater than the cost of her entire wardrobe.

"Geoffrey tells me you've made great strides since joining the guard. I can't begin to tell you how much it excites me to watch you, another woman, undertake this path in a place ruled by men."

"I'm honored he took the chance on me. To be honest, I expected to be dismissed once I was found out."

"Our princess would have been quite cross with me if I'd overlooked you." Geoffrey grinned.

Rae's lips parted, but her words were lost when the knight and his princess exchanged a silent look, broiling with unspoken words.

After setting down her tea mug, the noblewoman rose swiftly to her feet and flashed another serene smile to Rae before murmuring, "You'll have to forgive me. There's a matter requiring my attention."

"Of course, Your Grace. Thank you for having me."

The princess winked to Geoffrey and hurried from the room.

"I hope I did not come at a bad time."

"Not at all," he assured her. "She is never still, always with some project to follow up on. Besides, this gives you and me some time to talk."

"What shall we talk about, Ser?" His words renewed her anxiety in a surge of irrational worry, and then she realized she'd shown poor manners. "You'll have to forgive me for failing to inquire as to your health. Are you well?"

"Quite well. The healers are confident I'll return to my duties within the week. Now, on to our business. I have a question or two for you, and I hope this isn't too personal."

"Ser Ashcroft, you may ask me anything."

He nodded, but his eyes were thoughtful and intent, focused on her face. "What do you want for yourself? As a future."

Geoffrey crossed his broad arms against his chest.

Her future? She gave him a quizzical look but took a moment to consider the question.

She came from a simple farm family and had no dowry, special plans, or husbands awaiting her, handpicked by her deceased father. At the time of his death, she'd already been what most married women in Hindera would have called a spinster, doomed to a future of milking goats and mucking the barn instead of moving on to build a family of her own.

"I suppose I would hope to earn my way to a place of authority with the guard, Ser. To help make a difference in the city while supporting my family. To bring us some respectability so my sisters and my brother have the freedom to pursue their interests and lives."

"But did you have any other plans? Nothing set aside by you and your father?"

It clicked with crystal clarity, and Geoffrey's unspoken question became apparent. Swallowing a sudden, harsh and dry lump in her throat, she spoke without allowing emotion to enter her voice, "My father didn't believe in forced marriages, Ser. He met my mother without such a match, and they loved one another deeply. He wanted the same for all of us, to let us live the lives we wanted."

The knight commander left his armchair and joined her on the lady's settee. "Considering how well you swing a blade, that should surprise me little. I ask because there are many who will question what I intend to do, and while it's none of their business, I need to know you're prepared for whatever may come of it. For what may be said, for what may go unsaid, and for what will be thought of you and me."

"I'm not sure I understand." A hundred possibilities swept through her mind, ranging from the preposterous to the impossible.

"I'd like to offer you the opportunity to train alongside me. To become a knight. Andras has extended the same offer to Marik, so we'll be putting the two of you through your paces together, so to speak."

The impossible won.

"You cannot be serious."

"Do I appear to be joking with you?" His smile grew warm before he delivered an affectionate pat to the back of her hand. "I don't care if you're a woman. What I care about is that you're willing to lay your life down for our princess if the situation ever requires sacrifice."

"I meant every word of my oaths."

"I know you did. So, have a few days to think about it. There's no rush to provide an answer, and I don't plan to change my mind."

"Yes," she whispered. Rae told herself she wouldn't cry.

"You've decided so soon?"

She failed. The tears coursed hot and fast, joy and elation blurring her vision. "Ser Ashcroft, I've never wanted anything more."

He offered her a handkerchief, startling her with the gentlemanly gesture. The fine, linen square, stitched with the letters G.A., felt softer than silk against her skin. "I have one final offering."

"What more could there be?"

"It's no secret I left the Order of Ashta's Chosen, but I retain privilege to use all I learned through my blood, sweat, tears, and dedication. I consider it a gift freely mine to share with others, and so, I have decided, with the princess's blessing, to extend this offer to you."

Her breath seized in her lungs.

"I…" Her voice shuddered, and she took a moment to steady herself. "I don't know what to say. Magic such as yours… I don't have that."

"I think you do. More importantly, Raennia, you have a good heart. What the body lacks, the goddess will give."

"Would I have to join the Chosen?"

"No, of course not. Must we pray at the temple for our voices to be heard?"

Wordlessly, she shook her head.

"They may not honor that you're one of them, but they will respect what you can do once I've finished with you. That is, if you'll accept."

"How could I not? I only hope I can live up to the honor." She swallowed a dry lump in her throat. "That I won't disappoint you."

Geoffrey set his hand over her fingers, the touch warm and comforting as he turned her palm up to receive a handful of prayer beads, pristine pearls strung in on lengths of fine, silver cord. "Then take these and continue to honor your father's memory, care for your mother, and be good to others, like Jory, who battle their own demons. Training begins tomorrow at the sixth hour. Don't be late."

"I have no idea what to say."

"Go share the news with your family. You'll have plenty to say to them."

Pearls clutched tight in her hand, Rae rose to her feet and hurried from the room with good news to share.

MAGIC BELONGS TO NO ONE

13

Etienne emerged from his modest washroom to find Mystere's spirithawk on the headboard awaiting a response to the regent's anxious missive.

"Not yet," he told it. "We'll need time to write a response to him." He had already communicated several letters to Regent Mystere throughout the night without consulting the Hinderans.

"If you must," the raptor replied, making a disgruntled noise.

Possessing the intelligence to realize its presence would go unwelcomed, it stayed behind while Etienne sought Ysolde. A maid directed him to the woman's solar, where he often found her during the quiet hours of the afternoon once she'd delivered judgments, met Fingall over accounting discrepancies, and seen to any other matters.

It didn't surprise him to see her and Geoffrey in one another's company. Their close relationship reminded him of Fas Perran knights and their squires, incredibly close, eternally loyal.

For a moment, he was reluctant to interrupt them. He entered on the tail end of some joke between Geoffrey and Ysolde. The princess laughed, her knight's face lit up with glee, and then their eyes trained on Etienne.

"Good day, Geoffrey, Ysolde."

He bowed as Geoffrey rose to return the gesture. The man moved slowly, gingerly bending forward.

"I come with news of—"

"A moment." Ysolde hurried past him, peeked into the hall, and then closed the heavy wooden doors. "Our 'guest' has been loitering as often as he dares with a keen interest in making your acquaintance."

"Shall we give him what he wants?" Etienne inquired. As of the moment, no one but Regent Mystere knew of his whereabouts, and he dreaded the moment his father found out he'd fled to the cold, western reaches of Hindera to escape his responsibilities as the heir.

"Perhaps but not now. Lorwick and his marital ambitions can wait until more pressing matters are resolved. As far as I am concerned, who I hire into my employ is none of his damned business."

Geoffrey gave her a look. "And you warn me about my language."

"Who do you think I learned from?"

Ysolde directed Etienne to the settee, a generous host who invited him to sit beside her, as opposed to the impersonal high-backed chair adjacent to Geoffrey.

She leaned forward and eyed the parchment in his hands. "Have you brought news?"

"I have. Several letters, in fact."

"So, what did they say?"

"The news isn't good," Etienne admitted. "As you were both sleeping when the first letter arrived, I took the liberty to pen a response to Regent Mystere. Adrienne returned only moments ago with this."

"Does he admit to sending agents to Hindera?" she asked eagerly.

"No, he doesn't. In fact, what troubles me most is that he swears on the goddess herself to have no part in whatever has happened. Which means someone is acting unbeknownst to him or this is more complicated than it seems."

"With all due respect," Geoffrey said, "I know from firsthand experience how men will hide behind the name of their gods."

"He wouldn't lie. Not about this," Etienne insisted. "While I would love to believe the best about my countrymen, I know where to draw the line.

"You trust him at his word then."

"I do. He's been a second father to me. I didn't reveal my current whereabouts to him until our most recent exchange. Had he known war was coming, or that one would be instigated, he would have urged me to leave. I said nothing of swearing allegiance to you."

Etienne extended the two letters to Ysolde. Their disturbing contents detailed Regent Mystere's genuine surprise that any agents serving under his banner had journeyed to Hindera, let alone traveled to its northernmost city. Within, he'd vowed to investigate the legitimacy of Etienne's claims.

While he would have hesitated to reveal the truth to his father, he'd let down his guard in their ongoing communication and revealed the truth to Regent Mystere. He'd shared everything, excluding the presence of his bastard half-brother. When it came to Laurent, Etienne took no chances.

"He asked for one of the swords to verify its authenticity. I also told him to send his own messenger. Adrienne's worked hard enough, I believe." He managed a small smile. "His spectral hawk arrived with Adrienne and awaits any further correspondence from us."

Ysolde didn't laugh. Stress showed in the dark smudges beneath her blue-gray eyes and her stiff back. "I'm afraid that I don't understand. You swear Regent Mystere is not behind this attack, yet we found evidence to the contrary and blades belonging to his men. Where shall we look next?"

"Anyone else who may have cause to harm you. While I wish I had more information to provide for your father, deep down, I'm relieved to know my country may have had no ties to your attack." Etienne rubbed his chin thoughtfully and gazed out the window. "In fact, I can't understand what Fas Perra, or any regent, would have to gain by attempting to kill you."

"Harming Ysolde harms the king, of course," Geoffrey said. "She is his daughter. He may have adopted her, but she's been his daughter years longer than the children born of his blood. I don't believe Aldemar married the queen until years after Ysolde and her mother moved to the castle."

"That's right," Ysolde said.

"Interesting. If you don't mind my asking, how does such a thing happen? I've met many Marcogh in the past, but never one in so-called 'civilized' company," Etienne said.

"My mother once served Aldemar as a guide. He made expansive efforts to understand and respect the Marcogh way when previous monarchs hoped to tame them to Hinderan way of life. I suppose they fell in love on the trail, because when he asked her to see his home, she agreed."

Ysolde poured wine and offered Etienne a glass. He graciously accepted, savoring the taste of it.

"Did they not marry?"

"No," Ysolde said sadly. "My father had all manner of laws and rules to abide by, so my mother became his consort, and he was later forced by the nobility to accept Duke Riverdale's sister as a wife. Queen Rhonwen. My mother saw it as a sign and returned home ten years ago when the animosity escalated between her and the queen. Rhonwen was... She felt..."

"Say nothing further. My father remarried after the death of my mother, so I know firsthand the cruelty of stepmonsters."

"Stepmonsters," Ysolde repeated.

Etienne smiled. "It is fitting, no?"

This time, Ysolde smiled in return. "An apt enough term, I agree. If only they were the least of our worries."

After a chuckle, Etienne rose from the settee. "I leave it in your hands to respond to Regent Mystere."

Geoffrey broke his silence, pensive features matched by his contemplative words. "Could this be a plot by one of your other regents? In framing House Mystere, I mean."

"That is always a possibility, and one I've suspected since first discovering the sword."

Genuine sorrow filled Geoffrey's eyes. "I had hoped the tentative peace between our countries would last. Another war so soon would devastate both."

"Agreed."

Ysolde touched Etienne on the shoulder and murmured, "Thank you for this. I will pen a response and have it to you within the hour."

Before he left, Etienne paused at the door, his fingers inches from the knob. "I want to thank both of you for giving my brother a home. He means the world to me, and he's happier here in Hindera than I've seen in years. I swear, your faith in us has not been misplaced."

"A home for you both," Ysolde corrected.

"I would like to see this home remain ours, a place to start anew. Whoever is at fault, we'll get to the bottom of it."

***

Aldemar surpassed Ysolde's expectations, revealing a reasonable side to his personality she'd forgotten in the recent years. He didn't rage and muster the Royal Army to march toward Fas Perra, and the overall tone of his writing appeared calm.

The king asked two questions in his return missive: did Geoffrey trust her two Fas Perran agents, and what did they plan to do to uncover the true culprit?

In her response, she assured him of their trust and promised ample opportunity to personally meet the pair when he arrived.

Thankfully, Etienne was indifferent to the news. She'd found him lurking in the library, alone, one of her uncle's books spread over his palms.

"As you wish," he said agreeably.

"You're not worried about meeting him?"

"Should I be?" Etienne lifted one of his brows.

If there was one thing Ysolde admired about Etienne, it was that he always carried himself with grace and dignity. Rumors flitted readily around the estate, claiming him to be a warlock of the darkest caliber, but she sensed only goodwill, friendliness, and restraint.

And also sadness, uncertainty, and melancholy. No matter how he smiled, those always rose to the surface, as if he wore a mask for their sake to hide the rotting truth of what lay beneath.

"No," she said good-naturedly. "My father doesn't deserve the reputation made for him. It will be fine."

"Ah. Good." He shut the book and returned it to the shelf. "If I may ask, where did you study magic, Ysolde?"

"Father hired a tutor. He wasn't a bad teacher, and he never said anything, but I had the impression he disagreed with teaching a woman."

Etienne clicked his tongue in disapproval. "Magic belongs to no one people and certainly not to one gender. It would be a wise lesson for Hindera to learn one day."

"Change comes slowly in this kingdom."

"Come. I will show you a few things if you'd like."

Uncertainty crept into her voice. "Like summoning?"

She'd be branded a heretic if the members of the clergy knew she'd considered summoning a demon.

Etienne laughed, a warm, rich sound. "No. Summoning such as I do takes years of disciplined study. However, I can teach you some other spells you might find useful."

The offer intrigued her. "Allow me to fetch my cloak, and I'll meet you outside in an hour. Will the west training field suffice? Geoffrey should be finished with it."

"It should serve our purposes just fine," Etienne assured her.

He had also donned his cloak when they met outside. During the cooler months, moist air blew in from the ocean, and it could cut through to the bone. While the wind was still, they took no chances and dressed in multiple layers for a cold day.

"As I've trained in the sphere of death magic for quite a while, all spells within its domain come easily to me," he explained.

"I know nothing of death magic. It isn't learned in Hindera. In fact, I was given a choice between healing or undertaking study in the elements. My tutor would accept nothing else."

"With all due respect, your tutor was an ass."

A smile spread across her face as she mimicked, "Only Nirmad's Reapers are allowed to know the mysteries of the void, Ysolde, and it would serve you well to remember your place as a princess."

Etienne made a disgusted sound. "It isn't my intention to laud my kingdom and disparage yours, but where I come from, all citizens are encouraged to study the arts. Where you excel grants you the edge to become what you choose."

"Fas Perra must have no shortage of tutors then. As we have so few, many of our citizens, noble of birth or not, travel to the Magisterium to learn without limits."

"A pity for the misinformed if that's what they believe. From what I understand, the Magisterium has no restrictions when you're a *paying* student. Others aren't quite as fortunate."

"Your brother." She ventured a guess.

Etienne offered a tight smile in reply. "The Magisterium develops the talent they see to best suit their needs."

"I'm sorry. I didn't mean to pry."

"No, it is all right, but I will leave it to my brother to speak of his time there. I ask you to refrain from mentioning it."

"It will go no further," she promised. "Now…the lesson?"

Using battered training dummies in need of disposal and the help of one of the guardsmen, Etienne created a makeshift training ground. He made it look easy, reducing an old, disused sword to a pile of rust with the wave of his hand.

And somehow, he expected her to do it too.

During the course of their lesson, she discovered his staff was as much for intimidation as it was a focus to channel his most powerful spells. When asked about it, he explained, "For most incantations, it isn't necessary."

"Only the battlemages of the Royal Army are allowed staves, and the Wizard-General is responsible for their training," Ysolde said. Her brows knit. The weapon horrified her employees, but she was fascinated. "I was always told they're far too dangerous."

"Your kingdom enjoys hobbling its mages, I see."

"I never thought of it that way. Fingall told me their children use wands as they learn in the elven isles."

Etienne smoothed his thumb over a rune etched into the polished bone. "A dear friend helped me carve these years ago before I was drafted by Regent Sabatois into the war with your kingdom. He has a true gift for creating enchantments, and everything I've ever learned about them, I picked up from him."

"We don't have any enchanters here. At least none I know of. It's all outsourced to Iluminarel to keep trade flowing between our countries."

"The elves do amazing work, and Rhystheren is the best among their kind. He dwells in Crestoli now, Nymphalia I believe. I'd happily send him a letter and ask if he'll visit. He's the sort to always look for a challenge."

"I'm not sure if I should be insulted or complimented."

"Complimented. Now you've stalled enough. Try again."

Ysolde scowled at him and turned her eyes to the suit of maille covering the dummy. "I find our conversation to be more educational than my failed attempts at harnessing your magic."

"You have to mean it," Etienne told her with a laugh. "It'll never work if you're only halfhearted in your attempt. Try again. Imagine the metal broken to its most basic components, iron and earth, flawed metal. See it rusting in your mind's eye and becoming one with the ground again."

As Ysolde closed her eyes and concentrated on the imagery Etienne created for her, she felt a tiny spark, too small to grasp with her mind—a twitch of something new and alien. "It's difficult. It isn't at all like fire magic. It's as if I can feel it's there, but it's too slippery to hold."

"Agreed. If it makes you feel any better, I'm often reduced to fits of swearing whenever I'm required to cast a fire spell."

"Then perhaps you should be the student and I, the teacher, as I've been told I'm a natural at setting things ablaze."

"Does the king know you're learning forbidden magic?"

Ysolde whirled toward the voice to see Lorwick at the edge of the training ground, led by a member of the Ashguard and flanked by two of his own bodyguards. Sweat beaded on Guardsman Jory's brow, and his eyes darted back and forth between them.

Lorwick crossed the hard-packed earthen yard and peered down his nose at the pristine armor. "Not that the lessons seem to have taken."

The duke wore platemail with a purple cape draped from his broad shoulders. A crossbow hung from his hip, a sword on the other. Despite his polite voice and cordial smile, condescension bubbled beneath the veneer of civility.

No stranger to diplomacy among nobles, Etienne matched his smile and stepped into place beside Ysolde. "The pursuit of studies in magic isn't a race; it's a marathon cultivated by perseverance. Of course, such wisdom and understanding can only be gleaned by those with an aptitude for the art."

Ysolde wanted to grin. Her mouth twitched at the corners, and she glanced up at Etienne grinning broadly beside her. Despite all of her effort to maintain neutrality, he made no such attempt.

"Oh, excuse my manners," Ysolde said before Lorwick could retaliate. "I've forgotten to introduce you both. Scion Etienne Dufresne, allow me to present to you Gared Bowman, Duke of Lorwick. Lorwick, meet the Shade Knight of Fresna, my new spymaster."

"A pleasure, Lorwick," Etienne said brusquely with no pretenses of honoring the man's title. If he bowed, the movement was too brief for her eyes to register it.

Ysolde took pleasure in the tiny 'o' of surprise the duke's mouth formed as she gave him Etienne's full title.

Lorwick's mouth opened and closed, reminiscent of a fish. "Does your father know you've brought an agent of an enemy nation into your employment?"

An agent? As far as their rules of social etiquette went, Etienne was a prince among them and Ysolde's equal. That he respected her so deeply had endeared him to her.

"We haven't been at war for a long time, Lorwick."

The duke exploded, "Were those not Fas Perrans who attempted to slay you?"

"That's yet to be determined," she retorted.

"You appear to be dressed for battle," Etienne observed. "Were you prepared to slay more of my so-called Fas Perran brethren?"

"Hunting. I'll have a bear pelt for my floor before she manages this dark sorcery."

"Death is a part of the natural order. All things must one day come to an end, and there's nothing dark about it," Etienne challenged with a polite smile on his face. "Far more natural than some of the activities in which some men partake, especially against women and children."

The color drained from Lorwick's face. Then it flushed anew with red. He trembled with unspoken rage.

Raising her chin, the princess abandoned any pretenses of civility. "Your visit is neither wanted nor desired. Now that you've discerned the identity of my 'guest,' you're welcome to see yourself back to whatever hole you've crawled from."

"How dare you—"

Ysolde raised a hand to silence him, but then her anger swelled in a brilliant burst of scalding resentment. A single ring of brown, oxidized metal appeared in the center of Lorwick's chestplate, and then it spread like a wave, infecting all it touched.

"Do you see?" Lorwick blustered. "He's shown his true colors and attacked me!"

Etienne remained calm. "That was not my doing, friend, but I believe the princess has answered your challenge succinctly."

A stud fell from Lorwick's armor.

"You've been outwitted. Save your pride and leave," the sorcerer continued in a low voice.

With a purple face and no further words, Lorwick turned his back to them.

"Well done," Etienne said once the duke had stalked from the training yard, his armor disintegrating from his body with each step. He turned to her and smiled. "Shall we resume our exchange?"

"Fire?" Ysolde chirped in inquiry.

He bowed to her with an exaggerated flourish. "Of course. I am your willing student."

FOR LOVE

14

With a cup of tea balanced on the balcony railing and her dark hair bound in a loose plait over one shoulder, their princess watched over them from above.

Ysolde's observations had never unsettled Geoffrey before, but he found it difficult to keep his attention on their training and off of the woman above them. He barely raised his arm in time to ward off the blow swinging in for his chest. It struck his kite shield and rebounded wildly.

"Ser Geoffrey?" Raennia spoke up. It had taken nearly a week for her to adopt the more familiar name of Geoffrey over Ser Ashcroft, despite his adamant insistence.

"What?" he snarled as he whirled with his sword arm raised.

She shrank back a step, driven by reflex. "My apologies, Ser. You appear distracted. No, you don't *appear* to be distracted; you certainly are."

If she was anyone else, he would have had her running laps around the estate, bearing the largest burden she could lift.

Instead, the hostility drained from him as if sifting through a sieve. He sighed. At some point, he'd come to like the girl, and he didn't know when it had happened, whether it was the nature of her gender or her sheer perseverance—but he'd grown fond of her.

She was smart. Sincere. Compassionate. Everything he'd admired in his little sister. The little sister who hadn't lived past adolescence.

And now she had become his personal protégé, one who he encouraged to speak her mind.

"I am," Geoffrey agreed. "Give me a moment, and we'll resume."

"We will not," Rae said. "Are you all right, Ser?"

"No, I'm not."

"Then you should take your leave until such a time as you are fit to train," she pointed out, raising her chin.

Blast. Rae learned too quickly.

"You're right," he said. "Andras, please carry on. I have another matter to attend."

"Of course."

Geoffrey tossed the shield aside and made his way inside. The layers of fabric beneath his armor clung to his skin, his blond hair curled slick over his perspiring brow, and he smelled exactly like a man who'd spent four hours battling in a courtyard on a surprisingly warm autumn day.

And he also planned to make the most foolish move of his entire life.

"Ysolde?" Geoffrey called at the door. She often took tea in the solar, but he'd never dreaded entering the room before.

Anxiety compressed the air from his lungs and covered his palms with fresh sweat. There wasn't time to bathe, to change his clothing, or to continue rehearsing the lines he'd practiced a hundred times in his head since their night at the play. If he took one moment longer, he'd lose all courage, and then he'd never forgive himself.

"May I have a moment of your time?"

"Of course. Is something the matter? You look harried."

A mess. I look a disgusting mess, he thought, filling in the words Ysolde was too polite to say. "Yes. There is something wrong, and I cannot remain silent about it a moment longer."

Worry furrowed a familiar crease in her brow. "You know you can always speak to me about anything. What's upset you?"

"You can't marry Lorwick."

She blinked. "Geoffrey, I'm afraid my father's mind is set. You saw his letter. The duke is already in town."

"I don't care what your father has decreed. It would be wrong. An injustice of the worst sort."

"And what would you suggest I do then? He has ignored my pleas begging him to give me more time."

He glanced away, directing his attention to the cold fireplace as he redoubled his courage. "Simple. I gave it consideration since his decree arrived. I care for you deeply, Ysolde, and as you said to me mere weeks ago, my duty is to protect you from all things and do as I deem necessary. I won't allow you to marry Lorwick." He met her eyes again. "Marry *me* instead."

Silence greeted him, and for a moment he wasn't sure which was worse—her shocked stare or the laughter he had almost expected. "Don't be silly, Geoffrey. You don't honestly mean that."

"Have I ever lied to you? Am I not charged with your safety and wellbeing?"

"A duty you perform admirably, but one that has nothing to do with my current predicament."

"It has everything to do with your current predicament. Once King Aldemar arrives and declares your betrothal to Duke Lorwick, my days will surely be numbered. The very moment he raises a hand to strike you, I will kill him."

"He wouldn't dare," she whispered. "Those are exaggerations, surely."

"They're not mere tall tales. They are truths. You will become a pretty figurehead to sit beside him as he unravels four years of your hard work," he spat vehemently.

Ysolde sighed and looked away. "It does not matter. If it is as you say, he is father's choice, and I've failed to find a satisfactory substitute. While noble in thought, I cannot in good conscious allow you to do this."

Geoffrey silenced for a short while, devising his next course of attack. "Is the prospect of marrying me less appealing than wedding the duke?"

"No one could be less appealing than that man," she grumbled.

He took her hand. "Is it my reputation?" Of course it was his reputation. At least Lorwick wasn't a whoring drunk. Seconds later, he withdrew the castigating thought with a renewed sense of confidence. He hadn't visited the brothel or tavern in weeks.

"You're a fine man, Geoffrey," she replied, sidestepping the question.

"I know how you feel about my visits to the Moonlit Primrose. You've made your stance on the matter crystal clear."

"I have, and there's no sense in repeating it. You're an adult."

"Then trust and marry me," he said again, dropping to a bended knee.

Geoffrey held his breath, the moment between them stretching into eternal misery. Ysolde didn't answer. He said nothing more. He waited in front of her with his soul laid bare and his heart exposed.

"Excellent. I approve," a voice answered from Geoffrey's right. In his distraction, he'd never heard the doors open. He snapped his attention away from Ysolde's startled expression to the grinning features of their King.

Bloody hell.

"An unexpected match, to be sure, but not a displeasing one. You have my blessing."

King Aldemar was a fit man well into his sixties with a stocky, thick-shouldered frame and hints of gray touching the temples of his ash brown hair. And when he laughed, the entire world felt compelled to chuckle with him, for the sound was truly jolly, rich and warm with pleasure.

In a panic, Geoffrey quickly rose to his feet, only to bow down again. "Your early arrival is equally unexpected, my King."

And he would certainly strangle the guardsmen who failed to notify him that Aldemar was on the premises, allowing him to sneak into Ysolde's castle like a thief in the night.

"Father," Ysolde greeted, flustered. Her fingers briefly tightened over Geoffrey's hand then dropped away. "I'm sorry. I should have anticipated your early arrival and prepared a proper welcome."

"Oh, but you have. What a joyous occasion to witness with my own two eyes. Now I understand your reluctance to accept Lorwick as a match. Or any match at all!" Aldemar strode forward and embraced Ysolde. "Of course, the wedding

151

must occur within the month. Or even sooner. Will a week be sufficient time to plan?"

"Father—"

"Of course it will be. I shall inform everyone at once and pay my visit to Divine Father Hershel for a special license."

With a purposeful stride, the king left the room, giving them no chance to argue.

"Oh no!" Ysolde clasped her hands and paced across the room. "No, this cannot be happening."

"It could be worse," Geoffrey offered.

"I fail to see how anything could be worse than trapping you in a marriage." She ran a hand through her hair, displacing the neatly twisted style. "Please excuse me. I need to make sure everything else is ready before his jovial mood sours."

"Of course. Don't let me keep you."

Once she was gone, Geoffrey collapsed into one of the oversized chairs and stared at the open balcony doors.

What had he done? More importantly, had it been the right thing to do? In his heart, he believed there could be no other choice.

"Geoffrey," Fingall's stern voice called from the door. The elf swept into the room, the frown on his face creasing his features like wadded paper. "Of all the selfish things to do."

"Selfish?" His voice cracked with surprise.

"Allowing us to sweat and toil over a dozen suitors when you very well could have done this weeks ago."

"Ah, yes, well…"

Fingall cut in without allowing him to finish, all business in a brisk tone. "Naturally, she will continue to govern these lands, you shall maintain your authority over the duchy's defense, and of course, you will exchange your deplorable habit at the Moonlit Primrose for conceiving an heir with the princess."

Geoffrey crossed his arms over his chest and leveled a stoic gaze on Fingall. "I haven't made a visit in weeks and… We haven't even wed yet, but you already speak to me of heirs?"

"What other purpose could you possibly have to Ysolde? As often as you pay your visits to the Moonlit Primrose, you most of all should understand what occurs between a man and a woman once they are married," Fingall uttered in a droll tone. He rolled his eyes.

"I know what the bloody hell happens between a man and a woman, you spade-eared ass." Geoffrey rubbed his face and glanced out the window. News of the engagement would reach the city streets before the day's end.

"Good, then let me speak plainly. The king is appeased, which means Lorwick will have no further reason to haunt this city. As the *native* firstborn son of a baron, you're as good as titled yourself, thus the nobles will cease their bickering once you've assumed the title of Duke Ashdale. For now. An heir from a respected man of Hinderan blood will quell their unrest entirely, regardless of the mother's origins."

"Fantastic. I'm thrilled to know that you're on our side, Fingall, and that this is my new purpose in life."

"You speak with sarcasm, Ser Ashcroft, but you fail to realize that I *am* on your side, as well as the side of our princess. Since the first day she came into rule of our city, I have wanted nothing more than for her to succeed where her predecessor failed."

"Don't you have a family of your own in Iluminarel to boss around?"

"I do. Two daughters, a granddaughter, and a great-grandson. I direct them quite efficiently from here."

The elf's reminder took the wind from Geoffrey's sails. He sighed. "Forgive me. I shouldn't take my temper out on you, old friend. I should find a carrier pigeon to take news to my mother and father. They'll be cross if they learn from another party."

Cheers and congratulations followed Geoffrey through the grand estate. A couple of the men clapped him on the shoulders and expressed their surprise.

"Secretly courting our princess all this time, mate?" Andras asked.

Geoffrey attempted to smile. "There isn't a woman more worthy of my time."

"A couple of her chambermaids are incredibly disappointed. Naturally, some of our men will have to step up to console them." Andras grinned and strode away, a man on a mission.

Geoffrey's sunlit stroll to the post office failed to alleviate his burdens. So nervous his hand shook, he penned a brief note to his father and set the bird to flight from its roost. Afterward, he paid a long overdue visit to the Moonlit Primrose.

"Ser Geoffrey! You've returned at last!" an alluring voice cried from behind the bar. "Have you come to visit Rose again?" Violet's demure smile widened. "Or is there something I can provide for you, kind Ser?"

The coy vixen twisted a blue-black curl around her index finger.

"I'd like to see Rose." Geoffrey cleared his throat. "I'm willing to wait if she's occupied."

Violet sulked. "She's free, but she rarely accepts business these days unless it's from you and our other priority clients. Buttercup, darling, would you lead Ser Ashcroft to a room?"

A sunny blond woman popped into the room, fresh, new, and unrecognizable. Her exuberant smile eased Geoffrey's downed spirits and encouraged him to smile in return. "Hello, Ser. Right this way. Gosh, you're a big one. Your tailor must earn a bloody killing."

Geoffrey chuckled and stepped into the open room. "She does," he agreed. "And she's worth every penny. Be a good lass and let Rose know I'm waiting."

"Of course." Buttercup bowed out of the room, and moments later, Rose arrived in her place. The feisty redhead wore a belted silk robe fashioned in the Fas Perran style. Its lace-trimmed hemline rode her thighs. She wore blue well, the color deep as waters off the coast of Crestoli, contrasted by pale blossoms the color of dawn clouds.

It did nothing for him. Not even a stir of arousal.

"What a pleasure to see…" Rose's nose turned up. "Oh. Ugh. I see you've come in need of our bathing services."

Geoffrey grinned bashfully and ran his fingers through his hair to sweep a few sweat-dampened curls away from his face. "I actually came not as a client, but to speak to you about personal matters…"

"But?" Rose prompted, sensing more.

"With Aldemar in Ashdale, I should look my very best."

She sniffed daintily. "Did you not once say the services of your chambermaid Maribeth were satisfactory? Why don't you go to her instead?"

He grimaced. "Rose…"

"Fine." She took a step closer and raised one hand to his face. Her thumb slid over the rough, golden stubble on his cheeks. "I hope she doesn't shave her nethers the way she shaves your face. If so, I pity the men who lay with her."

"Not everyone has as fine a touch as you."

"Well, if you would send the girl for lessons, we could certainly remedy that problem. I suppose Princess Ysolde would find it inappropriate."

"Must you be a critic of everything, or will I have to pay you extra to close your mouth?" Geoffrey muttered.

Rose was a professional when it came to the Sarangi-style bathing spa, enforcing stringent rules among staff and patrons to the facility. The deep, hot-spring fed pools were for bathing and nothing more. If a patron craved intimacy, they paid for the privilege of a private room.

Wasting no time, Rose assisted him herself with removing his armor and clothes, sending the latter to be cleaned. Steaming water welcomed him into its embrace while the establishment's mistress observed him from a velvet divan.

"You can't go back wearing what you wore in, Geoffrey. Shall I send the girls for new clothes?"

"Only if you don't pauper me in the process. I've seen the fancy smocks you wrap your clients in."

"Trust me, I will find something which suits you myself. In the meantime, I'll send in Zinny."

"What for?"

"I received a missive from Fingall, stating you're to receive a haircut as well."

Geoffrey stared at her. "Fingall writes to you now?"

"Indeed. It seems your lady's steward finds you to be quite predictable. I am to see you returned to the estate fresh, shaven, trimmed, and smelling good."

"All things I intended on my own without him looking over my shoulder." After making a disgruntled noise, Geoffrey settled back against the marble edge of the soaking basin.

By the time he was cleaned, dried, and led to Rose's solarium, she had returned with a folded stack of new clothes. He relaxed at last, pleased with the absence of silks or crystalline buttons in the pile.

"Come lie down, and I'll get the rest of you sorted out," she invited. "You've been rubbing your back since you arrived."

"With just cause," he retorted. "Some of us do more than flash our tits for a living."

Rose swatted him. "And I certainly do more than that, as you well know."

The end result was always the same with him lying face down on the stone table, and Rose walking her knees over his back, kneading his spine with her fingers, and using generous amounts of oil on his battle-scarred skin.

"How are you always so tense?" Rose rubbed her hands down his bare back. "Clearly you have something to share with me, so spill it and share your mind."

"I conceived a brilliant idea to become betrothed to the princess."

The words were a bandage ripped from a wound, exposing his truth and laying his heart bare to the woman who knew his worst secrets. His doubts. His fears. She'd learned hundreds over the years no doubt, from the richest merchant to the most powerful city baron. "I proposed to Ysolde."

"And she accepted?" Rose's voice rose in question.

"Well, not exactly."

"One either accepts or does not accept, Geoffrey."

"The acceptance was made for her. Let us leave it at that. Our wedding is to occur in a week."

For a whore, Rose took excellent care of herself, and she also had surprisingly strong hands. In return for his sass, her capable fingers buried into his knotted muscles with excessive force.

He flinched beneath her. "Ow!"

"Forgive me," she replied in her sugary sweet voice he didn't buy for a second. "How does that feel?"

Geoffrey grunted under another series of vigorous kneads with her knuckles. "Delightful."

"Are you not pleased with the arrangement?" Warm oil pooled over the back of his shoulders. Rose's hands slid through the scented liquid and spread it down his spine.

"She is displeased with the arrangement, and that displeases me."

"Then you have already taken your first steps toward becoming a competent husband."

Geoffrey sighed. "Perhaps. A little higher, please, love."

"Here?"

As directed, Rose traced her fingers from one tender spot to the next, moving from the aching spot above the firm curve of his buttocks, to the condensed point of misery between his shoulders.

He groaned softly and turned his face into the pillow. "Fantastic."

Weekly visits to Rose became a tradition. But of course, he hadn't visited in a month. Hadn't cared. Hadn't noticed. No longer needed it.

"Let's be honest—you didn't come for a fuck, Geoffrey. If you did, there's nothing I can do with *this*." She gestured toward his flaccid length.

"I didn't this time," he admitted. "Not that a little hard work would have deterred you if a romp were my intentions. You already knew of the engagement, didn't you?"

"Word spreads quickly when the king's messengers are about."

Geoffrey sighed. "Am I making a mistake?"

"I'm a whore. Why would you ask me?"

When he didn't respond, she became his silent but willing servant. Her hands never stopped, but the unspoken words between them became heavier with each passing minute.

"I hurt you dearly, Rose."

"Don't dwell on that. I don't."

"You told me what to expect from Ashlynne, but I ignored you. I made terrible accusations. I said cruel things to you and to Lucas. To all of her close friends."

"She was a good girl, Geoffrey, but of course you know that. I loved her like my own little sister, and I still do. My reservations were because I knew her head was always in the clouds. As much as she cared for you, her real love was for her arts—for her music, her sculpture, and traveling to new worlds. I should have tried harder to warn you."

"While I want to lay sole blame at my mother's feet, I know it was only a matter of time. I thought marrying her would be the anchor she needed to stay."

"And now you are marrying another. No wonder you're a mess."

"It seemed the best option. Unless, of course, you'd prefer Duke Lorwick ruling the city with an iron fist. Demanding free services, no doubt."

"I have two girls who are capable and willing to service him. Despite all of his bluster, I won't allow him to touch anyone else and have drawn that line multiple times since his arrival."

"They have odd tastes then." He shuddered. "The thought of anyone submitting to that lunatic puts me on edge."

"They're kinky little bints," Rose agreed.

Geoffrey laughed and sat up for the rub down to continue. She buffed him with a soft cloth until the excess oil disappeared from his skin and then helped him into his new clothing.

With her work complete, he stood admiring his own reflection in the mirror. She'd given him a close shave after the bath, and one of her girls had clipped away his lanky curls. The blue tunic brought out the emerald in his eyes, worn beneath a leather doublet trimmed with gold stitches.

"I suppose I'm handsome enough to meet the king and their family for dinner now, as they'll no doubt expect me to join them."

"You certainly are," Rose agreed. "To answer your earlier question, Geoffrey, no one but you knows if you're doing the right thing. Only you, darling. I can't advise you on the path to take, but before you stand at the altar, know that you chose this for the right reasons. Don't do it as an escape."

"Thank you, Rose."

After a generous payment to Violet at the front desk, Geoffrey took the scenic route home to the castle on foot, wondering about his reasons. As far as he was concerned, there was no greater justification to marry than for love.

An Honorable Man

15

G eoffrey had been to his whore again.

The princess sighed when her dutiful husband-to-be seated her at the table and kissed her hand. The subtle scent of exotic oils clung to his skin, a telltale sign of her knight's philandering. His preferred woman at the Moonlit Primrose used a particular blend that Ysolde had never encountered elsewhere, and while pleasant, she'd come to associate it with his less than desirable habit.

"Will your parents arrive in time, Geoffrey?" Aldemar asked, oblivious to her inner turmoil. He'd become incredibly chummy with Geoffrey since dinner began, dropping the knight's title for favor of using his Ashtarian name only.

"Mother and Father will arrive with time to spare," he replied. "I'm sure of it. We haven't kept in touch, of course, but I have no doubt they'll be present."

"Excellent. It's been too long since I've seen Lord and Lady Lakeshire at court."

Her father's presence meant the kitchen staff ignored the usual recipe plans for the sensible and moderate meals Ysolde preferred. The large, silver serving platter held a roasted chicken stuffed with herbed rice and dried fruits, as well as fat sausages charred black on the outside the way the king preferred them. Honey glazed carrots and red-sugar spiced yams provided a sweet counterpoint to a bowl of bitter greens tossed with lemon and olive oil. A custard and berry tart sat at the far end of the table, a delicacy to suit Geoffrey's sweet tooth.

The banquet was massive, a feast for too few people.

Ysolde picked at her food, pushing bits of chicken around on her plate. When Shyla came around to refill their wine glasses, she happily accepted. The key phrase for the evening became, "more wine please," and a saving grace to help her endure.

"Your Majesty," Geoffrey began.

Aldemar chuckled. "Please. There's no need for such a title now. You're to become my son in marriage, Geoffrey. If anyone has earned the privilege to call me by name alone, it's the man who brought such happiness to my Ysolde."

"Thank you, Your Hi— Aldemar."

Her father sat at the head of the table, as was the customary place among Hinderans to put their guest of honor. Ysolde, as his daughter and only heir present, sat at his right. She and Geoffrey would have normally been placed beside one another, but etiquette required a husband or courting gentleman to sit opposite his wife. He looked mournful and unhappy across the table, quieter than usual.

Across the banquet table, Queen Rhonwen toyed with her meal, as if the delicious bounty were beneath her, unfit for her royal tongue. Ysolde's younger brother had no such reservations about the food. Whether he was oblivious to his mother's distaste or unconcerned with her prejudice, Theodoric ate with gusto.

Her father cleared his throat before asking, "Is the food not to your liking, my dear?"

"Hmmn? No, it's fine, Father."

"You're hardly eating," Aldemar pointed out.

"I have a fitting this eve," Ysolde replied with a small, forced smile. "Anticipation has left me with little appetite."

She caught Geoffrey watching her, his green eyes thoughtful and brooding, despite the well wishes of her father. He must have been equally displeased with the king's spontaneous acceptance.

Contrary to her friend's claims, she'd bet every coin in the coffers that he'd made the offer to be noble, expecting her to humbly decline. If her father hadn't pushed his overly large Hinderan nose into her affairs, she would have set Geoffrey free from his obligation.

"A bite or two won't cause any harm, will it?" Geoffrey finally asked, much to her father's approval.

With both men's expectant and concerned eyes upon her, she swallowed back her unease and forced herself to take a bite. The chicken was dry in her mouth, the vegetables too sweet. Even her favorite wine tasted sour.

Everything was wrong, and she couldn't say a word without worsening the situation. The only one who appeared pleased was the king, who remained ignorant to their growing unease.

As she risked a glance around the table, she made eye contact with her stepmother and was subjected to Queen Rhonwen's baleful glare. Ysolde forced the steel into her spine and stared back at her, unblinking.

"Quintin and I brought you several casks of wine from Crestoli," Ysolde's sister Jocelyn cut in. Rhonwen looked away first.

Ysolde turned a victorious smile to her sister, welcoming the distraction. "We haven't had Crestolian wine for some time. Thank you."

Jocelyn beamed and looked across the table to her red-haired, Crestolian husband then back to Ysolde. "I remembered how much you enjoyed the sweet red I sent you last year. He insisted we bring you a half dozen."

"Plus a few new vintages to try," Quintin added. "Jocelyn inspired me to expand our vineyards after our marriage, and I hoped you might enjoy the first from my new stock."

"I'm sure they're all wonderful," Ysolde replied without false praise.

"Better than that bottled fishwater from Lorwick," Theodoric muttered under his breath.

"Theo," Aldemar snapped.

"The boy speaks the truth. Chastise Lorwick for daring to pass that tripe off as valuable drink," Geoffrey said.

Theodoric grinned. The boy was Aldemar's younger, mischievous double, as if he'd been conceived without the queen's help.

"You're going to be an excellent brother-in-law." His blue eyes twinkled with delight.

Her family's apparent approval with her future husband did little to ease Ysolde's nerves or her conscience. Rather than join the conversation, she took another half-hearted bite from her meal and washed it down with more wine.

"Surely it cannot be so bad," Quintin mused. "What do you think of this man's produce, my jewel?"

Jocelyn's mischievous smile broadened. "My brothers speak the truth, but perhaps Ysolde keeps a bottle in her cellar. Was Lorwick not among the great number of men courting you until recently?"

"He was. Do you really want to try the fruits of his labor?"

Rhonwen made a disgusted sound in her throat and tossed her golden hair over one shoulder. It was braided in a stylish updo with emeralds glittering amidst thick coils left to hang free around her collarbones. "Must we indulge in such childish behavior at the dinner table?"

Aldemar's prompt answer took Ysolde by surprise. "It's only good fun, my lady."

Watching her stepmother glower across the table inspired a sense of malicious glee. Ysolde twisted in her seat and called out, "Shyla, could you fetch—"

"Of course," her friend said, beating her to it. "I'll be back in but a moment."

While Geoffrey, Quintin, and Jocelyn discussed their vineyard's recent achievements, Shyla retrieved the aforementioned bottle of Alvidean Valley red. She returned within minutes, uncorked the bottle, and poured for Quintin alone. Geoffrey cupped a hand protectively over his empty glass.

"Here you are, my lord." Shyla set a fresh glass down. "A red blend promised by Duke Lorwick to please the most sophisticated palates."

Ysolde failed to suppress her scoff, and Shyla winked at her.

Within seconds of sipping from the glass of Lorwick's best red, Quintin's face contorted, and his hazel eyes squeezed shut with regret. When he swallowed, it was as if Ysolde were watching a man gulp down a rock. "That's... ah..."

Jocelyn giggled.

"Don't lie," Geoffrey coaxed him.

"As you Hinderans say, bloody awful. Why did you allow me to do that to myself?"

"Personally, I think it's educational," Jocelyn said with a sniff, tossing her golden hair over her shoulder. "Now you've savored drink far inferior to our own."

"I will happily give you the remainder of what he left if you'd like to take it for research," Ysolde offered.

"Oh, no. No, thank you. I couldn't."

Silent and unseen until she appeared at Ysolde's side, Geoffrey's chambermaid, Maribeth, leaned down and whispered, "Princess, the seamstress is here and waits for you at your earliest convenience."

The king overheard, and his bearded face lit with joy. "Excellent! Then we shall conclude dinner and let you get to it, my love. Come, Geoffrey. Let us stroll the grounds while this fine meal settles in our bellies. We must speak of my future plans for the kingdom. I also have many inquiries regarding my daughter's special guests."

Geoffrey shot her a helpless look. At any other time, she would have rescued her knight, but she had troubles of her own to face.

"I'll accompany you, kind sister," Jocelyn offered as the dinner party broke apart.

With slow steps, Ysolde entered the solarium to meet with the seamstresses, feeling more like a criminal sentenced to the gallows than a soon-to-be bride. They both rushed to their feet to meet her, one of them half-elven with a delicate frame smaller than Ysolde's slender body. The woman's snowy white hair resembled clouds. The second was a younger girl who stood even shorter, barely thigh-high to the princess. A gnome.

"Good eve, Your Graces," the half-elf said.

"Good eve, Madam Gidget. I apologize for the abrupt notice for your services."

"Think nothing of it, my dear," Madam Gidget said with a wave. "It's my pleasure to have been called. Now, come here please and stand on this stool so we can get some measurements. It's been some time since I created a dress for you."

"Hi!" the tiny gnome called up to both women.

Madame Gidget's expression flattened before she turned to correct her pupil. "That isn't how we greet royalty, Ifri. These women are princesses."

"Oh. I'm sorry!" Her tiny face fell. "I didn't mean to upset you."

"Forgive her, Your Grace. Ifri is my new apprentice. She came all of the way from Fas Perra to study with me. Can you believe it? Such a distance to learn from me."

"You have a good teacher, Ifri. Study well."

"Oh, I will…Your Grace," she added in a quick rush. "Here now, I have the measure stick."

As the two fussed around her and Jocelyn watched, Ysolde tried to keep the unhappiness from her face. They all brimmed with so much enthusiasm that eventually the sentiment became infectious, and she looked forward to seeing the finalized design herself.

"How will you ever assemble a suitable dress in a week?" Jocelyn asked, intrigued. "My wedding gown took nearly a month."

"My dear, you underestimate me. I have a brand new sewing contraption designed by Ifri's father. I shall have the dress to you within a few days for a fitting and the finished design after your breakfast the following morn. Ifri, check the measurements thrice. There's no room for error," the dressmaker chided her assistant.

"Yes, ma'am."

Ysolde touched the yards of silken, pale gold fabric and sighed again. It was beautiful, but there was a part of her that wished for a simpler service. A different man who wanted her with equal passion and desire.

No. Rhun had left her. Knowing the truth didn't make it any easier, but at least it hurt a little less.

Jocelyn clapped her hands with glee. "There couldn't be a fabric more suited to your complexion, dear sister. You'll be a dream given life and the envy of every man. Perhaps some women as well," the young woman teased. "If only gold were my color. I'd look like an enormous coin. All round."

"Your pale blue was stunning, Jocelyn, and Quintin's eyes nearly bulged from his head.

Her sister gave a self-satisfied smile. "They did, didn't they?"

Once the dressmakers were gone, Ysolde passed the rest of her evening with Jocelyn, lacking the courage to track down the men. According to Andras, her father and Geoffrey had spent most of the evening in deep discussion in the former duke's war room, a place Ysolde had little use for since accepting rule in Ashdale. She'd always left most matters of defense up to Geoffrey.

Knowing her father well, she didn't count on seeing him again. The two parted ways after Ysolde toured her sister through the flourishing garden, and she retired to the solar to unwind with a book. Shyla had stoked the fire until the log of silkwood glowed bright at its center, emitting the comforting, lavender light it was known for.

She turned two pages, settled deeper into the divan, read two pages more, and then knew nothing else of the evening.

"She's out cold, Ser. Let me get the door."

"Mmm," she mumbled drowsily, her lids heavy. Her head lolled against the solid wall beneath her ear, and she breathed in the fragrant, woodsy scent from Sarangi.

Exotic oils? Ysolde jerked her head up and looked into Geoffrey's eyes. They were in the threshold of her bedroom, Shyla standing a few paces away with a hand on the doorknob. The young woman's cheeks were flushed.

"I knew we'd wake her." Geoffrey smiled apologetically. "I thought you'd rather return to your bed than court an aching neck by the morning, so Shyla came to help, as it wouldn't be appropriate for me to undress you…yet."

His words prickled her skin with gooseflesh and added an extra thump to her pulse. Once he set her down, Ysolde smoothed her fingers against her dress and avoided eye contact. "Shyla, would you please give Geoffrey and me a moment to speak?"

"Of course." Her friend shut the door behind her.

"Did your talk with my father go well?

"It did." Unpleasant silence followed his words until he gently added, "I never intended to do that in front of him, Ysolde. Apparently he ordered the guardsmen to keep his arrival a secret. He wanted to surprise you."

"I know. You wouldn't stoop to such tricks. It was an unfortunate coincidence." She sighed and recalled the smile on her father's face.

"I wouldn't," he agreed. "At any rate, sleep well and rest." He bowed to her and moved to the door.

"Geoffrey," she called before he could turn the knob. "Please, a moment longer."

"Yes?" He faced her again, green eyes filled with compassion.

"There is a matter I feel should be mentioned." Her palms grew damp, and she resisted the urge to wipe them on her dress. "You've been at the brothel."

"Is that a crime? I wasn't fit to be in your father's company in my prior state." The corner of his mouth quirked. He cut an impressive figure in his finery, dressed in a style he only donned for special occasions. She'd grown accustomed to seeing Geoffrey in simple tunics while out of armor.

"Is your bath here inadequate? I mean, do I need to send for an engineer?"

"No, it's nothing like that. Rose is a friend, and I also wanted to share our good news with her. I don't expect her to receive an invitation, but it seemed only appropriate and polite to tell her personally—"

"I see."

Geoffrey's features darkened. "—that her services are no longer required," he finished. "Truly, you have little faith in me. Did you think I'd gone to pay for a lay with her a mere hour after proposing to you?"

Heat flushed through her cheeks all the way up to her ears. "I said nothing."

"You may not have spoken the words out loud, but I can see the question in your eyes," he muttered.

He appeared so wounded by the unspoken accusation that Ysolde wisely backpedaled and took another approach.

"You have no true wish for this marriage, Geoffrey," she said in a quiet voice as she turned away to face the fire. "I have faith in your honor, but you're doing this out of a sense of duty. I still don't understand why."

Within seconds, a change came over Geoffrey. His expression became guarded, lips pressed into a neutral line. With his spine so rigid and straight, the knight towered above her with his eyes focused on something beyond the window instead. "Why does it matter?"

"Because we are to be wed, in every sense. Did you think this would be in name only? They will expect children. They will observe all the usual 'noble traditions' on our wedding night. You have no reason to put yourself through it."

"Would you prefer to do it with Lorwick? The king has dealt you a rotten hand, and I understand certain traditions must be met."

Certain traditions that appeared to make Geoffrey equally uncomfortable. She could recall few times when she'd seen her knight blush, the color overtaking his face so brilliantly it couldn't be anything but embarrassment. Until then, she'd thought he was unflappable.

"Perhaps I should reword my question," he said, shattering the unbearable silence. "Which of us would you find the most tolerable? Regardless of what the king has said, this remains your choice, and I will gladly step aside."

She sighed and sank down into her favorite chair. "I always thought I would marry for love, but you know too well how that turned out. Rhun didn't—couldn't—enjoy this life, so he returned to the Marcogh. After that, well, I'd thought father wouldn't press the issue. Or, like so many tried to assure me, I would meet someone else I could love as much. I have no fondness for Lorwick, but I also have no desire to see my friend caught in a life he loathes. You may have given up on finding your Ashlynne, Geoffrey, but you deserve to find love again."

"I would take sensible happiness over true love any day, Ysolde. If you could bring yourself to be happy alongside *me*."

"It feels so unfair to you," she whispered.

Geoffrey moved closer and took both of her hands in his larger grip. His fingers dwarfed hers, battle hardened and scarred. "I'm going to tell you something I've never spoken about to anyone else, Ysolde, so I ask you to keep this to yourself."

"Of course. I'd never betray your trust."

"I told no one my true reason for leaving the Order of Ashta's Chosen," Geoffrey said quietly. "Not even Father when he questioned me about coming home. He thought I'd disgraced myself or done something foolish, but he couldn't be further from the truth. To this day, I've never felt shame for what I did. I want you to know that before I tell you the rest."

"You've never spoken much of your time with the Order, and I've always tried to respect that. But disgracing yourself? I'd never believe that, and your father shouldn't have either. You're one of the most honorable men I know."

"So it would seem at times." Geoffrey released her hands and eased back into his own seat. "It wasn't long after I completed training and took my vows that I and several other paladins were assigned to accompany our priestesses on a journey to find the Marcogh. Mother Ashley insisted. We were to take the word of Ashta to the so-called heathens and show them the way to the light. A dozen of us went with nearly as many of our sisters."

For a moment, she didn't know what to say. She frowned at first, her brow wrinkled, then shook her head and chuckled. "I can't imagine that going so well. My mother's people are… I remember days spent outdoors with hardly a stitch on. We prayed to the wind and the grass, not to divine figures."

"I know I've asked about the Marcogh before, but I wanted to hear it from your perspective." Geoffrey flashed her a fragile smile, his anxiety threatening to crush its existence in entirety. "Anyway, it took us nearly a month's time before we found their trail. We caught them in the south and met with the chieftain, and to our surprise, he agreed to allow us to take five women and five young men in exchange for an equal number of our own."

"Wait, you swapped people? How did that come about?"

"From what I understood, it was his wife's idea. She thought we could be taught as well and that each participant would return with greater wisdom. Most importantly, our people would perform their duties during the exchange."

"Much like my mother agreeing to come to Hindera with the king," she murmured.

"Precisely. We were there for two years. It went well at first, I must admit. They were curious and eager to learn, so we taught them Hinderan, clothed them modestly, and the sisters held prayer school twice daily."

"And the priests who went with the Marcogh?"

"After much argument, a few sisters agreed. The life of a Marcogh woman is vastly different, down to your clothing. So they compromised, and the Marcogh women made the priestesses very lovely, modest raiments with animal skins, but they worked our ten volunteers as they would their own people.

"Eventually, tales returned to us that two of our men ran naked through the prairie grass, drank wine under the stars, and generally broke every vow we've ever taken. It created a scandal."

"Celibacy does not exist among the Marcogh." It was another difference between their cultures, the final wedge driven between her and Rhun. He'd wanted to express his affection for her through physical means and had ultimately respected her decision to remain a virgin without understanding why the Hinderans valued purity until marriage.

Sometimes, Ysolde wondered herself. Why did something so silly alter her worth?

"Exactly, and their argument was that they were told to do as the Marcogh wanted. It was the beginning of the end of the exchange. We discovered from the two knights that they'd both found women, taken them as wives, and refused to return. One was soon to become a father, his wife already swollen with child." Geoffrey leaned back in his seat and gazed at Ysolde for the first time since his story began, green eyes burning with intensity. "Your women are very beautiful, as are you, so I could hardly blame them."

Something in his gaze set off flutters in her stomach, leaving her tongue-tied with no reply for the unexpected compliment.

"So," she said, clearing her throat, "what about the exchange prompted your change of heart? Obviously you did not stay with the tribe, or you wouldn't be here now."

"I can't remember why I needed to speak with our captain. It must have been some silly, trifling request," Geoffrey murmured. He ran his fingers through his hair and gazed distantly out the window again. "He didn't join us at evening prayer, so I went to look for him. We'd built shelters during the months we lived beside them, and our captain had the best home, the only one with privacy."

She waited, sensing a weight and tension in his words. Whatever he wished to tell her, he didn't need her prompting, only her ear.

"But he wasn't alone. He was raping her, Ysolde. One of our exchangees. I only had a second to think before plunging my sword into his back. All I could wonder was, what if it was my sister? My mother? I stabbed an unarmed man in his back, and my only regret is that I didn't make him stand to face me first."

The picture he painted with his words was horrifying. She didn't recall much from her childhood years with the tribes, but she did know that as free as they were with their sexuality, they never claimed anything by force. It was one of the worst sorts of crimes among the Marcogh.

Without thought, Ysolde leaned forward and set her hand over Geoffrey's clenched fists.

"She corroborated everything. It had happened for a while, but she was afraid to speak up. He'd shown her his magic and threatened to slaughter her entire family if she said a word. As for me, regardless of the circumstances, I'd cut down our commander. If my father wasn't a nobleman, I'd have been flogged for it, but instead, I was given the choice of leaving the Order or living in seclusion for ten years in the monastery to atone for my crime."

"So you chose to leave."

"I will never repent for it. Any man who will take an unwilling female deserves nothing less than death. I will never regret what I did."

"You have nothing to repent for. He would have suffered a far crueler fate were he a tribesman."

Geoffrey chuckled humorlessly and ran one thumb over the top of her knuckles. "My knowledge of the event ends there. As I was forced to leave that night, I never learned of what the Marcogh did, if they found out, but I suspect their reluctance to deal with Hindera now stems from that event."

"Geoffrey…"

"So you see, I've killed before, and not even Ashta herself could save Lorwick if he harmed you, Ysolde. I would gut him and happily go to the gallows knowing you were free of him."

Tears stung her eyes and threatened to spill over. Once again, words failed her, his words touching deep, so she squeezed his hand and took in a shaky breath. "You're a good man, Geoffrey. An honorable man. I'm lucky to have a friend such as you, and I count myself fortunate... to have a future husband such as you."

As she gazed into the green eyes of her best friend, Ysolde touched a palm to his cheek.

She could love him one day, couldn't she? But could Geoffrey set aside his yearning for Ashlynne to love her in return?

TROPHIES

16

Etienne turned his face toward the rose-scented wind, their surroundings warmed by what was predicted to be the last fair day until spring.

"Don't you find Lorwick's change of heart convenient?" he asked in their native tongue.

His brother lay swinging in a hammock strung between two strong Hinderan oaks in the rear garden. Ysolde had given them leave to enjoy the castle residence grounds to their hearts content, trusting them to wander wherever they pleased. It was a vast estate, but it paled in comparison to Castle Fresna.

Etienne shoved the thought away, too stubborn to fall prey to homesickness. From his seat on a nearby lounger, a book on his lap, he looked unapproachable.

"Far from convenient. Can you blame him for turning a new leaf and showing his best behavior? That poor sod is loved by none, loathed by all, and held in disdain by even the king now. He's ruined. Speaking of convenience, I'm used to shining my own boots," Laurent complained. "But that little ragamuffin fey child had his way with all of my footwear."

"Let him cobble your shoes if he must. It makes him happy," Etienne said. "He repaired the sole in mine. Grateful that he did it too. I paid a hundred salazars for that pair, and I'd like to get more wear out of them."

Laurent's head swiveled to stare at his brother. "I could have purchased a dozen—no, two dozen fine pairs of boots for that price."

"Ah, yes, but they wouldn't have been *my* boots."

Etienne turned a page. For five minutes or so, he tuned out his younger brother's complaints of noble privilege, only to catch the tail end of a rant broaching a new subject: the weather.

"One of the maids had the audacity to complain of the heat to me in passing," Laurent said. "Crazy woman. This weather is perfect."

"I read the paper. Their weathermage believes it will be the last warm day of the season before true winter arrives. It'll frost next week, so I hope you're prepared to attend a frigid wedding in the snow." Etienne replied, quick to dash his brother's hopes.

"Blast."

"I am told the people here go to great efforts to craft astounding figures from blocks of ice. It is supposed to be quite beautiful."

Laurent grumbled something Etienne didn't understand and turned the topic. "How can they have a wedding when assassins lurk?"

"If you were better at your craft, or at least half as talented as you proclaim to be, we'd have found the assassins, and they'd be swinging from that macabre tower in the center of the city."

"Then perhaps you should have left witnesses instead of eliminating each assailant you encountered," Laurent reminded him patiently.

At the time, the princess's safety had been the top priority, making it difficult to focus on keeping one of their number alive for questioning.

"I—"

Laurent interrupted him, speaking Hinderan in lieu of Fas Perran. "Do you hear tone he uses with me?" He leaned forward with his eyes directed toward the covered colonnade across the garden. "Never good things to say to his brother."

Etienne twisted in his seat to see Raennia beside a carved column. Her gray eyes widened.

"I didn't mean to interrupt," she called to them.

"We discuss weddings and assassins," Laurent informed her with a cheerful smile. "Come. Come speak with us. He is much boring anyway."

Upon receiving his brother's invitation, Raennia stepped down into the garden. Etienne studied her a moment, looking over her leather and chainmail Ashguard uniform. The drab colors dulled the red sheen of her auburn hair, which she wore in an unflattering bun at the nape of her neck.

"Drink?" he offered.

Raennia eyed his flask much as she might a poisonous viper. "No, my lord, but thank you."

Etienne chuckled. "It's nothing harmful. I've already had my fun with you lot."

"Still, I am on watch, so I must decline."

"She is too clever for you." Laurent grinned. "Here, share with me, Raennia."

Laurent pulled a knife from his boot and cut into an apple he'd picked from the trees earlier. He offered out a wedge on the blade's tip.

"I've seen a dagger like that before." Raennia accepted the fruit, but her gaze focused on the weapon.

"Oh?" His brows rose, and he offered the dagger out to her hilt first. "You know Fas Perran steel?"

"No, not well. It's only... My father had one." Raennia hesitated. "Hinderan soldiers sometimes kept things from the war. I always assumed your side did as well."

They had. In fact, Etienne had chastised a few of the men and women in his regiment for claiming all sorts of objects from the fallen dead. He'd found the habit disrespectful to the deceased and prohibited it.

"It was one of the knives I carried in the war," Etienne said quietly. He sat back and crossed his arms against his chest. Raennia's red cheeks told him much about her character—the confession had embarrassed her, or better yet, she feared they would judge her deceased father.

"They're beautiful weapons. Enough so to stick in your mind long after they're gone."

"If one you admired is gone, you keep this one, yes?" Laurent offered. "I steal another from him."

"I couldn't."

"Please. You keep and put to good use. Stab someone for Princess with it."

Raennia gave in and took the dagger in her hand. "Thank you, Laurent."

Something about Rae's admission burrowed into Etienne's thoughts, piercing through the fog until he bolted upright from his seat.

He gestured to the knife and launched into Fas Perran. "This is why the enemy had swords belonging to Mystere's agents, Laurent. War trophies taken by Hinderan soldiers. It was an attack on the princess from within their own ranks. By their own people."

"We would have noticed that."

"Doubtful. Once you have cut a man's throat, you rarely look behind you again," Etienne said drily.

"How will we prove it when the bodies have been burned? Had you not been taxed to the edge of your reserves, you could have recalled a spirit among the dead. King Aldemar will not accept speculation. He'll want cold, iron hard proof placed in his hands."

"Then we find proof," Etienne said grimly.

Raennia stared at them, a silent observer to their quick-paced talk. She cleared her throat, snapping Etienne's attention back to her curious face.

"Raennia, would you pass word to Princess Ysolde that we have dire need to speak with her and the king? Urgent need," Etienne said.

"Of course. Would you like me to ask her to come here to you?"

Etienne shook his head. "No. The war room would suffice. There is a map of Hindera there, no?"

"Yes, there is. I'll seek Her Grace out and let her know of your need, my lord." She bowed then headed off as tasked.

"Come, I want to look the map over before they arrive."

The war room was situated in the northern tower, two floors above the armory. Swords once belonging to Hinderan knights hung on the walls beside ancient shields. A massive slab of rock, polished to a smooth table surface, served as the only furniture in the room aside from a cabinet with dozens of slots. Each deep indentation held a tube with a rolled map. Etienne skimmed his finger across the small, brass placards labeling each until he found the one marked Hindera.

"Here, help me."

Together they rolled the large map out across the table and used the provided weights to hold down the corners.

"I have heard Ysolde speak fondly of the count murdered prior to our arrival. He was a good man and close to her."

"As was the baron who oversaw this village," Etienne said. "Another perished recently, but no one has relayed word to the princess due to superstition. They fear it will ruin the upcoming nuptials to spread word of death so close to the date."

"As I said, how can they have a wedding with assassins around every corner?"

"They believe the Hinderan gentry will turn against them, and what is a king without his supporters?"

"Speaking of." Laurent nodded toward the doorway.

"What is the meaning of this meeting?" Aldemar demanded. Ysolde and Geoffrey followed close on the king's heels. "Called to my own war room by two foreigners? Princes you may be, but you hold no power here."

Ysolde turned her eyes to her father.

"Erm…my daughter's war room."

"Forgive my impertinence, Your Highness, but I felt this matter could not wait," Etienne explained.

"Father, they have shown nothing but kindness and respect since their arrival, unlike others whom previously had your approval," Ysolde said. "Let us hear them out."

"Fine," he grumbled.

Etienne swept a handful of pins into his palm and peppered them throughout the countryside surrounding Ashdale on the map. The final pin marked Weathermore.

"Here, here, and here, nobles close to Princess Ysolde have been murdered. I suspect this is the work of someone within your own country."

"My country?" Aldemar bristled. "Yet we find Fas Perran blades and men wearing your kingdom's colors at each attack. The raid in the southern valleys, those men came across the border."

"With all due respect, those blades and colors were not donned by men of my kingdom. If Fas Perra desired war, they would bring it in large number. We wouldn't send petty thugs to hassle villagers and raid caravans. We have plenty wealth of our own."

Aldemar frowned, his heavy brows drawn together. "Then how do you explain what we have found? Everything points to Fas Perra trying to undermine us at every turn."

"This is not a clever ploy by Fas Perra to weaken you, Your Majesty. This is a very real threat—a play by someone within *this* kingdom. Perhaps a duke, or even a count thirsting for greater power," Etienne said. "And they have tarnished my country's good name, most likely hoping to ruin the truce between us and conceal their crimes."

"Go on."

The king listened in contemplative silence as Etienne explained his theories about war trophies and his correspondence with Regent Mystere.

"I cannot prove it at this moment, but the coincidences are clear, no? I will send my brother—" Laurent's eyes bulged, and he whipped his head to stare at Etienne. "—to investigate the matter. I merely ask that you grant him the power to act in your name, good King."

"You want me to invest my authority in a man who barely speaks our language?"

"I doubt he will need to speak often. A letter is all I ask, granting your authority and an understanding that his task is of a sensitive nature."

"Father, do it. You must. How else are we to ever discover who's behind these murders? Are we to stand idly by and allow another noble to die?"

"It would be wise to listen, Aldemar." Geoffrey broke his silence. "They've spoken nothing but the truth to you."

The king looked between the circle of anxious faces, consternation drawing his heavy, graying brows close together while he studied the marks on the map. "All right. If only he had your charismatic tongue. I will pen a letter of deputization."

"Thank you. It is my hope that while the rest of the kingdom focuses on Ysolde's wedding, Laurent may uncover the identity of the mastermind behind this chaos. Now I have something to ask of you, Princess. The men who recently died were all friends to you, but who among the nobles living in Ashdale's duchy remain in good social standing with you?"

"Well, Count Shadeglen has been a kind man, and rather helpful during my first years as a duchess."

"I sense an unspoken 'but' here," Etienne said.

"He wrote a rather scathing letter about the recent rise in taxes, decrying the urgent need to establish a current garrison at Fort Stonewall. I'd like to send a crew of stonemasons to repair the damage caused during the Dawn Wars," Ysolde explained.

"I see. So he is certainly not at risk."

She gave him a small, tight smile. "No."

"Who else dwells nearby?"

"My parents are Lord and Lady Lakeshire, and Andras is second son of Lord Eastmark," Geoffrey offered. "Both supportive, as far as I know. Father's never had a cross word to say about Ysolde."

Question by question, Etienne chipped away at the king's reservations until he joined them and supplied the names of nobles who had yet to warm to his daughter's title. He wrote his notes in Fas Perra while Laurent nodded and followed along, promising his brother understood Hinderan better than he spoke it and lessening Aldemar's concerns.

"When will he leave?"

"Today," Laurent answered the king. "Forgive me, Princess Ysolde. Your safety come first before wedding. I will miss it."

"I understand. Of course, there will be many disappointed faces at the celebration afterward."

The half-elf chuckled and stepped away, as if bashful, only to pause and bow before striding from the room.

Etienne turned to face the ones who remained. "All spoken here today must remain between us, and only us, and I give my word that you'll have your antagonist's head for a wedding gift, Princess."

Privacy and Moonlight

17

The arrival of guests from all over Hindera kept Ysolde too busy to worry about the plots against her. Jocelyn and Shyla maintained her sanity through the family dinners and final dress fittings. When her wedding day dawned, Ysolde hid in her private quarters and tried not to give in to second thoughts.

It was far too late to back out, not without humiliating Geoffrey and tarnishing her own image.

The day passed in a complete blur, from her small breakfast to meeting with the priestess of Ashta. When it came time to dress, Ysolde had managed to find a small measure of calm.

"I can't breathe," she gasped as Shyla, Jocelyn, and Maribeth tugged and struggled with her corset lacings.

"You're not meant to breathe. You're meant to be so bloody beautiful Ser Geoffrey will want to rip the thing off with his own two hands," Shyla told her. Jocelyn giggled.

The pale gold construct of silk and lace warmed her skin, and its corseted bodice gave the illusion of plump cleavage. The diaphanous skirts trailed behind her.

Maribeth had spent nearly two hours weaving elaborate ribbons and small crystals into Ysolde's dark hair, and it would take her another half hour at the least to remove them all after the ceremony.

"You're stunning," Jocelyn gushed. "If you thought Quintin was awestruck, I cannot wait to see Geoffrey's face when you walk down the aisle.

Would Geoffrey care at all?

A fist rapped against the door, and the king called out to them, "May I see you in your dress before the wedding?"

The long years had blurred the memories of Ysolde's natural father. He had been a man of the Marcogh, a warrior and horseman who'd died during her infancy. From then, her mother had attempted to educate and raise her all alone until King Aldemar had passed through their lands in need of a guide. Their chief had assigned the job to young Tegau, Ysolde's mother.

At twenty years of age, Tegau had known every grass blade, leaf, and bramble in the plains. Aldemar had become fascinated with their people and culture and then later returned to steal them away from the tribe. He'd paid the chieftain two dozen Hinderan horses to release her to his care, and she'd gone with him willingly, eager to learn the world of the fair-skinned Hinderans.

For a time, Ysolde's mother had been happy within Aldemar's castle. Tegau had lived as his consort but often refused the lavish comforts he offered her. By contrast, Ysolde had adjusted to city life in the palace and played with the other children. When she'd eventually showed signs of possessing magic, Aldemar had hired a private tutor.

It was more than any member of the Marcogh ever received on the plains. And that was why when Tegau had reached her limit years later, she'd returned to her people without her teenage daughter. It had been her idea to leave Ysolde behind. Despite her promises to return one day, she never did, and according to Aldemar, the Marcogh would no longer accept contact.

Thanks to Geoffrey, she now understood why.

"Let him in," Ysolde said to Shyla.

Her friend scurried to open the door. Once the king entered, Jocelyn and the servants hurried away. It was only the two of them—Ysolde and the man who raised her with no less affection than he showed for his own flesh and blood.

"You are breathtaking."

The first flush of pleasure seeped through her. "Thank you, Father. It all feels so extravagant."

"Every girl should be a vision on her wedding day. I thought the same of Jocelyn. Today, I see the woman I always knew you would become."

Tears filled her eyes and threatened to spill over.

"Is this really what you want?" Aldemar took her face gently between his hands.

"Geoffrey is a good man," she told him honestly. "He has been my friend and protector these past four years, after all."

"He'll treat you well."

She put on a smile that wasn't entirely forced. "He will, I'm sure."

"When that horseman left you, I despised him. It required much of my control to not have him sought out and found for breaking your heart. I wanted him drawn and quartered, yet I refrained because I knew you loved him."

"Rhun tried," she said, dropping her gaze. She couldn't even see her feet in the voluminous skirt. "He gave it a year and hated every moment of it."

"He did," Aldemar agreed. "Your mother made it several years before leaving, and she loved you and me both. How could I judge him when your own mother failed to adapt to Hindera's culture?"

"I wish she was here."

"Me too," her father confessed in a soft voice. She knew then that Aldemar had never stopped loving Tegau. "Geoffrey is a good man. You'll find happiness with him, sweetheart, but why did you never tell me he fancied you?"

Aldemar understood her too well to believe an outright lie. She chose clever words instead. "I didn't know. It was all very sudden, Father."

"Well, you have no complaints from me." He smiled and kissed her brow. "I shall send your maids back to you and see you in the cathedral."

"Father?"

"Yes, dear?"

"If you intended to wed me to Lorwick, why was he absent from your side when you arrived?"

The old man paused at the door. "I loathed the thought of subjecting you to what was done to me, but I knew no alternative. I wanted to see you first, though. To speak with you on the matter and make you see the necessity. Bearing witness to Geoffrey's proposal was a relief."

"Lorwick didn't argue?"

"One does not argue with a king, Ysolde, and I never officially declared the match. I merely mentioned it in passing to him as a possibility for our future."

"But he wasn't at all unhappy?"

"It doesn't matter whether he was or not. Unless you care about Lorwick's affections?"

"No!" she blurted, followed by a softer, "No. Nothing like that."

"Then don't worry about his missed opportunity. Look forward to your new life with Geoffrey."

Ysolde could only wonder how much would change between them. After all, they were no longer mere companions—they were to become husband and wife, and from everything she had ever learned in observance of her father and Queen Rhonwen, the two were never meant to be close friends.

***

A thousand faces watched her walk down the aisle in the Radiant Cathedral, but the only one that stuck in her memory belonged to Geoffrey. She focused on him and let his steady gaze lead her forward to the altar.

When he took her hands, she was almost relieved for his warm grip. By contrast, her fingers felt ice cold, and she trembled as he slid a simple gold band upon her finger. She almost dropped his when doing the same in return, cheeks flushed and eyes downcast.

Their kiss, short and chaste, brought thunderous applause.

Afterward, they endured an hours-long public reception, seated beside one another at Gilded Park in matching, velvet-lined chairs. As was customary among the nobility on the eve of their wedding, they received well-wishes from the commonfolk, who brought gifts of livestock, art, and even garments.

They returned to the castle in a white, open-topped carriage driven by Geoffrey himself, while Ysolde tossed leather pouches of gold solans into the crowd filling the cobblestone streets.

Geoffrey's smile rejuvenated her. Watching him direct the pair of pristine, all white stallions, she noticed the weariness of the day had melted away. He looked at peace, his green eyes bright, laughter on his lips as the crowd called out their affection for him. He'd truly been beloved while watch captain.

He hardly appeared the same man, clean-shaven and dressed in formal attire. His bronze velvet surcoat held a subtle shine, and the chainmail beneath gleamed in the late afternoon sunshine.

The season had gifted a final day of favorable weather after all, leading priests to murmur about Ashta's blessing and approval from the gods.

At the end of their circuit through the city, the festivities moved inside Ashdale Castle, a final grand bridal feast for those closest to the newlyweds and their peers in the nobility. Even Duke Lorwick attended, although his features were pinched and without humor or even feigned goodwill.

"A toast to the newly married!" Aldemar said. "I could not ask for a greater man to take the hand of my oldest daughter. Ysolde, you were the first light of my life, loved from the very moment your mother placed you upon my knee."

A warm feeling spread through Ysolde's chest. She and Geoffrey sat side by side on the dais, their hands loosely joined. The nobility able to join them in the week's short notice occupied seats at the colossal banquet table.

The bride and groom weren't intended to partake in the feast. After all, they would soon be engaged in their own activities upstairs. Instead, a portion of the meal was set aside upon an immense, silver platter containing only the choicest cuts of the meats, the first slices of each pastry and pie, and even generous bowls of side dishes, such as fluffy rice smothered in savory cheeses and asparagus spears roasted in herbed butter.

It was their meal to savor alone in the privacy of their marriage bed once their union was consummated.

"Dearest sister, I wish you nothing but the most profound happiness, both passionate and eternal. Take care of her, Geoffrey," Jocelyn said to him. "As you always have."

"I, too, have something to say." Theodoric rose from his seat, glass in hand. "Geoffrey, during these visits to my sister's duchy, you've shown kindness and everlasting patience to a boy who admired you from our first meeting. You've taught me to wield a sword when all others have failed. You've been a brother to me, and it is only fitting now that I may have the privilege to call you my true brother. Ashta's blessings to both of you."

Theodoric raised his glass to them both. As he did, Rhonwen's mouth twisted as if she'd drunk curdled milk. The queen may have raised her glass in toast, but she offered none of her own.

"And now it is time for the newlyweds to take their leave of us," Fingall announced. "Off with the both of you."

Cheers and applause accompanied their walk from the dining hall. In the upper hall, where they parted to enter their separate rooms, a priestess offered a final blessing upon them both.

Shyla assisted her once she reached her chambers. Her gorgeous gown was stripped from her body with care and her hair freed from its intricate plaits. Ysolde trembled while her maid wiped her down with sweetly scented water.

From head to toe, her flesh was a uniform shade of tawny brown with exception to the pale reminder of the most excruciating period in her life. Its contrast to the rest of her flesh reminded Ysolde of a black-and-white cow in a field.

Back then, Ysolde retained memories of her proud Marcogh kin who celebrated their scars as trophies of valor. She thought of the injuries as a badge of honor. She'd lived. Many of the men who had faced the ancient being hadn't survived the encounter or the extent of their wounds. A legion of city watchmen had died.

A proper Hinderan woman had no scars, for she didn't battle, did not raise a weapon, and most certainly didn't square off against demon-tainted dragon bones. But in the end, when the fight had tumbled into the city streets, it had come down to her, a stray agent of the Magisterium, and three surviving guards who lived with injuries exceeding her own.

She didn't want Geoffrey to see it.

The young woman helped Ysolde into a nightgown the seamstress had gifted her. Gossamer-thin silk floated against her skin as if she wore nothing at all, but it at least concealed the ghastly burns.

"Ysolde?" Shyla called her softly. "You're shaking."

"My stomach is in knots," she admitted. "Shyla, what's…what is it like?"

"Well, you surely know what the end is like. Virgin you may be, but I know you must have given yourself pleasure."

A much needed laugh welled forth. "Well, yes, there's that, but the rest of it… I'm told it hurts."

"Only for a moment," Shyla assured her. "And that's only if he's in a rush…and sometimes they are."

"Has that happened to you?"

Shyla grimaced. "It has, but not recently at least, thank the gods. You have a good husband, Ysolde. He'd sooner hurt himself than harm you."

Ysolde hesitated, nibbling her lower lip. "So there *is* someone now? Sorry, sorry, I shouldn't pry."

"It's all right," Shyla replied without answering the question. "Just remember that the man waiting beyond that door is a man who loves you. He'd never hurt you."

Ysolde huffed out quick breath. "You're right. I'm being silly. I may have spent most of my life in Hindera, but the customs continue to strike me as odd. Why should my virginity be praised and his lack of it lauded?" Ysolde muttered. "At least one of us will know what to do."

Prior to the wedding, a priestess of Ashta had received Ysolde's pledge, a spoken vow that the new bride would go to her marriage bed a virgin. Then the woman had blessed her and the bed, sprinkling sacred spring water over the coverings.

Shyla giggled. "See? There's the spirit. Now have some of this and think of how relieved you are to have escaped Duke Lorwick's clutches." Her friend offered a crystal glass brimming with ruby liquid. Hoping it would settle her nerves, Ysolde drained the sweet wine without pause.

"Thank you," she whispered as she set the glass aside. "For being here too. It's a little awkward, isn't it? But I don't know if I could tolerate a stranger sitting there. Listening."

"It is, but I always knew I'd do this for you one day. I've never sat a bride's vigil before, but I'll keep my back turned if it makes you feel better." Shyla hugged her tightly and adjourned to her corner when the door creaked. Geoffrey was coming.

Courage failed Ysolde and sent her hurrying to the bed. The heavy curtains had all been drawn back and replaced with sheer fabric that afforded a small modicum of privacy and moonlight. Before the door could open fully, she slipped beneath the sheets.

"Ysolde?"

"I'm here."

Through the gauzy curtain, Geoffrey's large frame came into view. He neared the bed and parted the drapes to join her, clothed in a blue nightshirt reaching his mid-calf.

Her fingers tightened in the blanket, but he peeled the corner back and slid beneath with ease, requiring her to make room.

With a wry, half-forced smile on her lips, she noticed he approached the act as courageously as he handled all other business, straightforward and without fear.

She shivered as her mind wandered to an old memory of the time she'd gone to seek his counsel and overheard him in his chambers with Ashlynne. Never, not once, had she spoken of it to anyone. Instead of knocking, she'd hurried away and returned to her room.

Would she make the same sounds? A twisting sensation in her gut made her believe otherwise.

"I could cut myself," she offered in a small voice. "We can pretend."

"And spit on Ashta's blessing?" he whispered back, aware of Shyla.

After enduring the rites from the priests, anything less than a consummation of marriage would be an insult to the goddess.

Ysolde sighed and regretted her offer. "You're right. I'm sorry."

"No, it's all right. Forgive me, Ysolde, habit." Geoffrey's quiet assurances didn't settle the disquiet and guilt building in her chest. After a pause, he added, "I *will* fib if it's what you want. I'll tell them whatever you'd like. It's no one's bloody business what we do now that they've gotten their wedding."

"No, I would never make you dishonor your vows. It was a foolish thought."

"Then I'll be quick."

Quick and without feeling. The thought hurt, but she nodded in silent acceptance.

Geoffrey gathered her nightgown in his strong fingers, but Ysolde pushed against his hand before the material rose above her waist.

Her heart pounded. Ysolde's quick and nervous breaths drew in the smell of plum brandy, making her crave another sip of it and wish he'd brought a bottle to share.

Her new husband moved slowly, his actions creating a hysterical image in Ysolde's mind. She imagined him as a hunter, stalking a frightened animal in the woods, a virgin wife his quarry instead of a fleet-footed deer.

Eventually, he maneuvered his greater bulk atop her.

He was heavy. Solid muscle honed by battle and training, a strong physique over a tall frame that fit more perfectly than it should.

Their bare legs touched at the shins, the rest clothed in his linen dressing gown and her thin nightshift. With his next tug, he exposed her to the heat of his body. Everything beneath their waists touched, thighs to thighs and hips to hips. The impressive length of him, hard and hot, nestled against her lower belly.

Quaking like a leaf in the wind, she forced her locked legs to part and turned her head to the side.

"I'm ready," she whispered. They only needed to get it over with.

His weight shifted off her then he removed the nightshirt—she'd never seen him don such a garment in four years. Her eyes widened at the sight of his expansive chest. Of course, she'd seen him shirtless before, but spying him at a distance in the halls at night or sweating in the training ground was no comparison to having the man above her.

"Ysolde, not like this. I'll only hurt you."

"We have to," she whispered. Her gaze darted toward the shadowed corner, and while she couldn't make Shyla's figure out, she was aware of her presence. Could she make Shyla lie as well?

Geoffrey didn't answer her with words. His fingers did the talking instead, as bold as the man himself, trailing without hesitation over the curve of her breast. While her mind shied away, her body had the opposite reaction, and her nipple tightened beneath the pass of his hand.

"You truly are beautiful."

"Geoffrey, you do—"

With one finger against her lips, he stalled her shy protest. The same hand then smoothed over the dark hair fanned over Ysolde's pillow. "I mean it. I've always liked seeing your hair down. This is how it should always be. Free and untamed. Much like you."

Little by little, she relaxed beneath each gentle caress, touched beyond measure by the tenderness of the kisses he feathered over her cheek. They made a trail, eventually reaching her neck where his lips lingered.

"I plan to show you the night Lorwick would have never shared with you." He dragged in a breath, nose skimming her throat, and she was suddenly thankful for the fragrant water Shyla had bathed over her skin. "You smell divine."

She'd known all along Geoffrey would be an experienced lover, but she'd never expected him to make her body come alive with anticipation. She squirmed, not in discomfort, but eagerness, growing anxious for the next touch.

Lying beside her, Geoffrey let his fingers wander and explore. He circled her stiffened nipples then traced the dark areola of each modest swell, visible through the diaphanous nightgown. When his fingers traveled lower, learning her curves, skimming her navel, and finding her bare thigh, Ysolde sucked in her breath before taking the plunge.

She twisted to face him and walked her fingertips up his chest, exploring the light dusting of golden hair over his warm, muscled skin. He responded by gliding his palm over her bared hip and squeezing one plump cheek. She squeaked in surprise.

Without a word, Geoffrey rolled her flat and leaned above her. His fingers traced a tingling path up and down her thigh until instinct nudged her into parting her legs. She couldn't read his gaze in the dark, but she felt its weight.

"Tell me you want it, Ysolde."

"Yes," she whispered, her voice so quiet it was barely a sigh of sound.

Geoffrey caressed her intimately, skillfully, and shamelessly between her thighs. His strokes came slow and leisurely, only to gradually gain speed when she failed to voice protest.

Her breath fluttered, and by the time he raised her leg over his hip, she was aching to feel the rest of him where only his fingers had traveled. She clutched his bare shoulder and wiggled close until even a sheet of parchment couldn't slip between their bodies.

"Are you sure?" he whispered, breath warm against her ear. "Last chance."

"Yes," she affirmed in a ragged breath, only to gasp when he filled her.

Their arranged marriage, Geoffrey's duty, and everything in between ceased to exist, blurred away by the euphoria sweeping through her limbs. It spread like wildfire, sheer bliss that dragged a triumphant cry from her lips.

Her husband lived up to his promises, making love to her with tender hands and even sweeter kisses that never reached her lips. The slickness of his seed slid the final, full hilted dive to completion, and then they were joined by every meaning of the word, breathing one another's air and moaning in mutual satisfaction until the last blessed second of orgasm.

Geoffrey remained above her for a few moments more while Ysolde struggled to cope with the reality before her. Among the night's many expectations, pleasure and fulfillment had seemed impossible.

And maybe with the bonds of friendship as their beacon through the darkest days, they would endure their sham of a marriage. She'd spent her first time with her best friend, yet nothing about it had shamed her.

"Did I hurt you?"

She shook her head. "N-no."

Ysolde waited for Geoffrey to speak, and likewise, he watched her as if hoping she'd break the silence first. Instead, she dipped her head and played with a single frayed thread of silk on the sheets.

"I should leave you to rest. Good night, Ysolde."

With only a parting kiss to her brow, her new husband left their marriage bed. She was too stunned by his exit to speak, and the door shut soundlessly behind him.

"Ysolde?" Shyla's voice drifted from across the room. "Can I get you anything?"

"No." Ysolde didn't want to bother with baths, company, or wine. "A hot bath in the morning is all. See the priestess and tell her it was done."

"It will get better," her friend said hesitantly from the door.

Would it? When she curled beneath the blankets and turned her face against the pillow, Geoffrey's scent filled her lungs.

THE WEDDING GIFT

18

Geoffrey took his breakfast alone, unable to face his wife. Ysolde deserved much better, but his hopes of assuaging her unhappiness had died from the moment he'd noticed she was unable to make eye contact with him after their lovemaking.

Believing Ysolde to be shamed by their consummation, he'd abandoned the room in disgrace to spare her further dishonor. Despite coaching from Andras, Maribeth, and Shyla, at different points of his wedding day, he'd choked. No words seemed adequate.

Years ago, Geoffrey's own mother and father had wed under similar circumstances. As the product of an arranged marriage, he knew what to expect, but he had hoped for something more. After the priestess of Ashta had inspected him for any illnesses wrought by his indiscretions, Maribeth had bathed him. She couldn't wash away the humiliation left by the cleric's judgmental gaze, as if he were beneath his new wife.

Wasn't he?

Gone were his convictions that he'd make a more suitable husband than Baron Easton, Duke Riverdale, or even Lorwick.

Most of the wedding had passed like a hazy dream, and he wondered when he would awaken to find Ashlynne snug against his chest, his arm around her, face buried in her sleep-disheveled caramel hair.

He had loved her. Loved her so dearly he'd spent every dime of his savings and the money set aside for their first home to find her. Then he'd taken every odd job he could find around the city while off duty, desperate to find her, until Ysolde funneled her money into the search efforts.

And when that hadn't worked, he'd gone to Rose and begged.

A knock at his door interrupted his musings.

"Come in," he called out.

"Your Grace." Shyla curtsied in the entryway. "Would—"

"Please don't," Geoffrey interrupted her. "I've heard enough of that since the wedding."

"Sorry," she apologized.

"What may I do for you, Shyla?" He topped off his glass with more brandy without looking at his new wife's personal attendant. Ysolde and Shyla, practically sisters, were inseparable, and he expected her to deliver a tongue-lashing for how he'd handled her mistress.

"M'lady inquires as to whether or not you will join her for a private tea with her family and your parents before their departure."

Geoffrey stared at her. "Of course."

He knocked back the glass and rose from his seat. Shyla curtsied again then left without judgmental words.

For the duration of his morning duties, he dreaded teatime and feared Ysolde would view him through accusing, dead eyes. She didn't. She raised her face, a silent invitation for Geoffrey to kiss her cheek. He did as expected then took the seat beside her.

Tea was informal, a private affair for enjoyable conversation between friends and family. Part of him wanted to relax, but the part of him who knew his mother best had wanted to about-face and stride from the balcony. He hadn't allowed himself to be alone with them since their arrival.

"Good afternoon," he greeted the others, barely gazing in Lady Lakeshire's direction. He'd once told himself she was forgiven, but seeing her unapologetic features swelled his resentment.

Ysolde served him herself, placing a few of the ham-and-cheese pastries he liked best onto his plate and skipping over the traditional clotted cream and sliced peach sandwich fingers. She spooned exactly four teaspoons of sugar into his cup, surprising him with her memory for such trivial details regarding his habits.

"Thank you."

"You're welcome," she replied.

"It's a shame you two cannot enjoy a proper honeymoon," Aldemar mused. "When things are settled here, I shall make it up to you. This spring should be a fine time to visit Crestoli during the festival season."

"I've never been to Crestoli," Ysolde said in a soft voice. "But of course, you know that, Father. Geoffrey has told me of their women warriors, though, as mighty as any man."

"It is true, Your Grace," his father said. "Geoffrey and I have paid many visits to the desert kingdom."

"Ysolde. We are family now."

"She's correct, Cedric. As I told your son, let's have no more of that Your Majesty funny business," Aldemar said.

"Old habits. As I was saying, I often took Geoffrey to Crestoli during his youth, and during one such visit, he told me he planned to marry one of their warrior women and free her from the arena."

Geoffrey's cheeks flamed red.

"Oh?" Ysolde peered over with curiosity.

"I was eight years old," he muttered under his breath. He practically chugged his tea before making an abrupt change in subject. "We have a woman now in the guard, taken to squire in my service."

"A woman?" His father straightened in his seat.

Ysolde brightened. "Yes, Raennia is her name, and Geoffrey has nothing but praise for her skills. It's unfortunate you'll miss the chance to make her acquaintance, as she's currently assigned to tower duty in the north as part of her training."

"I think it's amazing a Hinderan woman is willing and able to defend her home and country." Jocelyn angled a beaming smile at her sister.

"You'll have to come visit us in Acalia," Quintin invited. "Bring your new guard and let her see the arena battles."

"I find it quite barbaric and inappropriate for a woman to wield a weapon. Are we not Hinderan?" Rhonwen said.

Aldemar regarded his wife with an appraising eye. "My wife is unfortunately correct. She'll never have a man's strength and stamina. It is a tactic among the heathens to the east, placing a woman behind a knight's shield. What sort of man would disgrace himself by cutting down a woman in battle?"

Months ago, or even weeks ago, Geoffrey would have balked at the challenge from the king and queen. Something inside him snapped. "I honor skill and courage where I find it. Better an armed woman than a sword for hire."

"I must question your judgment. Are you truly comfortable with one of our women facing threats at the wrong end of a blade?" the king asked. He appeared oblivious to Geoffrey's veiled insinuation that he was wrong to hire the Iron Fist to fight beside them against Fas Perra years ago.

"With all due respect, they are women, not children. Were you to see her fight, you'd understand why I chose her. If the women of Crestoli may battle as gladiators, why should our own women be denied the honor? Why shouldn't Fas Perran women carry a knight's banner?"

Rather than further chastise him, the king laughed and bowed his head. "A bold move. Once again, you've proven the future of our kingdom is indeed in the hands of the younger generation."

Geoffrey stared at him and waited for the punchline to the joke. When it didn't come, he struggled to voice an elegant response.

"I would not want to steal Theodoric's inheritance, Father. He deserves to be crown prince," Ysolde said for him.

Theodoric laughed. "So you may say, big sister. Speaking of which, Father, if I may, I'd like to present Ysolde with her final gift."

"Please do."

Ysolde accepted a thick, vellum scroll from her brother and broke the wax seal. Geoffrey expected some obscure text, perhaps, or a diagram detailing out some rare, forgotten plant. Ysolde loved such things.

"What's this?" Ysolde stared down at the scroll.

"My gift to you, as I've said, with Father's full approval."

"But this… You can't mean…"

"Ysolde, what is it, love?"

Aldemar rose from his seat and lifted his glass in toast. "You are, as of this moment before all present and in attendance, Crown Princess Ysolde and Prince-Consort Geoffrey."

It was if the world turned upside down. Surely he must have heard wrong, or it was some kind of post wedding prank.

Cedric Ashcroft's eyes bugged from his head. "Prince-Consort? My son. My son is Prince-Consort?"

Aldemar smiled. "Indeed."

After opening and closing her mouth several times in a failed attempt to enunciate a response, Ysolde whispered, "I do not know what to say, Father."

Nor did Rhonwen. From the corner of his eye, Geoffrey saw the woman's white knuckled grip of her tea mug. Her fingers shook with rage too powerful to be contained, for she jerked from her seat and strode away without further word or congratulation.

Geoffrey's eyes darted around the table from one calm face to the next, the king and his children oblivious to the queen's abrupt exit.

"Say that you'll accept it."

"I couldn't. This is Theodoric's birthright. How could I take such an inheritance from him?"

"It was Theodoric's idea, my daughter."

"I have no want or need of it," the young man agreed.

"One day, you'll feel differently. You're not yet eighteen and won't be for another year."

"Trust me, I won't want it."

"Then what of Jocelyn? She was your firstborn."

Aldemar chuckled. "Jocelyn has been wed to a Crestolian magnate," he reminded them. "The king of a city-state."

Jocelyn beamed at them. "See? I'm already a queen, Ysolde. Now you'll be one as well."

Reluctantly, Ysolde accepted their generous offer, and within minutes, they were discussing the coronation to occur within the next two years, elevating her officially to the title of Queen-in-Waiting. Geoffrey remained quiet, a silent observer who numbly devoured pastries and chugged sweet tea.

By the time the clock tower tolled with the fourth chime, it was time for Geoffrey's parents to depart.

"You're certain you don't wish to remain another night?" Ysolde asked.

"No, my dear. We've imposed upon your hospitality long enough," the baroness said.

With his mind still reeling from the news of becoming Prince-Consort, Geoffrey rose from his seat. "I'll ride with you to the gates. If you'll please excuse me, Ysolde."

He had inherited his towering build from his father but his blond hair and green eyes from his mother. Thankfully, he didn't have her freckles.

She resembled a pixie beside her enormous husband, hovering beside him nervously with a hand on his arm when he struggled to rise from his seat. "Cedric?"

"I've got it," the man muttered. He used his cane in the end.

"I'm proud of you, son," his father said to him once they were riding for the castle gates, each sitting upon a massive stallion bred by House Ashcroft's stables. "You've surpassed your grandfather and me. Duke of Ashdale. Prince-Consort of Hindera. Sweet Goddess, I never expected it."

Geoffrey put a neutral expression on his face, recalling their explosive argument about shaming the family name. "The title isn't why I married Ysolde, Father. Some of us care about more than money, power, and title."

"Of course not." The older man's smile brightened his weathered features, crinkling his gray eyes. "For love, the sweetest reason of all to take a woman for your wife. And for that, I'm also proud of you, Geoffrey. You've done incredibly well for yourself since leaving the Order."

"I suppose I have and cannot ask for anything more. Lady Ashta has blessed me deeply."

"That she has. Go say goodbye to your mother."

"Why don't you ride in the carriage with her?"

"I still have some strength in these old bones yet, son. I'll join her before the sun sets, don't you worry." They were horse people by trade, breeding some of the finest stock in Hindera, and his father had spent so much time in the saddle his legs were permanently bowed.

Geoffrey nudged Blackjack with the inside of his calf, and the horse veered toward the carriage. He spoke a curt farewell to his mother, who gazed upon him with sad eyes, then rode back to the castle.

"Ser Geoffrey!" Crispin greeted him at the stable. "May I play with Blackjack?"

"Play?" He raised a brow.

"Yes. He wishes to play outside in the green grass without the shackles of a saddle and reins."

"Hardly any grass, but if you say so, lad."

"I'll take good care of him, promise!"

The fey child led Blackjack to the stepping block and climbed upon it to unfasten the stallion's girth. With surprising strength in his meager bones, he raised the saddle and bounced to the tack room with it in his twig-thin arms.

Geoffrey never tired of watching him maintain the stables. With Huxley dead, Crispin had assumed his responsibilities with the dedication of a man trained years to the task.

He found Ysolde in the solar, alone for a change, without family hovering nearby. She turned away from the window and smiled, but he knew her well enough to tell the expression was forced for his benefit.

"It was good to see your parents again, don't you think?"

"I'm glad they've left. No good ever comes of their visits."

Ysolde's smile faltered. "They're your parents, Geoffrey, no matter your hard feelings. They seemed like they tried to make amends at the very least."

"It's all because I've married a princess and elevated our family. Nothing more. That's all it will ever be with the two of them."

Her lips pressed together in a thin line. "That is not the impression I had."

Barely having the chance to enjoy the comfort of it, Geoffrey left the seat and stared at his new wife. "Then you're delusional."

Ysolde opened her mouth then snapped it shut. She turned on her heel and strode from the room while he watched her without chasing, too stubborn to accept anything beyond his perception of the man and woman who'd raised him.

Night Terrors

19

From the outside, people thought them a happy couple with the love match of the decade. From the inside looking out, they were near strangers. Geoffrey and Ysolde endured awkward shared meals, cordial chats lacking their usual banter, and none of their once comfortable affections.

Geoffrey hadn't come to her bed the previous evening, and she hadn't sought him. Her mind returned frequently to their wedding night, to the way their bodies fit together. The way his fingers smoothed over her skin and through her hair. The way it had surpassed duty and felt closer to…an emotion she refused to give name to. Not yet.

After a second restless night spent tossing and turning, she and Geoffrey barely spoke a word over breakfast. The rest of her day passed with her usual arcane studies until she could bear the silence no longer.

If Geoffrey would not speak to her, then she would have to speak to him.

"Please put Geoffrey's place setting beside mine at dinner tonight, Shyla, and let the servers know they won't be needed."

Shyla gave her a knowing look, filled with approval. "As you wish."

"In fact, if you'd like to take the night—"

"No need for that. I am more than happy to stay."

"We're not completely inept, Shyla. I can serve the meal," Ysolde insisted. "You deserve to have some free time away from your duties too. Perhaps some time to spend with your…" She searched for a word, but it wasn't necessary, since color lit across Shyla's cheeks.

"Allow me to help with dinner so you may focus on your husband, and I will take my leave for the remainder of the night. Deal?"

"A fair deal," she agreed.

The maid curtsied and vanished into the hallway as Ysolde set aside the scroll parchment. Etienne had her learning enchantment runes by repetition, promising what the hand learned, the mind would never forget.

He'd proven in so few weeks that her initial assessment of needing no mage was false. He and his brother were overflowing with knowledge in a number of studies Hinderan scholars thought improper for a lady mage to learn. And he had no qualms about teaching her, but thanks to her new marriage, she had no patience for runes, spellcrafting, or any other activity with educational merit.

When suppertime arrived, Ysolde was prepared to indulge her new husband in a quiet, more intimate setting.

"Good evening," Geoffrey greeted her. The broad entrance to the dining hall framed him, and firelight from the nearby hearth lit across his fatigued features. He eyed the table, the placements, and finally turned to his wife.

Ysolde held her breath until he crossed the room and politely offered her the chair. She sat primly, and then he pushed it nearer to the table.

"Thank you. Wine?" She picked a crystal decanter up and filled a glass to the halfway point with the pale gold liquid.

Arrangements had changed on the day of his proposal, and ever since, the servers had enforced the rules of dining etiquette by setting her husband across the table. It may as well have been a chasm between them, a canyon no amount of stretching could bridge if she wanted to pass the salt. The staff did that for her.

Geoffrey glanced dubiously at their side-by-side place settings. "What's this?"

"I thought it would be nice to keep our meals as they always have been, close, without the table between us." She offered out the wine to him. "Please."

"All right," he said in a quieter voice. Once he was no longer studying her as if she'd grown a second head, her husband took his seat and accepted the glass.

One by one, Shyla brought the courses to them and assisted Ysolde with serving their portions. When Geoffrey tried to fetch his own dinner, Ysolde swatted the back of his knuckles with the spoon. His expression, paired with Shyla's swift about-face to conceal her amusement, almost broke Ysolde into a fit of giggles. She treasured her tiny victory over him like a jewel, holding it close to her heart.

"I know Fingall to be a harsh taskmaster with little mercy when it comes to educating duchesses—or even dukes—in the facets of their new duties. You've worked hard, and this is the only time you're allotted to relax," she chided in a gentle voice. A glance at his plate and the memory of his afternoon training session in the lists prompted her to add an extra portion of roast beef.

He chuckled but dipped his head in an appreciative nod. "Thank you. Where are the servers, anyway? Did Ren and Alwen skive off?"

"I sent them away for the evening. I thought..." She hesitated and flicked her gaze up to his curious face. "I thought you and I might enjoy a chance to talk without additional faces surrounding us."

He said nothing, and the silence fell heavier due to his quiet, assessing stare. Disappointment surged through her with a visceral stab.

"It *is* nice," he admitted at last, dashing her worries. His lips spread into a grin. "When we're so far apart, I can't sneak you the things I dislike. Or steal from your plate the things I enjoy."

"And we don't have to near shout to talk." She half hoped their morning silence had been a result of the distance and not something worse. "You don't even shout at your guards during training, so I see no reason for you to do so here."

"I shout plenty," he disagreed. "You happen to be absent when it's done. Speaking of training, Duncan says that you were at the balcony again. You ought to come down to join us sometime. I'll have you swinging about a greatsword as long as you are tall in no time. Better than a staff."

"Don't let Etienne hear you saying that."

Geoffrey snorted. "The staff is for show. I think."

"What?"

"He's a knight in his own right, Ysolde. The man wields a sword and shield with prowess. I should know, since I asked him into the training ground with me once, and he damned near thrashed me." Geoffrey grimaced and muttered under his breath, "The little ones are always quick."

The idea boggled her. In all her years at Ashdale she had never, not once, seen Geoffrey come close to being beaten in a fight, training or otherwise. After a moment of silence, she raised her eyes and saw him watching her intently.

"I tried lifting your sword once. I dropped it." The confession came with a duck of her head and a blush at her cheeks.

Geoffrey grinned. "I had no idea."

"I swore Andras to secrecy," she rattled off quickly. "He was giving me a tour of the armory."

"My sword is made for my size and reach, Ysolde. Of course you dropped it."

"It's just as well. I wouldn't know what to do with your sword."

"Heh." Geoffrey quickly swallowed a mouthful of quail, his face reddened, and his cheeks pillowed with poorly contained laughter. "I can always teach you to handle it, you know. You don't have to be incredibly strong to hold a man's weapon. Once you get your hand around it, you'll see."

"I…" She paused, grasping to figure out if there was an underlying meaning to his words. Before she could stop herself, Ysolde's gaze dropped to his lap. Once again their wedding night came to her thoughts and her discovery that *all* of him was large.

"You…?" he urged, voice teasing.

"I would be appreciative for a lesson," she ventured with as much coyness as she could muster. "To learn what to do when such things are in hand."

Shyla released an uncontrollable giggle and overpoured her glass. Water infused with lemon and mint sloshed over the edge.

"So sorry," the woman stammered.

"It's all right, Shyla," Ysolde murmured.

Geoffrey put on a straight face and returned to the serious topic, leaving no doubt in her mind that it wasn't her imagination.

He'd flirted with her. He'd actually flirted with her, instilling a lighthearted sense of joy that made Ysolde's spirits soar.

"You'd do well with a long blade, I think. Shorter than a longsword, slimmer than a shortsword, and a little more threatening than a dainty dagger."

Ysolde took a quick swallow of wine, nodded, and offered him a small smile. "Whatever you think is best. I like to watch you train the guard, so I will no doubt enjoy being under your tutelage as well," she said, picking up the original thread of conversation. "You have a gift for getting them all sorted without bellowing like a slave-driver."

"I like when you watch," he said simply.

And just like that, the light had returned to his green eyes, and he was once more her Geoffrey, the tension between them banished.

With every day since his proposal, she felt closer to regaining what was once normal between them.

**

Ysolde didn't invite him to return to her bed. Most wives thrived on attention, and while he'd given it to her without question since the wedding, he'd been surprised by her decision to join him for a close, personal dinner.

Not surprised. Thrilled.

And for a moment, he'd thought she felt a fraction of what he'd sorted from his murky feelings, discerning their relationship hadn't been as platonic as he'd originally thought.

He wanted Ysolde. With absolute certainty, he wanted her beyond a friendly arrangement. If she didn't feel the same, what then? Could he remain content with what would no doubt become a series of infrequent, passionless visit to her bed?

Would Ysolde truly care if he resumed his visits to Rose? Sweet Rose with her words of wisdom, her well thought advice, and an even sweeter grasp of the ways to make his body thrum with pleasure.

No, he couldn't do that to Ysolde and pervert their marriage oaths to suit his own agenda.

Most noblemen had mistresses. His father did. Aldemar did. Monogamy was an archaic device for peasants who married for silly reasons like true love.

And he'd rather be a peasant than humiliate Ysolde in such a way, he realized.

She was his friend first, wife second, and no amount of personal need could send him to the Primrose for their intimate services.

He laid in his bed after dinner with Ysolde on his mind, fantasies of holding her again nourished by the memory of her kiss. At the end of supper, she'd risen from her seat and stood on tiptoe to kiss his cheek, but her lips had brushed the corner of his mouth.

And it took every ounce of his self-control to end their encounter without hiking her skirts.

Eventually, his attention wandered to the door separating their adjoined bedroom suites. Ysolde was there, less than thirty feet from him, also tucked warm in her own bed.

Tomorrow would be another day. Another chance to lure Ysolde to a quiet place, alone and away from their servants. To bear witness to her shy but sweet flirtation attempts.

As usual, he slumbered with his sword at the bedside and within reach, his sense of duty as her protector undiminished by their marriage and his new title. With assassins on the move, Geoffrey left nothing to chance.

The first shriek roused him from sleep at half past the midnight chime. He threw the covers away as his sword flew hilt first to his fingers. Sword magic came naturally for him, muscle memory that took a life of its own and entwined with inherited sorcery.

Ysolde screamed again as he burst into her room. He practically took the door off its hinges and raised his sword toward the first moving shape to cross his path.

He nearly killed Shyla.

"Geoffrey, it's me!" she cried, raising both hands as if they would fend off the strike.

"Shyla?"

"I heard her cries as I returned to my room for the night."

Bed sheets rustled noisily with Ysolde's thrashing limbs. In the glow of the nearby candle, he saw her eyes closed and features twisted into a terrified mask.

Shyla hurried to the bedside and blew out the threat to Ysolde's bed curtains, the unnaturally bright flame dancing too close. "Forgive me, Geoffrey, I will settle her."

Ysolde twisted and turned in the bed, pillows knocked from the mattress. Her fearful whimpers pained him.

"Is it only a dream?"

"A night's terror, common for her. Did you not know?"

Geoffrey shook his head and exhaled deeply. His heart raced, a wild rhythm wrought by fear for her safety.

"There's no awakening her during them. I've tried. Ysolde has fits until they've run their course."

"I'll settle her." Geoffrey set the sword on the floor by the bedside. He couldn't skewer a nightmare with cold steel. As far as he knew.

Shyla opened her mouth as if to protest then seemed to reconsider. Instead she bowed her head and dipped into a small curtsey. "As you wish. Be mindful of the fire."

The maidservant stepped into the hallway and closed the door behind her. Left with his wife and complete privacy, Geoffrey settled carefully onto the disheveled bed.

Unlike him, Ysolde wore refined bedroom attire, though the cream-colored gown twisted around her waist and the blankets piled by her feet. She whimpered again at whatever visions held her, crying out.

"Ysolde," he called to her softly. Geoffrey smoothed her hair back from her clammy brow, feeling increasingly helpless against the intangible threat. Twice he caught sight of a flicker in the hearth, reminded of Shyla's parting caution.

With one final, unnerving scream, his wife jackknifed upright in the bed. Her dark blue eyes flew open wide, glassy and full of fear, and each heaving breath trembled her petrified frame. She seemed oblivious to his presence, quaking more than she had on their wedding night.

"Ysolde? Are you awake now?" He barely whispered it, his mind delayed by finally recognizing the state of the bed's occupant. With candles all extinguished, his eyes adjusted to the darkness and swept over her bare legs. Her beautiful and long bare legs, the length of them stretching into eternity.

She turned and stared as he held his breath and waited. Then she reached out for him without a word, only a whimper.

Without delay, Geoffrey pulled Ysolde into his arms. She curled against him and pressed her cheek against his chest, dampening him with her tears. He held her for an hour, her silent protector as the sobs subsided and reality vanquished her terror.

"Do you want to tell me about it?" he asked after a time of silence.

"I never remember them," she whispered. "Not really. I only remember the fear."

Geoffrey stroked his hand down her hair again, threading his fingers through the soft waves. "How long have such dreams troubled you?"

"Several years ago, before I came to Ashdale, there was an accident in the Nirmashire repository," she began uneasily.

Nirmashire, the royal city of the dead which housed all of Hindera's past monarchs, lay to the east at the base of the Tyrwennian mountain range dividing their kingdom from Fas Perra.

"One of the archivists unwittingly released a dracolich from its tomb. He and several others died before we managed to contain it again." She hesitated and swallowed thickly. "The nightmares began after that."

"I never knew."

"Few do," she admitted. "Shyla has always helped with them. I'm sorry you were troubled."

"It's nothing. And you'll need never to fear disrupting my sleep, Ysolde. I'll always be there when you need me."

Once as her protector and now as her husband. The role didn't change; it evolved to something greater and more meaningful.

He suppressed the brief flutter of desire that blossomed when he drew her alongside him into a lying position. Geoffrey kept one arm cradled behind her back, holding her comfortably near.

"Please stay," Ysolde whispered.

"Your blankets are warmer than my own, and I've grown quite comfortable, thank you. You'll have to box me out of the bed like a Sarangese monk if you want me to leave."

"Promise?"

"I'll be right here. Any nightmares will simply have to go through me."

"Just another woe for you to tease me over, I suppose," she said in a halfhearted attempt at humor.

"I miss teasing you about getting into trouble. There's no one to skewer as long as you're in safety. It makes my job dull."

"Shall I go out and harry some yetis to give you something to do?"

He didn't need to see her face to know she was finally smiling. He heard it in her voice.

"Definitely not. I like you plenty as you are, whole, safe, and sound."

***

Morning sunlight on his face stirred Geoffrey from his sleep. Even without opening his eyes, he registered the differences from his normal surroundings. The bed was softer than usual, the blankets sewn from thick layers of satin.

And then there was the woman tucked against him, the top of her head just beneath his chin. When she shifted in her sleep and rubbed her cheek against the side of his neck, Geoffrey took it as a silent invitation to squeeze her closer. To let his fingers wander down the line of Ysolde's back and follow her lithe curves.

Ysolde made a quiet sound and nestled closer, which brought a new tension to his already taut frame. The innocent skim of her lips and the feathering of her breath across his throat drove him to near madness.

"You stayed." Her quiet murmur accompanied a stretch and shift of her body. Her cheek settled against his shoulder, and he took it as a good sign that she didn't pull away and put space between them.

"Of course I did."

Despite a list of chores and duties awaiting him, Geoffrey didn't want to let her go. Didn't want to release her, crawl from her warm bed, and face the tedium of being the new duke. On top of assuming his share of Ysolde's work ruling over their duchy, he'd yet to turn over full command to Andras. It felt wrong, dumping the load into his lap.

"Mm... You're so soft in the morning." Geoffrey's fingers trailed lazy circles over her back, occasionally combing through her dark hair.

"And you're not."

He couldn't believe the playful quip had come from his Ysolde. Stunned into silence, he pushed forward with his hips, introducing her to the unrelenting stiffness she had inspired.

How much longer would it take to discover whether or not she would be expecting their child? And would it hurt to suggest "practicing" until they found out?

While Geoffrey mulled the thought over in his mind, Ysolde traced her fingers over a thick, puckered scar on his chest, freely touching him. Before he could make good on the fantasy of his wife arched beneath him, a knock interrupted his train of thought.

"Geoffrey, we need to speak." Andras's clear voice carried through the door.

"Come back later," he growled back.

"I'm sorry, cousin, but you'll want to hear this, as will the princess. It's important."

"Maybe we should hear him out," Ysolde whispered.

"Fine. I'll be out momentarily."

"I will join you presently," Ysolde said to him, shyly huddling beneath the sheets.

He kissed her hairline and crawled from the bed, regretting the loss of her heat. The trip back to his bedroom was short but cold and one he had hopes of abandoning in the future.

Once he'd thrown on a tunic and trousers, he emerged from his room to find the corridor empty. Ysolde hadn't finished her morning routine yet and was no doubt awaiting Shyla's help to tighten her corset strings so he went ahead without her, jogging the steps two at a time.

Andras awaited him in the room where the old duke had once performed most of his ducal functions. Ysolde hadn't liked it, citing the scarce number of windows gave it a dark, foreboding feel. She preferred the feel of the solarium and the open, spacious audience chamber.

"What happened?" Geoffrey asked. One look at his cousin's grim expression told him something had gone wrong.

"Have a seat, Geoffrey."

"What happened?" Geoffrey repeated.

"Perhaps we should wait for the princess."

Rather than say a word, he crossed his arms and stared his knight captain down until the man cleared his throat and stopped procrastinating.

"We received news from Laurent." Andras spoke in a quiet voice.

"Already? Has he found the source of the weapons?"

"No, it's not that. There was an attack on the road. Your mother's safe now, but…" Andras hesitated, and a flicker of pain made his eyes briefly close before he finished. "Your father was killed during a battle on the eastern road. He's gone, Geoffrey. I'm sorry. I'm so sorry."

In the blink of an eye, his already uncertain life was reduced to complete chaos. "Gone?"

"Yes. From what I gather from the message, the attack happened overnight." Andras offered him the rolled slip of paper often brought by carrier birds.

Numbness spread throughout, and his body was awash with cold.

"What's happened?" Ysolde asked.

Geoffrey remained silent, reeling from the news while Andras caught Ysolde up on the tragic information.

"What has been done thus far?" she asked.

"I've sent messengers to the watch posts, and we plan to ride south to investigate the matter. Lakeshire has already devoted several dozen members of the city watch to comb through the foothills, and I plan to join them—"

"No, no. I'll do it." Despite his words, Geoffrey didn't move, unable to fathom anything more than the final words he'd uttered to his mother and father when their coach departed.

Ysolde's touch lit across his shoulders and smoothed over his back, a welcome balm against the war raging in his heart. "Geoffrey?"

He wanted to reassure her, but he made a choked noise instead.

"Andras, please send for Etienne."

"Of course." Andras stepped from the room and shut the door behind him.

"Geoffrey, I'm sorry."

"The last things I said to him. To both of them. It wasn't enough."

Ysolde moved around and took his face in her hands, turning his gaze up to hers. "Your father loved you, and no matter what was said, he knew you felt the same. I know this loss is grievous, but your mother needs us right now. We have to go to her."

"I know." Geoffrey drew in an unsteady breath. "I'll ride—"

"No, *we* will ride. Together."

When Etienne arrived, he knocked on the door and awaited permission to enter. His solemn features and apologetic eyes settled on Geoffrey. "Greetings," he said, in lieu of the usual good morning.

"I'm certain your brother has kept you abreast of the recent developments," Ysolde said in a quiet voice. She laced her fingers with Geoffrey's thicker digits. "Will you accompany us to Lakeshire or remain here?"

"Do you plan to travel by carriage?" Etienne asked.

"No, by horseback. It will be faster if we don't have to keep to the roads."

Etienne's cerulean eyes filled with compassion. "May I suggest a more convenient mode of transportation?"

"What better way is there?" Geoffrey asked.

"I possess the raw materials and spell components to create a portal to Lakeshire. It's within my practical range, so you'll arrive within minutes as opposed to days."

Ysolde's eyes lit with interest, only to become muted again by the severity of the situation. "Is it safe?"

"Incredibly safe. Meet me in the courtyard in one hour. I'll be prepared by then to open it. These things can be difficult, and it isn't guaranteed to work, but I'd feel better having tried and spared you difficult days on the road."

"I'll have Andras and Crispin ready the horses then, in the event the spell fails," Geoffrey said. After withdrawing from Ysolde's hold, he left the room in silence, aware of their troubled eyes following him.

An hour later, they reached the courtyard to discover Etienne had completed his arcane work. He'd used chalk, animal bones, and other bits of spell material Geoffrey didn't question and buried dagger-sized crystal spires in the moist soil. In the middle of it all was the portal, a creation both beautiful and chilling, composed of voidstuff and forbidden magic no longer practiced in Hindera.

"I've gathered some men to escort you through the portal for your protection," Andras said. "They'll keep guard at the other end."

"How long can you maintain this?" Ysolde asked.

"A day," Etienne replied. "You'll want to form a chain and hold onto one another as you travel. Go straight ahead, and do not leave the path before you."

"What happens if I let go?" Geoffrey eyed the portal uncertainly.

"Nothing harmful. Time in the void is relative. It may appear to be seconds to you, but time passes in hours for spectators beyond the gateway." Etienne flashed a comforting smile and opened his pocket watch. "It's noon and fair weather in the void according to Adrienne. You'll arrive by the second bell without stragglers lagging hours behind if you follow my instructions."

"Thank you, Etienne, for doing this."

"My pleasure, Ysolde."

"Link hands with one another," Geoffrey directed the two dozen guardsmen accompanying them.

The passage through the portal only took seconds, but the time seemed to stretch. The air pressed in around them, and a thousand gleaming motes sparked against their clothes and hair. The sensation tingled, both hot and cold all at once.

Then it was over, and they stepped from the oversaturated brightness of the portal into the middle of the town square.

People stared, and a few cried out in fear or awe at their sudden appearance. Guards donning the blue-and-silver tabards of Lakeshire Watch had the portal surrounded.

Their weapons hesitantly lowered. "Ser Ashcroft?"

"Duke Ashdale," another guard hissed in correction and elbowed the initial speaker.

"By Ashta's holy skirt, you gave us a fright, Your Grace. Your Graces," one of them babbled. The last sword sheathed.

"No one is to come near this portal, do you understand? I've given orders to my man on the other side to execute anyone who enters who is not part of our contingent. Six of my men shall remain behind to see this is done."

"Of course, Your Grace. We will support them with our own and escort you to the keep."

In the years since Geoffrey had left home, little had changed in Lakeshire. He visited sparingly, and even then, it had been mostly for the benefit of his mother until she'd committed what had been the ultimate betrayal in his eyes. Within a day of meeting Ashlynne and taking her aside for a private chat between women, his bride-to-be vanished on the day of their scheduled wedding.

Passing the square where he ought to have wed her was a strangely numb moment without pain. Ysolde squeezed his hand. She'd never let go after their arrival.

A pair of guardsman rode up on their large, winterbred horses. One leapt from the saddle and bowed. "Your Graces, please, allow us to lend you our horses."

"I'd prefer to walk," he said, voice polite.

"And you, Princess Ysolde?"

213

Ysolde flashed them an appreciative smile. "I will walk with my husband. Thank you."

The fishing township of Lakeshire was the secondary hub of all trade in Northern Hindera. Men with boats made a prosperous business for themselves, leasing their ferries and watercraft to merchants and travelers heading to the deep south of the continent. The eastern meadows provided the perfect environment for keeping and breeding horses.

It was home, and as the only surviving child of Lord and Lady Lakeshire, it would belong to Geoffrey one day. If he had any inclination of inheriting it, at least. It had always been his plan to gift the title and land to his cousin Andras, and that plan still remained.

The vast estate rose from the top of a hill, more of a fortress than a manor with its stone columns, north and south towers, and battlements atop the colossal perimeter walls.

Once they surpassed the keep's immense, wrought-iron gates, they crossed a vast space serving as both orchard and courtyard to the residence's doors where a butler, already informed of their arrival, greeted them with a deep bow. He led the way into the manor, to the Blue Room where guests were received, and announced in a clear voice, "Duke and Duchess Ashdale to see you, my lady."

Everything was as Geoffrey remembered it, from the cobalt rug on the golden wood floor to the wall mural depicting wild horses running through a stream. Lady Lakeshire rose from a velvet chaise and stared across the room at them. Her eyes shimmered in the sunlight streaming through enormous windows Geoffrey hadn't seen in the year since Ashlynne had left him at the altar.

"Geoffrey," she whispered. She rushed to him, and they met halfway to join hands. "How did you arrive so soon?"

"A mage's portal brought us," he replied. "Mother, I... Were you injured?"

"Nothing dire," she replied.

"Tell me what happened."

"We were perhaps only a few hours from home, and we ought to have stopped at Crestwich for the night. There's an inn there, but your father insisted we could push through and be asleep in our own beds by midnight."

He nodded, encouraging. "And then?"

"Riders came from the east and the south to surround us from all sides. Our men tried to fight them off, and your father was among them. The ride had made him drowsy so he wanted to sit on his horse in the cool breeze."

There were jokes among their relatives that Baron Lakeshire must have been born in the saddle, as few things could part him from a horse's back.

Geoffrey blinked away the stinging sensation. "How did you escape?"

"Your father shouted for me to run, and one of the guardsmen slashed the tethers to the carriage horse and set me on his back."

"No one pursued you?"

"I was." She released his hands to wring hers together nervously. "But an elf came. A half-elf, I think. He was far too large to be one from Fellwood and too far from home. As I was riding away, I looked back and saw him appear in the thick of them as if by magic."

Geoffrey and Ysolde exchanged glances.

"What is it? Your faces changed," his mother said. "Do you know him?"

Ysolde nodded. "We do. He's brother to our spymaster, sent to investigate the occurrences in the eastern veldt."

"The Fas Perran?"

Ysolde nodded again.

"Never would I expect the day to come when a Fas Perran saves my life. Would that he had arrived only moments earlier." Her shoulders shook, and with the next breath, she steeled her nerves. "I want to know who did this, Geoffrey. I want them punished."

"As do I, Mother."

Accomplices

20

That morning, a carrier pigeon delivered a note to Laurent from Ysolde, passing a simple and clear update to his instructions.

She knew of his part in rescuing Lady Lakeshire, and the princess had no intentions of taking prisoners or placing the guilty on trial to be judged by their peers among the nobility. Once Laurent collected the necessary information, she wanted the perpetrator to die afraid. He had to send a message to any other would-be assassins.

After allowing one of the mercenaries to escape, he followed the man north into the town of Shadeglen where he'd stabled his mare and made himself at home at the local pub. He'd been tracking his quarry for three days, a relentless revenant haunting the steps of his prey.

There, he waited until he learned a name and discovered the Iron Fist had been recruiting locally. If they were Ysolde's torturers, King Aldemar would want more than his word as proof.

The familiar architecture, reminding him of Ysolde's castle, made penetrating the defenses easy. He scaled bricks and melded with the shadows, flowing over the curtain wall and into the inner courtyard.

Guards never looked up. It was a poor oversight in both those experienced and the ones new to the job. They marched on a strict patrol route, always staring directly ahead. Geoffrey trained his men to know better, and Laurent respected him for it. It made sneaking around Ashdale Castle a humorous challenge.

Laurent crouched in the shadows of a parapet on Shadeglen Castle's main wing, unseen by all guards patrolling the stone beneath. In all of the time he'd carried out assassinations and work for the Magisterium as their dog, he'd never enjoyed the thrill of the hunt or felt eager to take a life. Until now.

He'd been fourteen when his jailors had sold him into bondage to the Magisterium, an organization of ruthless mages who dwelled in a floating city far above Terraina. Laurent hadn't yet served half of his sentence as one of their mercenaries when Etienne had offered him another way out.

"Gonna go to the Festival of Giving?" one guard asked the other.

"Planning to take the wife and wee ones," the second replied. He covered a yawn behind his hand.

His friend leaned against the waist-high stone wall of the bridge connecting the main castle wing from its east tower. "Bollocks to having the nightwatch. The rich pansy arsehole never asks this of us. What's he got to be afraid of?"

"Probably thinks the Highborn Slasher's after him next. Y'heard what happened to Count Weathermore, dint ya?"

Laurent had never endured such frigid weather, but the promise of solving Ysolde's troubles warmed his desert elven blood. It kept him lurking on the balcony ledge, concealed by darkness, until his crow returned.

Crows and felines, by their very natures, were the closest mortal creatures to the void. Their spirits resided partially within it, making them perfect candidates for a mage's familiar.

Hello, dear friend. Have you found the count? he asked it.

The count occupies a room below, its corners dark, its shelves aglow.

Laurent gave it a morsel of meat for its work. *And is he alone?*

One is one, and two is two. A single spark will double soon.

After offering a second reward, Laurent crouched and leaned over the ledge to scan the castle wall. Candle light shone from the window beneath him. He swung down and climbed to the lower level, gathered his will, and flowed like liquid shadow onto the balcony where the doors were ajar.

Laurent drew his dagger and waited to barge in and save the count's life.

"What happened? Is it done?" Count Shadeglen's voice drifted through the window. "Have you killed them yet?"

Laurent stilled. Cold rushed through his veins. Shadeglen wasn't the next victim, betrayed by a clumsy host of guardsman and ill-prepared castle security.

He was behind it.

So much for loyalty. He peered through the glass door and, with his gifts, was little more than a mass of insubstantial shadow. He saw Shadeglen, a count who had once supported Ysolde, standing before one of the men who had terrorized her duchy.

"An enormous elf slaughtered everyone. I was lucky to escape with my life."

Shadeglen crossed his arms. "But Lakeshire is dead?"

"Gutted the old bastard myself. His bitch escaped, but she shouldn't be an issue."

"Shouldn't be an issue? Are you mad? She'll warn people. She could describe you."

"'Nae trouble there; we don't wear Iron Fist colors while on a job. We're travelin' tonight to complete our next contract. I only came to let you know and to get my payment."

"Right. Your payment." Shadeglen moved to a side table and poured a drink. "Here, slake your thirst. As the only man standing, I suppose it's only fair you also receive the share of the others."

"I'll drink to that."

While the mercenary chugged down his drink, the count opened his safe. It shone from within, containing every kind of jewel Laurent could imagine.

The sloppy assassin shambled forward to claim his reward. "Be quick about it, would you? I need to…to…be on the r…" he slurred.

Pausing as if to clear his head, he took another step and staggered off balance, banging into an adjacent desk.

"In a rush to travel, are you?"

"What dith you gi…?"

"Did you really think I'd pay you for a half-arsed job, you little shit?" Shadeglen kicked the man and stooped low. "I won't pay a single silver. You were to eliminate Lord *and* Lady Lakeshire. Your boss will understand."

"You b-b...bas—" His words trailed off in a series of hacking coughs.

"Bastard indeed. One does not ascend to my level of success by accepting inferior qualities of work."

While Shadeglen watched the vitality fade from the poisoned henchman, Laurent slipped into the room and activated an enchantment for silence by setting his lucky coin on the table beside him. Nothing could be heard beyond its sphere of influence, although the space within would soon reverberate with the sounds of vengeance.

"About time," Shadeglen muttered. "They certainly aren't making it as potently as they once did."

Laurent closed a thin, leather cord around Shadeglen's neck and yanked sharply. The count panicked as all garroted men typically did. He clawed at his own throat, his hands feeble, ineffective. Laurent choked him until he was limp but alive, and then he used the same cord to bind the man's wrists.

Then he opened up his kitbag and prepared the workstation, whistling merrily until the count opened his eyes.

Laurent crouched before him and smiled. "Hallo."

"How dare you! Untie me immediately, you elvish scum. Do you know who I am?"

"Yes, I do. You are coward. Traitor." He removed his dagger and held it over the flames in the hearth until it glowed hot. "And now we have fun."

"Wait, don't!" Shadeglen shouted in desert elven. "Whatever you've been paid, I can meet. I can pay more."

"You speak my language?" Laurent was taken aback, startled. He'd yet to meet a Hinderan educated in more than their native tongue.

"Please. I'll double your payment. Triple it."

Laurent sank his knife into the man's thigh, searing and burning him with the vicious cut. "Unlike you and your deceased friend, my loyalty cannot be purchased. Your actions have hurt two very dear friends of mine, and I have been sent to deal justice."

Shadeglen shrieked. He twisted on the ground and thrashed in agony, though it did him no good.

"Where I stabbed will not kill you. Yet," Laurent said. "In fact, you could survive with some healing. You *do* have a healer nearby, yes?"

"Guards! Someone! Help me!" Shadeglen screamed in Hinderan.

Chuckling as he yanked his blade free, Laurent waited a breath before he slipped it between Shadeglen's lower ribs, spearing him like a fish.

"This is my favorite part. When your lot realizes you are completely alone and there is no one to rescue you. Agony, isn't it? Much like the grief Ysolde will feel once I am forced to reveal your treachery to her. Because of you, a great man is dead. Sons have lost fathers."

"I'll tell you anything. Just stop the pain," the man blubbered.

"The quality of what you reveal will determine how little I hurt you. Whether I allow you to live, kill you kindly, or if I strip the flesh from your bones one inch at a time until you are a slippery mess not fit to feed a dog."

Given his choice, Shadeglen talked, and afterward, Laurent killed him slowly anyway.

***

Ysolde and Geoffrey remained in Lakeshire long enough to light Cedric's funeral pyre. While they had both pressed for his mother to join them in Ashdale, Gwendolyn insisted that she remain in Lakeshire. Neither the family business nor the town could operate without her. They returned through the portal, burdened with the knowledge that the killer was still out there.

"Laurent has returned!" Crispin shouted merrily. The fey child rushed into the audience chamber and leapt onto Ysolde's lap as she and Geoffrey concluded their judgment in a debt claim between two merchants. "Look what he brought me."

While Ashdale was a port city known for its wealth and trade, Shadeglen was known for its musicians. The boy held up a fine, silver flute, for which he demonstrated a natural affinity by placing it to his lips and letting his fingers fly along the holes. His jaunty tune brightened even Geoffrey's mood. It was like magic given sound, bringing life to the dour halls.

"You play well, Crispin. Come here. I think you're crushing my wife." He plucked Crispin from Ysolde's lap and raised the fey to his own broad shoulders.

"He wasn't quite so heavy a few months ago," Ysolde said.

"I think you're right, but that's to be expected now that he's had many weeks of healthy meals in his belly."

Ysolde smiled. "You're right. Shall we go meet Laurent together? Hopefully he has the news we lack."

Hopefully Laurent had gutted whoever was responsible for wounding her husband so deeply. That, she didn't voice, having sent the letter in secret. Geoffrey would have wanted to let justice prevail.

Once the boy was on his feet again, Crispin led them to the courtyard, his small hand warm in hers. Pink and purple streaks colored the evening sky, and the twin moons shone bright, low over the horizon. Laurent awaited them in the courtyard below with an unfamiliar wagon behind him.

"Hallo." He waved. Beside him, Etienne looked somber by comparison. Then again, she thought, Etienne always looked serious and grim.

"You're back sooner than I expected and with gifts," Geoffrey greeted as they joined the brothers.

"Of course I brought Crispin gift. It is little one's birthday." Laurent ran his fingers through Crispin's curly hair and beamed.

"What?" Ysolde set her hands on her hips. "Crispin! You never told us it's your birthday."

"How old are you now? Eight? Ten?" Geoffrey guessed after glancing the boy over.

"I'm three," Crispin declared.

Ysolde's mouth fell open before she asked in a halted stutter, "Wh-what?"

"He's a brownie child. Did you not realize?" Etienne asked.

"I knew he was fey, but I had no idea they aged so differently." Her cheeks warmed, but she felt better to glance up and see Geoffrey had also been stunned into staring at their ward.

"We can speak further about it at another time perhaps. For now, you may wish to dismiss him for the news Laurent has come to share is grave indeed."

Ysolde crouched and met the young boy's gaze. "Go let Madame Quirre know that you can have whatever sweet you'd like for dessert."

"Really? Even the honeyed cream?"

"Whatever you'd like," she promised. "Go on now."

Crispin darted off, and Ysolde stood, turning to Laurent. Geoffrey wrapped his arm around her as she leaned close to his side.

"I know it was you who saved my mother, Laurent, and I can't thank you enough. There are no words to convey the depth of my gratitude for what you've done."

Shaking his head, Laurent waved off his appreciative words. "It brings me pleasure to help you, Geoffrey. I am saddened to arrive too late for father. Trust all—nearly all—who play part in murder are now dead."

"Laurent and I discussed his discoveries, and the news isn't good," Etienne said.

Ysolde's eyes darted from the wagon to Laurent. "What did you find? Who did this?"

"Show them, but place it on the ground. Best for everyone to see," Etienne said.

With a stoic expression on his handsome face, Laurent set the heavy bundle on the cobbled path and unknotted the tie in the thick canvas. It fell apart, the corners of it falling to each side, and within that, there was still more material composed of the water-wicking oiled cloth used in the rainy season's fashionable cloaks.

"I apologize for state of gift, but I do as Princess commanded," Laurent announced.

The last knot loosened, and the fabric fell away, revealing a corpse. The eyes were wide and staring, the mouth ajar in a silent shriek, fingers curled into permanent claws.

Ysolde's eyes drifted over the bloodstained silks and rich, brocade vest. At first, she didn't recognize the ghoulish face, but she recognized the signet ring on the left hand.

Startled, Geoffrey leapt back and bellowed, "What in the void is this?"

"A traitor," Ysolde said.

"By all that is holy," Andras breathed. "You've murdered Count Shadeglen."

"No. He executed Count Shadeglen for his part in my assassination attempts. He will receive no funeral pyre," Ysolde said in a quiet voice, simmering with rage. "Place this cretin's corpse in the gibbet at the tower and let all know of his deceit. He will remain there until he rots."

Etienne stared at her, as stunned by the change in her as Geoffrey and Andras. Of them all, only Laurent appeared to be unsurprised.

"He hasn't yet told you what Shadeglen is guilty of committing," Andras said.

"Is he responsible for the death of Baron Lakeshire?" she asked.

"Yes," Laurent replied.

"Then my judgment is just, and my father will understand. All will know this is the reward for treason." She gestured to the broken body and turned her eyes to Laurent. "Thank you."

Laurent bowed deeply. "It was my pleasure, but as Etienne says, there is much, much more."

Geoffrey and Andras, still gaping at the corpse and in mirroring states of shock, gazed at her with uncertainty. The latter spoke first. "Shall I personally deliver his body to the tower?"

"I would appreciate it, Andras. Thank you. Let's take the rest of this conversation indoors."

Too impatient to reach her solarium for information, Ysolde's brisk stride led the three men to the formal parlor, a room located just beyond the entrance hall for receiving acquaintances and dignitaries. Upholstered furnishings in sage and gold silk surrounded a low, dark wood table decorated with a silver tea service for four.

Once they stepped inside, she shut and locked the door behind them.

"Tell me everything."

Laurent launched into his native tongue, the words flowing and lyrical despite the presence of guttural, hard consonants, an odd contrast that melded both components of the desert elven tongue. Etienne listened at first before translating.

"Shadeglen was not working alone, but he revealed a list of his conspirators prior to his death," Etienne relayed. "Lord Hinderwell, Count Hargrave, and Dowager Countess Fishwell. Lord and Lady Marbury, Lord Southglen, and Lord Fairdale. They're all working with the Iron Fist Mercenary Company."

Geoffrey's spine straightened. "Count Hargrave and the Marburys were at our wedding. The count shook my hand. He congratulated me to my face and smiled while wishing us a happy marriage."

Ysolde's stomach twisted, and she tasted her bitter lunch contents attempting to rise. "The Iron Fist saved Hindera from Fas Perra. My father paid them handsomely during the wars. We'd have never won if not for them."

Laurent continued to speak, and though little of his desert elven was recognizable, a single word stood out with familiar clarity among the gibberish: Aldemar.

"What of my father?" Ysolde demanded.

Etienne's frown lines deepened. "The plans didn't end with assassinating you. Shadeglen also revealed the next stage to their scheme was to eliminate the king and his family."

Her spine stiffened. "These conspirators must be gathered to stand trial for treason. Now. I want them all arrested and brought to the new prison beneath the tower."

"They'll never surrender to an arrest on the words of an assassin and one murdered count who died in terror," Geoffrey said. "No one will believe it."

"If they have nothing to hide, then they also have nothing to fear in answering your questions. Truly, Geoffrey, I don't give a damn what the nobility believes anymore. They can riot at Ashdale's gates if they'd like. Shadeglen's life became forfeit the moment he plotted the assassination of my family!"

When Andras returned from placing Shadeglen's body on prominent display at the watchtower, he and his lieutenants were brought into the room and given their orders.

She penned a letter to her father, asking not for his permission but alerting him to the threat. The missive ended with an abrupt warning of what she had done, and that within two weeks, she hoped to have the last of the six conspirators clad in irons.

Ysolde did not ask his forgiveness.

By evening, Nedic, Torrance, and Harrigan had ridden out, each taking with him a company of armed men ready to do battle in her name if necessary. They carried decrees bearing the wax sigil of House Westwood, the royal family, declaring the treacherous nobles as enemies to the Crown, and they were told to cut down anyone standing in their way.

As for the mercenaries, they were to be barred from the kingdom. Blacklisted from working again. Etienne believed if Shadeglen had been their only source of income in Hindera, they would soon grow bored, penniless, and eager to set sail to more prosperous shores. Swords for hire never worked for free.

While each company of men departed from the castle, Ysolde and Geoffrey watched from the east-facing tower of the castle wall as Ashdale Castle's security tightened.

"This will all be over soon." Ysolde slipped her hand into his and squeezed his fingers. "One way or another."

Uncovered

21

To her surprise, Aldemar didn't belittle her decision. He stood by her with the full authority of the Crown. Letters flew to every corner of the kingdom decrying Shadeglen's actions and promising death to anyone harboring the refugee nobles. As a result, the accused found no quarter or safety anywhere.

The royal army rode out to the south, and her father's useless spymaster consulted the stars, divined with his crystal ball, and read tealeaves that told them nothing useful.

Harrigan and his men commandeered two ferries capable of supporting all of their horses, and they rode the river south where they caught up with Lord and Lady Marbury on the southern roads, hoping to cross the borders into Fas Perra to take residence with her sister, a cousin of Lord Sabatois.

The Fas Perran guards had already received orders from Etienne, and politely turned them back at sword point. According to the prince, even Regent Sabatois, the representative of the goddess of madness, knew better than to harbor fugitives for her husband.

Of them all, Lord Fairdale was the only one to escape apprehension, but it wouldn't be long before Torrance's men, hounds, and scouts captured him.

Count Hargrave had devised a clever plan of his own, and when Nedic reached the city, he found it as well as Hargrave's castle under lockdown. With some convincing, the captain of the city watch joined forces with them, and together, they initiated an attack.

Geoffrey and Ysolde awaited word on the outcome of the battle, receiving their last updates a day prior by messenger.

The other six miscreant nobles had been tucked into the darkest corners of the newly established prison, issued rough burlap garments to wear, and given paltry meals of goulash and kippered fish. They received no wine, no silks, no finery, and Ysolde refused to hold trial until the last perpetrator was found.

While observing the members of the Ashguard sparring in the open courtyard, Andras and Geoffrey discussed the matters at their leisure.

"I have to admit, having the Fas Perrans around has been useful. We'd have lost the Marburys otherwise. They turned meek as mice once I locked them in their cells, apart from one another," Andras said.

"Their usefulness gives all the more reason to consider a true alliance between the kingdoms. Only we know Aldemar will never tolerate the 'heathens' for long," Geoffrey muttered.

His cousin sighed heavily. "I admit I find it difficult at times, and I'm hardly the example of piety myself." Andras crossed his arms and frowned, studying Etienne from across the courtyard. "Look at his ugly staff. It gives the maids the shivers, and even the guardsman have sworn it glows at times. Simply glows, seemingly without warning or reason. As if it's watching them."

"I believe it's for intimidation, a fearsome object to strike terror into his foes. You know as well as I do the man has skill with a blade."

"That I do, cousin. I watched him properly thrash you until you caught the best of him."

"He's formidable, especially for a mage. Though I once believed as you, I wouldn't underestimate his talent with a weapon he carries so proudly."

"Let's find out then, shall we?" Andras cupped his hands around his mouth and called out, voice booming across the courtyard, "Hey, Fas Perran! Can you use that bloody walking cane, or is it merely for show?"

Geoffrey winced. "Wait, no don't."

Etienne's stride halted. He stood ramrod straight.

"Why not?"

"Because you've just issued a challenge."

"Of course I did," Andras said with a laugh. "You said it yourself—it's for appearances and shock value, right? I'll bash him into the dirt with my shield then the three of us will have a pint at the Goose and Tap."

Andras jogged down to the courtyard. Etienne had already cast aside his coat.

"No armor?" Andras questioned. "Or shall I use a wooden training sword to match your walking stick?"

He assumed his fighting stance, a cocksure grin on his face.

After an unsettling chuckle, Etienne flashed Andras a fragile smile in return. "My robes are enchanted, so no armor is needed."

He raised his hand to the skull capping his staff, untwisted the hideous thing, and set it aside on an upraised stone pillar, confirming Geoffrey's thoughts regarding the skull and that its presence was psychological. Beneath it, gleamed a jewel of enormous proportions, a jagged spire of opalescent color set within grasping claws of wood at its top, each shaped like a dragon's talon.

Etienne beckoned Andras with his other hand.

"Come at me." His tone was casual, at ease.

Andras surged forward with his sword. The crack of wood against steel echoed across the courtyard, loud as thunder. Geoffrey winced, certain the staff would break, but the weapon withstood the force of the blow, unbending and strong. Runes flared along its length.

A small crowd gathered, mostly guards and a few staff members. Jory and Marik moved up beside Geoffrey, the younger of the two staring with rapt fascination.

"The battlemages of Fas Perra are a terrifying sight," Marik said, voice low. "I'd forgotten how much. How the men around me would freeze in fear as they returned our dead soldiers to life and rained spikes of lightning from the skies."

"Does it trouble you to watch?" Geoffrey asked.

Marik shook his head. "No longer."

"He's not even using magic." Jory sounded disappointed.

"Andras would have a better chance against him if he did." Geoffrey laughed. "His shield is enchanted to repel spells and return them upon his attacker. Little good it does against this."

The spar wore on, with Etienne backing Andras toward the edge of the ring, his staff flying through the air in a series of spins and strikes with power as well as speed. It swept beneath Andras's legs and spilled him onto the ground.

Andras rolled to his feet again and lunged forward, feinting then swinging the blade. It crashed with another roar against Etienne's staff, and the jewel at its end flared.

Unceremoniously, with no precursor or warning, Etienne parried, and the blunt end of the staff cracked into Andras's face. Geoffrey, along with the other observers, winced in sympathy.

Andras managed to get in two more strikes, but another blurring sweep from the staff took his legs out from beneath him for the second time

He ended up flat on his back, with the crystal shard pressed down against his throat.

"Do you yield, friend?"

"Yield," Andras mumbled.

Etienne helped the defeated knight to his feet and brushed the dirt from Andras's cape, grinning the whole while. "I told you I'd need no armor."

Jory applauded the loudest. "That was great. I can't wait to tell Raennia when she returns. She'll be sore she missed it."

"Speaking of duties, we should return to ours." Marik nudged the younger man away after a respectful nod to someone past Geoffrey's shoulder.

Ysolde stepped up to her husband's side and slipped her fingers into his hand. "Etienne, that was amazing. I had no idea you were so efficient with a staff."

"You believe I'm good with a staff?" Etienne asked incredulously.

Geoffrey kissed Ysolde's cheek then said bluntly to Etienne, "You beat Andras into the ground with a stick."

Andras glowered at him. Shyla arrived with cloth to mop his face, which he took ungraciously before shooing the young woman away. She lingered, gazing at him with mournful eyes, and then hurried away without a backwards glance.

No one else noticed, but Geoffrey did, and it riled a simmering anger in him until he shoved the thoughts aside. Later, he would speak a warning to his cousin on Shyla's behalf.

"His arrogance lost him that fight." Etienne laughed. "He came into the spar expecting to thoroughly teach me a lesson and found himself bested. That's all there is to it. I would have lost, most certainly, had it been Geoffrey or even Marik."

While Andras concealed his thoughts beneath a mask of growing indifference, Ysolde only grew all the more curious. She eyed the weapon and raised a brow, expression reminding Geoffrey of when she suspected Crispin of conducting fey mischief.

"How did your wooden staff stand up against a sword?" she asked.

"Whoever told you it's wood?" Etienne retorted.

She remained unconvinced but leaned forward to study the weapon. "What else could it be?"

Etienne smiled. "It's bone. The whorls are not the rings of a tree's wood. You see not a branch, but a sliver of a dragon's bone polished and worked for many years."

"I had no idea bone could be used. But a dragon? Truly?"

"Indeed. Rare to find in our Age, when dragons no longer fill the skies," Geoffrey mused.

"It's lovely."

"You may hold it, if you'd like," Etienne offered.

Ysolde took it gently in both hands. "It seems so light. Lighter than I thought it would be."

Etienne chuckled. "It's dragon's bone, so of course it's light. How else would one soar across the skies?"

"Where did you get it?" Geoffrey regarded the weapon with equal interest.

"My good friend, Rhystheren, is a master stavecrafter, as they're the only ones with the skill to work dragon's bone. It can take a decade to carve one staff, years to polish, months to etch a single rune. I waited quite a long time to receive this one from him, and of course, it was worth it."

Ysolde's fingers gently touched the crystal held at the top. "What's this gem?"

"It's called a naiad's tear. They're found only in the depths of the Sea of Troubles."

"I've never heard of them, but it's beautiful just the same."

Geoffrey recognized the look in Ysolde's eyes. She'd scour her library for days in search of information on the unknown gemstone.

"They're rather malleable when it comes to magic. As offered before, I'd gladly write to my friend. Crafting staves has been his life's work for the past few hundred years. He collects the bones from old ruins found in the Crestolian deserts."

"An elf then? A few hundred years. He must be as old as Fingall."

Etienne nodded. "He's quite old. Five hundred, if I recall, if not nearer to six."

She considered the offer. "Write him, please, and extend my invitation. I'm certain Fingall will take pleasure in having the company of another elf for a time."

"Excellent. I'm most certain Rhys would appreciate the same." Etienne bowed to them and continued on his path while Andras sat on the steps, mopping the blood from his stinging nose. "Well fought, Ser Everly."

"You deserved that," Geoffrey said.

"I did."

"Pinch it and tilt your head back."

"He hits fast," Andras grumbled.

"Well, at least we share the experience now." Geoffrey laughed and clapped his cousin's shoulder. "We'll see you at dinner. Until then, get some rest."

Geoffrey decided to hold his words regarding Shyla until later, saving Andras a further loss of pride. He'd suspected for a long while something was brewing between them, a theory cemented by her haste to tend his injuries and Andras's surge of impudent ingratitude.

Once Andras was gone, Ysolde orbited her husband, swishing his cloak with one arm before she neared him from the front and pressed surprisingly close. Her palm flattened to his tabard, fingers splayed above his heart.

"Yes, my Queen?" he asked when she said nothing, only gazed at him.

"I'm not queen yet," she murmured.

"Soon-to-be. Our Queen-in-Waiting," he teased. "How may I serve?"

"I came out to ask if you want to join me for a ride."

As the clock tolled the tenth morning chime, Geoffrey groaned into one hand. "While that would be lovely, I've promised to meet Gregor. We've got bandit sightings in the countryside. If it's the Iron Fist, I hope to let them know they've overstayed their welcome in Hindera. They can either throw down arms or join those in prison."

"Must you go with him?"

"I don't have to, but I want to. He's paying a personal welfare check upon one of his lieutenants. The man lives with his family two hours north and rides into town each morn. Never fail."

"Until now?"

"If he hasn't returned today, this'll be the fourth morning he's failed to report. I thought I'd have a look at progress on the new tower while we're out."

"You'll take men along with you, I hope. And home in time for supper?"

"At least a dozen, and you have my word that we'll return by evening for dinner. Try to remain out of trouble until then."

After a chaste but affectionate kiss to her cheek, Geoffrey rode to the watchmen's barracks to meet their captain. He, Gregor, and a dozen men from both the local city watch and the Ashguard, devoted their morning to personally investigating claims of danger in the foothills, an allegation proven true once they saw smoke on the horizon and tracked it to a single smoldering homestead.

"This your man's home?" Geoffrey asked as they approached a home reduced to a skeletal frame of charred wood and a shattered, sagging roof.

"It is." Gregor dismounted and drew his sword. "Looks like whatever happened here, he took one of theirs."

He kicked over a corpse in dark leathers sprawled across the walk leading to the crumbling stone steps.

"This doesn't look like the Iron Fist. The armor is ill-fitting. Scavenged, by the looks of it," Geoffrey observed.

"Could be thieves capitalizing on the fear sown by the trouble among the nobility. With so many of our people engaged in battle to the east, this would be the opportune moment to strike," a young watchman said.

After their combined forces swept through ruined winter crops, they came upon the outlying buildings near the pasture. It was barren, cold, hard earth and mere rubble.

Gregor spit in disgust. "Not a bloody chicken left in the roost. All the livestock gone."

"They've kicked in the door to the storeroom here. Empty," Geoffrey called to his friend. "Not even a wheel of cheese remains."

"Cheese? That's an odd thing to point out. Hungry, lad? Has our princess withheld your meals?"

"I'm not hungry. I'm merely saying they've gotten it all," Geoffrey grumbled.

Deeper investigation discovered the charred remains of a hound but no human bodies to accompany it. "The occupants were taken, or they fled for safety."

"Knowing Samson, the latter. He'd want to get his family to safety."

"Yes, but why not send a bird? Pass a warning?"

"You know as well as I do those things can get shot down."

After riding farther into the country, they met with the heads of three more farming households. The owners of the other home had vanished without a trace. No one had taken them in, but everyone appreciated the warning.

Later that evening as Gregor and Geoffrey rode on the trail toward the city, the cool mountain wind swept down into the plains and cut through their heavy armor. An early winter was on the way.

"They're likely to be thieves dabbling in slavery, no doubt. It's happening more and more frequently," Geoffrey stated.

"And what do you plan to do about it, mate?"

"Train more men. I'll order guard outposts to be constructed in the hills to accompany the soldiers in the towers and commission more of those gnomish telescopes. I want them to stand watch in all places, at all times."

"Those are a lot of wants. You've certainly adjusted well to your new title," Gregor said dryly. "The mages are predicting the harshest winter Ashdale has known in a century, and you plan to put men in godsdamned towers."

"I do, and they'll be well-paid for it. Uh. I hope. I plan to speak with my wife once we return. I suppose eight additional silver a head should suffice for all, watchmen and Ashguard alike."

"You're the duke, mate. Clap your hands and make it so."

Technically, Geoffrey could execute any edict he desired, but he had yet to take advantage of his new privileges. At the city gates, he and Gregor parted ways, one to return to the barracks to issue new patrol orders, the other to return to the castle. Geoffrey tracked down Andras to relay the horrible news from the hills.

"Bandits, you say?"

"A larger band from the looks of it, capitalizing on the fear the Iron Fist has already spread. Unless they've turned to petty crimes to make their profits in the absence of Shadeglen's purse, it couldn't be them."

"What's the plan?"

"I'll let you know once I've consulted the princess."

Andras held out a hand for him to slow. "Hold it. I feel it's my duty as your friend and relative to warn you of emminent danger. It's about bloody time you arrived."

"What? Was there a rush?" Geoffrey asked.

"Your wife's asked me twice of your whereabouts since supper, and she's quite pissed," Andras warned him.

"Damn. How long since supper?"

"Nearly three hours," Andras replied.

Ysolde would be in bed by now or curled up asleep in her study with a book. After peeking into the study and solar, finding them empty, Geoffrey headed upstairs.

Maribeth awaited him in his personal chamber. She'd served faithfully as his chambermaid and personal bath attendant for as long as he'd been a knight in Ysolde's service. They'd developed a strange friendship filled with sometimes genuine flirting, and yet it had never become anything more. He had no more desire to bed his half-elf maid than he did to sleep with their elderly but eccentric cook.

In the days after Ashlynne had ended their betrothal, he'd fielded veiled offers and subtle hints from among the female staff.

"I've run you a hot bath, Your Grace. May I help you with your armor?"

Geoffrey scowled at her and received an impish smile. Each member of the staff, in their own way, had found humorous methods of adjusting to his promotion.

"If you were a child, I'd swat your arse," he muttered.

"Then as an adult, I say you're quite welcome to do it," she teased. "Or rather, you would be if we weren't under threat of fire and doom from your princess."

One by one, she relieved him of his armor and clothing. The clothing was set aside to be laundered, but she returned his armor to the stand and set his blade by the bedside where Geoffrey preferred it. The years as his personal servant had afforded Maribeth an understanding of his preferred routine.

The soothing, aromatic fragrance of the Hinderan gum tree wafted from the steamy water. It was known for its soothing qualities and ability to loosen tight muscles but difficult to extract, an extravagant purchase. He stepped down into the deep basin and let the menthol scent surround him and pervade every aching pore. Maribeth rolled her sleeves above her elbows and perched on the edge, finding a delicate balance providing the reach she needed to attend his back.

"You're so tense," the maid murmured.

Geoffrey sighed and tilted his head forward when her fingers reached the base of his neck. "It was a long day of hard riding, and yet another one awaits me tomorrow."

In the past, she'd sometimes knelt behind him in the tub, her soapy, warm breasts pressed against his back as she applied firm pressure to his shoulders. Maribeth remained clothed, and for that, he was oddly relieved.

Marriage to Ysolde had changed the dynamic of every relationship he held among staff and friends alike. Andras had spent a day calling him Duke Ashdale, but he'd made the prestigious title sound like a taunt. It had stopped after Geoffrey had punched him in the chest.

"I take it that means you'll need another of these now that you no longer visit the Primrose."

He hadn't been to see Rose for a massage since his wedding, and it was beginning to show in his aching muscles and joints. He'd have to make up for it soon. She didn't rely on his money, but they enjoyed the casual, friendly company.

"No doubt that I will. How are you enjoying your lessons at the Primrose?"

"It's splendid. Thank you for arranging it, Your Grace."

He groaned. "By the gods, I promise to drown you if this has to persist."

Maribeth squeezed his left shoulder, her touch tender yet friendly, a reassuring gesture he'd needed. "I'm sorry. You know we do it only in jest. At first, I never knew what to call you anymore. In a way, this is awkward for all of us."

"You didn't have to attend me anymore, Beth. Go on. I can finish." He'd spear a sponge onto a stick to reach the places he lacked the agility to reach on his own before he forced her to endure further discomfort.

"No, no. It's all right. It isn't the bath that's awkward. I've been scrubbing your back four bloody years now. That's not the concern. It's just…" She chuckled. "I suppose most of us were expecting you to change once you became Duke Ashdale. It seemed natural you'd want your rightful title and all you've earned. But no, you've aspired even higher than that. Prince Geoffrey. It would have turned most men into arseholes."

"Sorry to disappoint," he said with a laugh. "I'm the same man I've always bee—"

"Geoffrey?" The door connecting to Ysolde's room opened. "Is everything all— Oh."

"You're not asleep?"

"You can go, Maribeth."

The girl opened her mouth then cut her eyes toward Geoffrey for instruction.

"Out!" Ysolde snapped.

"I'd do what she says, love," he suggested, hoping to spare her Ysolde's wrath.

"Good evening, Your Graces." Maribeth stepped away and curtsied in perfect form to Ysolde, who remained silent and stiff until the door to the room closed.

"I did not realize you bathed with company," she finally said.

"Don't you?"

"No. Our wedding night was the first time I was fully attended. I find bathing pleasant because it is the only time I am ever truly alone, for at least a little while. No one watching. No one listening. No one expecting me to be without flaw."

Geoffrey hesitated a moment before voicing the thought on his mind.

"You *are* flawless, my lady. For me, ever since I first became a squire, it was the one time of the day when another serviced me instead. I looked forward to it." He remained submerged in the tub, watching her from across the room. "How different we are when it comes to bath time."

"Would you like me to send her back to you?"

"Does it trouble you?"

Ysolde's silence spoke volumes. Of all the things he'd sacrificed to improve her happiness, losing his bath attendant seemed minor in comparison.

"You came for something," he prompted. "What may I do for you, my lady?"

"You were gone a long time. Longer than I expected," she rambled. "When I realized you were back I thought... I wanted to be sure you were well, Geoffrey."

"Gregor and I underestimated the trouble in the foothills. I apologize if my tardiness upset you," he offered. "Knowing your bed schedule as I do, I thought you'd be fast asleep by now and planned to join you once bathed."

"I couldn't sleep. I'd hoped to find you... Well, it doesn't matter. I'm sorry I interrupted."

The realization struck him, painfully clear, a startling lance of truth.

Ysolde was jealous.

He'd never seen it before, never witnessed her jealousy, but the existence of it startled him. He stared.

In an urgent voice, he quickly spoke out, "I seem to be found. Whatever you wanted, surely you can ask it now."

Geoffrey shifted in the tub, and with a washcloth, resumed the task Maribeth had left unfinished.

"May I help with that?" Ysolde asked instead.

After he beckoned her closer, she took up the wet sponge and claimed a precarious perch on the ledge, too shy to join him, too short of limb to kneel beside the basin.

Despite the steaming water, Geoffrey shivered when she touched him. Anticipation made him hyperaware of her presence, so he directed his attention to another topic. "While you're here, may we speak of a few matters?"

"Of course."

Ysolde didn't massage his shoulders the way Rose or Maribeth did, but her soothing touch glided over his bulky muscles. Fortunately, semi-opaque suds floated on the scented water and concealed his arousing state.

"In light of the bandit problems in the hills, I'd like to hire a few stonemasons to construct a dozen additional towers throughout the duchy. As Ashdale grows, we'll need more city watchmen within as well."

If only the watchtowers had been there weeks ago for his mother and father.

"That seems wise and reasonable. It will provide additional safety for our citizens and also supply jobs before the snowfall. Fingall will help arrange it."

"Thank you. They've worked hard for a pittance. Would you be amenable to increasing their weekly wage by eight silvers, my lady?"

"Certainly."

"That's it?" He'd expected questions at the very least.

"Geoffrey, you know what's needed." She ran the sponge down his spine, beneath the water all the way to his tailbone.

A second later, her fingers traced over a scar. He knew the scar's placement, able to guess at her fascination without seeing her. He'd been slashed down once in training as a squire, a hard lesson from a battle-hardened paladin about watching his rear. The old man had wanted Geoffrey to learn early in his career to never expect his opponents to bear the same honor he upheld.

Some men were always willing to cut another in the back.

"I do, but I've grown accustomed to seeking your permission."

"You're Duke Ashdale now." Ysolde worked lather through his hair. "If I disagreed with you at every turn, how would that look?"

The smile was in her voice again, but this time Geoffrey peered over his shoulder to see it.

"Besides, I value and trust your opinion. You have a smart head on your shoulders, Geoffrey." Ysolde leaned toward the faucet, gave it a turn, and filled the bowl with lukewarm water. She rinsed his hair with a whispered warning to close his eyes then asked in a louder voice, "Was there anything else that came to your attention?"

"Nothing at the moment."

While he soaked for a while longer in the bath, Ysolde remained alongside him in conversation. When the level decreased, she turned the hot knob and added another capful of the alchemical mixture Rose had prescribed for his back.

Would Ysolde loathe it too, if she knew of its origins? Once the heat had diminished his lingering pains to a dull ache, he removed the plug and began to rise. Ysolde jerked to her feet as if to leave.

Geoffrey circled his fingers around her wrist, keeping her from moving away. "Why are you leaving?"

"You've finished."

"But you haven't," he teased. "Would you fetch me a towel?"

His wife crossed to the rack in two long steps and fumbled down a fluffy towel. Having Ysolde near taunted him, an unintentional seduction that made him hard as his sword's hilt.

As the water spiraled down the drain, Geoffrey rose boldly to his feet. He had no blankets, no smallclothes, nothing at all to conceal him.

His body glistened from head to toe. Rivulets of water ran down his muscular thighs, and he saw her eyes track the movement before flicking back to his face.

Ysolde held the towel against her chest. Her eyes were wide and midnight blue, contrast against the rosy flush coloring her cheeks.

Geoffrey wanted her to see him. All of him. Bared in the lantern light without curtains, sheets, or a scrap of cloth between her eyes and his body. Part of him expected her to flee, but she surprised him by stepping forward to buff his body dry with the same towel she'd clutched like a life rope.

"I lied," Geoffrey murmured.

"Oh?" Her blue eyes lifted to meet his gaze.

"I've one final thing for your consideration: we are to try to conceive, are we not?"

Ysolde nodded without a word.

He took a step closer without breaking eye contact. "Bed me again."

"If you give me a moment, I'll have Shyla ready me for you—"

"I don't want to wait." The words left him in a rush, quicker than he could bite them back.

She blinked. Confusion crossed her features. "I require her help unlacing my stays and taking down my hair for the night."

"As luck would have it, I have fingers," Geoffrey reminded her, impatience seeping into his voice. Aroused tension filled him as he maneuvered behind her. He plucked the laces to her corset and loosened them within seconds, a skill acquired with years of practice. It dropped to the ground, and moments later, the midnight velvet gown pooled over her feet too, leaving only her matching dark blue slip.

"Not my shift," she said quickly, resisting his attempt to draw the fabric down over her shoulders.

"I want to see you," he insisted while slipping the strap down her left shoulder.

"Please," she whispered, trembling.

Her trepidation took the wind out of his sails and stopped him cold.

"As you wish, Ysolde." Even if he wanted otherwise, he wouldn't press her to fully disrobe. "Come here."

Geoffrey took her smaller hand and led her to his bedchamber. Rather than take her to the bed, he settled her on a chaise near his hearth, the flames warming his freshly bathed skin.

Lacking a brush in his personal chambers, he began the tedious process of releasing her hair from its intricate styling. His fingers loosened her braids and ran through her glossy strands. Black curls danced around her shoulders and down her back, darker than the midnight sky.

Little by little, Ysolde relaxed beneath his tender ministrations. After her hair flowed neatly down her shoulders, he plaited it in a single braid, well-practiced from nights when Ashlynne once shared his sleeping quarters. His heart pounded as he took his wife by the hand and led her to the massive bed. Maribeth had turned back the covers on the way from his room.

"You have a choice now, Ysolde. We sleep in my bed, or we sleep in yours. In mine, there will be no clothing between us."

"Geoffrey…"

He cupped her cheek and swept his thumb back and forth over her smooth skin. "Surely you are not so shy as to always hide from me. The choice lies with you, my lady. My bed and only our skin, or we go to your chambers. Choose."

"I have scars," she whispered as her gaze dropped away.

"As do I."

"Men are meant to have scars. They're badges of your honor, proof of your strength and all you've accomplished in the service of others." Ysolde raised a hand to his shoulder where the jagged marks and indentations from her demonic assailant's teeth remained.

"Are they not the same for women? Why should scars detract from your beauty but enhance mine?" he asked in a soft voice. "Do you think me to be so shallow a man that scars would trouble me?"

He hadn't seen them, and he couldn't begin to guess at their severity. As Ysolde calmed, he loosened the ties at the front of the thin camisole until it gaped at the front and exposed a single, full breast. It slipped from her left shoulder, revealing more almond brown skin. With the next nudge from Geoffrey, it glided to the floor.

"Behold. The beauty. My wife in all her glory," he whispered, standing too close to appreciate the full view of her nude form. He leaned back and drank her in, the sight of Ysolde's body setting him ablaze with desire.

If disgust was her expectation, he gave her none, only awe and profound appreciation for what had been only mystery until now. His hands ran the silhouette of her ribs, his thumbs beneath the subtle curve of her breasts.

A burn scar. Taut and shiny, the pale contrast against her golden brown complexion swept like paint toward her navel.

"Was that so horrible?"

"I didn't want you to think less of me," she confessed, her voice small.

Geoffrey pulled her into his arms and held her close. When she melted against him, he took it a step further, letting his palms smooth up her bare back.

"I could never think less of you, Ysolde."

Because he thought the world of her. At some point, she'd transcended the role of the dear friend and princess he had sworn to protect, becoming a beloved wife instead. He struggled to find the words and give breath to them, so he kissed her instead.

He hungered for her, taking his cues not to stop when her fingers curled against his shoulders, gripping instead of pushing. Her lips parted first without coaxing, and the intuitive flick of her tongue urged him to mirror her.

He'd thought her shy at first, or even inexperienced, but he quickly learned kisses were where Ysolde excelled. She raised to the tips of her toes, elongating her body against him. Her small, pert breasts were warm against his chest, her nipples tightly budded.

"Gods," Geoffrey groaned, turning his mouth from her lips.

She sucked in ragged breaths, her cheek to his shoulder. "I didn't speak the whole truth before."

"Then speak it now."

"I couldn't sleep because I missed you there beside me."

"And I wanted to be at your side," he whispered.

Their mutual confessions brought silence and more kisses, subtle exploration of fingers creeping over flesh, tracing muscles, following lithe curves, pressed so closely he couldn't examine the naked bounty of her body with anything but his hands.

Step by step, he guided them closer to the bed until the edge of it struck his thigh. Ysolde didn't receive a chance to argue or resist. He swept her from the floor and placed his wife onto the cool sheets.

"You're beautiful," he said as he sprawled beside her.

The scarring began to the left of her navel. There, the flesh was pinkish and shiny, old burns healed but lacking the pleasant brown hue covering the rest of her body. It crawled upward, a testament to her willpower, that she'd known such pain and survived.

"Beautiful," he said again. Before she could protest, he lowered his lips to the scarred flesh beneath her breast and kissed it.

"Stunning." He kissed higher, brushing his lips against the gently rounded curve.

"Exquisite." Higher, he found the dusky peak, untouched by her old injuries and stiffened with desire. His lips closed around it, and he sucked, releasing it with an audible pop.

"Perfect, Ysolde." He kissed the broad plane of discoloration wrapping her ribs. "Mine. Tell me what you want."

"I want to look into your eyes this time. To kiss your lips and have your whispers. I want you to take me to bed because you want me, not out of duty for a child."

His hand fell to her wrist, thumb tracing the inside of it before he guided her fingers below his waist. "Would you believe this to be inspired by duty for a child alone?"

Ysolde's breath hitched. Agile fingers traced over the hard column of flesh, hesitant at first and then with unconcealed curiosity.

"*Yes,*" Geoffrey hissed between his teeth. "See how you rouse me, Ysolde? See the things you do to me?" He claimed her mouth again in his hunger for more. Her lips were sweet, and kissing her had become his new addiction.

"I want us to have the night we both deserve."

"We will." He groaned and thrust forward against her hand. "Gods, we will."

When she gave no opposition to his touch, he traced her slick divide, encouraged by her breathy, sweet sigh. All the while that he explored her petal soft flesh, there was a desperate, all-consuming need for more, to sate himself in in the treasures of her body and know her once again as his wife.

"Have you ever touched yourself this way?" he asked.

Hot color flooded her face.

"I… That is to say…" She squirmed beneath his next teasing stroke and the entrance of a second digit. "Yes and no."

His restraint waned.

"Have you or haven't you?" he teased. "There's only one answer, love."

A feverish heat radiated from her receptive body, bared and open to him without reservation or shyness. Desire made his mouth as dry as sand, so he whet his thirst by lowering his head between her thighs.

"Geoffrey, what are you— Oh!"

Ysolde's hands clung to his fair curls and tugged at the roots. His tongue took the place of his fingers, fervor in his pace until her body stretched rigid over the sheets and throaty cries passed her lips.

Across the room, the flames in the hearth blazed white-gold and spiraled high into the chimney. Chuckling, Geoffrey turned his face and kissed the inside of her thigh. The slender limb quivered and tensed beneath his mouth.

"Why are you stopping?" she protested while tugging his hair. "Don't stop."

"I want to feel my wife shudder around me."

He needed to feel her spasming around him in climax, to watch her head fall back in rapture, her eyes wide in startled surprise. He wanted to hear his name from her lips. It was a visceral pang that hit him so hard that he was startled by the very real and true ache of blossoming love.

There was no apprehension of hurting her this time. While she was no less tight, her snug embrace yielded to his size. Ysolde responded beautifully beneath him, amenable to his guidance whether by voice or touch.

Each hesitant shift and startled gasp reminded Geoffrey that he was the first to know her so intimately, and the humbling thought filled him with a renewed resolve to show her every delight he could offer.

Recompense arrived with the sheer bliss of her body's tightening hold. Her heels pulled him in closer while her back arched up from the bed, her head tilted back against the sheets. As sweet as her mewling cries were, they lacked the one sound he wanted to hear—his name.

Their moans mingled as Geoffrey quickened his tempo, his chest crushed against her firm, rounded breasts. Her nails dug into his back, pinpricks of pain that he happily accepted. He groaned long and low, his seed spilling in her with a rush. When it was done, he slumped down upon her equally relaxed body.

"I cannot move," Ysolde mumbled in a sleepy slur, eyes already closed. Likewise, he was content to lie still upon her, his body sapped of energy and limbs no better than leaden weight.

"Why would you want to?" he questioned.

She answered him with a lazy kiss. What was meant to be gentle and tender evolved into something profoundly deeper. Ysolde's fingers anchored him by a handful of his hair, but Geoffrey had no inclination to pull away. Not for as long as he drew breath.

"Gods, I want you again," he moaned against her lips.

He made love to her a second time with her atop him, slower and less frenzied, but no less thorough with his touches. Afterward, as they lay cooling together, they barely stirred when Maribeth tiptoed inside to tend the dying hearth fire.

Untested

22

 **F**amiliar warmth greeted Ysolde's slowly waking state. She burrowed closer to the source and blearily opened her eyes when a rhythmic beat intruded upon her senses.

Geoffrey.

He held her tight as if she were something dear and wanted. Even though she was trapped, Ysolde experienced a quiet enjoyment and sensation of belonging. Her body ached, but it was different than the morning after her wedding, akin to the weariness she felt after a long day of riding.

Did he always have so much stamina? How did any one woman satisfy such vitality? The reflective thought led her to wonder if that was why he frequented the brothel.

As he slept, she took the opportunity to study him. Geoffrey's leg hairs tickled her toes as they rubbed against him, quickly warmed by the heat he radiated. Following her silent wishes, Ysolde lifted a hand to his face and smoothed an unruly golden curl away from his brow. She traced his face without touching, fingertips hovering a hair's breadth above his skin while she learned more closely the features she had seen for so many years.

Geoffrey was a handsome man, and she had always thought so. Now, up close, she admired the length of his thick lashes and the slight bend to his nose. It had been broken once. The skew was subtle, but she found it intriguing and suiting to his features.

The moment he displayed signs of rousing, she dropped her hand.

"Good morning," she greeted when his eyes finally flickered open.

"Mm… good morning." While the window curtains in Ysolde's room guarded against the morning sun, Geoffrey tended to awaken with the dawn to begin his day. The room, aglow with warm sunlight, didn't permit sleeping in for long. "Fancy meeting you here."

"Yes, well, I found myself quite agreeably trapped and rather cozy."

"Oh, did you?"

The door flew open with a bang. Ysolde made a startled sound and dragged the sheets up to her chin.

"What is this nonsense of increasing pay to the watchmen? This duchy is not made of gold, you witless p—" Fingall came up short and stared at the two wide-eyed lovers in the bed.

"What was that, Fingall?" she said from beside Geoffrey. Was he truly insulting Geoffrey behind her back?

"Your Grace." The elf bowed and spun promptly, putting his back to them. "I came to discuss this talk of pay. Rumors have already spread through the castle from the city itself of a sizable increase."

"Eight silver a head will hardly break us, Fingall." Ysolde attempted to sound as authoritative as a woman could when huddling naked beneath bedsheets. Usually, she dealt with Fingall while dressed. "My husband made a fair point. We pay the men too little for the important job they provide."

Geoffrey snorted.

"We discussed it at length and were going to bring the numbers to your attention, weren't we?" She turned her head to Geoffrey.

"Very right," he confirmed.

"We will speak of this once you are available, Geoffrey," Fingall said darkly. He shut the door behind him.

"I'd better make myself decent and pretend to seek his counsel," Geoffrey said moments after the elf had left them in peace. "It'll hurt his feelings if I don't."

"Don't allow him to bully you," she warned as her nude husband moved from the bed and stretched beside the window, daylight shadowing each dip and highlighting muscular planes. She watched him with a blissful smile on her face.

At times, it was difficult to believe he belonged to her. Geoffrey was a paragon of honor, the very model of masculinity, a man any woman would feel blessed to take to her bed or stand beside in marriage.

And he was all hers.

"He doesn't scare me, Ysolde. You don't want to know how we converse when away from your presence, and frankly, I wouldn't have it any other way. Too many others have changed, blinded by my new title now. There's a chorus of 'Your Grace' wherever I go now from people who once called me friend."

"Duke or not, he should have always accorded you respect," she grumbled as she slid to the mattress's edge and tested the reliability of her legs.

"Fingall and I have known one another long before you came into rule. Take no offense."

"Yes, as I am often reminded," she sighed. "Fingall disapproves of my 'disrespect for tradition.'"

Geoffrey crossed to her in a few steps and placed his hands upon her hips.

"He is an old elf and set in his ways. He cares for you too." He paused, only to grin and add, "Did you see how quickly he spun about when he realized you were naked?"

"Maybe he'll stop barging into rooms," she huffed in reply. Geoffrey's touch, while innocent, set off a chain of fluttering ripples in her stomach.

"Would you like…" His words trailed as he glanced aside. "Nothing. I should tend to my duties."

"I'll let you go see Fingall then."

Geoffrey watched her a moment longer, his expression indescribable, confusing. He reminded her of a man clinging precariously to a ledge, unsure if he should take a leap of faith or continue to cling to safety.

Ysolde's back was suddenly to the wall, his lips crushing her mouth. He nudged her with his hips, introducing her to the part of him she'd craved since awakening.

"Geoffrey," she groaned against his mouth. The swift intrusion startled her but was not unwelcome. She grasped him with both her fingers and her body, eager for the unspoken promises lavished by his slow movements.

"I swear to the gods you're like a bloody drug."

Once they were finished, he left her covered in a light blanket while he enjoyed a necessary wash in their shared bath. Ysolde dozed again, useless, spent, and absolutely ruined for the rest of her day. No other activity when measured could hold a candle to the lovemaking they'd shared.

Their newfound affection, or rather, the transformation of it from friendship to marital bliss, provided the ideal distraction Ysolde needed from the dangers plaguing the city—a temporary distraction, nonetheless, as life and work carried on, forcing her to bathe, dress, and attend her court.

Orders were given to the staff, and despite the growing temptation to peek in on Fingall and Geoffrey, she hurried outside and to the guard barracks to search for the newly titled Knight Commander.

Andras thrived under the mountain of pressure thrust upon his broad shoulders, and as Geoffrey's replacement, the soldiers of her duchy flourished. He performed his former duties and Geoffrey's work without complaints, laboring harder than necessary to save the duke and duchess the stress of appointing a second-in-command.

"Andras, I'd like to go into the city. Are you available to escort me at any point today? I'll gladly wait until your time is free."

"I'm available now, Your Grace. But perhaps you'd enjoy having another escort in your company."

Ysolde's brows rose. While there had been no further attempts on her life in the recent weeks, she could name few guards with whom Geoffrey would entrust her safety. "Who?"

He nodded toward Raennia. Across the courtyard, she stood facing a training dummy. Her posture was without fault, strokes flawless and concentration focused. Ysolde took pleasure in watching her train, and she found there was art in it, much like watching a master perfecting his craft.

How long had the woman developed her swordsmanship skills before pursuing employment in the Ashguard? According to Geoffrey, Raennia's father had taught her, and what she lacked in experience, she offset with a voracious hunger for learning. She was their battle sponge, and the men quickly treated her as one of them.

"Raennia?" she questioned.

"It's what Geoffrey has trained her to do, Your Grace. She's returned from her time spent at the watchtower and appears quite ready, and more importantly, she needs to be tested."

Tested. The word sounded as forbidden as it was alluring. Her eyes darted to Andras and studied the self-assured smirk on his bearded face. "Geoffrey has no idea you've suggested this to me, does he?"

"He intended to do it in time, I'm sure. He's mentioned it to me in passing, but the girl will never have the chance to prove herself if the towers are the only travel she sees beyond the estate. It's a waste of talent, is what it is."

"Geoffrey would never allow me to leave the grounds with a single guard. Not unless that guard was you. Or him." Ysolde pursed her lips, realization coming to her mind. "Yes, I do believe I will. Good day to you, Andras."

He bowed. "Good day, Princess."

The Duchess of Ashdale had always done as she pleased, and with that thought in mind, Ysolde strode from Andras with purpose. Shoulders squared and head held high, she sought to defy her husband for the first time since their new marriage.

Was it true defiance? She didn't think so. It was shortly after the panicked coach ride and failed abduction when he'd confessed taking pleasure in knowing she could defend herself. If necessary.

But she wouldn't throw all of the rules in his face. Even dukes, with exception to Duke Riverdale who was known for his exceptional skill with blades, traveled in the company of a knight protector. Aldemar found the company of his brother-in-law intolerable and hadn't ordered him to change his practices.

Ysolde smiled as she thought of her father, wondering what he would think if he knew of her plans to strike out into the city in the company of a female escort.

"Your Grace," Raennia greeted her upon arrival. She sheathed her sword and bowed deeply, chest heaving. Sweat shone upon her brow, dampening stray wisps of auburn hair slick against her forehead and ears.

"That won't be necessary, Raennia. No need for that."

The young woman wore no knightly plate, but like all soldiers of the Ashdale duchy, she had been fitted and equipped with light chainmail beneath a black tabard emblazoned with a golden sunburst.

Smiling brightly, and with no shortage of amiable envy for the armor-clad woman, she said, "Your new armor suits you."

"Thank you, Your Grace. I need it to survive your husband's training. He hits with the might of a mountain giant."

"Would you believe he's tried to convince me to join him in the sparring ring?"

Raennia laughed. "With you, I believe he would go more gently."

"Perhaps."

"Is there something you need, Your Grace?"

"Yes. With your training coming to a close, has Geoffrey spoken to you of the duties you'll be asked to perform?"

"Not to any detail, Your Grace. I'd assumed I would shadow him for some of it."

"A good guess. Knowing Geoffrey, he'll still assign you a regular shift rotation. It will let you see how the day-to-day dealings go around the castle. The faces that pass through our gate. Then, of course, there will be your lessons with Geoffrey, but I would ask a personal favor of you."

"Anything you need."

"I'd ask that you, when available, accompany me beyond the gates when I visit the city. With the Festival of Giving approaching, I prefer to see things firsthand rather than rely on reports, and I know Geoffrey cannot always accompany me. I'd like you to join me in his stead."

"I'd be honored."

"Splendid. We can begin today."

"Excell— Wait. Today?"

"Is there a better time to begin?" Ysolde jittered with nervous energy, giving Raennia no time to answer the rhetorical question. She linked arms with the woman and strode with purpose to find Crispin.

Once he and the new groomsman had prepared Ysolde's light carriage, he accompanied them in the handsome steel-and-dark wood vehicle. The fey child had a fondness for bearing her purchases.

As the coachman navigated the streets, Ysolde explained her plans for the morning to her new chaperone. They would shop along the route to the magistrate's office. Then their path would curve into the temple district. Afterward, she planned to enjoy a walk in the brisk afternoon air and a snack from a vendor before returning home for tea.

They left the carriage at the city stables and continued on foot toward the busy marketplace. The first half hour passed with little conversation except for intermittent remarks from Crispin about the city, its weather, or the people. He had come a long way from the dirty, starving ragamuffin she'd rescued.

A swarthy-skinned shopper lurked at the edge of the herbalist's tent, clothed in dark, tactical leathers with numerous pockets and pouches ideal for storing tools. His long hair fell around his shoulders, framing a handsome face with chiseled features, full lips, and impossibly blue eyes on the verge of becoming green in the right setting. The pointed tips of his ears peeked from his dark mane.

Laurent.

It was a fine day for a shopping trip to the markets. Of course he would be out as well. She couldn't blame him.

"What do you think of this?" Ysolde asked her companion.

"I like the green one," Crispin chimed in. He lingered at Ysolde's side, eager to fulfill her first request.

"Your Grace, I—" Raennia stopped. Her gray eyes flicked to the colorful scarves and shawls on display.

"It's all right," Ysolde assured the hesitant woman. "You may be my escort, but you're allowed to speak with me, Raennia."

"I think the golden one with the dark red embellishments would suit you better. Bring out your blue eyes."

"Do you wear such fancies?"

"Nothing like this, Your Grace. They would be spoiled beyond repair working the fields, and I have no need for them in my armor."

"Does Geoffrey—" She halted, remembering their transferal of responsibilities. "Does Andras not grant you days away from duty?"

Deciding Crispin's good behavior was deserving of a gift, she neatly tied the green scarf around his neck, humoring him by making a makeshift cravat like the ones Etienne favored.

"He does. I fear I spend my free day either in the barracks or with my family. I tend to wear pants and tunics still."

"Are you not fond of women's clothing? Even with family?"

Raennia hesitated, and color crept up her neck into her cheeks. "I haven't much occasion for dresses."

Ysolde moistened her lips and glanced away, wary of offending the quiet woman. "Forgive my curiosity, Raennia. I only meant to learn more about you."

Letting the subject drop, she settled her bill for the three scarves and had one packaged as a gift, a peace offering to Maribeth.

Was she forever bound to be surrounded servants who viewed themselves as inferior and noble females who despised her true lineage? Ysolde loathed it. All she'd wanted since the day Aldemar had brought them from the tribes was to have a friend. Even Shyla had her moments of fulfilling the role of a servant over the duty of a friend. But in Geoffrey, she'd found that at last.

After donning the new scarf, worn as a hood over her dark braids, she continued on foot for the magistrate's office. The man worked out of a courthouse near the watchtower, where he presided over the city's criminal element. The underground jail, which had once been the modest temporary home for no more than a three dozen criminals, had been expanded to hold as many as a hundred occupants.

They spoke at length about her plans for the city and his reluctance to abolish *all* executions from Ashdale. Like Geoffrey, he found it impossible to believe they could become a province free of the death penalty, but he supported her ideas to restrict its use. Shadeglen and the corruption festering in the kingdom had opened her eyes to its necessity, and their meetings had revealed he wasn't the bloodthirsty judge she'd originally thought him to be. He cared about Ashdale and her people.

Ysolde emerged from his office to rejoin Raennia and Crispin in the foyer.

"Business complete," she announced. "We'll head to the temple and home."

Circling the watchtower brought the gibbet containing Shadeglen's mouldering old corpse into view. It had bloated beyond recognition in the two weeks since his death, staining the fine surcoat and trousers muddy brown.

Gregor had affixed a flyer to the brick wall behind Shadeglen identifying him, the word TRAITOR spelled below his name in oversized letters. His crime had been described in greater detail below that.

"What a waste," Raennia murmured.

"My thoughts as well," Ysolde agreed.

On the nearby street corner, a man in resplendent mage robes perused the day's headlines near the newspaper boy. They were black, worn over matching leather breeches, their silver trim fetching against the thick material. If her attention hadn't been drawn by the breadth of his shoulders or the gleam of his dark hair, then with certainty she would have noticed the ivory staff crossed over his back, an ashen, misshapen skull at its tip.

Both of them?

Her mood darkened. Of course Andras wouldn't court an altercation with Geoffrey by sending her with only the newly trained recruit.

"I suppose I should be the one glowering," Raennia said in a low voice beside her. "It's no offense against you, Your Grace. Your life is treasured, by your people and Ser Geoff— the duke."

"But it is an offense against you."

Her stoic guardian offered a quick, wry smile. "I am new and untested."

"It's deceitful," Ysolde murmured.

"Then I suppose all we can do is prove them unneeded."

Once they were home, she had every intention of exchanging words to the conspicuous pair of brothers shadowing her throughout Ashdale.

"The temple is our last stop, unless there is someplace you wish to visit afterward?"

"None I can think of," Raennia replied, more at ease. "Though I'd certainly be agreeable if you'd show me where to buy those cherry tarts His Grace favors. He shared one with me once, and I can never find the stall."

Crispin's little face lit up. "Those are my favorite. Can we get some? Please?"

"It's my hidden gem, but I'll share the location with you so long as you swear not to show Geoffrey. Otherwise he'll buy the poor man out every day."

"I swear on my sword," Rae vowed. Her solemn voice made the topic seem a matter of life and death. Then her expression broke into a smile as the two women and fey child continued to a brick path in the sloping hill.

Ashdale's Temple of the Trinity sat on the second highest point in the city, only the castle above it. Built from pale stone brought up from the southern desert, it gleamed a rosy gold during the sunrise and silver beneath the moon.

"My family offers prayers to Nox every season," Raennia offered without prompting when they reached the entrance chamber. Taking it as an attempt to initiate a conversation, Ysolde eagerly latched to the subject. Religion in Hindera had always been a fascination to her.

"Do Ashta and Nirmad hold places in your prayers as well?"

"Oh, yes, of course. It's only that Nox represents the life of a farmer so well, the struggle and hard toil involved in growing and harvesting crops. Mother still thanks her at the evening meals. What of you, Your Grace?"

"I try to remember all three in my prayers, but it is to Ashta I feel the closest. Come, they should be expecting me."

The temple had been divided into three levels, a celestial upper floor dedicated to Ashta, an earthly ground level for Nox, and a consecrated subterranean level where urns of the honored dead lined stone shelves chiseled from the mountain cradling the city. Each spacious room displayed a frieze carved into the stone walls depicting stories of the Trinity.

Ysolde led the way inside, smiling at Crispin's awed expression. He skipped ahead, running to the walls to trace his fingers over the gilded carvings.

"Please don't touch, young man," a sharp voice called out. "You'll smudge them."

"But I'm only looking."

When Ysolde reached the boy's side, she ran her fingers through his curls. "Crispin, please do as Priest Ferdinand says. Look with your eyes, sweetling."

"But they're so shiny."

"I'll keep an eye on him," Raennia assured her. As she flashed Ysolde an encouraging smile, she stepped into place behind Crispin and set both gloved hands on his scrawny shoulders.

The tall, elderly priest took his time approaching them, his steps slow. Ysolde waited, patient as ever, but she wondered at his seeming reticence.

"Your Grace, I hadn't expected you."

She arched a slim brow. "I sent a missive stating I would be by to help with arrangements, as I always have done."

"I was under the impression Duke Ashdale would join us to plan a budget for the upcoming celebration," Priest Ferdinand said. "Your Grace, perhaps this matter is better to be delegated to your husband while you attend to issues of lesser significance."

Ysolde's smile faded. "Pardon me, Priest. Would you kindly repeat that?"

"We would prefer to discuss matters of such importance with the duke. Surely you must understand our hesitation to move forward with the festival's plans without Duke Ashdale's say so," the priest said.

The elderly priest's words cut through her like a blade, leaving chill in their wake.

"You discussed the matter with me last year. And the year prior."

"And now you are married, Your Grace, with a husband to preside as leader of the city. I mean no offense—"

"Don't you?" Ysolde interrupted. "Isn't that precisely what you mean when you imply the addition of a husband to my duchy strips my word of its value? I was Duchess Ashdale long before Geoffrey Ashcroft placed this ring upon my finger."

"It is not how things are done. Please, I beg you to return home and send the duke in your stead. Celebrate your love of Ashta in a way beneficial to you and your new husband. In the meantime, know that we eagerly await news of an heir to bless in our lady's name."

"An heir," she repeated drily.

The priest continued, unfazed. "Indeed, Your Grace. We hope to ring the bells in your honor when you bring the word. Now, with a duke present, we should—"

"You men of Hinderan stock shame yourselves. You venerate a goddess, but when faced with a woman of flesh and blood, your words are proven to be little more than lip service. You disgrace yourself and Ashta's name."

Ferdinand's face purpled. He bowed deeply, clutching his prayer beads in a frail, white-knuckled hand. "My apologies, Princess. My profound and sincere apologies."

"Thank you," Ysolde said curtly. "Now please, let us view the plans for the festival as intended."

Tension remained between them until the conclusion of the planning stages. He avoided eye contact to stare at the gold tassels on his robes, giving short and abrupt answers. Once the final agreement was in place, Ysolde bid him a curt farewell and left the chamber.

"What you said in there," Raennia said after they reached the bottom of the stairs. "It was inspiring, Your Grace."

"I only spoke the truth of my mind."

"Which is more than what most would do."

Something made her pause and turn to study the guard at her side. Without further thought, she took Raennia's hands in hers.

"Ever since my arrival I have had to work harder to prove myself capable of overseeing this province because of my sex. Just as you have had to do. We've earned our places, Raennia. We shouldn't have to fight every day to keep them. Don't let them treat you different. Fight for every scrap of respect and show them no quarter."

"I will, Your Grace. Thank you."

They wound through the city and collected their promised pastries, but Ysolde could not shake the sour mood from her time at the temple. She wandered along in silence while Crispin chattered and stuffed his face with his treat.

Without warning, she jerked to a stop, pulled back by a firm grip on her arm. Raennia stepped forward and thrust Ysolde behind her, sword drawn.

A man in dark leathers stood in their path, a sword at his hip. The stranger's eyes burned with fury, and his hair hung lank around an unshaven face. He stank of ale, the smell wafting off of him in odorous fumes with old perspiration and the stench of livestock.

"Step aside," Raennia ordered.

"I have a bone to pick with her. This little savage bint let my brother dangle in the gallows. She let him die over a whore's word."

Raennia kept herself between the man and Ysolde. "Whatever your grievance may be, you can take it before the magistrate or attend an open audience like everyone else. I suggest you step back and let us pass."

He spit to the side and narrowed his dark eyes at Rae, drawing his sword. "What good is a bloody open audience when she's already killed him? Oh no, I want more than that."

The blanket of spectators to the stranger's rear made Ysolde reluctant to resort to magic, its use known for inciting panic in crowds. One misplaced jet of flame could mean doom for one of the onlookers surrounding them.

It was, of course, part of the reason why the king decreed it necessary for her to have a bodyguard. A mage's self-defense could mean doom for all in their presence, and she lacked the precise aim to confidently take down her assailant without endangering innocents. Tackling a demon with Geoffrey had been child's play, the alley empty, void of all other life.

Blades clashed, the sharp song of metal against metal whistling in the air, singing a cry of battle Ysolde had heard for years in their training yard. Raennia's longsword danced and swept her opponent's attack from its mark. Her riposte came swift, a sharp slash over the man's chest that bit a deep groove through his leather armor.

"This doesn't concern you, wench. Step aside."

"If you want her, come through me."

Ysolde's eyes darted to the streets. The crowd had distanced from them, the faces all blurring together to create a sea of color observing the spectacle. No one came to their aid.

A city watchman blew his whistle and shouted for the tide of onlookers to part. The thick throng of bodies reminded her of cattle grazing on a grassy knoll. Oblivious and unconcerned.

Where had Etienne gone? Or even Laurent?

The man fought with a skilled precision at odds with his unkempt appearance. Raennia couldn't break through his defenses, and the city watchman who had stood on the street corner may as well have been a mile away. Above the din of the crowd, Ysolde heard him threatening to use his blackjack to force their compliance.

The attacker drew first blood. Raennia cried out as the sword swept past her cheek and cut a thin line. She blocked, and then her next strike found a gap between the hard plates of studded leather.

Before he could recover from the sharp sting of her blade, her shield crashed into his chest.

He stumbled back from the blow, off balance and taken by surprise, only able to recover on account of fancy footwork maneuvering him from her next stroke. Otherwise, Raennia would have taken his head off. She missed by so narrow a margin a line of blood glistened on his throat.

Fire sizzled at the tips of Ysolde's fingers. The two fighters weaved in and out, their dance of blades witnessed by all. The crowd adjusted only as necessary, hoots and hollers for blood filling the busy streets.

Where was the watchman?

Her palms itched, hot and eager to release a spell, but she couldn't risk including Raennia in the inferno.

She didn't need to. In one smoothly executed move, the female guard disarmed her attacker. His sword flew from his hand to the pavement. Then the tip of her blade pressed to his throat. A drop of blood beaded from the indent in his flesh.

"Out of the way, people! Move!" A trio of watchmen pushed their way through.

Raennia stepped forward, forcing the man down to his knees. The watchmen broke through the crowd's edge, took in the scene before them, and rushed to secure him.

"Was the princess injured?" one demanded as the other two hauled away their struggling assailant.

With a heaving chest and perspiring brow, Raennia whirled to face her. "Your Grace, were you harmed?"

"No. No. I'm uninjured," Ysolde assured her, voice tight. "Not a scratch. He didn't have a chance to do anything to me after you interceded. I felt so helpless, but perhaps I should be asking if you are all right. You are the one bleeding."

Ysolde quickly removed a kerchief from her handbag and pressed it to Rae's cheek.

"Barely more than flesh wounds, and the battle wasn't any worse than sparring with your husband," Raennia admitted. "But perhaps that makes it all the more terrifying. I haven't been so afraid since bandits raided my family's home. I thought…"

Further explanation wasn't needed. Ysolde read it in her eyes, a mix of excitement and fear, confidence and terror.

"You performed admirably, Raennia. Perfectly. I wish I'd done more than stand there like an idiot while you fought for our lives."

"That's what I'm here for, but what of the boy?" Raennia turned sharply on one foot. "Where has Crispin gone?"

They found Crispin cowering out of sight behind a stall on the roadside. The child had fled, and neither of them blamed him for it. Ysolde coaxed him out and, with several tight hugs, convinced him neither she nor Raennia detested him for running.

"Come, we should return and report what happened. Then I'll visit the watch captain's office."

They endured the return trip to the castle in silence, too many thoughts weighing on Ysolde's mind to make conversation. While she had escaped the incident intact, she had no doubt in her mind that unless she fought for it, her first trip to Ashdale with Raennia would be the last.

"Thank you again for today, Raennia. For your company as much as the rest."

"I am happy to accompany you anytime." Raennia bowed then departed, purposeful steps carrying her toward the barracks where Andras had taken over Geoffrey's office.

Ysolde drew in a deep breath then headed inside. Ever since their return to the estate, she'd seen the guards whispering behind their hands, respectful as always, courteous and bowing to their princess, but holding conversations too low for her to hear. They knew.

From the corner of her eye, she spied Maribeth lingering at the edge of the entrance room. Her tense posture, stiff spine, and forced smile painted a portrait of obedience Ysolde never enjoyed to see in the staff.

"Maribeth?"

The girl stepped forward and dipped, curtsying low enough for her strawberry blond braid to touch the floor. "Pardon my intrusion, Your Grace, but your husband awaits you in the solarium. He desires your company for the midday meal."

"Has he said anything about my visit to Ashdale?" Ysolde asked.

"Sincere apologies," she murmured without raising her eyes from the carpeted floor. "Not to my knowledge, Your Grace. I know nothing but the command given to me." Her hands shook.

Ysolde produced the package from the shawl vendor. "I would like to give this to you. After my poor display of temper last night, this is the least of what you deserve."

"Your Grace owes me nothing."

"Please, look at me."

Maribeth raised her eyes, wariness etched in her delicate features. Her slender, tapered ears twitched.

When Aldemar had first titled her as duchess and sent her to Ashdale, the castle had been staffed generously with servants devoted to not only the former duke, but those loyal to the Westbrook name, and by proxy, Ysolde as well. She'd found the residence occupied by only smiling and supportive faces. Maribeth had been her uncle's personal chambermaid as well, a sweet girl, a few years younger than Ysolde, thrilled to have a job to help support her ailing human mother.

"You and Geoffrey did nothing wrong," Ysolde assured her, "but until you've heard otherwise from me, I will assume your evening duties. You're not to blame for my failure to learn my husband's preferences."

If Geoffrey enjoyed bathing in company, then he would receive company. His *wife's* company. Every night if she could help it.

The idea of meeting him for the evening bath thrilled her, sending shivers of anticipatory delight sliding down her spine and tingles to her fingertips.

But it wouldn't be the same for him, would it?

She knew from memory he preferred the famed bathing pools of the Primrose, where she imagined the attendants delivered a particularly personal service. Her, perched on the broad rim of the tub, would lack the appeal of a nude woman, slippery from suds and soap, water sluicing over exquisite curves and lithe limbs.

Ysolde set her lips into a tight line, considering her options. She'd have no choice but to join him in the bath.

"Your Grace?" Maribeth repeated.

Ysolde snapped out of her thoughts, cutting her eyes back to the beautiful half-elf. "Please accept my gift, with my apologies."

"Thank you, Your Grace. I accept your apology most humbly. If you'll come with me, I will take you to your husband."

Ysolde fell into step beside Maribeth, a lightness in her heart and a smile on her lips. Ysolde waved Maribeth off before she could knock on the half-open door and announce their arrival. Instead, she peered inside, her smile widening to see Geoffrey occupying his oversized armchair with a thin, leather-bound book spread over the palm of one of his huge hands.

He mouthed the words as he read. "'...and then he ripped my bodice, and all that I knew came undone, his hands fire that alit my skin with a thousand sensations as sharp as glass. My thoughts warred within, divided by the blasphemy of our courtly improprieties whilst I shuddered for breath.' What in the name of the void is she reading? Not remotely accurate," he voiced the latter out loud. "That shouldn't feel like glass."

Maribeth's giggle alerted Geoffrey to their arrival while Ysolde froze in place, red from head to toe. Somehow he had found the wrong book, one she'd wedged between two spellbooks out of his sight. Geoffrey leapt up from his seat, a guilty smile on his face.

"Forgive me. I was just doing some, er, reading. How was your morning?"

"Eventful," she replied, stepping inside. Maribeth closed the door behind her and left them alone. "I stopped by the magistrate's and the temple."

"Ah, so that's where Andras was all morning. I had wondered." He took the cover off the large platter on the table, revealing a variety of sandwiches and sliced fruits.

"What do you mean? Andras didn't tell you?"

Geoffrey's smile faded. "Tell me what?"

"Raennia accompanied me during my rounds through Ashdale. I haven't seen Andras since this morning."

"What? You took Rae—"

She held up her hand to forestall his incoming reprimand. "You selected her as your squire with the intent to assign her as my guard. If she is to take on that duty when you cannot, she has to get used to being with me. She didn't lose me even once."

Her husband grunted and crossed his arms. "Did you even try to lose her?"

Ysolde smiled brightly and fluttered her lashes. "No."

Geoffrey laughed, and the tension in his frame vanished, giving way to shaking shoulders. He pulled her in close and dipped down to kiss her lips. "My clever wife, using my own logic against me."

"There is something you should know. Before we sit to eat."

"What's that?" He turned his face into her throat and delivered another kiss.

It would be easy to put off the bad news and enjoy more pleasant pursuits, but she knew Geoffrey too well. He would be furious if he found out later. Especially if someone else brought the news to him. So she kissed his cheek and stepped out of his embrace.

"There was an attack in the marketplace, but Raennia stepped in and brought the man down before any harm could be done."

She detailed out the encounter, a little surprised at how calm Geoffrey remained through it all. He looked her over, head to toe, when she finished then tugged her in close.

"I'm happy you're safe."

"You're not upset?"

"No, I'm not. In fact, I was the one who arranged the encounter."

"You what?" Her voice rose and cracked.

"The man Rae battled is a friend of mine from the monastery, Brother Cartleton. I wrote him weeks ago and asked if he'd pay a visit to test a squire of mine, and he arrived just this day."

"Why?" She threw her hands up in the air then lowered them to her hips, staring her husband down.

"It was nothing against you, love. I had to see how Raennia would react under legitimate pressure."

"She could have skewered him!"

"Which is why Etienne was on hand to throw up a magic shield before she could."

"Little good it did her," Ysolde grumbled. "She was sliced across the cheek."

Geoffrey winced. "Yes, well, the idea was to keep either of them from killing each other, not from averting all harm.

Raennia is a smart girl. If no blows landed a hit, she would have known magic was involved. I had Gregor explain to the watch before their shift turnout that we'd be conducting a drill and not to become actively involved."

"Fair enough, I suppose. Still, you could have told me about it."

"Apologies, Ysolde, but you're a piss poor actress," he said with shameless candor. He grinned wide and enfolded her in his arms, ignoring her stiff presentation to squeeze her against his chest. "I've seen you pretend that you're not sore about some matter or another."

She wrinkled her nose and stuck her tongue out at him in a childish gesture that earned her another kiss. Her annoyance mellowed. The wrinkles in her brow smoothed, and the hard stare, at times seeming sharp enough to leave puncture wounds in him, finally eased.

"Was it all really necessary?"

"It was. The truth is I cannot lock you away in a golden tower, and now that my duties have changed, I can't stand beside you each day. I trust Rae, and today she's proven herself capable."

Relief flooded through her. "Thank you, Geoffrey. I'm glad you think so."

"And if she doesn't skewer me for your shared ordeal, she'll be your new personal guard from this day forward."

FORGOTTEN MISERY

23

After three days of unrelenting rain, the day of the executions dawned bright and clear. The crowds cheered, accepting the arrival of the sun as a sign of the Radiant Lady's blessing.

The damp air had not been kind to Shadeglen's remains, and it was there beneath the dangling gibbet on the wooden platform where the treacherous nobles were paraded in their prison garments. While Geoffrey lent his support and strength to her decision, he balked at the idea of executing ladies.

It was unprecedented in Hindera. He cautioned her against turning the crowd to her disfavor, warning abrupt changes could unravel the public's trust.

"Listen to your husband, Your Grace. While change is a good thing in small measure, think of it as a fire given an excess of kindling. Too much before it's ready, and you'll smother the flames," Fingall advised her.

For the old elf and Geoffrey to come to an agreement was so rare an occurrence, she accepted their guidance, and the three collaborated over a more fitting judgment, unbeknownst to the eight facing trial.

One by one, their crimes were read, and Geoffrey, known for his kindness, his benevolence, and especially his ability to hear only the truth, questioned them.

"Count Hargrave, you have heard the crimes for which you stand accused. How do you plead?" Geoffrey stood before the line of men and women chained on the raised stage while Ysolde sat above them in a spectator booth. Her mouth pressed into a flat line.

"Innocent, for each crime was done in the name of our kingdom for a righteous cause."

"Then I declare you guilty and sentence you to death."

Geoffrey turned to the next noble. "Baron Hinderwell, how do you plead?"

"Please, I beg you, I had no idea it would come to this. I thought we merely intended to chase her from the kingdom. Force her to return to the savages—"

"Guilty," Geoffrey interrupted.

And so on it went, one man after the other, some pleading mercy and others spitting vitriol against Ysolde and the king, earning jeers from the crowd who urged the executioner to carry out his duties.

"Kill them!" a man in the crowd screamed.

"Traitors! Bloody traitors! All of them deserve to hang. The axe is too good for them!"

"We want a quarterin', Princess!"

The ghastly idea of drawing and quartering anyone turned Ysolde's stomach. She'd never witnessed such barbarism and had recused herself from spectating a single execution since taking over the city.

"I must say," Lorwick said as he took a seat near her. "It surprises me deeply to discover you have the conviction to order death among our peers."

Her skin crawled, having him so close.

"We must each do what's necessary to guarantee the security of our kingdom."

She forced herself to look at him, to truly look at the insidious beast beside her, and realized he didn't scare her. Never had. She'd always seen him as a spoiled child.

With that in her mind, she smiled. "Wouldn't you do the same?"

"Yes." Lorwick stared at her, taken by surprise. "I would. And I shall."

Geoffrey returned to his seat at her other side. Count Hargrave was taken to the block. He knelt and lowered his head without argument. The blade came down, and swift justice was served.

Ysolde flinched. Out of sight behind the wooden ledge, Geoffrey took her hand in his large grip. Lord Hinderwell was dragged to the block, sobbing every step, and Lorwick chuckled beside her once he died.

"You need not watch," Geoffrey whispered. "Anyone would understand if you looked away."

"No." Ysolde inhaled a deep breath. "I must watch. If I have the will to order their death, then I must have the will to witness it."

The next man was brought to the block, his eyes defiant and hateful.

"A she-beast can never rule Hindera. Killing us changes nothing!" Marbury screamed up to her.

The executioner kicked the baron in the back of his knee and brought him down to the ground. A guard forced his cheek to the block, and then his head tumbled to the stage as well.

When the last head rolled across the wooden stage, Ysolde shivered, palpable relief rushing through her veins like death's chill. There had been no gratification. She felt cold instead, although the act had been necessary and empowering.

She rose from her seat above the crowd and two remaining women. "As for you, you shall not be put to death to join your husbands and families. Your remaining days in this world shall be filled with toil and labor. High Templar Felix and his men shall escort you personally to the convent in Ackleton."

"No, please, Your Grace. I would take death instead," the countess pleaded. "I knew nothing of what Shadeglen planned. Nothing. We only gave him money!"

"Please, dear Princess, have mercy upon us," Lady Marbury wept. "Is it not enough you have taken my husband?"

Ysolde watched them. She thought of Lady Lakeshire, Geoffrey's mother, and the pain etched in her face. How she'd held the baroness for an afternoon and listened to her stories of Cedric's kindness. How he'd once taken mistresses at the start of their arranged marriage, but when he'd come to love her, it had all stopped. How she'd watched him change. How their affection had become genuine and she'd come to love him in return. How she knew not how to carry on without her best friend.

"No," the princess answered. "It is not enough."

The female conspirators were spared death but handed over to the Devout of Nox, bound for the convent in Ackleton near Hindera's deep southern border, where the simmering heat could blister the skin in seconds on the hottest afternoons. Their remaining days would be spent in the service of others, and for nobility, who had never worked a day in their lives, the fate was deemed crueler than death.

The citizens cheered her. Word had already spread throughout the land about her upcoming coronation, that she was soon to become Hindera's first Queen-in-Waiting, a momentous occasion to be celebrated by all. While she took little satisfaction in spectating the execution, she'd felt an abundance of elation when High Priest Ferdinand swallowed his pride and consulted her regarding the event.

Applause continued long after the carriage took them away.

"Smile, my love. You gave them a kind death. May Nirmad shepherd them to brighter places so that they may repent in death for what was done in life."

Ysolde gave Geoffrey a small, tight smile. "I thought I would be prepared for it, but I have no regrets. What's done is done, and we've delivered our message."

As the groomsman directed their coach onto the mountain road, it curved the upward slope, and she watched the city shrink through the window on the right. The sun shone over the historical mural chiseled into the rough stone at their left, and Ysolde thought one day, her image would be immortalized in rock as Hindera's first queen in her own right.

With every positive thought to uplift her spirits, a bleak memory darkened her triumphant mood with the sour notes of forgotten miseries. Of all the people she loved most, one person wouldn't be present during her finest achievement. The one person who, indirectly, was to thank for all she'd ever received in life.

"Geoffrey? I want to know your thoughts about something of importance to me."

"Yes?"

"Lately, I find myself dreaming about my mother, and I wonder if she thinks about me too." Ysolde bit her lower lip. She couldn't tell Geoffrey the loss of his father had inspired a whole new spectrum of emotions for a woman who had long ago become a stranger to her.

"I'm sure she does, love. You're her only child, after all."

Ysolde nodded. "I sent a letter to Brychas, an invitation really, to our wedding. I hoped a messenger would deliver it to her, but no response ever came."

Could she blame her mother for refusing to tolerate another day of living as the king's consort while he made perfect, pale-skinned babies with his new wife? She couldn't. At the time, Ysolde had been approaching her eighteenth birthday, and she'd spent all but the first three years of her life in Stormwatch. Fifteen years. Long enough to forget her native tongue.

"Darling, what were you hoping for if she'd answered?"

"I don't know. Ten years ago, I resented her for bringing me here and abandoning me," Ysolde admitted. She inhaled, letting the air fill her lungs and calm her. "Now I am glad. Had my mother never brought me here, I wouldn't have met you, Geoffrey. Had she taken me with her, I would never have known this, being with you as your wife."

"I sense a 'but' is coming."

Ysolde gazed out the window, avoiding eye contact. "Rhun would never take me to see them unless I swore to forsake Hinderan ways and return forever. Once, many months after Mother left us, I ran away from the castle and tried to find them. I couldn't. It was impossible. Tikiina and I wandered alone in the east hills until the royal guard and Father found us."

"You want to search again."

"I want to send Etienne. He knows how to find the clans, and Fas Perra remains in good standing with them."

Geoffrey's voice softened. "And if he finds her, what then?"

"I need to know whether she wants to be a part of my life at all or if she's happier without me. The silence isn't enough. I need the closure to move forward and know I've exhausted all reasonable options to know her."

"Are you asking my advice?"

"Yes," she said without hesitation.

"If it brings you peace, then send him."

"You don't think it's silly, sending away one of our most valuable allies when all has gone mad around us?"

Her husband leaned down and kissed her cheek then the other. "No, Ysolde. 'Silly' isn't a word I would ever attribute to your feelings."

"Thank you. Besides, we have the conspirators now. It should all be over. What's the worst that could happen?"

THE MAELSTROM

24

After a four-day journey to Lakeshire and three days aboard a ferry sailing down the Nirmean River, Etienne enjoyed a ride on his fellsteed into the deep southern province. During the winter months, Ackleton became tolerable—less of a sweltering death trap and more of a temperate holiday getaway from the frigid north.

Eventually, rolling hills gave way to rocky paths strewn with sand and swaying palms dancing in the balmy breeze. Nearly three weeks after embarking on his journey to the south, Etienne reached his destination.

Brychas was the Marcovian jewel of the desert, and finding it only became possible when one knew where to look. Etienne had met them in the past, years ago when he'd served in Fas Perra's military forces and led his own regiment of troops into the mountains. Then, he and his people had been taken in one cold, hungry night, and he'd never forgotten the neutral Marcogh's generosity.

He'd learned the wild folk built temporary dwellings at the foot of the peaks dividing Fas Perra and Hindera's northern borders. At the time, he'd been fascinated, and curiosity had inspired a search for them years later. He'd learned their language, listened to their stories, and a little less than two years later, he'd parted ways with a new respect for life beyond Fas Perra and invitation to return whenever the winds brought him to their trails again.

To the untrained eye, there was no oasis south of Ackleton. Only sand, shimmering air, and heat capable of boiling the hair on an unprotected head. Etienne followed the familiar markers taught to him during his guest stay, and he crossed the illusional curtain veiling the village of the wilderkin from their civilized brethren of the cities.

The buildings in Brychas shone under the sun with a soft lustre, crafted from peach-hued sandstone. Ancient sentinels—large winged-serpent statues—flanked the bronze gates leading into the city. Years of wind and blowing sand had polished most details away into a smooth mask.

Narrow channels of water ran parallel to the stone pathways through Brychas, the shallow canals routing water from a small lake between their city and the edges of Fellwood. The Marcogh settlement lacked a village square, or rather, it had improved upon the concept, and in its place there was a communal garden of vast size, filled with every green delight, fruit, and vegetable. Herbs grew wild in a state of edible, organized chaos beneath windows and beside doors.

"Welcome, wayfarer."

"Greetings to you," Etienne replied. As he dismounted Belle, the gatekeeper studied her with skeptical eyes. The man's shoulder-length braids shifted with the breeze, dark as night and tipped with clay beads. His russet skin was weathered from the sun over a lean frame with deceptive strength beneath fluttering silk robes worn open at the chest.

"You travel with the same creature. I remember you from many years ago. You came with your warriors from Fas Perra and were lost in the cold. We sheltered all of you and fed you warm meals that night."

Etienne exhaled a relieved sigh. "You have a long memory."

The gatekeeper's gaze mirrored the evening sky, dusky blue with glimmers of orange and fuschia. Legends said the Marcogh were descendants of the last storm spirits of the skies and the blood of the vespers gave them their unique powers.

Following custom, he offered the gatekeeper a small wooden box. Inside, seeds set against damp cloth had already begun to sprout.

"Sweetwater thorns. Quite generous. Very rare and difficult to find, even for our best gatherers."

"A gift to the Marcogh and their horses, to seed along your trails."

The gatekeeper bowed and gestured them inside. "Your beast may graze with our herds, if grass is to her favor. If not, she is welcome to dine with the hounds."

Etienne turned to his horse and rubbed her snout. "Your choice."

Once he unsaddled her and removed the burden of their traveling equipment, Belle pranced away with a playful nicker, shedding her magical disguise. Her charcoal locks danced without wind, twisting and twirling like living flame around a slim equine face. Jagged teeth took the place of blunt equine incisors, canines arising where only smooth, pink gum had existed before.

"Ah, we have a visitor!" the dog handler cried when Belle raced after a shank of meat he'd tossed into their pen.

"My apologies!" Etienne called after her.

The houndmaster waved it off dismissively. "All are welcome, even the occasional surprise guest."

A woman stepped from the adjacent house, took in the scene of the meat-eating horse, and then flashed Etienne a bright smile. A few beaded braids decorated her shoulder-length mane, the rest freely framing her oval face.

"It has been a long time since we have hosted such a magnificent steed. You honor us."

Etienne bowed. "The honor is ours, for your acceptance."

"Come, you will dine with us. Certainly you must be hungry to have traveled here from so far. Fas Perran, aren't you?"

"Are my people so easy to distinguish?"

"It's your smile," she told him, "that sets you apart, and yours is one that could light the night sky. The people of Fas Perra are always the friendliest. Come."

And the Marcogh were natural born flirts. He grinned and let her beckon him to join her family. The house was small, a quaint hovel by even Hinderan standards with tile floor and mud brick decor. The windows remained open to the elements, and the evening breeze blew through, tousling his dark hair as he introduced himself.

"I am Maire, and this one is Kinia, my daughter. My son, Takekka, and my beloved, Virin." Afterward, she named the extended members of her husband's family and offered Etienne a place at the low table to eat.

"What brings you to us?" Virin helped his wife to pass the components of their meal, the wooden bowls each featuring a different item.

Etienne helped himself to a portion from an assortment of diced fruit and chopped herbs then chuckled as the girl, Kinia, placed a generous portion of meat on his plate.

"Thank you," he murmured to the young woman before answering her father. "I seek someone among the Marcogh."

Eyebrows raised. "One among us who travels with the herd or one who dwells?"

"She may be a migrator. Has this woman entered Brychas within the past few years?" Etienne revealed a small, charcoal pencil portrait of Ysolde's mother, Tegau, forever captured at the age of thirty. She couldn't have changed much in the years.

"Ah. Her. She ran off with the Hinderan king years ago." The curt reply came from Virin's father. "Never returned to her kinsmen."

"No visits?"

"Took her child and chose to become a citydweller."

"Is it possible a northern clan could have taken her in? A clan who weathers to the north during the winter?"

The men and women around the table shrugged.

"Igritte might know. She runs messages between clans. Why do you seek Tegau?" Maire asked.

"Her child grew to become a fine young woman, and she's asked me seek her mother. Tegau disappeared as of ten years ago with promises to visit the clan and return to her loved ones of the city one day. They would like closure, to speak with her again."

Expressions, which had become stern and closed at the mention of Hindera, softened gradually. They didn't think well of the western kingdom, and Etienne could only wonder what had Hindera done to earn the Marcogh's disdain.

"Then seek Igritte. She will be with her mother, Huanna, our foal teacher," Virin said.

Etienne dipped his head in respect. "Much appreciation."

"After dinner, Kinia will show you the way. Then you will stay here with us for the night."

Following dinner, Maire's daughter led him from the home with her fingers possessively clutching his robe sleeve. Brychas wasn't large, but their winding paths created a puzzling maze between homes too similar to pick out landmarks.

As he passed several beautiful women, their braided hair and gossamer garments dancing in the breeze, he made a note to barter for gifts. He thought Ysolde would like a dress crafted from her people, even if she'd never, or rather, *couldn't* ever publically wear it.

"This is Igritte's home," Kinia said. "I'll wait for you here, and then you can return to sleep in my bed."

Letting Kinia down without causing an insult would become a problem to tackle later. For now, he merely flashed the teen a charming smile and moved ahead.

"Igritte?" he called at the entrance.

The Marcogh disdained solid doors and closed windows, leaving their homes open to neighbors instead. Wooden and bone beads clinked gently each time the breeze stirred them.

A woman appeared with an infant on her hip. When she parted the beaded curtain and stepped into the breeze, the diaphanous black silks she wore danced around her slender limbs. The garment billowed around her torso, revealing a heavy, full bosom, and metal rings in her hair chimed.

"Greetings. I do not mean to interrupt you, but I've come bearing questions."

"Hello," she said uncertainly, watching him. "Are you a visitor from the east?"

"I am Etienne, a traveler from the northern plains of Fas Perra," he corrected with a smile. "I seek one of your people, a woman by name of Tegau, daughter of Tiga."

Her eyes widened, and then she called over her shoulder, "Mother, this one asks of Tegau."

A Marcogh elder emerged from the rear of the darkened hut. Deep, rusty red streaks threaded through Huanna's otherwise dark hair, and she moved with nimble grace despite her age.

"Tegau trained foals with me in her youth before she chose the runner's way. Before the city king came and charmed her away. Like a daughter, she was."

"She left the king ten years ago. Has no one seen her?"

Igritte took a seat beside her mother. "No. Not once. I pay my visits to many of the clans as a messenger. Her face has not been among them."

"Tegau loved her daughter. If she is not among us, and not with Tisola, then her spirit flies with the wind." Huanna lowered her head. "She promised to visit. To return one day and tell us of the city. Now I understand. She is gone."

"Tisola?"

"Her little one."

He wondered if Ysolde recalled her birth name and if the royal family would accept the words of two Marcogh women as proof of Tegau's death. Etienne doubted it.

"With your blessing, I would like to try to call on her spirit."

The women exchanged glances. "If Tegau is with the winds, it seems cruel to pull her away from them."

"Crueler than depriving her loved ones of truth? Of avenging her death if needed?"

Igritte placed a hand on Huanna's arm. "Mother, this man speaks the truth. If Tegau flies with the winds, we must know what took her from us."

Torn between a desire for knowledge and Tegau to rest in peace, Huanna looked away from them both. "Tegau was a sweet girl. You have my blessing."

"My thanks." Etienne bowed. "Do you have anything of hers? Something treasured."

Igritte set her child in her mother's arms and hurried to rummage through a leather satchel. She produced a blade with a fine, glistening white edge, a polished wood handle. "I have this. Will it do?"

"What significance did it hold to her?"

"It is bone from the thigh of a horse lost under our care. We slew a wyvern together to save him, but we were far too late. Tegau made this knife to honor him as I mourned, a token to lighten my heart so his loss was not in vain."

"It may be enough to touch her spirit, to speak with her again. May I borrow it? I promise to return it to you as it is."

"Of course. Is there anything else?" Igritte asked.

"I require a quiet place for the ritual where I won't be disturbed."

"Our gathering circle will be empty. No one will disturb you there. Come, I will show you." Huanna gestured for him to follow her outside. Kinia straightened away from the wall, only to be ushered away by the elder. "Tell your father his guest will be busy this night, youngling. He will see you on the morrow."

They took him to a wide amphitheater-style meeting place with a curving, crescent-shaped wall behind rows of stone benches in increasing height, its position ideal for blocking the high noon sun. The ashen remnants of the fire pit glowed at the center, surrounded by colorful bricks in a rainbow array spaced by golden sand. Another semi-circular bench stretched across the opposite side of the pit, a place for elders to sit.

"Will this suffice?"

"Yes, thank you. Would you like to remain?"

Huanna's eyes lit up. "To see Tegau again? Yes. Though my prayers are that you will fail."

"So are mine," Etienne murmured.

Above them, the sky had become an endless sea of midnight dusted by patterns of celestial silver. Etienne sprinkled ground dragon scale upon the charcoal remnants then crouched and lit it with a tinder stick. The flames leapt high, twisting in columns of dancing green and white.

With Igritte's dagger held in his left hand and his right raised toward the smoke, he began a prayer in his native tongue while Huanna stood at his side.

"Lady of Death, your humble servant searches among the lost for a woman missed by many. Tegau, I hold a bone from a creature you once cherished and stand beside a woman who loves you."

The air remained still, the night silent aside from laughter down the hill, drum beats, and evening song.

"Perhaps she is not dead," Etienne murmured.

"Perhaps not," Huanna agreed.

"I can send Adrienne out with her scent, but it could be weeks to fi—"

Clouds rolled in without warning, blotting out the stars, and a cold wind whipped through the amphitheater to extinguish Etienne's fire and leave only plumes of gently rising smoke drifting from the smoldering coals. A hazy figure coalesced within the gray cloud, wavering in and out as the wind stirred through the air.

An oval face with high cheekbones and almond-shaped eyes formed before them, the resemblance uncanny to the woman who'd sent Etienne on his journey.

"Tegau," Huanna whispered.

When she spoke, the words came, not from the spirit, but from the winds surrounding them. It howled in the distance, fierce as a storm, and lightning flashed overhead with the threat of rain.

"Why have I been called? Who pulls me from the maelstrom?"

"Etienne Dufresne of Fas Perra. I call your spirit to give closure to your loved ones. What is the maelstrom?"

"The calm winds are denied me." Her voice was a tempest's screech, whistling through the air and piercing his ears.

"No rites given to her body," Huanna whispered in explanation. "Spirits of the lost go to the storm, not the tranquil breeze. Her bones must be blessed by the soothsayer, or she'll never return to the wheel of life."

"Tell me where to find your remains, Tegau, so I may put you to rest and grant your family peace."

The spirit moved in a restless pattern above the fire. "I hear the river. I saw its shining curve, the singing falls, and then saw no more."

"Who killed you?" Huanna demanded.

Tegau's eyes smoldered in the insubstantial mist. "His wife."

Etienne's gaze jerked back to the spirit. "The queen?"

"Jealousy brought my life to an end. I should have seen it. I should have never accepted her toast, but for my Tisola, I wished to leave with peace. Now I cannot even visit her upon the breeze to caress her face and whisper my love. I may only find her in the most violent of storms."

Fury welled within Etienne's chest when he thought of the treacherous queen's superior attitude, how she'd smiled in Ysolde's face, and the disdain she'd made no attempt to conceal. "I give my word to you that your bones will be put to rest. I will see it done."

"You will have your place amongst us again, Tegau," Huanna promised.

"Give Tisola my love. Tell Aldemar I forgive."

With the next cool gust, the spiritual form of Tegau dissipated, and the clouds unleashed a ferocious torrent of rain.

***

Etienne carried the news as a burden. The truth had pierced him, the knowledge weaving misery where once there'd been hope.

Years ago, as a child, he'd overheard the murder of his own mother, and he felt her loss no less keenly as an adult than he did thirty-five years prior. His hopes of bringing favorable news to Ysolde had been dashed.

How could he tell her that the woman who had loved her more than anything had been assassinated by her rival and wife to the man they both loved?

Would anyone believe him? Would King Aldemar charge his own queen with the murder of a consort who gave him no true heirs?

Adrienne popped her head out of his travel bag. "There's a robbery ahead."

As Etienne veered into the trees, a cloak of darkness shrouded both rider and his mare. "So?"

"Will you do nothing?"

"What business is it of mine?"

"What lodged itself in your rear?" the cat countered.

"I have naught but poor news to deliver a friend, and my journey south was in vain," he growled.

"No, Etienne, your travels were not in vain. You will bring closure to Ysolde and deliver news she will greatly appreciate. She will no longer worry about her mother's well-being or believe the woman she's loved most abandoned her."

He glanced down at the cat. In her smallest form, she balanced on the horn of his saddle, appearing as a kitten would.

"The tidings are grim. Do you really think she'll find closure in them?"

"Your mother may be gone, but you have always known Amelie's fate and never questioned her unerring devotion to you. Imagine yourself in Ysolde's place and that you have wondered for years."

Etienne said nothing.

"That Amelie and Tegau share similar fates strikes me as little more than destiny," the cat continued, "and marks you as the one best suited to deliver such news."

He answered with grudging agreement, "You're right."

"Of course, I'm right," she replied as he left the darkened path. "How is it I, a demon from the void, have become your voice of conscience?"

"Because you are my truest friend. And you're right again. I should do something about this."

Etienne leapt down from Belle's back. While his brother could go great distances in the pocket of nothing between the Void and the Real, his ability to skim between dimensions was limited. Stunted.

But it was enough to have an advantage over a bandit.

"Let's have those silks too, pretty. Take off every scrap," the highwayman said.

"Please, sir."

"All of it. Better to be nekkid and alive than layin' on the ground with your throat slit. You wantin' to join your driver?"

Etienne's eyes drifted from the corpse of the coachman to the blade that had slain him. The thief held a rapier, a Fas Perran sword once held by a woman. Had one of his countrywomen met a similar fate, or had it been a stolen war trophy liberated from one of the dead?

It made his blood boil, and in a second, he was upon the man with his sword drawn and the cool tip at the man's nape.

"Drop the weapon."

After it clattered to the ground, Etienne reversed his sword in his grip and slammed the pommel into the bandit's skull. He fell with a thud to the dirt road. Inside the carriage was a girl on the cusp of womanhood and a guard with a bleeding hole in the center of his chest. An escort. She trembled and shrank away as if he'd finish what the thief began.

"I'm not here to harm you. Please, come out from there."

He coaxed her outside the carriage, away from the bloodied body, and gave her a quick look-over. Slapped around but largely uninjured.

"I'm going to unhitch your horse. Are you able to ride?"

"I've never done so without a saddle, but I'll try my best."

"Brave girl. Kirkwood is less than an hour's ride north. If it was your destination, you're nearly there."

"It is, sirrah. I'm to spend the season with relatives."

"Good. Up you go then." He gave the girl a lift onto the palomino's back.

"I am Alannya." The young woman moistened her lips and shyly glanced down at him. "My father will want to reward you. What name shall I give of my savior? How will we find you to give our thanks?"

"Scion Etienne Dufresne, Shade Knight of Fresna." He bowed to her. "This cretin is no countryman of mine, a wolf in false clothing. I require no payment to do what is right."

Her eyes widened.

"Th-thank you, my lord," she stammered.

Once the girl was gone from sight, Etienne turned his attention to the groaning figure at his feet.

"Adrienne, my sweet, find us a bit of privacy for the night. We need to have a talk with our new friend here."

INTEGRITY AND HONOR

25

Andras crossed his arms and gave the stockpile of dusty weapons a dubious look. "I don't think it's going to work. Even if you find it, she'll never lift it again."

"She will," Geoffrey insisted. "I wish that I could blame you for the state of this armory, but this is my fault. I should have fired Omran and hired a quartermaster worth his salt, able to function without a bottle."

But of course, every time he'd visited the armory and its pitiful, half-drunken caretaker, he'd felt pity for the man and left him to his mourning.

"It is," Andras agreed. "Look at what that brainless git has done. Blunted and rusted the blades. Bows needing to be restrung. I began seeking a replacement last week among the men for someone eager to experience thankless, hard work."

Constructed of heavy stone and mortar, the castle armory had stood for centuries as a storage room for weapons of all variety from the shortest dagger to the heaviest greatsword. Somewhere in a haphazard pile of longbows and weaponry lay the subject of Geoffrey's hour-long search.

"I'm sorry, all right? I should have sacked him long ago."

"Would you know it if you saw it?" Andras asked.

"I would. I've watched her shoot it enough to recognize it," Geoffrey said. "Besides, it's not as if we have many elven-crafted bows."

"You mean like this one hanging up on the wall?"

Geoffrey abandoned the pile and turned on his heel. There, on the support pillar behind him, hung the prize he sought. The pale, silver wood gleamed even in the dim lighting.

"If it was a troll it would have squished you." Andras made no effort to conceal his humor. "Now what will you do with it?"

"I have a plan."

"I've had prior witness to your plans in the past, Geoffrey. Your scheme may very well have you sleeping with the hounds this night."

Geoffrey shot his cousin a dirty look. Despite the negativity, he emerged from the armory with the bow in hand.

It was a handsome piece carved from lightning-struck lunar cypress. Fingall had sent for the branch from his homeland in Iluminarel and crafted it with his own hands when Ysolde had outgrown the bow of her childhood, blending elven talent and Marcogh crafting technique.

"It certainly is lovely. I couldn't draw this string if I wanted to," Andras muttered. "It's a wonder she ever could. Won't it need some care before she shoots it?"

Geoffrey shook his head. "No, that's the glory of elven bows, mate. Once made, nothing but a sharp axe or the fires of the void can destroy them."

After admiring it a moment longer, Andras shook his head. "I recall many afternoons of watching her shoot from astride Tikiina, but I'll believe it when I see it."

"Do me a favor?"

"What?"

"Fetch Raennia and set up the archery targets. I have to lure Ysolde down without rousing suspicion."

"May want to give me that then." Andras took the bow and quiver.

"Take a training bow as well for Rae."

Geoffrey expected to find Ysolde overseeing accounting operations with Fingall, but he encountered Shyla in the hall and was sent toward the kitchen instead.

"Ysolde?" he called.

"In here."

Geoffrey stepped inside and spied her by the counter, laying down a tray covered in sweet glaze. "What are you up to?"

"I walked the walls for some fresh air and brought the guards warm honeyrolls from the kitchen."

"So you're the culprit who spoils my men," he teased.

"You've already given them casks of mulled wine. If anyone's spoiled them, it is you. At least now they've got something to dull the alcohol sloshing in their bellies."

On a fine winter day, or rather, as fine a day as Ashdale winters came, the men enjoyed their training between rounds of mulled wine. When a visiting duke had disapproved of the tradition, asking how any man could train with several mugs of steaming, sweet wine in him, Benedict Westwood had only laughed and cited the barbarians of the north regularly slew their enemies while inebriated with far stronger drink.

"My lady, they'd hang me in the gibbet if I broke your uncle's tradition."

Ysolde smiled at him. "I know, and I have nothing against it. It's not even that strong, truth be told."

Before she could shrug her cloak back from her shoulders, Geoffrey surrounded his wife with both arms, catching it. He kissed her first and then refastened the heavy, fur-lined garment.

"Don't take off your layers yet. I want to show you something outside."

"Oh?" Ysolde's upturned face and hazy eyes lured him down for another kiss. "Perhaps I would like to show my husband something inside."

He paused, conflicted. "Much later." Or so he hoped.

After taking her by the hand, he led Ysolde outside. A full course of archery targets awaited them, some on posts, others dangling from branches, and some mounted on stationary objects and dummies.

"What's this?"

"An archery lesson. I'd like Raennia to have a firm grasp of how to handle a bow, should the need arise, and I thought, who better to teach her than you?"

Ysolde pulled her hand from his grasp. "I can't."

"Love, you're the better archer out of the two of us. Better than anyone here, except maybe Fingall. Aside from that, you, ah, can better understand any unique issues."

"Unique issues," she repeated.

"Balancing issues," he clarified. He smiled, took a leap, and dropped his gaze to his wife's modest bosom. "Hers are significantly larger."

"You're an arse."

Her concise summation broadened his grin. "An arse you adore. Tell me I'm wrong, and I'll gladly take this bow and teach her myself. Poorly, of course, as you know my nearsightedness impedes my aim. Then the men who claim her to be inferior will have adequate proof."

Ysolde's expression changed, and the good nature at his ribbing faded, replaced by determination. "I'll have her outshooting your best rangers by month's end."

"I know you will."

Raennia stepped onto the training grounds while Geoffrey moved to the fringe and fetched himself a generous mug of mulled wine. The spiced drink warmed his belly, the heat of it chasing the chill from his hands, and he watched from the sidelines while his wife tutored his squire in the fine art of archery.

Ysolde shined in her natural element. Her carefree features and bright eyes brought to mind the euphoria she displayed whenever they went for a ride in the hills and raced across the meadows.

"Told you," he muttered to Andras.

"Don't look so smug. It isn't too late for our princess to have a change of heart. You'll be begging Blackjack to share his blanket with you by evening if she discovers your betting."

"You know, it'd be worth it."

The women met again the following day and the day thereafter, startling Geoffrey with the ferocity of their training.

"Whatever you said to our princess has done its job," Andras whispered to him. "I've never seen two women more dedicated."

"I appealed to their spite," Geoffrey said, voice low. "They would walk across hot coals to see us men proved wrong."

"A dangerous gamble." Andras chuckled. "Jory has been watching too, had you noticed? I may see how he handles a bow tomorrow after his patrol of the hillsides."

"A good decision, I'd say. I had my eye on him for a time and had considered placing him in a rotation to one of the watchtowers in the midlands. The time away from Nedic and some of these other arseholes would do him some good."

"You read my mind. He seems a quiet sort. Given a knapsack of books and a good watch partner, he may be happy there."

Geoffrey nodded. "I have a few thoughts on the matter, but ultimately the final choice is yours."

"Lucky me."

"The joys of command." Geoffrey's grin widened.

"Ha ha." Andras pushed away from the wall. "Looks like their lesson is over."

Geoffrey followed him. "For one of them at least. Time to see what else my squire can do."

Had Geoffrey not developed such a liking for Marik, he would have poked fun at Andras for choosing a squire who was magically stunted. They'd tested the man with all manner of magical tricks, and even the spell scrolls Etienne scribed had been useless in Marik's hands. Nothing worked. His drug addiction had scorched the very core of his magical essence.

Rae was Marik's direct opposite, a fount of limitless potential according to Etienne, who had watched the girl and appraised her magical aura. According to the brothers, she shone like a lantern in the dark.

"I don't suppose you're in the mood for another lesson," Geoffrey called out to his pupil.

Raennia adjusted her path away from the barracks and veered toward him.

"Of course, Duke Ashdale." She offered a pleasant smile.

"Geoffrey," he reminded her. "Let's tackle something difficult today. You've been fighting with a sword for a while now, and I'd like to progress to one of the first things we learn as paladins. To smite evil."

"I can't do that. I wouldn't know where to begin."

"If you can master meditation, you can do this as well. It's the next step, after all. A paladin attuned with his inner self can open his heart to Ashta." After his assurances, he guided Rae to the center of the sparring arena where they were clear of other guardsmen for her to potentially harm if anything went awry.

"There's no evil to smite."

He glanced to his left and saw her large-eyed expression. He barked out a laugh before nudging her with his elbow. "Of course there isn't. Did you believe they sent us out to battle demons and learn in the heat of battle?"

"But how do you practice something if there's no way to make sure it works?" Her skepticism remained, brows shooting up beneath the wisps of auburn coming loose to frame her face.

"Perhaps I should have worded my intentions better," he said. "What I mean to teach you is how to channel Ashta's blessing to your sword. It's how we smite evil. To do that, you have to open yourself to her guidance."

Geoffrey grasped his sword around the hilt, and upon drawing it from the scabbard, the blade erupted in a blaze of golden fire. A hush fell over the training yard, and all eyes turned toward them. His displays of prowess as a paladin were so infrequent many of the guards had forgotten he had the training.

"Now you try." He returned the sword to its sheath and watched her. "Take a deep breath. Clear your thoughts."

Eyes closed, his squire took a moment to center herself. Determination took its place upon her features as she opened her eyes and drew her sword, but no spark ignited. Raennia held the weapon out and focused on the blade, as if she could will it to burn with righteous flames.

"Nothing is happening."

"Need I tell you it takes practice?"

She shot him an unamused glare but tried again.

"You aren't merely holding a blade, Rae. You're an extension of Ashta herself, committed to dispensing justice to those who would do wrong."

"I can't," she huffed, shoulders dropping and hands trembling. "I'm not a paladin. I don't have the years with the Chosen that you do."

"My ability has nothing to do with training in the monastery and everything to do with a strong devotion to Ashta. Walk with me for a bit," he encouraged her.

Sheathing her sword, Raennia fell in at his side, gray eyes downcast.

"Speak with me honestly, Rae. Forget that I'm the duke or even a man of noble blood. Tell me how you feel about raising your sword in Ashta's honor."

She glanced away, taking a moment to give the question real thought. "I suppose, in my mind, it shouldn't only be for the honor of a god or goddess. I raise my sword not for glory but to protect the ones I love."

"But why do you protect them?" he pressed.

"Who else will?"

Geoffrey stopped to set one hand upon her shoulder.

"Then if you understand that, the goddess can't ask for anything more. You need no church, no organization of pious men, or official title to do what is right, Rae. As long as you feel it here," he said, touching a hand to the metal above her heart. "That was the biggest lesson I took away from my years at the monastery, the only one of true importance. Your integrity and doing what is right matters more than any deed carried out for appearances or honor."

"And magic? Doesn't that come from Ashta herself?"

"Yes and no. Your magic is the spark, but think of Ashta's gift, her blessing to you, as the fuel to create an inferno." He paused and collected his thoughts. "Maybe I've said this wrong. How much do you know of Marik's history?"

"A little," she answered, voice quiet. "He doesn't speak of it much. I know he lost his family during the war and returned home a broken man. He used glow to dull the pain."

"He did," Geoffrey confirmed. "The insidious thing about glow is that it doesn't waste the body or sicken the mind. Aside from his shakes, you couldn't tell at a glance he was a user. Prolonged use of it kills the magic inside you and your connection to it."

"It makes you numb," she countered. "I had no idea it affected magic, though.

"It does," he agreed. "It makes you numb in every way, smothering the natural magical spark inside of you until there's nothing left. If Marik were gravely injured, there isn't a healer in this world or the next able to heal him. Something must remain for the magic to grasp. I don't think anything could help him, short of Ashta herself."

Raennia stared at him, eyes wide. "You mean it stops him from casting spells and people from using magic on him?"

"He can neither cast magic from items nor can he invoke it from scrolls, Rae. But according to the Dufresnes, you're quite the opposite."

"I… Well…" She blinked rapidly, flustered. "They believe so?"

"Indeed. Etienne more so than his brother. I'd dare to say he even sounded impressed."

"I've never done magic before."

"You'd be surprised how many people have the potential without ever realizing it," he confided. "Think about what I said today. Find your own inner peace. Then we'll try this again."

THE BEST FORM OF FLATTERY

26

 Etienne crouched in front of his captive. The merc he'd apprehended in the midst of unsavory, roadside activity goaned on the floor with his hands shackled behind his back.

"Awakening now, are you? Good. Good. I have a feeling you and I will become very close in the coming days."

"Piss off, Fas Perran dog."

"If I'm a dog, what does that make you? There is a phrase among my people, said often by those in the art trade. 'Imitation is the best form of flattery.' Judging from this weapon liberated from your possession and the phony Fas Perran accent I overheard, you have gone to exquisite lengths to compliment my countrymen. I would like to know why."

He spoke casually, scraping a layer of rind from the exterior of a juicy, purple fruit he'd plucked from a nearby tree. The knife glinted, reflecting the torch fire above them.

"Your lot will get what's coming to you soon. We kicked your arses once."

"Do you see what I'm doing to this fruit?" Etienne asked casually. "In five minutes, my companion and I will have finished eating it."

He sliced a sliver of the pale golden inner flesh and offered it to Adrienne. She licked it up from his fingers.

"And then you're next. You'll live through it all, of course, every excruciating second, so whoever it is you're hoping to protect, I hope they've paid you well and that you enjoyed every silver to the fullest."

The mercenary stared at him.

"Let me have him." Adrienne's eyes flashed in the firelight, orange and red.

"In time." He offered her another sweet wedge and ate one himself. "I know how you dislike unwrapping your gifts, *ourabette*. So I shall have to do it for you."

"But I want him fresh. What good is a dead toy?"

"Oh, he'll live. Trust me." Etienne's eyes darted back to their guest, and he smiled. "As a priest of Fresna, goddess of the dead, I assure you, you won't die until we've had our fill of your torment."

"You won't do that. The bloody bint who hired you would never approve of it. She's soft. A child. She's got no business ruling Ashdale."

"Ah, so you know who I am. Good. As for my employer, the noble *woman* who hired me will never know what I've done."

"Let me taste him now. A finger," Adrienne urged, voice a velvet purr echoing with the power of the void.

Etienne rose and gestured. "As you will."

Wetwork had once made him sick in the past, but he'd come to understand some situations called for a hardened heart and a stronger stomach. He left the room, wondering if he and Laurent had inherited their callous natures from their supposed peace-loving father.

He knew Adrienne had begun when he heard the first bloodcurdling scream.

Fifteen minutes later, he and the imitator became the best of friends. Adrienne had removed the first and middle digits of his right hand, and with flames of the void, she'd also cauterized the stumps. He breathed ragged, choking breaths, sobbing on his side, the fight gone from him.

"I-I'll tell you anything. *Anything.* Please get the demon away from me."

Etienne smiled and intentionally avoided looking at his feline. He hated when she had blood on her mouth.

"What she did was only the beginning, I want you to know. If at any point I feel you have been dishonest with me, you will have lost your purpose. And then I will allow her to have you, but first I must warn you of her love for entrails."

"No! Please, for the love of the gods, no!"

With unyielding patience, Etienne waited for the mercenary's hysterics to end. Once he no longer shook and sobbed, the questioning began.

"What is your name?"

"Henwell. Pietr Henwell."

"What a pleasure to meet you, Pietr. I am glad we could do this and converse as men. Now tell me, weren't the Iron Fist not exiled from Hindera?"

"We were, but the boss didn't care. We were given orders to operate quietly and hide our origins to complete the job."

"I see. Tell me who hired you."

"I didn't know the names of the people who hired us until they were executed. It was always code names and phony titles. The boss frequently met with nobles and relayed our instructions at camp."

"Code names?"

His captive nodded, desperate for Etienne to believe him. Etienne was aware of movement to his right, a snapping noise, cartilage ripping, and bones crunching. The man turned green.

"Tell me more of your plans. We already know of Shadeglen. Tell us something new."

"We were told to make trouble along the border and paid a handsome sum to attack the river valley farms."

"Were you also hired to harass Ashdale?"

"Yes. Whoever hired us, they have a hatred for the princess. Wanted her to look incompetent."

"And to kidnap her?" Etienne pressed.

"I think. Fuck. I wasn't part of that operation." He tilted his head back against the wall, gasping in his breaths. "I don't know anything but this job."

Etienne pressed his lips together thoughtfully, dissatisfied with the answer. "Where were you to go once you completed your work? Surely at some point, you would have been recalled to report in."

The man hesitated, but after a growling hiss from Adrienne, he changed his mind.

"There's an old fort somewhere north. I don't know the exact location. When they called us in, we were all going to meet in the mountain foothills north of Eastmark and travel from there. Please don't let her eat another finger. Please! I swear that's all I know."

"You and I will make a visit to Kirkwood. The authorities there will take a great interest in what happened on the road."

"They'll hang me there! Have mercy, mate. Haven't you taken enough from me? That was my bloody sword hand!"

"Then they are merciful. For what you planned to do with that young woman, you would have lost more than two fingers in Fas Perra."

TAKEN FOR GRANTED

27

There was nothing, Ysolde decided, more exhilarating than an afternoon ride through the hills. With the duke preoccupied by matters of state, Andras and Raennia rode with her in Geoffrey's stead. And while their company was enjoyable, nothing compared to the presence of having her husband alongside her.

"How do you do it?" Raennia asked.

"Do what?"

"You ride with no saddle, but your speed never wavers. It's as if you're affixed to the horse's back by glue," Raennia said enviously.

"I was riding ponies before I could speak full sentences. Even after I went to live in Stormwatch, a saddle always felt strange, so father never made me use one. I can't connect with my horse with all of the leather and cotton between us." She flashed Rae a genuine smile. "If you'd ever like to try it, I can teach you."

"Maybe when the weather is fair and the wind no longer cuts like a thousand frozen knives," Rae teased.

"It'll snow soon." Andras glanced toward the north, a frown on his face. "They've predicted a blizzard will lay as much snow as I am tall by this week's end. We'll be buried in it."

"Is it awful of me to admit I'm glad I won't be stranded out in the country this winter?" Raennia asked.

"When I was his squire, I pissed Geoffrey off and spent a complete season's rotation in the Lakeshire west tower. The wind would blow in this godsawful chill from Lake Amanu, and I'd spend more time huddled beneath a blanket than watching the west. My uncle felt pity for me, and he'd ride out with a basket of hot food to supplement my rations once a week. Those days were a blessing."

The female squire laughed, her expression sympathetic. "Once, when the snows to the south were at their worst, we had the goats and our plow horse inside with us because the snow was up to the eaves."

"Speaking of snow, we should head back. I have a feeling it will arrive sooner than a week."

"We best listen to him, Raennia," Ysolde said, laughing. "I've come to discover Andras is better than any weathermage."

Her guardians escorted her home, and Crispin ran out to greet them from the stables. "Did you have a good ride?"

"A lovely ride," she assured him. "Next time, you can come with me."

Crispin's impish features brightened.

"Excuse me, Your Grace, I have an urgent message for you." A young guardsman stepped over and extended a wax-sealed scroll.

"Thank you, Jory. How long—"

"The hawk arrived only moments ago. Knowing you were eager for the news, I was going to ride out, but your return saved me the trip."

Etienne's graceful script written across the paper sparked a sudden nervousness. As she broke the wax seal bearing the crest of House Dufresne, she wondered if the news was good or bad and hesitated to open the letter to see. While she didn't need Geoffrey standing beside her, she wanted him. In her wildest dreams, Etienne was writing to tell her he and Tegau were riding for the north and that soon they would see one another again.

Letter in hand, Ysolde headed down the hall with a smile and a bounce in her step. Despite the uncertain future on the horizon and recent troubles long behind them, she took comfort in an improved relationship with her husband.

"Maribeth, have you seen Geoffrey?"

"He's... ahh, the duke is in his study, Your Grace, but there's—"

"Has he ended his meeting with Lord Faringdale and Lord Clarkston?"

Since becoming Duke Ashdale and acquiring the confidence to lead as their reigning noble, Geoffrey had taken to meeting with professional acquaintances in the gentlemen's study. When she'd left the castle, he and the local lords had been discussing the winter season and providing for the poor.

"Yes, Your Grace, they left half an hour ago."

"I'll go find him then, thank you, Maribeth."

"You may want to—"

Ysolde didn't wait. Her heart was bursting with enthusiasm as she hurried down the halls, letting portraits and tapestries fly past her. She had a letter with news about her mother, and when she opened it, she wanted Geoffrey standing beside her. She had him to thank for it, his encouragement and Etienne's efforts yielding the payoff she'd craved for years.

Her palm nudged the heavy wooden door open when she reached it, but the call for her husband died on her lips. She heard his voice and saw he wasn't alone.

"It's so good to see you again. I wish I'd been there to help when you needed me."

Her husband stood beside his neglected desk, neither writing a missive to the guard nor handling citywide affairs. Geoffrey held a brunette in a close embrace with her cheek pressed against his shoulder. As Ysolde tried to take in what she was seeing, her gaze fell to the woman's familiar face.

It was as if someone had split her chest and wrenched the beating heart from it. She stepped back from the half-open doorway, numb all the way through as hot tears blurred her vision. She blinked them away quickly and forced cold, hard logic to surface.

Geoffrey would never betray her, and in all of their marriage, all of their friendship, he'd never told her a lie.

"Welcome back to Ashdale," she said in a measured voice, infusing calm into her tone.

The voice cracked, unrecognizable to Ysolde's ears, but it held the power to jerk both Geoffrey and Ashlynne apart. Her voice brimmed with unwanted emotion she hadn't felt in years. Not since Rhun had walked away from their engagement.

"Ysolde, I thought you would be riding still."

"My ride is over," she said. "I was unaware we had a guest."

"I'm leaving, Your Grace."

Ysolde hadn't realized she was backpedaling until Ashlynne spoke. Her eyes darted from Geoffrey to Ashlynne and saw gray eyes staring back at her in horror. They quickly averted in shame before she wiped her tear-streaked cheeks

The Ashlynne of Ysolde's memories was a vivacious artist with glorious caramel waves down her back. She'd changed, and perhaps that was why Geoffrey never found her. She wore her hair short, a mess of pixie's curls surrounding her heart-shaped face.

Jumping to conclusions would dishonor herself as much as Geoffrey. Ysolde suppressed the malignant accusations swirling in her thoughts.

"Please, don't leave on my account. I'll let you two finish." Ysolde turned away.

"Ysolde, wait a moment, love—" Geoffrey's hand closed around her wrist.

"Yes?"

"It isn't how it appears," he said awkwardly. "Ashlynne is sailing from Wysteria to Valekesh. She came to say goodbye before leaving the continent."

After Ysolde disentangled his fingers from around her wrist, she flashed him an uncertain smile. "Then there's no rush for her to leave. Take the time you need, Geoffrey. I am going to ride a little longer, I think."

"Are you certain?"

"Of course I am." She drew in a deep breath and felt some of the tension in her chest loosen. "You two will have lots to discuss, and I think it better you do so alone. Then, if all is well, I'd enjoy it if she stayed for dinner."

She stood on tiptoe to kiss his stubbled cheek, stunning both Ashlynne and Geoffrey when she left the room. Within moments, she had returned to the barn to find Tikiina's head over the stall door and large, brown eyes watching for her. The mare knew. She always knew.

"Are you riding again, ma'am?" Crispin called from where he lay on a pile of clean hay.

"Only for a bit, Crispin." He came to her for a hug, a puppy trailing behind him. He and the canine had been sharing a snack of rejected portions from the evening's meal. Crispin liked the parts of the animal no one else enjoyed. Although offal was a delicacy in southern Hindera, Ysolde had no love for it, and the cooks readily surrendered those bits to the fey child.

Crispin fetched the stepping block while she freed Tikiina from the stall. Blackjack snorted and made noisy objections to their departure, as he always did whenever left behind.

"He wants to run free too." Crispin's brown eyes watched the black steed. Then he fell into step alongside Ysolde and Tikiina. He bit his lower lip. "You should stay and play games with me."

"We'll play games when I've returned. Promise. After dinner before I tuck you in."

His small face pinched with worry. "I don't want you to go."

Crispin accepted a fond tousle of his messy hair. His horns, which had been tiny nubs months ago, had finally begun to protrude from his chestnut curls. When she rode away, she glanced back to see him still watching her at the barn opening.

Andras caught up with her before she made it to the castle gates. "Your Grace? Going out again?"

Ysolde gave him a shaky smile. "Yes. I need a moment to clear my head."

The knight commander studied her, concern etched in his features. "Shall I fetch Geo—"

"No, that won't be needed. He is occupied," she interrupted. After a moment of thought, she added in a quiet voice. "Ashlynne returned."

"I see." Andras spun Zephyr around and flashed her a gentle smile as the stallion fell into step beside her. "Then I'll have to accompany you myself."

To his credit, he was an excellent silent companion who laid no judgment during their ride into the hills. He didn't complain about the biting wind, didn't try to coax her back to the castle, and made no effort to slow her down when she urged her mare into a swift gallop.

The cold air whipped through her hair, tugging a ribbon free, but she didn't care. She urged Tikiina faster and charged across the meadow.

Riding brought clarity. With a horse beneath her, the world flying by in a blur, her worries and fears seemed far away.

Ysolde didn't stop until Tikiina slowed on her own.

As the breath rushed in and out of the princess's lungs and the lush velvet beneath her woolen cloak clung to her perspiring skin, she stroked her fingers down her mare's dampened neck. Tikiina tossed back her head and whinnied with elation.

Hinderan winter twilights painted the sky in deep purples and smoky gray smudged with pink. She smelled the promise of snow in the wind, a sharpness blowing in from the eastern mountains.

"Lunara for your thoughts?"

She made a soft sound, not quite a laugh. "I suppose I'm a little afraid. They have so much history."

"I assure you, when I look at Geoffrey, I see a man content with his life—no, a man grateful for his blessings and the woman he loves."

"He's never said those words to me, Andras." She picked at the tiny snowflakes drifting down against her coat. "Only her."

"He loves you," Andras insisted.

"I know."

"Just as I love Shyla," the knight continued.

Ysolde's startled lean backward brought her mare to an abrupt halt. "Shyla?"

A pair of solemn, brown eyes studied her. Zephyr intuitively stepped alongside Tikiina and stopped too.

Andras was waiting for her reaction, and at first, the absurdity of Shyla's persistent silence struck her as hilarious.

Then she laughed and clapped her hands. "I knew it! I knew Shyla was spending her time with one of the guardsmen, but she'd never tell me who."

"Apologies, Princess. That was my doing. I thought…" He dragged in a deep breath and gazed ahead. "I am a baron's second-born son, a knight, and thus there are high expectations regarding the lady I am to wed."

"I understand all too well."

"I had hoped… That is, I mean to say… I'd like your blessing, Your Grace. I want to marry her, if she'll have me and forgive my recent behavior."

"Of course you have it, not that you need my permission." She smiled, heart lighter. "And if your family has anything to say, they can do so knowing I fully stand behind you."

"Thank you."

"When will you ask her?"

"Tonight, I hope. We planned to meet after dinner."

"Then you'll need flowers." Ysolde slipped down from Tikiina's back and gazed at the thin tree line where vines wrapped around the oaks in thick cords of green accented with blue and purple flowers.

"Shyla loves those purple ones," she pointed out. "If you gather a few of those, I'll search under the pines for some snowdrops."

She rummaged through forest debris and brushed aside pinecones to reveal the tough, white blossoms that thrived in cool weather. Healers prized the thick, silken petals as a component of the poultices they created for burns, but Ysolde enjoyed their sweet fragrance.

"Is this enough?" Andras called.

Ysolde turned. He stood behind her holding a mass of flowers in his large hands, claimed with no skill. "Did you yank down the entire vine?"

Andras blushed. "Maybe."

"She'll love them."

"I hope s—" The flowers dropped from Andras' hands, replaced by his sword. "Behind me, Your Grace.

At first, Ysolde saw nothing, but then the sound of many hoofbeats reached her ears. Andras and Geoffrey shared similar gifts, a sense for when danger was present. Shielding her behind him, he stepped forward.

"Ho there! What business do you have in Ashdale, strangers?" Andras called.

At the lead of the group, a man rode a dappled gray stallion with a stocky frame and powerful legs. His scarlet cloak was fastened by a colorful, gold brooch at the left shoulder, the shape of a black fist imprinted in the metal. He watched from the saddle, an enormous man with blue-black skin and tusks curled over his lower lip. He made a terrifying example of what happened when orc and human blood mixed.

"Our business is our own, and that pertains to the pretty you're shielding behind you."

"Is it?" Andras's sword arm was unwavering, and his calm voice echoed across the small clearing. "I would have expected the Iron Fist to be long gone, setting sail to more profitable shores. Why do you remain when the purse strings have been cut?"

"Is that what you think?"

Ysolde stood tall behind Andras and refused to cower. Her fingertips tingled with unreleased magic.

"I think we've put your employer to the death, and it would be unwise to show your faces near Ashdale without worthy recompense for the time."

The half-orc grinned, revealing a set of uneven teeth. "Ah, you're smart for a Hinderan, but Shadeglen was never our employer. You have our appreciation for removing him from the equation."

"Then maybe I should do the same for you."

"Don't go over there," she hissed at him, grasping at the knight's elbow.

He shrugged her touch away and stepped up as a company of men emerged from the thick of the forest. They had come in force. As her eyes swept over their ranks, she counted at least two dozen.

"We don't want you, you dumb git. Get out of the way, and we'll let you carry on with your life. Even take a message back to the castle."

"The princess goes nowhere without me at her side."

The man laughed. "Your choice, but we're only taking one prisoner today."

He gestured with his sword, and arrows whistled through the air in a small, precise number meant to eliminate Andras from the fight.

They struck his shield instead, harmlessly splintering over the enchanted wood.

"Ysolde, run!" With only that cry of warning, Andras charged forward into the fray. His sword cut through boiled leather and met flesh. One man fell, and many more surrounded the commander with bloodthirst gleaming in their eyes.

With Andras occupied in battle to her right, Ysolde focused her magic on the left flank. Fire and wind swirled together in a violent maelstrom, a flaming twister that broke over their ranks and brought men to their knees in agonizing pain. She fought to keep the inferno between herself and her attackers but away from Andras.

"Someone shoot the knight!" the leader roared from horseback.

Upon abolishing the fiery tornado, Ysolde aimed a line of flames through the air as the archers released their next volley. The arrows charred and fell to ash before they reached their intended target.

The commander was unstoppable, her knight unflinching despite eminent danger from the archers. Unerring in his trust for her, Andras gutted another man while Ysolde defended his back at a safe distance—a mage's casting distance.

A sharp sting exploded in warmth at the back of Ysolde's neck. She stumbled to the right and caught her balance against a tree, abrading her palm on the rough bark.

"Andras!" she cried, searching for him through a haze of bleeding colors.

"Run, Your Grace!"

She snapped her head toward his voice, saw him surrounded on all sides. The mercenaries were numerous, and they seemed to spill from the woods without end. She blinked her eyes rapidly and willed her vision to focus.

Andras was Geoffrey's protégé, his student in every way, and with a blade, he had few equals among the men serving under her duchy's banner. She'd watched him take on all of the recruits at once, an exhibition to prove their potential to them.

These were not trainees, and he was not Geoffrey. He took down two men to his front and knocked another off balance with a powerful slam from his shield.

Then a sword sank into his thigh. He staggered, recovered, thrust forward, and took down another attacker. The others closed in on him, and together they rained strikes with impunity as the fallen knight cried out for his princess to flee.

She tried to help, but her focus failed, and she summoned nothing more than a few quick-burning embers to her fingers. Nausea roiled in her gut and threatened to drag her into the abyss of unconsciousness.

"No. Andras." Her words slurred together, and she stumbled to her hands and knees in the grass.

"Grab the bitch and toss her over the back of her mare. Boss wants her unspoiled."

"No," she whispered. Her magic became a spark too weak to ignite.

Laurent and Etienne had been right all along. Her adversaries hadn't wanted her dead.

As the world dulled into shades of gray and finally black, Ysolde was gathered from the ground into a pair of strong arms, and she knew nothing more.

***

"No sign of her or Andras toward the lake." Raennia dismounted and accepted the warm mug passed to her by Crispin. Geoffrey studied her reddened cheeks and brought over a woolen blanket.

"I rode south along the coast with similar results," Geoffrey told her. He'd hoped to return to find Ysolde warming by the hearth with a cup of chocolate. "Get yourself warmed up, and I'll send Marik out on the next run."

"No, I'll be fine," she countered. "I can go out again, and it will be easier than trying to explain what paths I already searched."

"Geoffrey, you've done all you can to search for her. Remove yourself at once from this awful weather and go inside." Fingall looked as haggard as Geoffrey felt.

"Agreed. We'll continue to look for her." Marik clapped him on the back and tried to steer Geoffrey from the stable, but he didn't budge.

"No." Geoffrey shook his head. "There will be no resting for me until I know she's safe and somewhere warm for the night, whether it's here, the city, or elsewhere."

"I know," Marik said. "I know."

At first, no one had worried when sunset had arrived and Andras hadn't returned with the princess. Dark fell earlier in the winter months, spreading shadows over the land by the sixth evening chime. Easy to lose the time, easier for Ysolde, if she'd been upset, to venture into the city to clear her mind.

Then dinner had come and gone without a sign or a word from either of them.

Geoffrey and a few soldiers of the Ashguard had visited the city and spoken to the watchmen. None had seen her, but all promised to report in at the first sighting.

"Was she upset?" Marik asked.

"I thought so, but she wanted to allow us time to talk."

"Would she have told you the truth?"

"Yes," Geoffrey said without hesitation. "She would. It felt strange to let her walk away, but I believed her. It's not like her to run away from problems."

Laurent stepped into place beside him, his dark brows furrowed with consternation. The half-elf shivered, despite wearing multiple layers of garments, including an insulated cloak. "Were that I have quick way to contact brother. He would find Ysolde," he said. "I am sorry, Geoffrey. Very sorry."

"It's all right. Thank you for all you've already done, Laurent. I know this isn't your season."

"I cannot track in snow," he agreed.

Geoffrey looked down at the folded letter in his hands for the hundredth time. Crispin had brought it to him after finding it on the stable floor, fallen from Ysolde's purse during her departure. The troubling news it bore weighed on him.

Had she come to him for comfort, needing his shoulder, and instead she'd found him with his former lover in his arms?

What Ysolde had witnessed was her husband holding a friend in need, tortured by the recent upsets to her new life and freshly heartbroken. He felt no glee, no satisfaction in learning Ashlynne had lost the man she loved. He'd held her as a friend without resentment, proving to himself he no longer loathed her for departing on their wedding day.

And she'd sought him for closure.

Sighing, Geoffrey tipped his head back and closed his eyes. "I only want Ysolde to return to us safely."

Raennia set her gloved hand on his arm. "We'll find h—"

"Rider coming!" the sentry yelled. "I can't see much through the snow."

"Open the gates!" Fingall ordered before Geoffrey had the chance.

Geoffrey rushed onto the courtyard to see Zephyr pacing the cobbled path. The horse tossed his head and reared, splotches of rust brown darkening the silver fur of his face. One stain in the suspicious shape of a handprint, marred the stallion's throat.

"Ashta's Tears, that's blood."

Zephyr charged past them again, shaking his mane and snorting steam, his nostrils flaring.

"Zephyr's never scared of anything. Andras is always braggin' on that," Nedic said, staring.

"Keep back! A kick from him will kill you." Marik jerked a gateman away from the horse's rear.

While dancing in place and stamping with his hooves, Zephyr made an intimidating sight. Like his father, he'd kicked down doors in the past, a horse too intelligent to be given to anyone but Geoffrey's most devoted former squire.

"Whoa there, boy." Raennia held out one hand toward the wild horse and the other to keep the rest of them at bay. "You're home now, and we're going to get you warmed up. Yes, what a good boy you are. Let us care for you."

Speaking with a low and even voice, Raennia advanced on the horse with slow steps, accomplishing what no other had done in the past. Zephyr and Blackjack were extraordinary animals but often said to be mule-headed and stubborn. They didn't listen to anyone but their riders.

Zephyr's large hooves struck against the cobbled ground, but he didn't charge again. Raennia worked her way closer until she set her hand against his nose.

"There now, it's all right. Come with me."

With a light touch and more gentle words, Raennia guided the war horse into the stable and to his stall. Every second that passed until the animal was soothed enough to approach dragged on like hours to Geoffrey.

"Shall I give him a bit of feed, Ser?"

"Just a bit, Crispin," Geoffrey said.

The fey child scooped a handful of molasses-coated oats and offered it on a palm. With the other hand, Crispin touched the brown residue on Zephyr's neck, made moist again by snow and the perspiration on his coat. He rubbed his fingers together, sniffed it.

"It's blood," he confirmed.

"Is he hurt?"

"Scared witless and cold, but I don't see any cuts on him."

"He's got brambles in his mane," Raennia observed. "Silverthorns. We always do our best to clear them out in the southern hills because they choke out farmland and tangle up the animals' coats. Ruin them for selling."

"Are you saying they were in the southern hills?" Geoffrey asked. "That's hours away, and they haven't been gone that long."

Crispin bounced up to his feet.

"I know where!" he announced. He continued once every set of adult eyes had turned to him. "I mean, I can ask the silverthorn."

"You talk to plants?" Raennia cocked her head to the side.

"I know you mean well, Crispin," Geoffrey said, ruffling the child's hair, "but we need to find Ysolde and Andras."

"But I can help!" Crispin scrunched his face and took a burr from Zephyr's mane into his hand. He brought the fuzzy, silver-blue thorn up to his face and stared at it. "This one says it's from the thicket in the northern wood, by the glade where we pick berries."

"The northern wood." Geoffrey turned and grasped Blackjack by the reins.

"It's a blizzard out there." Jory panted as he stumbled into the stables. Raennia hurried over and draped a blanket around his shoulders. "North of the tributary it's a complete white out, Your Grace." His teeth chattered. "I wager the storm will be over us within the hour."

Geoffrey swore under his breath and moved to the door. Despite the hour, Ashdale Castle remained brightly lit by dozens of magical lanterns glowing at every stone corner. They also shone like small beacons along the main roads where the enormous iron constructs kept travelers safe.

"I have to get out there."

"You'll freeze to death," Fingall chided, a voice of reason. "You won't do your wife any good if you're frozen or hurt."

"The princess knows fire magic, doesn't she?" Jory asked, bright eyes hopeful within his youthful face. "If they've found shelter, they'll be warm."

"The lad is right," Marik said. "Perhaps Andras is merely injured, and they're weathering the storm. I've seen numerous caves to the north while hunting bear."

They were right, all of them, but it galled him to stay when Ysolde was lost. "We'll leave at dawn."

FINDING STRENGTH

28

Ysolde awakened to unyielding, cold stone behind and beneath her. The chill seeped through her dress and numbed her unresponsive limbs, but that wasn't the worst of it. Rough iron shackles trapped her arms over her head. The metal cut into her wrists and left her fingers without feeling.

"You couldn't have made my job easier, Princess."

Her eyes snapped to a dim room without windows, lit only by two torches burning at opposite ends of the cell. Duke Lorwick stepped from the shadows, and his outline clarified, bringing his gloating face into view.

A migraine stabbed behind her left eye, a methodic pulse discouraging the use of magic. She tried to sense it. Tried to form a spell by twitching her fingers; instead, the knife only twisted in her brain.

Whatever they'd used to drug her had a lingering effect.

"What did you do to me?"

"A simple poison laced with glow." Lorwick's smile broadened. "Courtesy of friends I met in Sarangi. It's quite the useful little drug, although it's primarily used by their monks during religious rituals. I had some doubts about it, but as we traveled, your body remained in a state of stasis. You were on the brink of life and death itself and absolutely harmless."

Harmless was the last word she would have used.

"Coward."

He crouched beside her, one hand pressed down on her legs to keep her still. His repulsive touch made bile rise in her throat.

"Can you blame me for taking preventative measures? I've tasted your magic before."

Lorwick trailed the tip of a knife down Ysolde's dress, gliding through the black laces binding her corset. It gaped open to reveal plum velvet beneath. The lace edge of her chemise made a flattering appearance from the neckline of the sumptuous dress bodice.

"When I'm finished with you, you'll wish you'd have accepted my proposal. I would have brought respect to the name Aldemar ruined. Westbrook," he said in a bitter laugh, "has become the joke of the kingdom. A lover of two-legged mongrels. I would have made the people see you as human."

"I *am* human."

He scoffed. "You are no more human than my hound is a wolf."

"To the void with you. If anyone here is an animal, it's you—a disgusting pig."

Lorwick leaned in closer and sneered. "The Marcogh are horse people, aren't they? How poetic that I should have the opportunity to break you like a fine filly. I wonder how harshly you will dare to speak to me once I've had my cock in your mouth."

"I'd bite it off before I allowed you to dishonor me that way."

The dagger dipped, and the sharp point traced a circle over the tip of her breast. He poked her nipple through the velvet hard enough to bite without breaking the skin.

Ysolde wouldn't cry out. She wouldn't give him the satisfaction and reward his taunts with her terror. Instead, she stared into him without breaking eye contact, eyes burning with hate.

"Like a true Marcogh."

She thought of Geoffrey in those moments and how she'd never get to tell him how she felt. Her mind flew to sweet Andras who had died too soon, too early, two years her junior. Shyla would be lost without them both, losing her lover and best friend in one narrow period.

And she thought of her father. Losing Tegau had nearly broken him. *Had* broken him. For years, he hadn't been the same man again, and he'd blamed himself, hating his obligations to the Crown.

Most of all, she feared for her city and what would become of them once she was gone. If Geoffrey could lead without her and bring happiness to her duchy alone.

The first tear wet her cheek, and it had nothing to do with her fate. Had this been how the Marcogh girl of Geoffrey's story felt, terrified for the life of her family and what would become of them?

Lorwick touched her throat with the ungloved silky touch of a man who hadn't worked a day in his life. "I'm going to fuck you like the dog you are, and there's nothing your knight can do about it." He unlaced his breeches. "All the while, I want you to remember this wasn't necessary. It didn't have to happen this way."

A man popped into view, wandering past the dungeon's cell door. "Hey! Lorwick! General Karvempfen wants a hollar at ya. Says it's all important like."

Fastening up again, Lorwick swore and hurried from the cell. "Keep an eye on this bitch. She's drugged, but take no chances."

The new jailer shuffled into the cell and eyed her once Lorwick was gone. He wore the armor of the southern duchy and Lorwick's colors. Traitors. Traitors to the Crown, all of them.

"Please," she called over to him. "If you let me go, I'll grant you clemency."

"Nice try." The soldier chuckled. "No idea why I gotta watch ya. Ain't like yer goin' anywhere," he muttered before turning his back on her to take a piss by the wall. The burning stench of strong urine stung her eyes. "Ahhh."

It couldn't end like this. She couldn't die alone in a fetid dungeon cell, surrounded by the smell of piss.

She wouldn't allow Lorwick the pleasure of watching her succumb.

Ysolde reached for her magic. As she willed her fingers to cooperate, she pushed through the blanket of agony woven by the drugs. The pain was excruciating, a thousand glass shards in her mind at once, each one sharper then the next.

Every time she moved her arms a fine drift of dust rained down over her head. Ysolde peered up at the rotting timbers and old stone overhead.

One entropy spell, even a weak one, would be enough to reduce the wood to dust and stone to pebbles. The thought materialized, a sudden flash of inspiration in the dark. The spell Etienne had taught her took every bit of her focus as pain pierced through her skull. Her arms shook, her eyes watered, but her magic responded.

The iron pin fastening the shackle to the wall clattered to the ground, and like that, Ysolde's arms were free. They fell at first, leaden and dead. Discomfort rushed from her fingertips up to her elbows as sensation returned in an explosion of pins and needles in her palms. She bit her tongue to stifle a cry.

"No sense in trying to get loose. They built forts like this one to last."

Too drunk or too lazy to notice she had freed herself, Ysolde sent up a silent prayer for her guard's incompetence. The brittle shackles crumbled around her wrists until they were nothing but reddened dust.

She rose, pushing past the pain. Ysolde surrounded her fist with fire, creating a brand of living flame. It continued beyond the length of her fingers, the heat of it matched only by the excruciating throb exploding from the center of her skull. It ebbed and flowed like the tide and threatened to pitch her into oblivion again.

Step by slow step, she crept up on her unsuspecting jailor. As the stream of urine slowed and drizzled, Ysolde thrust toward the man's unprotected back with all of her weight behind the blow.

Her jailer died in silence with his eyes wide and his mouth twisted in terror. She swayed and staggered back. Then the ground closed in on her, a blurry stretch of gray stone rising to meet her.

An unfathomable time passed before Ysolde stirred from where she had fallen. Her victim still lay beside her, eyes staring and mouth open. An ashen crater smoldered in his back.

A hollow ache pulsed within her, but when she attempted to reach for her magic, the nausea threatened to lay her back against the ground. Hot tears trickled down her cheeks, but she wiped them away and searched the corpse for a weapon. She took his knife and keys before hurrying through the open cell door.

Ysolde passed empty cells, their bars veiled in thick layers of spider webs and dust. The dank chill settled into her bones again, and her slippered feet sloshed through a puddle of cold water leaking from the crumbling mortar above her.

Only a few feet away from the end of the corridor, Ysolde came to an abrupt stop. Lorwick stood in the archway leading to the stairwell, arms crossed and a dangerous gleam in his eyes.

"Going somewhere, Princess?"

He unclasped his heavy cloak and tossed it aside. Ysolde eyed him warily, her gaze dropping to the sword and knife sheathed at his waist.

Everything about Lorwick was at odds with their surroundings. His thick, velvet doublet was suited for a high feast at a royal hall rather than a dank dungeon infested with vermin. He was the model of sophistication, a handsome man with an ugly soul. His smile oozed charisma, but it didn't reach his eyes.

The dagger in her hand seemed a pitiful defense against his brawn and various armaments, but it was all she had. Without a connection to her magic, few options remained at her disposal.

She couldn't overcome Lorwick by physical means. She couldn't outrun him, and now that he'd seen her escape attempt, she couldn't hide in the dank levels of the fortress's dungeons and pray her abduction had been noticed by Geoffrey.

"Ah, there it is," Lorwick uttered as he came in closer. "You've finally realized you have nowhere to run. Nowhere to hide. I can see it in your eyes."

"Stay back."

"Shall we make a deal, Princess?" Lorwick stepped closer, forcing Ysolde to backpedal. The dagger trembled in her hand.

"You have nothing I want."

"I know otherwise. Look at how your hand trembles. The way you shake."

He took another forward step, and with Ysolde having no alternative but to swing the dagger blade in a wild arc in front of her, he laughed.

"Your failure of a knight hasn't taught you to use a weapon, I see."

She made a silent vow that if she survived, she would accept Geoffrey's next offer to teach her. "What do you want?"

"Come to me, Ysolde. Set down your weapon and become a docile pet. And when I'm done with you, I won't let every man in this camp have his turn. It would be worth it."

"I'd rather die fighting," Ysolde hissed.

"But what will your death accomplish for Hindera and your loved ones? When I finish with what I have planned for this kingdom, you'll wish you were on my good side. As we speak, your father is living his final moments before my future queen rids the throne of him. That is why you're here, my pet."

"What?" An icy grip clenched down on her heart.

"Had you married me instead of that imbecile, your father might have lived. When he proclaimed you his official heir, he sealed his own fate. Rhonwen will need a strong king at her side, a better king, and she has already chosen me. With your coronation only in the planning stages, the bishops and high priests will have no choice but to accept Rhonwen's decree."

"No." She mouthed the word, too stunned and heartsick to do anything more.

Ysolde let the dagger fall from her listless fingers. She couldn't fight him, she had no magic, and she couldn't run. Her empty belly ached, and her mouth was parched.

"Come to me of your own free will, and I promise I'll grant your supporters quick, clean deaths. Your Geoffrey won't be drawn and quartered in the square. Your little maid won't be reamed by my best knights." He leaned forward and dropped his voice. "If you won't do it for yourself, sweet Princess, do it for the ones you love. A noble sacrifice."

"If you've already won and taken our kingdom, why do this to me now? Why does my obedience matter? Why do you need me here?"

"Why?" The handsome man chuckled, teeth white in his perfect smile. "Because I want to. This business between us has nothing to do with Hindera. Come to me now, and I may even be gentle."

Ysolde swallowed, throat tight, and took one small step forward after another. She didn't look up when Lorwick dragged her in the rest of the way. He took her by the chin and forced her face up, his lascivious grin twisting his otherwise attractive features into something disgusting.

Without waiting, Lorwick kissed her hard and thrust his tongue into her mouth while she tried not to choke. His hand groped her breast.

Eyes open, she suffered through it all. Her fingers crept over his belt until the hard pommel of his dagger filled her grasp. The knife slipped free from the scabbard, oiled and maintained to perfection.

In an effortlessly glide, it slammed beneath Lorwick's ribs, and Ysolde's meager strength, as little as it had seemed to her, was more than enough to bury it to the hilt.

His scream was both magical and musical to her ears, a pleasure worth every ounce of pain she experienced when the back of his hand crashed into her cheek. The blow rocked Ysolde back and crumpled her to the floor.

"You bitch!"

"I would never lie with you of my own free will! You're not fit to rut a pig!"

As she struggled to find footing, Lorwick kicked her in the side. "I should have killed you instead of taking pity."

Pain exploded in her ribs in an exquisite wave of agony. It rocked the wind from her lungs. In a desperate bid to remain free, she writhed onto her back and kicked at him, catching his unprotected groin with her heel.

After scrambling to her feet, she bolted down the corridor in the opposite direction with Lorwick in pursuit. Instead of shouting out to the guards, he swore and cursed behind her, his booted feet pounding over stone ground.

Ysolde pushed herself, putting on a final burst of speed. She passed through the doorway first and turned, shoving her full weight against the wooden door as Lorwick reached for her.

His scream followed a sickening crack as the door slammed against his arm. The furious, agonized sound raised goose pimples across her flesh, but she refused to let up the pressure. Neither did he.

There were stairs behind her, a small flight of seven or eight descending into darkness. In her weakened state, she had no hope of overpowering even a one-armed man. The bottom of her slippers skidded and slid, providing no traction.

Ysolde let go. When she surrendered her hold of the door, Lorwick's momentum carried him through and into her.

She was prepared for it, and as he slammed into her, she threw herself backward toward the open archway to her rear. They tumbled and rolled toward the bottom, striking the walls and edges of the steps.

His knee landed in her thigh, and her elbow buried in his ribs, creating a jumble of limbs when they reached bottom. Pain flared through her left leg, radiating upward from her ankle.

She'd hoped the fall would kill one or both of them, but Lorwick groaned beside her on the floor before he pushed up on one palm and glared at her with murder in his eyes.

Unable to run from her captor, a rage overtook her. Ysolde launched herself at him with her fingers curled into claws.

The sound of her pulse raced in her ears, and adrenaline flooded her body. Lorwick roared as she jabbed a finger successfully in his eye. Then her head skipped off the stone floor, blurring her vision behind a curtain of black. She struggled, kicking and punching.

Ysolde pushed at him, and her hands came away slick with blood.

After tumbling across the floor, he came out on top, straddling her hips with his knees, his good hand pressed against her throat. Her fingers scrabbled at the dusty floor in search of anything she could find.

Black spots danced in her vision, and her starved lungs burned as Lorwick's fingers tightened. His face was a twisted mask of fury, bloody spittle foaming at the corners of his mouth.

Her hand closed around a cold, broken stone brick. With her final vestige of strength, Ysolde swung her arm upward and bashed the rock against his temple. Blessed air rushed down her throat, and she wheezed as Lorwick slumped against her, limp and immobile. Too still.

At first, all she could do was lie beneath him, dragging in precious breaths of air while tears streamed down her cheeks. She waited until her head stopped spinning then tried to push Lorwick off, but he was heavier than he looked.

With some difficulty, she rolled the duke onto his side. Open, blue eyes stared back at her beneath a bloody gash splitting his brow. She beat him again with the rock for good measure then a third time, too furious to leave anything to chance. She wasn't satisfied until the meaty, wet sound of his cracking skull indicated he was dead.

Hot tears trickled down her cheeks as she sobbed, the ragged sound echoing against the walls. As much as she wanted to huddle on the floor and cry, the danger of her position struck her with terrifying clarity.

Help hadn't arrived to save Lorwick, and she wouldn't linger to discover why.

Ysolde returned to the main dungeon floor and claimed Lorwick's abandoned cloak. Afterward, she limped toward the archway at the far end and the stairs beyond. They curved in a semi-circular path, sloping upward to a higher level.

She kept close to the wall where the shadows were thickest, avoiding the pools of light cast by torches on the walls.

The fort had been built during a time before the invention of the mage lantern and after the dwarves had made their reclusive retreat into the mountains. Dwarven stonecraft *would* have withstood the test of time.

On the next level, she slipped through an alcove, the corridor leading past a makeshift barracks reeking of tobacco and alcohol. Two mercenaries laughed and played cards. Two more slept in their beds.

In her mind, it seemed like hours passed as she tiptoed through the dusty corridors in search of an exit. Each time she heard a noise or voice, she ducked into the shadows and tried to make herself as small as possible until the sense of danger passed.

The layout struck her as familiar, and a fleeting memory came to mind of her father taking her on a tour of Ackleton's border defenses the year before she received Ashdale's duchy. If their designs were similar, she could expect to find the main doors with a left turn through another corridor.

Boisterous laughter filled the hallway from a room ahead. Ysolde peeked around the corner and felt her heart plummet. At least thirty men occupied the great hall, standing between her and the main doors—thirty armed men with athletic builds and military experience who would be without mercy or compassion if they spotted their prized prisoner making a getaway.

Despair and desperation threatened to overwhelm her. Fate couldn't be as cruel as to end her escape when she'd come so close to freedom.

A cool wind touched her face, a draft from a source she couldn't see. Her eyes cut toward the direction of the current, where a crack of daylight shone radiant and inviting.

The corridor's postern door opened without a creak, exposing her to winter air. She pulled it close behind her, left just as she found it, then limped down a trio of steps leading to the paved walk.

The wind tousled her hair, cold and biting, yet surprising in how it refreshed her spirits. Ysolde shook off the fatigue in her aching body and pressed on at a crawl while the long edges of Lorwick's cloak dragged through the frost layered on the stone.

On a wall up ahead, two men chatted and laughed, one smoking his pipe while the other held an enormous turkey leg.

He bit into the succulent meat, and Ysolde's mouth watered. How long had it been since she'd eaten?

"...sack Ashdale when we're done with this mess. Boss promised it. The bint down below ain't got 'alf an idea 'bout running a city. They won't be prepared for us," the smoker bragged.

His companion, a heavyset man with a barrel chest and a gut overflowing the top of his trousers, chuckled and continued to eat.

"Have you seen the women?"

"Lots of pretty faces and plenty of whores to pass around. We'll make a killin' in slaves. Just you watch. When we reach port in Sarangi, they'll go for at least twenty gold a head. Fifty if they're unspoilt."

"Like they'll make it far before someone's plundering 'em," the portly smoker said.

The pair erupted into lecherous laughter. Ysolde crept beneath them on the ground below, hoping they remained ignorant to her presence.

No one had screamed about Lorwick's death yet, restoring her hope of escaping with her life.

Due to the unforgiving cold, most of the mercenaries and Lorwick's men seemed to have settled inside the fort, with only the pair of lookouts on the high wall. Occupying the old, forgotten fort had made them lax in their duties.

Ysolde could have wept when relief when she found Tikiina among a line of horses under an old, derelict stable's sagging roof. They had all been tied with rope and lacked saddles.

Tikiina's small whinny sent lances of fear into Ysolde's heart. She ducked behind the rotting wooden shelter while her ankle sang in disapproval. It had swelled to twice its usual size, bloated and hot with pain.

"Quiet, girl," she whispered to the mare.

"What was that?" a voice called.

"Just that bloody fleabitten mare. Lorwick said to take an axe to the fucking thing if it keeps up that racket through the night. We'll eat it tomorrow."

Tikiina knelt in the messy straw, allowing Ysolde onto her back. She crawled onto the horse and lay against her, eyes closed.

"Take us home," she said in a hushed voice.

The courtyard stretched empty and abandoned, neglected by the combination of mercs and guards. She saw one man in a watchtower at the opposing side, but he shouted down to another fellow on ground level.

"Give 'em a week! They're forgin' through snow and what else."

"A Narkanthi army ought to be used to snow," the man on the ground complained.

Tikiina hurried through a gap in the palisade while both were occupied.

With so much snow all around them, they couldn't be anywhere but Fort Stonewall, the site of the final battle between Narkanth and Hindera decades ago. With no food, no water, and no magic, the only thing Ysolde had left was her prayers.

Tikiina forged through the snow, and behind them, the alarm split the afternoon sky.

They knew she'd escaped.

BLOOD ON THE SNOW

29

orning dawned with a suspiciously still day, the blizzard leaving a meager blanket of snow in the city streets, which salt and a little work would remove in time. The worst of it had been dumped in the hills and mountain pass, though it wasn't too much for their mounts to forge through.

Raennia had ridden Zephyr. It was Crispin's idea, the young fey promising Zephyr would remember where he and Andras had parted. He led them fearlessly, proud stride cutting through the freshly fallen snow.

"Ho, guardsmen! I see something!" Jory called. "To our left!"

True to Crispin's word, Zephyr had already veered left, leading the rest of the guard. In the distance, something pale and gray protruded from the snowbank.

"It's a…it's a hand," Rae whispered. A fair hand, bloodless and white. Her throat clenched as she dismounted Zephyr's back. Every beat of her racing heart roared like a thunderclap until she brushed aside the layer of newly fallen snow.

Lifeless eyes, once brown but now glassed and gray in death, stared up at her. Rae cried out and stumbled back into the snow.

"Oh no. Ashta's Tears, not this," Jory moaned into one hand.

The commotion drew Marik next with Geoffrey coming in from the rear on his massive horse.

"No," Geoffrey breathed. "Andras."

"He was struck down by multiple blades, I'd say." Marik glanced up at the commander and narrowed his eyes. "They were attacked."

Zephyr nosed at the still body and whinnied.

"Ysolde! Ysolde!" Geoffrey tore at the snow with his hands, a frantic man with desperation in his eyes, "Don't bloody stand there. Help me!"

Jory shot Rae an uncertain look but moved over and started sweeping through the snow. Raennia joined him, Marik not far behind. The thick drifts made their task slow, laborious, and cold, numbing their fingers within moments of beginning the search.

Each time they found a body, Raennia's stomach tensed. She uncovered several armored men and her companions a dozen more but no sign of their princess. They found only forest debris and old leaves, as well as the thriving snowdrops that would eventually push through to the surface and flourish in the cold weather.

There was no sign of Ysolde or Tikiina, any tracks long covered by the snowstorm.

"These men were burned alive," Marik said. "The princess wields fire, does she not?"

"She does," Geoffrey confirmed.

"These here around Andras were slain by a blade. He made a final stand here." Sorrow dimmed Jory's admiration. "There must have been an army against them."

"She's dead." Geoffrey slumped against a tree. "I failed her. I failed her when she needed me most."

"You don't know that, Your Grace," Marik said, his voice uncertain.

"We've found no sign of Ysolde, and her guard lies dead before us," Geoffrey said in a tremulous voice. "My dear cousin. It should have been me to travel with her. I should have been at her side. I—"

Taking hold of Geoffrey by the shoulders, Rae steadied him and looked into his face. "Get ahold of yourself and listen to me. Ysolde isn't here, and for as long as we haven't found her body, I refuse to believe she's dead. She's out there somewhere, and she needs us."

Time held still, teacher and student, mentor and mentee, squire and knight, the others silent bystanders holding their breath as Geoffrey stared at her with wide eyes. He shuddered once, and the last anguished groan fell from his lips before he leaned back against the tree again.

"You're right. Gods, you're right. Grant me a moment to think."

"Take what you need."

They fashioned a litter from branches and a spare blanket to move Andras's body. She glanced at Geoffrey once while they set their fallen comrade to rights. The duke's eyes were closed, and his lips moved silently in prayer while he clutched his prayer beads in one gauntleted fist.

While he had guided Rae through several rounds of meditation and prayer, she had yet to experience the tranquil sense of control he'd promised. But within moments, he had changed, and he stepped forward again with the grief washed from his face in lieu of a determined set to his jaw.

Geoffrey crouched by one of the corpses they had uncovered and flipped the body over. "Do you recognize this armor, Laurent?"

"It is Iron Fist. It does not surprise to find them here. They take any job offered for right amount of gold."

"Including the abduction of a princess," Geoffrey muttered. "Marik, I'd like for you and Jory to return Andras to the castle. Redirect the bulk of the search parties and tell them to travel north. Laurent, Raennia, and I will continue on from here."

"Aye, Your Grace," Marik said.

After he'd given more instructions for Marik to relay to the lieutenants at the castle, Geoffrey mounted his horse and turned to the north.

"When you killed Shadeglen, did he give you any reason to suspect he hadn't worked alone?" he asked Laurent.

"No. He was petrified. I thought he tell me full truth of everything."

"Then he withheld the name of one of his conspirators. Perhaps he hoped to survive your interrogation and feared retribution at his cohort's hands."

"Yes," Laurent agreed. "If Iron Fist take Ysolde, they do for money and orders of another man. We will find her." He drew his cloak tight and remained tall on his borrowed horse, despite the occasional tremor.

"Will you be able to travel in this weather?" Raennia asked the elf in a quiet voice as Geoffrey moved ahead of them.

"I would wrestle yeti for Ysolde."

The three of them set out, aware of what lay before them. At any moment, they could stumble upon a camp of hardened mercenaries with a bloodthirst for coin, and the fate befallen to Andras could become theirs.

Would the three of them be enough?

By nightfall, the unforgiving wind had numbed the tips of Laurent's ears. He rubbed them and frowned, his tall body huddled in his saddle for the warmth exuded from his horse.

"Laurent can't take more of this, Geoffrey. There's an orchard nearby where we may take shelter for the night," Raennia called out.

Geoffrey grunted but turned his horse in the right direction, revealing his familiarity with the area. The moon shone high in the sky by the time they reached the modest house set in the middle of the sweet apple orchard. The owner stepped outside with a lantern in one hand, an axe in the other.

"I know him." Rae dismounted her horse and hurried forward.

He wasn't yet elderly, a man of his early sixties with steel gray hair and a face creased with the heavy wrinkles of a hard life. He squinted at them. "Raennia? What brings you out at such a later hour?"

"Tracking bandits, Howen." She remembered the older man from her childhood, when her parents had done a seed trade with him. "I come with the Duke of Ashdale."

"You jest."

She shook her head, expression solemn. "No trickery, on my word. Can you put us up for the night?"

Geoffrey stepped forward and bowed courteously to Howen, whose eyes grew increasingly large in his weathered face. "It would do us an honor to have shelter in your home for this eve."

"The honor is ours, Duke Ashdale. Kaven!" Howen called.

A lanky youth came up behind him. The boy's eyes grew round when he saw the three visitors.

"Take their horses to the barn. Get 'em warmed and fed. I'll do the same for our guests."

"Yes, Father."

Laurent shook for an hour by the hearth, insisting to Geoffrey he was able to go on with them. A desert elf belonged in the scorching heat, and despite being half-blooded, he showed most of their tendencies. Raennia kept him supplied with hot cider, courtesy of their host.

"We saw a host of men traveling northeast not a day past. Too many to be bandits."

"Did they cause you any trouble?" Geoffrey asked.

"No, they passed by us with little issue, thank the goddess. I'm missing a goat and lost a few chickens, but it wasn't worth our lives to protest it."

Geoffrey raised a brow. "How many were there?"

Howen considered. "From what I saw, perhaps a dozen. Maybe two. You understand, I wasn't standing outside and watching. Spied them from the windows until they cleared the orchard.

"Very wise of you to do," Geoffrey said.

After a dinner of thick stew and fresh baked bread, they managed to convince Howen that giving up his bed for the duke wasn't necessary.

By sunrise, Laurent had recuperated from his frosty ordeal to ride with them. The generosity of their hosts carried into the morning hours, as Howen's benevolent wife awakened early to scramble eggs and brew black tea, which the three famished riders accepted. The meal warmed their bellies, and they exited the cottage to find Kaven loading their horses with camping gear.

"I can't let you leave this way." The old farmer chuckled and patted Zephyr's side. "You may not find warm lodgings where you're going, and the way I see it, Ashta sent the lot of you here for a reason."

"You have our deepest thanks," Geoffrey told the man. "How can I ever repay you?"

"You can buy out his stock of ciders and apple wine for the castle cellars," Raennia suggested, giving Howen a wink. "No one makes better."

"Done."

Howen bowed. "Thank you, Your Grace. Good luck hunting those scoundrels."

Their steeds picked their way through the frost until they ran afoul of muddy trails on the northern highway. The snow had begun to melt, a warmer day banishing the blanket of white and turning it to slush.

Geoffrey spoke little while Laurent and Raennia filled the silence with idle conversation regarding Hindera's history with Narkanth.

"I read of them," Laurent admitted. "So much hatred for foolish reasons."

"If these mercenaries took the princess across the border, it'll mean war," she murmured.

"Pray it is not so," the half-elf replied.

Raennia prayed it every moment. Their northward search provided few clues. Few homesteads were established near the start of the cold tundra, and the two they passed had seen no sight of their quarry.

After the first eight hours in the saddle, Geoffrey turned his worried eyes to the horizon. The sun set soon after, and when its loss proved too much for Laurent's sensitive desert elven constitution, Raennia found a cavern to make camp in. The shallow depression in the rock provided barely enough room for them and their horses, but it sheltered from the biting wind.

She worried for her mentor. Dark circles smudged Geoffrey's hollow eyes, and he spoke infrequently as his determination cracked and the despair seeped through.

He slept poorly that night. Whenever she awakened, she saw him pacing at the mouth of the cave or slumped by the fire twisting his wedding band around one finger.

By evening the next day, Geoffrey's optimism returned. It took the word of a traveling merchant who saw a band of men for hire on the road.

"I can only tell you they wasn't goin' to the south or travelin' the coast, Your Grace. Looked like they were goin' thataway."

"We must part ways to cover greater ground. Rae, travel northeast toward the remnants of Fort Stonewall. I'll continue north to Fort Blackvale. Laurent, I'd like you to check the cave systems on the eastern range, and if either of you find anything, do *not* engage them. Use the dragonbreath beacon and take care until help arrives."

They'd each set out with one of the alchemical flares when leaving from the castle.

Raennia patted her leather supply bag and nodded. "As you wish. May we have good news when we meet again."

They separated at the fork in the highway, each forging on to face the bitter cold alone. A long trail lay before her with few lampposts along the way. She knew the path due to Geoffrey forcing her to learn every main road. She, Jory, and Marik, as well as the other new guards, had been tasked with memorizing Hindera's map.

Raennia jerked her eyes toward a copper shape moving beneath the gray sky. She'd never seen any other horse such a brilliant shade of burnished red, the color unique to the Marcogh.

It had to be Tikiina.

Without waiting to verify her thoughts, Raennia removed the dragonbreath capsule from her pack and shook it briskly before aiming it above her. It required no application of fire, only a removal of its cord with a sharp yank, causing the lid to pop free and its contents to burst into the air.

It was glorious, a sight she could have appreciated under better circumstances. Radiant color in green and red shot upward into the sky with showers of gold surging over the clouds. It streamed until the cylinder grew unbearably hot, and even then, she didn't dare to release it until the last glimmer of color streaked skyward.

Anyone, friend or foe for miles around, would be able to see the signal. She prayed Geoffrey and Laurent would be among them.

Urging Zephyr into a gallop, Raennia chased the distant figure but never made progress. She called out, shouted Ysolde's name, shouted Tikiina's, but to no avail.

Zephyr plowed through a copse of trees, and when they emerged, the copper shadow was gone. He slowed and pranced in place while Raennia stood in the stirrups with a hand shading her eyes. She searched for tracks, any disturbance in the snow and slush, but saw nothing.

"I'm sure I saw Tikiina, Zeph."

He nickered gently and picked up speed. His nostrils flared, snorting steam into the cool air.

"Zeph?"

The stallion transitioned from a trot to a jog. She let him lead, placing her trust in the horse who had led them to Andras's body.

Tikiina emerged from around the rocky outcropping, a slumped, cloaked figure on her back.

"Ysolde?"

The rider stirred and looked up, Ysolde's pale face peering out from beneath the furred hood. The princess stared past her, glassy-eyed, then slid from Tikiina's back into a graceless heap on the ground.

Swearing, Raennia dismounted and rushed over to kneel beside her.

"Ysolde! Ysolde! Stay with me," Rae begged the princess.

She pulled Ysolde to a sitting position in the snow while Zephyr and Tikiina nickered nervously. The princess's lips were blue-gray with cold, as were her fingers, despite the heavy cloak worn over her shoulders. Beneath, rusty brown stains soaked her dress.

"They're coming," Ysolde whispered. Her wind-chapped lips had cracked. "Too many. Too many to fight."

With strength she hadn't known she possessed, Rae lifted Ysolde onto Zephyr's back and climbed into the saddle behind her. The silver horse shot off like cannon fire, a streak against the darkening trail.

Rae didn't dare to look behind her. She'd seen no one at first but Ysolde, but as the fine hairs on the back of her neck rose, she knew they were no longer alone.

Risking it, she glanced over a shoulder and spotted five men riding their horses hard and fast, whipping them and shouting. Their words, a foreign tongue she'd never heard, carried to her on the wind.

"Five of them," Rae said.

"Can't outrun," Ysolde whispered. "Slowing you."

"I won't leave you behind. Not when I've come so far to find you."

Rae had never raced a horse so swiftly, but Zephyr was true to his name, a natural on the cold ground. His limitless endurance continued to the mountain path, and their pursuers failed to gain ground.

If they were mercenaries from Kigi and other warm places, they weren't trained to ride in the snowy conditions. They'd have little experience with the combination of Hindera's frigid climate and the rocky, uneven ground.

Raennia veered left down the mountain path, trusting Zephyr to maintain his footing.

One of the mercenaries, unskilled with navigating the mountainous terrain on horseback, skidded over the ledge, his horse resisting him all the while, tugging back at the bit and kicking out. They both tumbled down the ravine and out of Rae's sight.

Four.

She didn't question their small number, but as she fled with the princess, Tikiina racing behind them over stone and ice, she concocted a plan. Less than ten miles away, she was bound to encounter one of the northern watchtowers.

They closed in as she formed her fragile scheme, one of the mercs at Zephyr's left flank. She took a sharp turn right, weaving down the rocks and tightening her arm around Ysolde's thin waist. The princess felt small and frail.

A crossbow bolt ripped past Raennia's shoulder, missing by a narrow margin to embed in a tree trunk.

She gasped and leaned forward, guarding Ysolde with her body. The road before them stretched into the horizon, an endless, risky path she couldn't continue for long. They closed in again.

Like Andras, Rae had no choice but to make a stand. With a touch of her right calf to Zephyr's ribs, she coaxed him to make a sharp turn. He rolled back and spun to face the horsemen who sped past them.

As she slid from Zephyr's back, Ysolde gave a feeble protest.

"Stay on the horse, Your Grace," she whispered. "Take her to safety, Zeph, if the opportunity arises."

When Andras and Geoffrey confessed they had staged the confrontation in the city, Rae had been furious with them both. They'd terrified her. For all of her confidence with a blade, what she'd feared that day hadn't been losing her life, but Ysolde coming to harm.

Now, she understood. A strange sense of tranquility came over her, loosening her stiff spine and rejuvenating her exhausted muscles. She drew her sword and assumed a defensive stance, watching the man in the lead.

He was an enormous, rugged brute with dark green hair fashioned into thick locks. The tusks poking over his lip told her he was half-orc, and according to Laurent, the Iron Fist was led by two of them—Tuwaktu and Tiwekmir.

The man in front of her couldn't have been more than thirty. His face was unlined by age, almost handsome despite the deeply masculine chiseled angles and too-strong jaw.

"Tiwekmir?" She based her guess on Laurent's description of the two brothers.

He started. "You know my name?"

"I do. As we speak, there are dozens—no, hundreds of soldiers combing through the hills for the princess. They've seen the beacon I released, and they know we're here. If you leave now before they arrive, you'll have your life and whatever you were paid."

One of the men barked out harsh and loud laughter. Even Tiwekmir cracked a grin. He glanced to his left at a pale man with a long, hooked nose. They spoke in an indiscernible tongue. Then the fair-skinned man shook his head.

"Where are these soldiers? You're alone. My companion's hunting hawk can see for miles." His eyes dropped to Rae's chest.

She wore a furred cloak over her shoulders, dappled black-and-gray fur from the longhaired rams that frequented the mountain ranges. Beneath it, her woolen tunic and boned leather doublet failed to convey her rank in the Ashguard pecking order.

"They'll come," Raennia insisted.

The men all chuckled, and their leader nodded toward her. "Knock the bitch out and toss her over the back of her horse. We'll have another whore for the auction."

Two of the men dismounted and approached. Rae backed up and raised her sword.

"Don't," she warned.

"You even know how to swing that, little girl?"

Answering with a vicious stab and sweep, she disarmed the first mercenary and smashed her hilt into his face. He staggered back into his companion.

After that, the mercs learned their lesson and split up, coming at her from both sides.

She had seconds to act before her opponents realized the depth of her skill, that they couldn't underestimate her and survive. She reversed the sword as a third merc came up behind her—ducking his fist to the back of her skull by swaying to her left—and plunged her blade behind her into his abdomen. She spun to rip it free, spilling his guts.

Three.

Rae fought with a ferocity that had startled most of her peers. Some of the others newly inducted into the Ashguard had shied away from her during spars and training. She was quick with a blade, displaying a proclivity for disabling her opponents, and what she lacked in strength, she offset with cunning.

Tiwekmir dismounted his horse as her blade whistled. Steel sang against steel, and she twisted and swung again, slicing one mercenary across his throat. Blood pulsed to the rhythm of their battle frenzy.

Two.

From the corner of her eye, she saw him stumble and grasp at his spurting neck. He swung a feeble stroke while she ducked beneath his blade, rushed him, and thrust him toward their leader.

Tiwekmir jerked back, giving ground, but his alarm lasted only for a moment. His tusked mouth widened in a cruel grin.

With two against one, the odds weren't in her favor. Hoofbeats pounded behind her, and Raennia realized Zephyr had left as directed, galloping away with Ysolde passed out on his back.

She didn't care. She trusted him to take the princess home. Raennia only needed to make her final stand. If she could cripple both men, Ysolde would be safe.

Tiwekmir was a monstrous beast of a man, taller than Geoffrey, with an enormous barrel chest and tree trunk limbs. Unlike the others, he'd donned armor before the pursuit, and his plate shone with well-maintained luster.

His effortless parries forced Raennia back with each failed strike. Fending off both assailants wore her down.

"You're quick. Good. I like it when a woman has some fight in her."

Tikiina lurked nearby, the mare watching from the edge of the fight. Suddenly, she charged from the rear, taking the second mercenary by surprise.

He dealt a gash to her shoulder, slicing through copper fur and staining her coat with rich, red blood. She twisted and leapt, drove both hind hooves into his chest, and bolted away. Her trick wouldn't work twice.

One.

Raennia dragged in a ragged breath and eyed the hulking mercenary commander. Calculated cunning and anger replaced the earlier amusement in his eyes.

He rushed forward and put her on the defensive, forcing her to scramble back until he broke through her guard. She twisted her body but turned her head too late. The slice glided over her cheek, cutting deep into tissue and muscle beneath. If she hadn't whipped her head back, it would have also taken her eye.

She screamed out in pain and stumbled back as the blood welled to the surface, barely raising her weapon in time to fend off the next swing. Their swords crossed and remained locked.

Pressing his advantage, the half-orc drove a small dagger into her shoulder. The excruciating pain nearly caused her to drop her sword, but she pressed through it and gripped the hilt all the more tightly.

"Give up, and I'll show you mercy."

"No!"

"Mule-headed woman. You should have been one of our females. Here in this dismal wasteland of snow, your skill is wasted on the Hinderans. Maybe I'll keep you for myself. Train you to accept our ways, whether you want it or not."

Raennia spat in his face. "I'd rather die."

"As you like."

Tiwekmir backhanded her. The blow caught her in the face, forcing her back until she fell heavily into the snow. Hot blood streamed down one nostril, and her eyes watered from the pain. He'd broken her nose.

It couldn't end like this. She was all that remained between him and Ysolde. Between him and those she held dear. Determination surged through her, accompanied by a strengthening fount of calm.

As the jagged, black blade descended, Rae thrust up with her sword to parry.

In an explosion of radiance, the steel blazed like sunlight, golden and vibrant from its hilt to the blade's tip. Holy fire crackled along its length, and new strength surged along her aching arm, thrusting Tiwekmir off balance and shattering his weapon into glittering fragments that fell around her in the snow.

Raennia leapt to her feet and lunged forward. Her blade pierced through his cuirass and slid into flesh while Tiwekmir's startled eyes locked on her face. He couldn't believe it, and neither could she until he was choking on the blood filling his own lungs.

With blood streaming from her face and shoulder, Rae abandoned her sword and stumbled forward toward the blurry shape of the mare in the distance. Tikiina trotted toward her to little avail, as the world around the Raennia spun, a disoriented haze.

DOMINIQUE KRISTINE

She collapsed in the snow before reaching the horse, praying not for herself, but for the woman she had saved.

A Light in the Dark

30

G eoffrey had nearly reached the fort when he saw the magical beacon light the sky. He turned Blackjack toward the eruption of color and galloped hard across the rocky terrain. In his mind, it was a race against time with an unknown number of dangers lurking ahead.

He didn't find the girls, but snowy tracks beneath the origin of the flare took him southward along a rocky ridge trampled from a half dozen or more travelers on horseback. He saw disturbed snow near its ledge and dismounted to look below. A man lay at the bottom beside a dead horse.

Blackjack snorted and stamped.

"I know, mate. We've got to find them. We *will* find them," he murmured.

Geoffrey followed the tracks of multiple horses until he found four corpses in the cold, one of which still sported Raennia's sword in his chest. The blade had pierced through armor, flesh, and bone, then armor again, skewering the brutish half-orc. Blood stained the trampled snow a fresh crimson.

With daylight dwindling and the remnants of her flare vanished from the evening sky, Geoffrey released his beacon as well.

"Ysolde!" he hollered. "Raennia!" His voice echoed across the uneven terrain, met with silence.

After retrieving Rae's sword, he turned Blackjack around and searched for any sign of her passage. Bright droplets of blood mingled with unshod hoof prints, and with no other clues, he followed them.

An hour passed before the trail came to an end, and the building pressure in his chest eased when he spotted Zephyr and Tikiina lying in a hay-filled lean-to.

The exhausted horses nickered. Without prompting, Blackjack trotted to join his kin, and Geoffrey dismounted to head inside the only other available shelter.

Only three walls of the dilapidated cottage stood, its roof half sunk. The hearth was cold, but a lingering, strange warmth in the air felt, like magic skimming across his senses.

Rae lay beside Ysolde beneath a blanket stretched over two aged, wafer-thin mattresses.

"Ysolde!"

His wife stirred, opening her eyes and blinking up at him. "Geoffrey?"

Sword and fears cast aside, he dropped to his knees at her side and pulled her against him. Tears trickled down his cheeks without shame.

"It's truly you?" Her arms tightened around his neck, and her body shuddered in his embrace. "I thought I would never see you again."

"And I feared the same. What happened?"

A glance at Rae over Ysolde's shoulder told him a story of her survival. The unconscious woman's nose was skewed and her eyes shadowed with purple smudges beneath them. A new gash crossed over the thin scar she'd received weeks ago.

"Raennia found me and fought them off while Zephyr bore me away. The last thing I remember is…there was a woman. A woman helped me inside."

Geoffrey surveyed the area and saw no one. They were alone. "There's no one else here. Sweet Ashta." He touched the cut strings of her dress bodice then her bruised cheek. "Who did this?"

Holding her in his arms wasn't enough. He wanted to run his hands over every inch, inspect her for any injury. The state of her clothing made his mind jump to the worst conclusions, a terror no one wanted to face. He'd kill whoever had hurt her.

"Lorwick," she whispered, a tremble in her voice. "It was Lorwick, Geoffrey, and h-h-he tried…" Her lower lip quivered, and fresh tears spilled down her cheeks. "He's dead now. I killed him when I escaped from Fort Stonewall."

He drew her closer and held her head to his shoulder, his cheek against her hair. "I'm sorry, Ysolde, I should have known. I should have been with you."

"No," she said with force. She leaned back and brought her palm against his cheek. "You were where you needed to be. Just as you are now. Andras… They… Geoffrey, they killed him."

"I know," he whispered. "We found him as we searched for the both of you. If Lorwick weren't dead, I'd make him wish he were for all that he's done."

"It wasn't only him." Panic filled her voice, and she pulled back, looking up at him with wild eyes. "Geoffrey, he wasn't working alone. My father is in danger! He said Rhonwen was going to kill him, and there was a general from Narkanth."

"Slow down, love. Etienne's letter said he should be with your father."

"Letter?" Her brows furrowed. "I didn't read it."

A new knot of tension twisted in his gut, but he kept his silence regarding the letter's heartbreaking contents. Now wasn't the time. "There's nothing we can do for your father from here. Let's get you both back to the castle."

After drawing the blanket back to her shoulders, Geoffrey moved to the opening in the cottage's wall and waited for help to arrive.

***

After two days of riding, the wearied company returned to Ashdale with a full escort. Word of their arrival spread like wildfire through every district until citizens lined the streets all the way up to the castle, crying out thanks and praises to the gods while tossing flowers into their path. They welcomed Ysolde home with open, loving arms.

King Aldemar met them at the castle gates, dressed in full battle regalia. He'd arrived hours ahead of them by ship with Etienne in his company.

"Father, you're alive!"

"Ysolde!" Aldemar rushed forward and helped his daughter down himself, crushing her close. "Thank the Trinity."

"No," Geoffrey said. "Thank Raennia."

Marik and Jory assisted Raennia down from Zephyr's back, the latter holding her steady with an arm around her shoulders when her legs threatened to give out beneath her. She had insisted on riding back with Geoffrey and Ysolde rather than wait for a wagon. "I'm only glad I was able to find her. Ysolde rescued herself long before I came across her."

Aldemar looked between both women with a mixture of wonder and respect. He kissed Ysolde's brow before finally releasing her back into Geoffrey's arms. "Have the ones responsible for this been eliminated?"

"Duke Lorwick is dead," Geoffrey told him. "I've commanded the troops to storm Fort Stonewall, where he and the Iron Fist set up their base. His body will be brought back here to display beside Shadeglen."

Ysolde gave no argument when Geoffrey directed her inside to a warm bath and bed. He promised to relay the story of her miraculous escape for her, and once Raennia repeated her part in the rescue, she, too, retired to a guest bedchamber in the main castle residence at his insistence.

Once the women were settled, he met with Etienne and Aldemar in the war room.

"Now that the needs of the women have been addressed, let us speak regarding this travesty. Ysolde would have liked to stand here with us, but she's earned the right to sleep in her own bed."

"You'll hear no complaints from me," Aldemar said.

"Ysolde told me Lorwick spoke of the queen, of her role to kill you." Geoffrey sank into his chair, weary beyond belief, but certain matters needed to be addressed. "Is she under guard in Stormwatch?

Aldemar and Etienne exchanged looks, but it was the king who answered with a heavy voice. "Rhonwen escaped."

"Prior to my arrival," Etienne added. "If only I rode as quickly as a hawk could fly. I foolishly kept Adrienne by my side. If I'd sent her—"

"Don't blame yourself," Aldemar cut him off. "I underestimated my queen's sympathizers, and for that, the blame resides with me alone. After Scion Dufresne's letter arrived, I confronted her about her involvement in Tegau's disappearance, her...death. When she stood before me in silence, defiance in her eyes, I saw the truth." Deep lines etched Aldemar's brow. "I had her confined to her room, under guard, and still she escaped."

"Then she's likely gone to Narkanth. They've sent one of their generals to Stonewall. Lorwick was in contact with him."

"Do you know which? No, never mind. One or another, it makes no difference. Narkanth has always acted as a single mind, with few dissidents among their ranks. If a general entered Hindera, it was by order of their king."

"Then it's war," Geoffrey said grimly.

"Fas Perra will stand with you," Etienne said. "I will see it is done."

Aldemar turned to face Geoffrey. "I will leave several ships under your command, my son. We'll fortify the northern towers and show them Hindera is no easy target."

Discussion fell briefly to matters of security, until the king noticed Geoffrey's heavy eyes and haggard features.

Ordered to rest, Geoffrey took his leave. He had long surpassed reasonable exhaustion. First, he peeked into Ysolde's room and saw her snuggled beside Crispin in bed.

Geoffrey chuckled and continued to his personal chamber, moving as stiff as a poorly oiled suit of armor. He trudged through the darkened bedroom and enjoyed a long soak without attendants or a wife to care for him.

The whole while he lay there, submerged to his shoulders in steaming water and surrounded by the scent of menthol and herbs, his mind traveled to Ysolde's ordeal, her survival.

"Thank the Goddess," he said out loud.

His muscles hummed a song of disapproval when he emerged from the tub, as the long soak had given every inch of him the opportunity to stiffen.

A fresh hearthfire glowed, courtesy of Maribeth, he thought. Its heat spread throughout the room, radiating into cold space and warming his skin. His joints protested moving, but he approached his bed to find a lump distorting the heavy fur blankets.

"Ysolde?"

His wife lay curled beneath the layers of fur and silk with only the top of her head visible to him. Her appearance in his bed didn't surprise Geoffrey. Crispin was not a peaceful sleeper, often wiggling, squirming, and turning about during the night.

She said nothing, so he presumed her to be asleep and slid beneath the covers to remain a casual distance from her. After a few seconds, she bridged the gap and moved nearer.

"Why are you so far from me?" Ysolde asked.

"I thought you were asleep." Geoffrey rolled to his side and faced her.

Her midnight eyes watched him, dancing flames reflected in her gaze. It wasn't Maribeth's doing, as he previously thought; the fire was connected to Ysolde's sorcery instead.

"He didn't...spoil me," she said in a quiet voice.

"Sweetheart, no, that never—" He swallowed back the lie forming in his throat. "Even if he had, it wouldn't change my feelings for you, Ysolde. Or my desires for you. My only thought was in letting you rest, undisturbed."

"I thought maybe..." She sniffled, the small sound tearing at his heart. "I was afraid you wouldn't—"

"Ysolde, stop and listen to me." He cupped his palm against her cheek and swept away a teardrop with his thumb. "Nothing in this world could change what we have."

"When I first saw Ashlynne, I was afraid. Then later, in the dungeon, I thought of you and wished I had said more. Let you know that I never doubted you."

"Seeing her was a shock, but I realized something." He pushed up on one elbow and lowered his palm from her cheek, taking her hand instead. "The love and affection I once felt had changed. It didn't hurt the way I imagined it would, and we parted as friends. But when you failed to return, Ysolde, I have never known such fear."

"Nothing scares you," she protested.

"This did, and I realized that we've wasted enough time. *I* have wasted enough time without speaking my mind and my heart." Geoffrey clasped her hand between large palms. "I love you, Ysolde."

The hearth flashed as the slow-burning cinders combusted, shooting up toward the chimney.

"Geoffrey…" Ysolde's eyes shone, glossy with unshed tears and the pattern of the night sky across her dark irises.

"And I am ashamed it took nearly losing you to understand I can't live without you. How much I look forward to your smiles and your laughter." His arm slid around her, and he gathered her close against his bare chest.

"I love you too," she whispered in the dark. "Sometimes I think I always have."

Relief and elation swelled in his heart, banishing the cold, clinging doubts and fears. A part of him had worried she would never see beyond the forced arrangement of their marriage, whether affection grew between them or not.

No longer.

With laughter and lightness in his voice, he held his wife all the more tightly and declared his love a second time against her ear and then a third against her throat, knowing he would never tire of saying the words.

He had his princess back—his light, his life—and he would never let the shadows take her from him again.

At Peace

Andras was laid to rest before a crowd of hundreds, his battered body beneath a velvet sheet in Nirmad's colors. Fragrant oils soaked the wooden funeral pyre and scented the air, awaiting the touch of flames to send his soul to the veil beyond.

Ysolde stood with Shyla by her side, arm around her friend's trembling shoulders. Grief left Shyla pale, her eyes puffy and red, her cheeks wet with tears.

His funeral was long overdue, delayed by the troubles in the kingdom. They couldn't put him to rest while Ysolde and Geoffrey, as well as so many among the guard who loved him, were gone.

Geoffrey approached Ysolde and Shyla from where he'd stood with the priest of death beside the body during the final rites and prayers.

"Shyla, he would have wanted you to have this." He opened his fist to reveal a pendant depicting the sacred moon of Nirmad, a silver crescent stamped into an onyx medallion. Andras had worn it every day without fail.

Fresh tears rolled down Shyla's cheeks as she accepted the pendant, clutching it close to her heart.

"Thank you." Her voice cracked.

"I know it isn't much, considering how much you meant to him—"

"No," Shyla interrupted, managing a faint, brief, watery smile. "It is more than enough. Part of me feels as if it should go with him, but I will wear it in his honor and his memory."

The priest in black, silver-trimmed robes stepped forward with a burning torch and set the pyre aflame.

Shyla tried to stand tall and brave, but the effort became too much. She broke down, shoulders sagging, and wailed into her hands. Ysolde pulled her close while her friend wept against her shoulder

"I'm so sorry," she whispered against Shyla's hair. "I wish I'd been alone. That he hadn't ridden out with me."

"No." Shyla uttered the word amidst her sobs. "He died in the service he held dear to his heart. He would not want these tears." But they came just the same, whether she tried to suppress them or not. Her shoulders quaked, and a fresh torrent spilled down her cheeks. "Gods, I miss him."

"I know," Ysolde whispered. "He loved you, Shyla, and that love will always be with you.

Ysolde took small pleasure in knowing two of the men responsible for his death had been slain, and she prayed for the others to face justice as well once the Ashguard returned from retaking Fort Stonewall.

"I promise you, Shyla, his death won't go unpunished."

But would Tegau's murder receive the same vengeance? Geoffrey had broken the news of her mother's death to her on the morning following their return, but there had been no grief, only a hollow sense of acceptance. Deep down, part of her had always known.

As a tear slipped down Ysolde's cheek, she thought of the lives lost to Rhonwen's treachery and vowed to do anything to bring her former stepmother to justice.

***

If Etienne and Laurent were nervous, they concealed their apprehension beautifully. Raennia trembled as she stood alongside the two brothers.

She'd declined magical healing of her face, wearing the scars earned in the service of the princess with pride, though the healers had straightened her nose to the best of their abilities. It would always have a small bump, a slight skew, and in that similarity, she and Geoffrey matched.

Clad in his royal regalia, heavy furs, and jeweled crown, King Aldemar stood before them with a smile. "So it would appear I have the three of you to thank for the survival of my family. Each of you played a vital role in the events recently come to pass, and you have my gratitude."

"It was our honor," Etienne said.

Laurent nodded, prone to giving silent agreement when alongside his brother.

Aldemar turned to Raennia, who straightened with dignity.

"You are the woman who saved my daughter," Aldemar said.

"Yes, Your Majesty," Raennia said in a tiny voice. She bowed deeply and held her pose, afraid to lift her head.

She wore men's clothing tailored to her shape, leather leggings beneath a black surcoat trimmed in silver. It laced down her back and at the sides, defining her figure as feminine—a request from the tailor who could not bear to conceal her curves in full.

Weeks ago when Andras had instructed her to purchase funeral garb to honor her fallen brothers, she hadn't expected to wear it to his own pyre.

"When Geoffrey first described his decision to take a woman to squire, I thought him foolish and short-sighted. What honor could there be in sending a Hinderan woman to her death? You stand no taller than the shortest man in this room, your body weaker, incapable of wielding our largest weapons."

Rae's spine stiffened.

"Yet you stand here before me days after we have lost a man of great physical strength and battle prowess. You alone stood between Ysolde and a company of mercenaries. Slayer of a half-orc captain."

She blinked up at him.

"Please never bow to me again, Raennia. On this day, it is I who should bow to you, and yet even that seems insufficient for the undertakings completed by you three proud men and women. I would grant upon you each a boon of your choosing. From now and henceforth, I am Aldemar to you and never Your Majesty again."

Aldemar turned his gaze to Etienne. "What might I give a mage of your skill? My libraries are forever open to your perusal, but it seems so little for what you have done and for the task ahead of you. Recovering Tegau's remains will bring peace to her restless spirit, and for that, no prize will ever be enough."

"I ask nothing for myself," Etienne replied. "Only that my brother always has a home in your kingdom, and if he should ever need protection, it will be given."

"Granted," Aldemar said without questioning. "But surely you desire something for yourself, Prince of Fas Perra?"

Etienne shook his head and smiled. "The honor has been restored to my kingdom's name, and my brother is safe. I need nothing more."

"I also ask nothing," Laurent said. "I have spent much of life in dark work for gain of others. It is pleasure to do good deeds to help a friend."

"Then I shall bestow a gift upon you of my own choosing for your unwavering service to the Crown," Aldemar said, stunned by their modesty. "To you, Laurent of Fas Perra, I bequeath the title Count of Shadeglen, so that none ever question the value of your words and honor again."

Laurent's eyes bugged. "I could not— I do not know Hinderan law. What things to do."

"A steward will advise you, and in time, you will learn our tongue as well as any other. May you always have a home in Shadeglen, Laurent." The king bowed deeply, nearly to the floor.

"Take it," Etienne advised him.

"Yes, of course. I accept, Aldemar. My many thanks."

Raennia's eyes darted to Ysolde and Geoffrey, who sat in their thrones on the high dais of the audience chamber. The princess's reassuring smile lent her courage when the king turned his attention to her next.

"Perhaps you should receive the greatest gift of all," he said to Raennia. "Ask anything of me with exception to my daughter's future crown, and it is yours. Would you like to become a princess? I have a son who, although he's never met you, is quite taken with you."

"A flattering offer, but one I must respectfully decline. I have no aspirations to royalty. I only ask to remain here, in Ashdale, and continue my training. To serve the princess."

"Only that?" Aldemar questioned. His incredulous voice made Ysolde smile.

"Yes."

"As you wish. However, I pray you will allow me one indulgence, young lady." Aldemar's eyes twinkled. "Today you are Raennia, squire in training. Tomorrow, however, I would see you as Ser Raennia, knight of Ashdale."

From that point forward, everything changed.

As a token of appreciation and part of her elevation in title, Ysolde made a prompt change in the residential assignment. While Geoffrey saw to the last-minute preparations for her knighthood, Maribeth and other members of the maid staff moved her belongings into a private bedchamber with a stunning, deep, porcelain bath.

After a brief visit to share the news with her mother, who fretted over her facial injuries, she returned to the castle, to thunderous applause. Her knighthood brought the good news they'd needed in the wake of Andras's loss, a reason to celebrate and raise their spirits once more.

The seamstress arrived to tailor the traditional, blessed, white-and-gold vestments she would wear during the ceremony. Raennia soaked and washed for hours before attending a night vigil alongside Geoffrey in Ashdale Castle's small chapel devoted to Ashta.

"Are you excited?"

"I couldn't sleep were I even allowed," she confessed. "I can't believe…"

Her voice trailed, and her eyes lifted to the remarkable, lifesize statue of Ashta depicted in pink granite. It glowed rose gold in the lantern lights.

"None of this feels real, Geoffrey. Using magic. Becoming a knight. I'd have never dreamed up any of this. Would the Order of Ashta's Chosen even accept me?"

"Ashta chose you, love. It matters not whether they accept you, but they'd be hypocrites if they were to disrespect a woman chosen by our goddess. You wielded her holy fire,

Rae. She accepts you, and the opinion of mortals pales by comparison."

Raennia dropped her chin and smiled, tears pricking her eyes. "It comes easy now, as if it was always a part of me, there and waiting." After a pause and silence between them, she added, "You don't have to stay, Geoffrey. Jory said he'd pop in to pray beside me."

She was only allowed one companion in prayer at a time. Otherwise, she was to spend the night alone.

"I know. But I want to. I have my own thanks to give, after all, and you happen to be occupying our chapel." He flashed her a grin. "I've prayed every night since we brought her home. I can't help it."

Raennia recalled nothing after the battle, although Ysolde swore a woman had helped her down from Zephyr then later appeared with Raennia draped across Tikiina's back. Geoffrey and the soldiers who'd found them had been convinced Rae's knock to the head resulted in her loss of memories and that Ysolde's mystery savior was a figment of her delirious imagination.

If she tried, Rae could remember warm arms around her, but in truth, the vague memories tugging at her subconscious seemed planted by Ysolde's recollections more than anything. According to the princess, a woman with golden eyes had brought them inside a home with solid stone walls and a roaring hearth.

Perhaps it had been a witch afraid of persecution. Then again, Geoffrey insisted he'd found them in little more than a ruined shack.

Maybe it was a product of Ysolde's imagination and the two women had saved each other after all.

At dawn, King Aldemar himself came to escort them from the chapel to the audience chamber. As her sponsor, and almost as an older brother, Geoffrey presented her to the princess. Rae lowered to a knee and bowed her head respectfully.

"On this day, I present my faithful squire to Princess Ysolde, Duchess of Ashdale," Geoffrey declared to all in attendance. Her fellow members of the Ashguard packed the hall, her mother and siblings standing in the place of honor at the king's side.

"Rise, Raennia," Ysolde directed.

While her insides quaked, Raennia rose and faced the princess. A tumultuous buzz hummed through her veins until it became an exercise of will to keep still.

"Not only have you demonstrated all qualities desired in a knight, but you've saved my life and reunited me with my husband. For that, no title, no amount of gold seems adequate."

"I am honored to be of service, Your Grace."

"I am the one who is honored, Raennia. Ashdale was blessed the day you decided to test for the guard."

A prickling sensation in her eyes threatened to bring up tears, so Raennia swallowed them back and bowed her head.

The ceremony continued with a blessing from an Ashtarian priestess. With each repeated word, Raennia experienced a sense of warmth, a glowing radiance, all around her. It brought a sense of peace and belonging and reminded her of the same serenity she'd experienced in the battle when she'd called on Ashta's holy fire.

As if Ashta herself were with her.

When prompted, she recited the maxim of all holy warriors who served in the name of their goddess, her voice strong and clear. "With faith as my shield, love shall be my armor and dedication my sword."

The flat of the blessed blade touched her left shoulder then her right. Its cool weight was a comfort.

"I knight thee Ser Raennia," Ysolde murmured.

She passed the blade to Geoffrey, who then girded it around Raennia's waist with a fine, leather sword belt emblazoned with the golden sigil of their goddess.

Cheers and applause erupted in the room as the new knight turned to face her audience. Upon locating her family again, thoughts of her father surfaced, twined with wishes that he could have been among them. For him to see all the countless hours indulging her in swordplay had not been wasted.

He would be proud of her, she thought. But he always had been.

***

Tegau, daughter of Tiga, was laid to rest a month later, once Etienne unearthed her remains and the business in Fort Stonewall was finished. The Ashguard had swept through the northern hills and wiped out the few remaining mercenaries within the old garrison but found no Narkanthi soldiers among them. Like the leader of the Iron Fist, they had made their escape, likely across the border.

By then, Ysolde had recovered from both the mental and physical wounds of her ordeal, and with her faithful knight Raennia standing alongside her, the princess and her loved ones had traveled south to Brychas with a small contingent of the Royal Army.

Despite their skepticism regarding Hindera, Etienne had convinced the gatekeeper to permit them inside. The Marcogh had welcomed Ysolde into their fold with open arms and larger hearts. Faces from memories long past stirred from her subconscious.

It was a bittersweet moment in time, seeing her mother's bones settled. All those years believing Tegau had left her behind without ever looking back, when the truth was much more painful and abolished any hope of reconciliation.

She'd always wished her mother would return to her with apologies and love, and now hope had been dashed.

With her father at one side of her and Geoffrey on the other, Ysolde watched the village shaman lower each bone to its final resting place. The Marcogh lacked cemeteries, but they treated their dead with respect.

For Tegau, they chose a small corner of grassy trail just beyond Brychas, where the desert sand blended with green oasis. Their people believed that by burying their kin on the paths taken during their migration, they would always be beside them, a guardian spirit of the air guiding them even in death.

When the other Marcogh left, Ysolde seeded precious succulents in the freshly mounded soil with her father's help while Geoffrey, Raennia, and Etienne toured the humble settlement.

"I wish things had gone differently." She patted the last seed into place.

Aldemar smiled and offered her a hand up. "So do I, but I will treasure every memory I have of your mother. She lives on in us. I see her in you each time you smile."

Arm in arm, they returned to the village of her birth as the sun began its slow descent behind the horizon. The other members of their traveling company waited in the gathering circle, enjoying flavorful kebabs roasted with desert spices.

A young girl offered Aldemar and Ysolde one upon arrival, along with a bowl of cool refreshment. To celebrate Ysolde's visit, the Marcogh matrons had put together an elaborate feast. They brought out casks of sweet cactus wine and played music, both as a farewell to Tegau and a welcome home to her daughter.

Ysolde hoped it signified a mending between her people and Hindera.

Geoffrey flashed her a welcoming smile when she stepped up to his side. "We've been challenged to play in the games after sunset. You should join as well, since Etienne declined his invitation. If I didn't know better, I'd say the old mage is terrified of looking poorly on his little black horse."

"Your husband fancies himself a true horseman and plans to participate in the races," Etienne said with a derisive snort. "Trust me when I say it would hardly be fair if I competed with the rest of you."

"I think Tikiina would love a race. What about you, Raennia? What have they suckered you into joining?"

Raennia looked over and grinned. "Archery."

"Laurent will be sore that he stayed behind with Fingall," Etienne mused.

"Learning the ins and outs of running a city, even one as small as Shadeglen, is bound to keep him occupied." Geoffrey claimed another kebab. "I'm absolutely certain Fingall is taking great delight in playing instructor."

Etienne snorted, and they all shared a laugh around the campfire. The sound of flapping wings intruded, and a raven landed upon the mage's shoulder. He regarded it with a glance, tilting his head.

"News?" Ysolde asked, voice filled with hope.

"Good news," Etienne confirmed. "Our spies saw Rhonwen as she reached Narkanth's shores, Aldemar. She's there, no doubt causing mischief, but at least we know where the disgraced queen has gone and with whom she's allied herself."

"Then there she may stay until she rots," the king replied. "She and the Iron Fist shall remain forever exiled under pain of death, should they return."

"They'll only take their business to more prosperous shores, or worse, recuperate and return with Narkanth's army," Geoffrey said.

"Then let them return and face their defeat. Hindera will not bend to them."

Ysolde took her husband's hand before tilting her face up to the sun. A gentle breeze caressed her skin and absolved her mind of worries. "Then if the Iron Fist and Narkanth want war, war is what they shall have."

ABOUT THE AUTHOR

As a fantasy novel and horror movie enthusiast, DOMINIQUE KRISTINE enjoys writing as an outlet for her creativity. The works of Tolkien have inspired her and remain some of her favorite novels. She blames her love for reading on her mother, who introduced her to the worlds of Stephen King, Pern, and Xanth.

www.ingramcontent.com/pod-product-compliance
Lightning Source LLC
Chambersburg PA
CBHW051327250626
47155CB00007B/2488